SOMETHING FOR EVERYTHING

SOMETHING FOR EVERYTHING

BY BP GREGORY

Something for Everything
Copyright © 2015 BP Gregory
All Rights Reserved

ISBN: 978 0 6458265 2 4

This is the second edition, published 2016.

ACKNOWLEDGMENTS

Thank you to my dedicated proof readers: Ahren Morris, who was first this time (it's only a race if you're winning); the talented Nola James who proudly returned the manuscript smeared with delicious food; Diane and Martin Gregory for such hard work and identifying the typos in salacious words; and of course the triumphant return of Jason Steen.

Something for Everything cover image by Extradeda, Orotund cover image by Alex Malikov, The Town cover images by Pavelr and Tim Bird, Flora & Jim cover image by Marcel Jancovic, and Visit the House image by Peter Dedeurwaerder all courtesy of Shutterstock.

Old Skipping Rhyme is by Ahren Daniel Morris and used with permission. Ahren Daniel Morris retains all copyright on the rhyme.

CONTENT ADVISORY

This story features adult themes including addiction: alcoholism, agoraphobia, animal violence, child neglect, mental health issues, and sexual harrassment. It may not be suitable for all readers.

TABLE OF CONTENTS

OLD SKIPPING RHYME

Walk and jump and skip and run
The Blessed are coming, under the sun
Run and climb and get real high
The Blessed are coming, bye bye bye
Climb and jump, stay at the top
The Blessed are coming, smell of rot
Jump and run and don't look back
The Blessed are coming, all is black.

WITHIN THE LATEX BUBBLE

JOHN'S ADULT LIFE was passing in a series of incomprehensible bursts.

Sporadically he clawed at the blurred dioramas speeding past, trying to make sense of them. Branded across the forehead with the invisible mark of a hero. Luckily everybody talked to the mark, not the gravel-rash eyes.

There had been this grizzled fellow who approached him in a bar, back when he would morosely still visit such places. Back when he'd still been fooling himself.

'Excuse me, Surgeon? Sir?' Shyly fumbling for all that stolid girth. The chipped physique of a tradesman, which demanded its own respect. His body language broadcast on a wide frequency how badly he wished to grasp John's thin arm in the hearty way of his tribe, assert physical reality, with a mitt that would go right 'round the bicep. Knowing full well it would be the last thing he would ever do, touching a Surgeon. Calamity for them both.

Clammy from taking even this mild risk of approaching. Good on him. The other patrons were clustered right up the other end of the bar.

'Oh, hell.' Shifting restlessly from foot to foot. 'One of you Surgeons saved my boy. Of course, they won't ever tell me *who*, but I … just wanted the chance to say thanks to one of yeh. He's a good boy, my boy.'

Real men would brusquely shake hands. Stupid John didn't even think to buy the grateful sod a drink.

He simply stood there like an idiot and his withered fingers in their latex casing padded sadly at his leather palms. Stood there, wishing he was drunk and verbose. Stood until the mystified fellow shook his head angrily and stalked away.

John was a Surgeon, and Surgeons were heroes. Or at least his fucking hands were.

Often in dreams his hands would separate from the wrist entirely, finally conceding he was no part of them and their grandiose future. Severed appendages that freed themselves in the deep wallow of night when his raw eyes finally closed.

Then they would come creeping up his bedclothes, groping their way blindly along his spindly hirsute body. Yellowed nails scratching through the coarse greying hair of his chest. No—Go away! What do you want?

Still, fear didn't prevent folk gathering to peer curiously from a murky distance, as though through aquarium glass. To witness him drowning in public idolatry, cheer his submersion with their idiot applause.

That's right, he asserted within the grim privacy of his

long skull. Clenched his teeth into it and refused to let go. *I save them. It's what I do. It's all they need me to do.*

Curious eyes poked at him, hungry for a piece they could nibble off and take home. Shoulders back, he had to remind himself, chin high.

A woman at a café giggled, her colour high. She had a napkin clenched in hand, smeared with her fashionable lipstick.

'Surgeon,' she tittered, holding it out. Streaks on her teeth. 'Would you kiss this for me?' Friends at the table egging her on, the bold spear-tip of their social wedge. They laughed because they were scared, and it was a high.

Kiss me, kiss me by proxy. Everybody loved to be desired. And what lust burned greater than that ever-denied?

Overtaken by a sort of addiction they jittered. Would take to their beds afterward and gulp water as their brains melted in a gooey rush. *Look at my body, Surgeon, let me pretend you're touching me. Ooh, let me be your nursie nurse?* The flush on them so strong, an aggregate of grasping hands and wet lipstick mouths, it was difficult for John to even see them as people.

He finally abandoned the warm noisy hubs of life. He'd no right to go messing with ordinary folk, he was ruining everyone's night. Surgeons must not be touched. Not outside the mysterious act of surgery. And surgery was only safe because the patient's mind became untethered, lost to the world. Just insensate meat slammed on a gurney.

Comfort, reassurance, *contact*; that precious warmth the human animal can't remain sane and functioning without. It was a heinous crime for a Surgeon, with swift and pitiless punishment. Awareness of this peeped just below consciousness, and by great exhausting effort John kept it there.

The days when things made sense seemed long ago. Snippets of impossible nostalgia, steeped in a rosy haze. He'd had the friend along all that time, he supposed, flapping and dangling at his coattails. But even she wasn't entirely sane anymore.

A morning happened.

Probably the same as most mornings.

John jerked awake with teeth sunk in his forearm to bite back a scream, leery of the neighbours even as he slopped out from the thick waters of slumber. Without thinking he raked the bedclothes down in a panic. The horrible, creeping, severed hands would be bundled in them and flung from him.

Of course the disembodied appendages were not there, he was trying to throw away his own hands. Any thickhead would know that.

His sheets, John realised, were flooded.

This was not the way a hero would sleep. He lay in a rapidly chilling sweat and piss bath, rank enough to peel paint right off the walls. Quaking, unable to even be disgusted until he'd calmed, he rolled to the dry side like a man washed from a shipwreck. His fists were clenched lest they dare touch anything.

It was the beginning of a brand new day.

CHAPTER ONE

TACTILE

'**SO, A FEW NURSES** from the census came by mine.'

The friend was a blur, scarcely understandable. Shaking and blue to the gills because the city's heat cycled down at night. It was no time to be wandering about with fever on the brain.

'Asked if they could take a quick poke about my ladybits. You know, to check if there's any issue. Because there hasn't been. Any issue. And they laughed like drains, like they hadn't trotted out *that* old chestnut at every house.'

Even through the vibration you could sort of guess she'd squandered a striking youth, but ah, that face. Already sagging off its bone scaffold, circus pavilion coming down.

The friend and the city, both.

John winced at the telling, knotted fingers until latex squealed. He was vastly happier to imagine her *sans* bits, but to mention so was a rookie error. He'd get twice the earful. 'Did you tell them to take themselves on a long walk, or what?'

'Ha. It's amazing where, "Fuck off, my mate's a Surgeon," gets you. You seem to have an effect on people, Johnny. When your brain's in gear, that is.'

At three in the morning he ought to be rehearsing surgery, or dead to the world. Instead, bursting in, she'd caught him staring apathetically through the wall, his behaviour hung like a cheap toy.

Didn't she fall on her ass cackling at the sight. Annoying, but hyperactivity was typical of the city's mounting hysteria; if he wanted to condemn her, he'd have to shriek it to the streets. A wave of thundering panic built and he alone of the masses became lethargic and depressed. Perhaps he'd started off lower.

The friend, however, was clearly getting worse and he was running out of blind eyes to turn. Thoughtlessly bare toes waterlogged on plush carpet. Ought to feel lucky she'd remembered pants. He'd seen his own fingers appear just as dead and white any number of times, peeled from imprisoning gloves with the nails all spongy.

Only music should stir on the streets in the wee hours, especially around here in *The Cutters* surgical district. They got tinkling music, from frost rimed speakers. Ethereal confections of piano and flute playing to themselves in the bitter concrete night.

Out this way, for your sanity in the grey breaths before

dawn you closed your eyes tight beneath bedclothes. Those sweet chimes acted fine on punk vandals and kids, but they wouldn't dissuade the downstairs folk from creeping about.

If the downstairs people were real. Nobody John knew had ever been brave enough to look.

Silent, they were, in case you stirred. In case you betrayed yourself as awake and listening, in which case something would have to be done, dear, wouldn't it?

Their music erased thought. It was the crash and thunder of vast stamping pistons; cogs the size of buildings that rolled ponderously, filling all of creation. A chorus of overwrought machinery crying out for relief, for a moment's rest that would never come.

From the moment of her launch their city, *A New Life*, had been in flight. Her very purpose for being. Fleeing mindlessly, like all the cities, from something only the downstairs folk could claim any contact with.

The friend's teeth clattered audibly as John ushered her into the lounge with little sweeps of his arms, snapping on a fresh pair of gloves from the steel dispenser by the door. He no longer noticed when he sent a dusting of talcum in silent rain, and tracked it about everywhere he went.

A crown of dreadlocks piled atop his head, secured by string. It gave the impression his attached body ought to be of the robust, caber-tossing variety; but in reality that great ginger noggin sat more like a lollypop on a stick. Most people had eaten meals with more meat on them than John.

'Johnny,' she chattered dazedly, still in the throes of what had driven her from her safe home, driven her to bring it *here*. 'I don't know if the visitors triggered it, I was so *angry*, but it happened again. It happened while I was yelling at them, I'm sorry. I was asleep … or awake … or—I don't know, I don't know what! I woke up suddenly and it was dark, and the nurses were gone!'

Probably out of there like their wimples were on fire.

Tranced is what she would have been. Every man and his dog were *au fait* with the symptoms. Everybody knew to flee.

Some trancers returned to bed, seeking comfort on autopilot, but most stood as the friend had, wherever they'd been hit. Staring off into infinity, probably drooling. Breaking out in jelly sweat as their temperatures shot up and up. It would end in seizures, if that went on too long.

For something to do John busied himself topping up the kettle, water hammering on copper. She rubbed gooseflesh on her wobbly white arms. Night had trailed her in, with its marrow-cracking chill, a damp tang that was slow dispersing.

'I remember thinking I had to calm the hell down. I was still in my house, after all. Still in the city and nothing could get me here. Not here.'

Not here. Only out there.

The world rolling by with all its wonders remained a shunned void, the antithesis of bustling life within the walls. The majority of citizens had never glimpsed the natural sky. Only the comforting embrace of a solid grey ceiling. Sane and credulous by day, but the lights couldn't stay on all the time.

When you closed your eyes all bets were off, your mind could wander anywhere. Grim legend held that if the monsters out there, the Blessed, seized you in their great square teeth before you could wake yourself up ... Something had to explain the waves of sleep-death that swept the population, defying all analysis.

But these day-trances, this thing happening to the friend, anyone could be prone to it. There were those who tranced and tranced helplessly, every day. Growing haggard and bony, sheets stained yellow. If the neighbours caught you stuffing that linen in a dustbin you'd be shunned; disposal had to be secret, it could take months.

Made up of dark hints and rumours to the uninitiated, there was even a terminal stage. Vague legends of the underbelly, down there where the downstairs people crawled. An unvoiced suggestion that there might be a way, there was always a way out, but only for those desperate and overwhelmed. Only they were ready to find it.

They became the folk who stepped from life one day. Vanished, like they had been wiped from existence.

Generally that became the cue for all those who had studiously ignored the warning signs to send up wails of grief. Friends and family. Petitions underlined and tear-stained, demands scored through the paper. The lower levels must be chained off, for the love of God. Cordoned, gassed, something! Plug that hole. Down there. Somewhere between the immense grinding treads that pounded the landscape to rubble.

Like it would do any good. *A New Life* was immense, a grand old lady, and those pilgrims dragging their exhausted hearts could always find a way to slip through and be gone.

For what it was worth, John was determined to do everything in his power to prevent the friend becoming one of them.

He slapped the kettle on the stove, a declaration of war. Coffee. That was step one. Things kept skittering away from him, like cockroaches when you flip on what ought to be an illuminating light.

He fished a couple of mugs from the cupboard. The purple one hers, on its own shelf, as though touch were a contagion a Surgeon could pick up off crockery.

'Hey, Johnny.' She threw a pillow at him. 'You listening?'

'Nope.' He lied. 'It's boring. You're boring.' He waved

latex-shrouded hands, conducting an orchestra of one scared woman, bundled up in a guest blanket that had never shucked off its crinkly packaging for anyone else.

She switched tracks. Stopping and thinking were hardly the friend's forte these days; she lived in dread of it. Racing faster through life to beat awareness to the finish line.

'Seems like we never thought about the other cities when we were little.'

'To have identity there have to be others, right? You and me. Us and them. And that's why our city's the best.'

She sighed explosively, a great blowing-out of tension. 'Do you reckon we'll hit the Flagship soon?'

'Reach. Reach the Flagship, not hit.' Very superstitious. 'Weeks at least, they say. We're gaining gradually. You ought to be excited, instead of … whatever you are.'

'I'm reasonably confident *excited*'s not the word. More like starts with *fucking* and ends in *terrified*.' She'd turned green. Her pulse beat visibly in her neck. He was getting sympathy cramps just looking at her. 'After all this time we'll finally know what happened, why they went silent. All those other cities. And when it might happen to us.'

The lights on the comms board stuttering out one by one over the decades. Sometimes heavy breathing came in over the roaring static, and once … once it was a kind of *giggling*, you'd swear. And whispering, the way you do when you're scared of being overhead. Only nobody knew what it was saying.

The final connection to the Flagship had been lost only recently. They were still scheduled to meet, though, and that made her the only chance of finding out what was going on. Nobody was about to stroll out there and look.

'Your morbid nature's showing,' he scolded. 'It's unladylike.' He suffered a chill nonetheless, and ploughed on. 'We don't know *anything's* happened to anybody. There are at least a thousand perfectly solid explanations why lines or even the navigation squawks might go down. We're all tooling blissfully about on old, old equipment, after all. Ancient stuff. Nobody's manufactured anything wonderful and new since the glory days of Son.'

Her face drooped further. It would be on the floor at this rate. 'We could do with the likes of Son now. You know, when I was a kid I used to pretend I had him as a secret friend. Like he'd been hiding all this time, just waiting for me. Another lonely kid to play with.'

'Of course you did. Children are such egomaniacs. Especially girls.'

'*Son and the Marvellous Machines*, do you remember that? It was my favourite show.'

'You can't seriously wish Son was around. Here, now? I can't think of anything worse.'

She clapped a horrified hand over her mouth. *Blasphemy!*

He hurried to his point. 'No, really, think. We owe him everything, right? Son built the cities and he saved us from Outside, from the Blessed. But all that was such a horribly long time ago.

'Technology just handed to us, so precious and shining, and what have we accomplished? We don't even know how to take care of things properly anymore. It's all falling apart. The masses proved happier with their merry-go-round of shopping, fucking, and raising brats.

'So if you ask me, yeah, it'd be *awful* if Son were somehow alive to see what we've done with all he left us.'

'You're really shit at cheering people up. Anybody ever mentioned?'

'Daily.' He set the mug down in front of her. Enough caffeine and she would slide into sleep, a rag doll on his couch.

'Drink up. If you don't mind, I'm going to get some practice in while there's still night left.'

'Be my guest. It's your house.'

That lasted all of two seconds. Bored, she came to his elbow.

'Uh, would you mind staying over there?'

'Do I look like an idiot? No touchee the Surgeon.'

'Just … step back, then. More.'

'Shut up, I can't even reach you from here. See? *See?*'

Taking off his gloves and exposing the stewed digits to the air always felt horribly lewd, let alone with someone else in the room. Stirred up urges he'd rather do without.

But she wasn't going to bugger off, so he took a deep breath and got on with it.

His patient, a furry little beastie engineered to house a human heart, beamed groggily as he lifted it from the carrier. Warm, soft fur. A faint mousy whiff.

Despite his tension he couldn't help returning the foolish toothy display. The heart animal wasn't about to notice the cracked ruin of his hands. Or flinch, as the friend did, from the high unearthly whine of the laser scalpel heating up.

Couldn't blame her. Even after all these years a thrill of unease shot through him every time the surgical tool woke to life, like *this* was the time he was going to poop his pants. Beneath fissured fingers and visible to his altered eyes only, the scalpel set to bloodlessly parting warm living tissue cell by cell.

Only the ornate silver handle was visible to the friend's sight, there wasn't much point trying to see what he was doing. If it weren't for the drugged little animal gradually skinning open on the bench she would hardly have been aware of the dangerous instrument at all.

The friend had no way of knowing the inflamed needling

irritation the blade brought to John's carefully altered sclera. A spike through his head. The Surgeons clasped their secrets close, and that secret was always pain. Pain for experience. Pain for efficacy.

Who wouldn't want every patient to thrive? Who wouldn't cast themselves gladly on a pyre to see suffering scraped out, until in the entire city only theirs was left?

In skilful hands whole structures could be transplanted without a single pierced membrane. Slide to a finer edge and you could shave the axons from a neuron. Finer still and you'd be messing with molecular components, something even a Surgeon needed special licenses for.

LeMars, the laser scalpel's creator, had used the cursed singing prototype on his own arteries, spreading them wide. It was said he'd had a vision of the future. It was true that a live dropped scalpel would plunge through the depths of the city, and everything it encountered. Until it emerged from *A New Life*'s belly to fall, humming and spinning, burying itself in the earth. Earthquakes. Catastrophe.

Nonetheless the inventor was posthumously lauded a hero, patron saint of the circulatory system. Every scalpel carried his name *LeMars*, in ornate curling script on the handle.

Picking coyly at her nails, she found something new. 'Well. I went to High Estate this week.'

Telling heat bloomed in sallow cheeks. He didn't need to glance to confirm her wicked grin, sharp uneven teeth bared at his spine.

High Estate ranked as the greatest of John's obsessions, a guilty moral addiction he mustn't indulge in. Society permitted scant leeway for a Surgeon to be weak. Or human. Cry me a river.

Best crush sweaty daydreams and act his age. No spring chicken. Cram them away in some back pocket and smile,

smile as the friend teased his tail feathers. Smile through gritted teeth if necessary.

His long-boned hands never faltered, despite her best efforts. If anyone deserved accolades, it was those Surgeon's hands for dragging the rest of him to success.

'There was a rave, you know.' Coyly.

'There's always a rave!' He couldn't help assuaging discomfort with a jab of his own. 'Why were you flouncing about High Estate parties instead of home with hubby?'

This time her smile came without humour. 'My dear *husband* was working. Be kind to him, Johnny. He always works.'

Instantly ashamed. Bending over his work to hide it. Charles had been his friend, too, back in the day. Nobody made the decision, but she'd inherited him in the end.

Now the happy couple devoted their time to methods of staying apart within the confines of one small flat. Easiest for Charles—he just set about working himself into an early grave. Marital joy being an obligation, the friend's bitter glare reminded him, that a Surgeon stood exempt from. If "exempt" was the word.

The pause gave her a breath to recover. Bringing Charles into it had been cruel, and neither of them were used to him being cruel. It was normally her remit.

'So, do you want to hear about it or not?'

A petulant, unfair question. She knew damn well he lived for these recitals, addicted, stretching out the days. Although she'd taken a bitter edge, when she rambled on about parties the ghost of her adolescent irrepressibility returned. A stupid force of spirit he found frustrating and gladdening in equal measure. Insufferable to his threadbare nerves, he wished a thousand times a day she'd grow up—but it at least proved not everything could be crushed down.

'The rave, it was brilliant. All splashy neon and sound. Loads, and I mean *loads* of people showed up. So many bodies packed in, all breathing and moving together. Sweat thrown up in a spray against coloured lights …'

Breath hissed through teeth a little faster, though he tried to hide it.

'… and I could *smell* all those people, rank funk down the back of the throat, like foul musky animals …'

He wondered where she drew that from. Weren't many animals roaming the city; excluding Frankenbeasties like his little patient here, wriggling impatiently against the straps.

What she described were beasts of nightmare. The very reason for the walls. Great, hulking animals with hot hides and wild smells. Wicked horns. Volcanic eyes.

When he realised his devious subconscious had thrown up the Blessed he hastily squashed the notion. More than enough in the day to be leery of already.

'Exotic animals,' the friend was crooning dreamily, still lost in her neon fantasy. 'So much skin to be seen. Glittering eyelids. Dyed hair in spiked crests. Cocks so heavily pierced they dragged along the ground.'

Bypass practice was almost over, his furry patient doped to the eyeballs and counting its tiny clawed fingers drowsily. Its own heart batted shyly beside the grafted interloper, which bulged monstrously by comparison.

In fact, that human heart filled so much of the chest cavity that lung expansion was visibly cramped, digestion retarded. The miracle of science, hey?

All that remained was to restore blood flow and set the seat of human love pumping again. Easy as pie. Its motion shook the beastie like a motor in a too-frail building.

He set to silently knitting his "patient" back together

with mesh.

Returning to her perch the friend snuggled into the couch cushions. The furnishings of *The Cutters* far outstripped anything to be found down her end of town. 'C'mon, big shot Surgeon. You finished yet?'

John snipped the last wire and thrust his hands in the air like a triumphant gymnast. 'Aaand—I'm done. That's a new time trial.'

Switching the scalpel off, nervously aware of the cooling molecules where the blade had been. Only once had she attempted to touch it. Off her tits on whiskey, she was. Although it hadn't been live he'd still lashed out in a panic as though to slap her away with his bare hand, only pulling up at the last second.

If it hadn't been so serious, the identical shock on their grey faces would have been comic. Never saw her drink whiskey again after that.

'Can I hold him now? Can I? Can I?' She held out her arms, a child eager for its new toy.

On with fresh gloves. 'Sure, but be gentle. Don't put pressure on its belly.'

That earned him a look. 'I'm careful all the damn time. I was born careful.'

The beastie submitted its round body for petting, even blew a few contented spit bubbles. Delighted, she smiled down at it. Curled up on the couch like that, button of a thing in her arms. Was that how she'd look if Charles had given her a baby?

Her next question ever so innocently fired his way. 'Why not tag along next time?'

An air pocket in his glove was more important. He fussed, muttering. 'Uh, sure. Tag along to ..?'

'A rave. Come to High Estate. Stay for the food.'

He scowled thunderously. 'You know better than to suggest that! Especially here!'

'Oh, quit being such a crotchety old grumpy pants. Society peeping through the keyhole, are they? Or are you wetting your shorts that they might suspect the hero of being human?'

'I'm not human. I'm a *Surgeon*.' But his catechism, lately repeated with such despair, rang hollow.

If she noticed his despondence, it earned no further concession than blunt irritation. 'Zippedy-do, bully for you. Look, it's just you've always been so *fascinated* with how the shady half lives. And now, what with the Flagship coming up and all … You may never get another chance.'

'I am **not** fascinated.'

He might as well have stamped his foot. It didn't warrant a response. Only a mental self-kicking; no chance she'd tell him about the rave now. And he'd rather bite his tongue off than ask.

Those wild melee parties always ended the same, anyhow. Some gang, whichever was hot property at the time, took over. And it was all downhill and into the shit from there.

'Johnny, look at it this way. Don't you want to try something exciting before we all die?'

Now he'd reason to trot out the indignant. 'You just watched me hold a *living human heart* in my hands!'

'Uh, hardly attached to a human, though, was it?'

'To date I've performed twenty-nine *highly* dangerous procedures and *hundreds* of tiddlies, with, excuse my ass, a *one hundred frigging percent* success rate! Exactly how exciting do I need to be? Have you got some kind of sliding scale going?'

She wasn't backing off. 'Ever talked to any of them? Given a patient whose life you so *heroically* …' He closed his eyes at the sour spray. '… saved a chance to say thanks?'

'Get to your point already.'

'All you do is repair unconscious meat the way you'd unblock your garbage disposal. What are they to you? Of all things, High Estate at least seems to *matter*.'

When there was no counter-offensive, when he didn't even open his eyes she sighed, visibly trying to let go of her agitation.

'Look, I'm sorry. I know what you do is really important. It just seems unfair, you know?'

Nothing.

'Would you look at me when I'm talking to you? I'm talking happiness, marriage, love. *Fun*. You're always stuck off to one side, or in the distance. Just because there's no other way doesn't make it right.'

Inwardly he quivered at her clumsy attempt at sympathy, but couldn't reply. They were both too old for such emotional flapping about.

She sighed. 'We're getting closer to the Flagship, Johnny. Maybe none of this will even matter once we get there.'

He didn't like arguments, but John's rooms were very quiet after she left.

As quiet as they could be. Not quite the soundproof luxury of the sunlight suburbs at the top of the city—he could still hear *A New Life* groaning all around him.

Most of the city's inhabitants could not consciously register her mechanical pulse. They had known it in the womb, and would die without ever experiencing such a strange thing as silence.

It was a Surgeon's poor luck to move between states,

neither fish nor fowl. Unbearably sensitive to such realities.

The gentle vibration caressed the spine, the steady *baoum baoum* of immense treads. Of those who could hear, some odd ducks were disturbed by it. Tympanic reconstructions were by far the most common surgery done.

On top there was always the dull hissing ventilation, a genius system for drawing the external in safely through a series of spiked traps and filters. The whining lights. And of course innumerable consumer appliances being fired at once.

Only appliances, though. The days of the modern miracles, the living thinking machines, were long past, no matter how covertly longed for. Not even *A New Life* had capacity for thought, although hippies and radicals claimed that she dreamed. Dreamed away her long slow journey. Only Son would have known for sure.

As though she scented the grey trend of his thoughts a message from the friend flashed up on John's screen. Couldn't resist one last dig.

ANOTHER HIGH ESTATE
PARTY TOMO NIGHT
COME PLAY
YOU CAN JUST WATCH
TRY SOMETHING
EXCITING
BEFORE WE ALL DIE.

He tried to clamp down on his anger, and shocked the

beastie as much as himself by kicking the couch.

'Fuck!'

Why this infuriating compulsion to stir things up, things that ought to lie decently dead? All ignorant, the friend would end up getting them both killed.

The heart animal burbled in its strange, wordless voice, becoming more active as the ether drained. It groggily rubbed its sutures.

'No!' He lightly smacked the pink paws. 'Naughty!' The damn thing had been unzipped more times than his coat. Ought to know by now not to fiddle with the stitching.

Way back before regulations got so strict about claw length, a heart animal had been found dead at the bottom of its crib. Guts all tangled where it had stupidly tried to flee its mistake. The things were bloody priceless, nobody even knew how old they were. The mysteries of the eternal cell had been lost with the thinking machines.

You never heard so much as a murmur of discontent when you returned them to their plain sterile cribs, where they might wait months. Some kind hearted minder might hang an infant's glittering mobile, for the beastie to coo and chuckle at.

Kind hearted. Certain daft minders were known to cry plenty when their charges got hauled off for surgical practice, and never mind that that was what they were *made* for.

He deposited the rotund creature back in its carrier, all ready for somebody else to practice. It wet the newspaper with a gush of ammonia, and then curled up to sleep with its butt in the air.

When gloved hands lingered on soft fur he resolutely recalled them. Touch. It was so easy for the bloody friend to take for granted. A perfect buddy for a Surgeon, she couldn't stand anyone too close, like she'd been rubbed all over with ground glass. It made John want to scream at her. She never used to be like this.

Of course, she never used to be married.

It wasn't the sort of thing you could say, but in his secret heart he suspected *there* lay the font of all ill. But what else was she supposed to do? Society, the very institution he upheld, dictated marriage. She was hardly in any position to ask "How high?"

Once your date arrived you got a selection, delivered on a list all fancy around the edges. Some of them you would even know. But hell or high water you had to pick one, and marry them. Supposedly all that hardware in the city's cranium only spat out nice clean matches for healthy bouncing bubs, but who knew how it schemed?

So the friend went on her merry way, and John downed taller and taller glasses of chilled vodka in an effort to get to sleep at night. When he dispensed with the glass he knew he was in trouble, but anything topped lying in the dark with visions of High Estate dancing in his head, feeling a right pervert.

The snowballing disaster was en route to see him broken at the bottom of the mountain, if he couldn't find a way to sort himself out somehow.

John's frantic, gnawing thoughts were interrupted by a rap at the front door, which made a welcome change from the friend's more dramatic entrances. But seriously, he glanced at the clock. Didn't anyone *sleep* anymore?

Relief was short lived, as a voice like a decade in the desert crackled through the panels.

'Don't ignore me, Surgeon. I know you're in there.'

He could only hope to live to an age where he could give so few fucks. Sighing, he opened the door to confront the Captain on the front step, before she put a chunk of rock through the window under the mistaken impression she was still spry enough to climb through.

Red rimmed eyes peered at him from a face as grey and lumpy as unstirred tallow. The porch light wasn't doing her any favours. In her prime the Captain would have towered over him, before the years buckled her spine into its present C shape.

Others, especially women, turned to cosmetics or surgery to mitigate time's impact but never the Captain. She shoved her increasing frailty in your face. Each indignity heaped on that snowy head only served to make her sour spirit burn hotter.

A single concession, the silver flask hung around her wattled neck.

'Surgeon,' she acknowledged coolly as though he were the one calling on her for favours at four in the damned morning. Unused to wearing gloves she plucked absently at the void teats at the ends of fingers, with the nerve-wracking squeaking of a freshman.

She always donned gloves when she wandered into *The Cutters* to visit a Surgeon—"blending with the natives," she called it. John felt the gesture sent a darker message: that Surgeons couldn't be trusted to control themselves.

'Captain,' he responded in kind.

Her crumbling body appeared as a series of errors awaiting correction, rather than the result of a natural process, and his fingers itched for the scalpel. She'd rather sip strychnine than take him up on it, of course.

'What can I do for you on this fine chilly morning?' Their steaming breath rose all around them.

'Just making sure you're around.'

He raised his hands. *Where else would I be?*

'Don't be smart, Surgeon. We are expecting some new data

in the next day or so, something critical. I'm going to want your expertise when it comes in. So don't go wandering off.'

'New information? On the Flagship?'

The old goat was too canny to feed that rumour one way or the other. By way of response she turned and shuffled her way back down the drive. The cold air couldn't be doing any favours for those joints.

Her purpose had been served—the vigilant neighbours would have witnessed her visit, the interaction noted. He'd just been boosted into a new social circle. Privy to secrets he was sure not to want.

During a crisis the Captain would never sit idle while others flapped about in a tizz; the cunning biddy would be drawing all strings to her. It felt comforting, in a way. No matter what the city faced, she would be ready.

Turning back into his apartment John blanched and for a moment was afraid he might faint. The hallway dipped and swayed.

The friend's innocent-sly, vastly incriminating message was still all over the screen.

He hoped like fuck the Captain's aged eyes hadn't been able to read it over his shoulder.

TRY SOMETHING

With a sweep of his hand he erased it. Would that a thought could be wiped so easily.

BEFORE WE ALL DIE.

Later that day, with an iceberg of clear spirit drifting in the waters beneath his belt, John typed a reply.

He went. God knows why, but he went.

CHAPTER TWO

THE GREATER OF TWO EVILS

FOR ALL HIS fascination with the sordid, John had never been to High Estate. In truth he'd barely ventured a foot beyond *The Cutters* since becoming a fully fledged Surgeon.

That was how the suburb was designed: the hermitage of convenience. He had rich food to distract, booze to dull himself to sleep and thick, bitter coffee to kick him awake each morning. Contained, where eyes could be kept on his simple habits.

It wasn't until he sallied forth and felt the first trembling stab of anxiety that he realised how sedentary life had become. Funny thing that, in a city that couldn't stop moving.

Even to be entering the bustling commons with its arcades and cheap sodium-laced food felt new and strange, never mind he'd grown up here. A right mess, caught between the smooth luxury above that beckoned him back, and the sheer degradation below.

Already the architecture's heavy lines went unsoftened, the shops mere neon specks at the foot of the grey immensity of layered apartments that loomed up into the gloom. The inhabitants milled through blocky corridors as an afterthought, ants in an ant farm.

Great gusts of dank air moved along these halls, puffing back and forth as though playful beneath cavernous ceilings. Artificial light beamed. The commons smelled like a damp linen closet, and its concrete pressed down firmly upon your brow.

This was new: hand-drawn wagons were everywhere, fluttering with black ribbons. Parasites selling the hope that trancing could somehow be undone. They called out, competing to spruik the old tale about Son's wife, who'd suffered the sickness. But Son himself had led her home with a black ribbon around her neck. These very ribbons! This special dye. Wouldn't you hate yourself, if you don't?

John struggled to cling to enough dignity to keep gawping to a minimum, but the friend was more used to the stuffy air, and picked up his cowardly scent at once with a tiny superior smile. These dim halls were her territory still; aberration rather than fate to aspire higher. No doubt his trembling presence made her feel awfully streetwise and tough about it.

When he came slinking around the corner she broke into her widest crook-toothed grin. *Boggle* at the sight of her: tarted up as he'd never seen, or imagined, or in the slough of deepest nightmare wanted to see. Modest breasts hoicked to the ceiling for all their worth in cups of blazing colours. Height boosted by heels into something of Amazonian pretension. If he knew her an inch she'd be carting them before the evening was out, limping and moaning.

Funnily enough, his reaction to the obscene getup was to remember how she had looked all rumpled, drifting off peacefully on his couch. He neither liked nor trusted this flashy stranger standing in his friend's place.

Typically she didn't give two hoots for his opinion one way or the other.

Tapping a gladiatrix boot impatiently, 'Take off the damn gloves. You can't wear those out, everyone will know what you are.'

She was probably right, much as he eternally hated to admit, but he clasped his hands protectively. 'Bulldust. Loads of people wear gloves. I've had kids run up to me in latex all the way to the elbow, carrying on about how they aim to make Surgeon one day.' Mainly kids who'd lost a parent, or playmate. Stupid kids.

'Not where we're off to they bloody don't. Hate to bruise your tender ego, but the cult of Johnny doesn't extend much more than a block around your apartment.'

True to form nothing was to be taken seriously, not for long. She strutted and hammed like a drag queen ruling the cocktail hour stage. 'Well. Let's go get a cart, then.'

He was pathetically grateful. His stomach felt light and unstable, and he might have stammeringly backed out given any more smart commentary. Looking longingly back at his gloves, abandoned and shrivelled on the pavement with the rest of the trash, he still might cut and run. Never live that down.

In the spirit of their venture, after much searching she

managed to turn up the most clapped-out bomb in the entire suburb. Generations of over-breeders had used it as their little run-around sedan, used it to death.

Springs groaned as she began pumping coins into the battered meter, and he eyed it doubtfully. 'C'mon. I've got credit to manage a little better. We'll end up pushing the damn thing home.'

'And you could totally use the exercise. This is my treat, Johnny. Do you really fancy a cart on your account getting traced to High Estate?'

The hand waving his card drooped. She had a point.

'Besides.' A grimace toward the slick models, the shiny carts he regarded with longing that would slip through a keyhole and park on a dime. 'They'd be nicked the second we stopped. We wouldn't even have time to get out.'

He patted the clunker's bonnet gingerly, then wiped his begrimed hand on his pants. Normally it would be a case of stripping old gloves off, a clean pair on, but not here, not tonight. He felt so *exposed*.

'You've got one thing right. Nobody's going to steal this baby. But hey, at least let me pay you back.' Funds travelling from his account to hers were hardly novel. He wondered if Charles cared, or even noticed.

She rolled her eyes. Some debt couldn't be tallied up so neatly. 'You can buy me a coffee sometime.'

'You're really into this, aren't you?' John shook his head, swallowing against the nerves in his gut, little panicked fingers searching for a way out. 'This is insane. I should never have let you talk me into it.'

'Damn straight, sunshine. Let's try and enjoy ourselves anyhow, shall we?'

Surely this couldn't actually be happening. John wouldn't do anything so utterly, irredeemably *illegal*—not the

Surgeon, bastion of propriety. Not after so many nice safe years.

Springs shrieked within threadbare seats and poked him spitefully in the back as they climbed into the cart. The upholstery let loose a mildewy gust of baby spit. And at all this, the friend grinned. Of course she was exhilarated, flying free: what did *she* have to lose? A mercy she didn't raise the skull and crossbones over their rickety vehicle. It was going to be hard to drag her kicking and screaming back into normal life tomorrow, that was for damn sure.

She drove, which was nominally good. His nerves would have rocketed them straight into the nearest wall.

He sat back and attempted not flinching every time she yanked her way through the gears, slapping the side of his chair and yelling, 'Shut up!' even though he hadn't said a peep. Every surface felt oddly greasy, like an emptied takeout container. His skin crawled around and around in an effort not to touch anything. His pulse was thundering in his ears so hard it was difficult to focus.

Boldly defying all odds that wanted to turn them into a runway smear, they shot down an express lane into the bowels of *A New Life*. Bright, well-maintained lights gave way to an energy saving yellow.

More and more graffiti began to put in an appearance, as nobody could be bothered painting over it. A bold evolution from hurried tagging to full-blown cultist illustrations and gang signs. About two kilometres beyond the last of the "nice" lights it hit absolute cliché. Should you venture into High Estate all walls became their storybook, indoctrination for those who couldn't read.

Heat tainted John's cheeks, although they were so puerile it was funny. Crude cartoon people scrunched together like wadded paper, leering down at the motorway on a massively disproportionate scale. Some of them must have taken generations to complete, any number of foolhardy vandals smashed flat by the speeding carts. Old blood splashed up, to join the depicted revelry.

Soon he became aware of a faint thumping that wasn't his pulse or the muffled jouncing suspension. It reverberated in breastbone and jaw, his high-strung heart quivering to match the beat. After only a minute of it he might have been running a marathon, he was so short of breath.

'Do you hear it?' The excited whites of her eyes flashed.

He ran his tongue around a papery dry mouth. 'I do.'

A tiny secretive smile slid across her chops.

'We're close.' She shoved a crumpled flyer at him. 'This is where we're going.'

John smoothed it on his knee and gaped disbelievingly.

A sloppily printed ink demon capered before a city block. Its long twisted horn betrayed the genus of such a nightmare. Beneath, *THE SEX IS IN THE BASS* glared in cheap lipstick red.

'*Where* did you get this?' It didn't gel with the friend *he* knew.

'Oh, you know.' She shrugged and the cart wobbled, causing the air to catch in his chest like fishhooks.

'I really don't.'

'If you must know, it was taped to the back of a toilet door.'

'*What?*'

'Forget it, Johnny. These things get posted in out of the way spots all the time. It's really clever. See that building over the monster's shoulder? You have to recognise its profile to know where the party is. And you punch the pattern of shadows on the street into this free program hidden in a chatroom to get the date and time.'

'A *public* toilet?'

'Stop it. Most just come for the dancing.'

'It *was*, wasn't it? The *sex*, posted in a *public* toilet!' He dropped the flyer. 'Ugh, I want to bleach my hands.'

She laughed, despite the ripe tomato blush scaling her cheekbones. 'We'll be out of there long before things get bad.'

His return chuckle was falsetto, even to his ears. Now she did glance across, probably taking in the beads of sweat he felt running down his forehead. The smile dropped off her mouth.

He had a real talent for stripping the fun out of life.

'Trust me, Johnny, nobody's going to touch you. Appearance to the contrary I'm not stupid.'

He felt a pang: of course she was looking out for him. Reckless, blundering; but if she ever saw him in true peril, the whole city wouldn't halt her charge to the rescue.

'I'd trust your ass a whole lot better if you managed to keep your eyes on the road for ten seconds.' Most of his bravado came from the sea of vodka he had swishing about his circulatory system. It was evaporating far too fast for his liking.

Halting their downward plunge the cart left the arterial road for narrowing streets, that wound between cluttered grey buildings. Down here people had ceased struggling against *A New Life*'s uncompromising aesthetic and inhabited it like squatters. A messy organic blight on pure form and line.

On waves of dank air that gusted through the window, he could gradually discern layers to the noise they'd been hearing. He'd never known music could be an assault, yet here it was, this hammering pulse-beat. Challenging brain and balls in a language beyond words. Both shrank away, appalled.

It gave terrifying fidelity to all those tales the friend had related. Primal, provocative, and most of all *violent*. The concept had seemed titillating in the bland confines of his lounge room. Now it dawned on John that closer to the racket was the last place he wanted to be. Years of training protested, *no no no …*

He moaned and half-lurched from his seat, flinging the door open so that it rang sparks against the wall on that side. The friend shrieked and slammed on the brakes. She felt her heart stop.

Ignoring her, he lunged from the still-moving cart, fetching his shoulder a fine crack on the doorframe before he tumbled out of sight. She really squealed now, stomping the brake pedal through the centre of the earth, sure he'd gone under the wheels. *OhmyGodohmyGodohmyGod.*

Luckily it was just the ill-kept road teasing. John was already back on his feet where the sidewalk opened to foot traffic. A little scraped and with one arm hanging numb from a bruised shoulder. Threading his way in fits and starts through the pedestrians, hunched and pushing back their whispers with his good hand. Fingers curled into palm with the white-knuckled terror that he might knock against somebody, might touch their *skin*.

Hopefully the jaundiced light concealed his distress but nothing could gentrify the friend's spitting and swearing as she hauled the cart into the first available spot.

She eventually found him sitting against a pillar as the locals tramped past, his head sagging forward and a hand clamped to his face. The front of his shirt was sodden with crimson so theatrical it could only be blood.

'Johnny, oh my God!'

'S' ok,' he managed nasally, grimacing to forestall a hysterical outburst.

All that blood. It streamed from both nostrils in warm coppery rivulets, coating lips and chin. He could rub his fingers in what slimed the digits, dark and rich like secret wet earth.

'...?'

'The. Music.'

He was trying to stay monosyllabic to avoid swallowing wads of the stuff. At least the crushing pressure in his sinuses was relieved. In fact the pounding beat, which was coming from quite nearby, had become bearable. Intriguing, even.

'Well, hell, don't let them see you bleed.'

With an aggressive glare around she shoed him down a dingy side alley, using little fluttering motions as though she would push but kept remembering hands off. A good deal of unease slithering about. He wasn't the only one having second thoughts.

The odd nook between buildings was at least sheltered and dim, even if the cheap plank fence trembled with the rattling music. Hope nobody in the block was expected up early for work tomorrow.

Once she had him safely out of sight with only bins for company the friend began fussing and scolding unbearably.

'Pinch your nose. Up here between the eyes.' She demonstrated, in case he'd forgotten where his face was. 'That's where you want the clot to form. Otherwise it'll just drop straight out onto the road. And while we're on the topic don't you ever, *ever* pull that shit while I'm driving! No, tilt your head *back.*'

'Wives'. Tale.'

'What?'

It was getting easier to breathe. 'Head's got to be forward for a bleed, not back. You don't want the red sticky running down your airway. Or your throat, fastest route to an upset stomach.'

'Wonderful.' She shook her head, taking a visibly calming

breath. Extremely visible, given the outfit. It was hard not to feel embarrassed. 'Are you sure you want to go through with this?'

'Here, aren't I?'

'I guess you are, at that.'

'Well, you couldn't push me into anything I genuinely didn't want. Maybe I'm finally ready.'

'Or as close as you'll ever be. One last hurrah before we all die, huh? You're going to have to lose that shirt.'

He spat a wad of clotted tissue, no standing on manners. 'Why?'

'Johnny, I'm serious, you can't let them see you've been bleeding, not the people down here. They're not likely to offer you a hanky.'

Suck you dry, her eyes warned gravely, and he found the frisson of fear strangely thrilling.

'Here, get the shirt off. Use the clean bits to wipe your face. No point coming over all shy—there'll be plenty of jerks wearing far less.'

Gooseflesh stippled bare skin as he stripped it off, mostly nerves. He'd never been this exposed. As though he'd peeled off his skin. 'I liked that shirt. It was my Sunday shirt.'

She held out an impatient hand. 'Give.'

Scrunching the rather expensive weave she set to scrubbing the alley's squalid crannies. Perhaps she'd decided they were staying for the night and was trying to make the place more homely. No—that was a stupid idea.

She hoicked up and spat on the ruined fabric, rubbing it in for good measure.

'If you didn't like it, you could have just said.'

'Hardy har har. I'm messing up your blood sample, dumbass. Don't want anybody finding this and whipping up a little black magic with your DNA.'

'Aren't you a bit old to believe in dusty hoodoo rituals? I thought you were into modern parties, dancing, music like all the young 'uns do.'

'Oh, but down here it's all the same thing, Johnny-boy.'

Other women would hide those teeth, but not the friend. Nothing could be too bad in a world where she could flash that grin on demand. She'd never let anything happen to him. Not while he owed her a coffee, at any rate.

Re-emerging into the milling foot traffic—people about, at this hour!—John discovered how close they had come before his cowardly bailing out. The building from the tacky flyer loomed right across the street. A notable leviathan in a cluster of towering monstrosities. Hulking its misshapen shoulders up and up, it probably pierced several of the city's layers. Demanding in its construction that all give way before it.

Both their necks creaked. Finding broken windows, the peeling remnants of asbestos hazard stickers, even streaks of bird shit which really dated it. The last of *A New Life*'s inbred pigeons were generally believed to have vanished during a fierce famine decades ago.

The final fancier leaped to his death from a rooftop clutching one of his empty coops, the scandal being that by the time authorities arrived the pavement had been licked clean. Shuddering, John wondered if it had been this very building. Perhaps he was standing right where a starving multitude had once used their fingertips to scrape one of their fellows off the road.

It certainly looked a place where bad things happened. The memory lingered, a nasty half-seen miasma about its looming blunt head. The building probably hadn't been renovated since a priceless bottle of champagne shattered on *A New Life*'s bow and away she crawled. Glittering suds and glass thrown into the air.

'Bad news, cowboy. We're taking the stairs.'

'Why?'

'Grown men don't whine, Johnny.'

'I'm not whining. Waaaaaah. Why can't we take the elevator?'

'This is High Estate, nothing *works*. Even if we pressed that button and the elevator *did* move, I sure as hell wouldn't go gambling our lives by getting on the damn thing. Not in a million years, not if you paid me.'

The steel clad fire door to the stairwell was just flat out gone. Its toothless dark gap, stinking of fermented cask juice, looked the sort of pit junkies crawl into to die. Unfazed by the likelihood of getting mugged, shanked or raped inside-out the friend marched straight into the squalid darkness and began climbing.

Was this sort of place *normal* for most people? John found it terrifying. Only his pride, and fear of being left alone on the street where he was clearly the juicier target, enabled him to follow.

'Kids do, you know,' she called down over her shoulder.

No matter how he hurried, when she turned back to him her features grew dimmer and dimmer, as they clomped away from the light. The omnipresent music was muffled to dull booms beneath her words, like somebody slamming a door in rage, over and over. Should there be anyone nefarious haunting this stairwell they'd sure know they were coming, but he couldn't think of an excuse to shush her. She didn't take kindly to shushing.

'Kids do what?'

'There's this whole subculture of bored thrillseekers who spend their time riding old stuff. Escalators, elevators, dumbwaiters. Whatever they can run a voltage through and get back into creaky, dusty life.'

'What happens when somebody's hyperactive son or daughter plummets to their death or gets churned up in the gears?'

'The rest of the idiots hold a party. They gaff the death trap back together, don't even bother to wipe the blood, and it's a point of honour to see who rides it next.'

'But ... why?'

'You did hear me say "bored thrillseeking" kids.'

'But it's so pointless!'

'Not to them. They get to feel alive. They've got some crazy legend they're chasing, of people stepping into junk and just ... just disappearing. Not dead. Just poof! Through some hidden gate to nowhere. Never send a postcard back. They all reckon there's somewhere to go, if they can only find a way to slip through.'

John desperately wanted to inquire, Do they trance? These kids, standing there with eyes flickering, when they should be awake? But it wasn't a topic he wanted her dwelling on. Keep it out of mind. Bar the gates.

They just climbed for a while, feeling the music shiver in the crumbling stairwell. She ran out of breath for chatting pretty quickly. He was even more unfit, a life spent on the couch hadn't adequately prepared him for midnight adventures. Cautious of breaking out his nosebleed he took it easy.

She forged impatiently ahead. Her daring outfit forced him to keep his eyes modestly on the steps ahead, and by the time they approached the top you could tell the same had occurred to her. Traffic-stop red, she hurried to yank open the door on the landing. John saw the beast, the icon from the pamphlet stencilled on the pebbled surface in thick red spray paint that had spattered and dripped, rendering the thing almost illegible. A threatening, exploded Rorschach.

The door opened. Blazing multicoloured light and the deep-throated roar of music rushed out. The friend beckoned and hurried through to point out the party.

There at the top of the wall, out of breath and slightly light headed, John saw his first High Estate rave. They were above it here. Dizzyingly perched on the shell of the great hollowed out building. Everything had been knocked out, floor upon floor, regardless of structural support. In his imagination the hulking structure suddenly seemed paper thin, pressed flat on a pamphlet. Swaying dangerously and ready to collapse in on itself at any moment.

Looking down, with a twist of nausea he realised that had they opened any of those other stairwell doors, doors without the dripping red mark, they had stood a good chance of plunging helplessly into empty air. Screaming as they plummeted down. An empty coop shattered on the ground and only the drab grey feathers of an extinct bird left, pinwheeling softly through the thin haze.

The ghastly open expanse ought to have taken his breath away. Rarely in the city did you see anything so vacant and exposed. But the base of it, down there, was safely filled. Packed wall-to-wall with moving bodies. With *people*, he realised in a sort of stunned amazement.

John could not have been more bewildered if he'd woken to discover he had hallucinated his whole life, while standing tranced in a corner.

From way up here you had to squint to resolve the bright compelling detail. They were even above the lights, which pointed needle-thin beams down at the crushing, heaving mass. Haphazardly wired to bring the building down in a blazing inferno. Beams that jittered and zagged wildly.

The globes blazed, more than enough to hurt his sensitive altered eyes, and if you looked directly at them they seemed to be rushing toward you. Coloured, moving, pulsating lights. Sparking off suspended mirrors and bits of glass, flashing, spinning …

'WHOA Nellie!'

The friend barred his way with her arm and he recoiled from the threatened contact, recoiled like someone given an electric shock. Recoiled just in time to avoid taking a fatal plunge over the edge.

He'd been leaning impulsively forward, drawn by the hypnotising dazzle. A seductive lure to just let go. God, what must it be like down there under the full force of it?

'Hey. You ok?'

He nodded numbly. *Not even slightly.*

Relieved, she pointed out over the suspended cage of the rigging, shouting to be heard. 'That way. There are safe spots for voyeurs to nest in. Nobody comes up here to be pawed, so you'll be fine.'

'Why do you come, then?' Suddenly it seemed an important question.

She had known about it all along, but he could never have imagined such a chaotic, blinding, deafening space. A place to be swept right away and be gone.

Grinning maniacally into a compact mirror she ignored the question and applied tiger bars of luminous paint to her sunken cheeks, which immediately began to glow in the ultraviolet backwash. No more immune to the thumping music she breathed it in, right to her core. Perspiration sheened the bare curve of her neck and shoulders.

'How do I look?' she asked pertly.

His opinion couldn't have been more irrelevant.

Without waiting for an answer she tossed her sweat-blackened hair and was gone. Descending the steps at eager breakneck speed to find her way into the party, the hungry maw that devoured all those people below.

Places for voyeurs, hey?

He shaded his eyes and yes, there were thin aluminium walkways strung over the steel pipe lattice. Distressingly thin. Intended for veteran tradesmen in full safety harness, with plenty of insurance and a wary eye at the back—some spouses weren't averse to giving a shove, matchmaking hardly an exact science.

It seemed only a pitiful few came to watch, compared to the immeasurable surging mass below. Perhaps thirty at most. And each sat alone, encapsulated in their own private world. Hunched shapes that clung like roosting gargoyles, their avid faces turned down, hungry, ripe to swoop. Splashed with reflected neon that clung like foam.

It was so bloody high up here!

John couldn't bear the prospect of walking upright over all that *nothing* and instead crawled abjectly on his hands and knees, flatly refusing to focus beyond the pitted aluminium to which he clung. Too close to the steaming lights the rungs burned his hands, and left tired burgundy smears.

He wiped them one at a time without letting go the other and tried not to picture what a cowardly figure he must cut. Luckily his slow progress took him among true human islands. To the other voyeurs, John hardly existed.

Dear Lord, he wished he could blinker his own awareness so readily. Every square millimetre of skin was horrifyingly alive to the mighty space below. He could only bring himself to venture a short way, scarcely clear of the wall, and then wind both legs tight to the ladder. *I'm never moving again*, he promised. Sweaty hands clamped down like vices, sealing the deal.

The moment he glanced down into the heaving mass,

vertigo smacked hooks into his brain.

There were so *many*! Individuals no longer existed, they were simply *together* in the dull stamping lullaby of the herd mind, the pack mentality. Where majority was permitted and no-one accountable for anything. Movement lubricated into synchronicity by the heaving sweat of the many.

John had thought himself acquainted with sweat. During surgery a patient's wracked secretions chemically outlined their failing health. But oh no, not here. There was no information to receive, it all garbled senselessly into one enormous *stink*. Gelded by his life of sterile soaps the primitive olfactory centres of his brain stuttered into stumbling panic. This was sensory paganism, and it jeered at the safe filtered world his body was conditioned to.

No chance of spotting the friend in that hectic crush of skin on skin, even with the keenest eye, but he bit his lip and strove anyway. Desperate for a glimpse of the familiar. But of course there was nothing he knew, his cardboard world didn't exist here. No wonder she mocked him. The people below were alien, moving like burning stars to the frenzy of alien music.

A bone pale flank. The brutish stamping of a cloven hoof. The crowd was an open mouth, screaming up at John, wanting him. And worst of all, on a podium in the erection of a naked fat man he saw a twisting bloodstained horn, ready to impale its victim.

No need to witness what great and terrible beasts might roam beyond the city's walls. They were all right here, a construct of hot cries and thrashing limbs that raged unchecked. It was everybody's waking nightmare. Invoked in this heated bedlam the Blessed had sculpted themselves anew in humanity's very flesh.

From deep within the black cage of John's chest, a small

broken piece began to groan in kind. Longing to be reunited with the whole.

He trembled, breaking out in a sweat of his own that was sallow with desperation. Wrestled for clear thought and control.

The urges buried deep in his soul rose from their starved stupor, painfully aware of imprisonment. Limbs truncated to prevent escape; crawling like a worm in darkness, going nowhere. Shackles creaked under strain. Consciousness was a puny add-on, icing to the cake of the true, throbbing, vital creature. Yet John resisted.

Years of training, of sacrifice were behind him. A grizzled unyielding veteran in a war against himself, he had long ago conquered the fresh impetuosity of boyhood; left the blood-fever of adolescence, far behind. He was a man, and true humanity was control.

He bent his forehead to the hot ladder. Trembling became palsied shuddering, threatening to flick him off his perch but slowly the beast inside was pushed down. It rumbled discontentedly as the breath of freedom brushed by but John gave it no choice, no choice but to subside back into the muck, trailing its chains behind.

Little by little his aching fists unclenched. He had justified their faith in him, those Surgeon hands. They became loose and relaxed on the rungs.

The outer world intruded. Vibration, a shaking of the scaffold made him look up with his heart in his mouth.

The other voyeurs had no such qualms to hold them back. Not a single soul here was concerned with maintaining the delicate thread of reason—no, they fled it. Embraced the bestial, one and all. Escaping from their lives, if only for this night.

All on their feet, moving to the music's whim like fearless

puppets. John could only discern silhouettes against the larger dark, barely enough to distinguish their gyrations. Should the scaffold be jerked away their strings would hold them, surely. Whirling in mid-air.

A kid who couldn't have been older than thirteen whipped out his little noodle and pissed off the edge. Whooping soundlessly and spraying it about like a fountain. Droplets sizzled on hot lights.

Caught in the drifting back spray, to John's primed nostrils the acid exuded a provoking musk. His balls tightened, the creature bound limbless in darkness bellowed its challenge. He fought an urge to jump to his feet and do the same, make the crowd his own. Drench the presumptuous kid so thoroughly, his hairless scrotum would never climb back out of his throat.

But letting go of the ladder would be clearly insane.

Light turned the falling droplets to flame. Those subsumed in the pit below only raised their arms to the downpour and writhed more frantically. Revulsion inverted by frenzy. Looming above it all like possessed gods, who deigned to rain their essence on mere worms, in a sky of thundering lights the voyeurs stamped and shook.

John saw her go, the voyeur closest to him. The girl. Even with his altered eyes scorched and blazing he saw her foot slide off the rail, before she herself knew what was happening.

Instinct kicked in and he lunged forward explosively. Muscles knew their job far in advance of his dithering brain, squashed its attempts to ruin the fluid process. At the furthest extent of his reach the girl's flailing wrist smacked dead centre into his palm. Into his gloveless palm.

The girl, young woman or whatever she was, completed her motion with long hair fanning out behind. Arms spread wide as though she possessed wings and was about to leap joyously into the air. His imposition registered before imbalance did, and her dimly seen mouth twisted angrily. The beginning of an ugly outrage she'd never get time to finish. No time. For her, time had run out.

Her centre of gravity drifted on its way out past the edge of the scaffold. Momentum dragged them both forward through the lights.

Dire awareness flooded in, too damn late to do anything now and she clutched at him, opening painted lips to wail.

For a moment John thought he caught a glimpse of somebody skulking beyond the lights. The merest hint of rich gold hair gleaming in darkness, a colour he'd never seen before. An observer, crouching like a spider on the lattice. Something eerie, with limbs that didn't seem jointed quite right.

'Help!'

But his desperate croak went unanswered, and when he blinked sweat from his eyes there was nobody. Merely his own flicker of hallucination that anybody might intercede, might give a damn and save them both. Their slow motion ballet came to an end. Gravity asserted itself.

'Gaah!'

John's chest hit the metal with all the girl's falling weight, plus his. It really seemed something in there would snap like a wishbone. But arms and legs stayed firm, holding them.

The girl dangled from his overstretched arm like an unwelcome graft. She clawed frantically at his wrist, twisting and pinwheeling in the empty air. It seemed the vast churning sea below had noticed them now: if he focussed beyond his burden the upturned faces, the countless eyes and mouths were all eager black holes.

'Help us!' he yelled, but couldn't hear his voice. And he

feared, oh so very much feared that to help was not what the crowd wanted at all.

All of the lights swung jerkily around. With the rest of the building plunged into darkness the struggling woman was lit into a living rave sculpture. A glowing chameleon in space that flashed red, yellow, purple, seeking the colour that would allow her to slip away and escape.

Her only cry was the avid roar of the crowd, but John could see her mouth making desperate, mindless shapes. Panicked beyond thought. To save a drowning person sometimes you had to knock them out, lest they drag you under. But clinging in place was taking everything he had.

John held her frail wrist.

John held her.

He held.

It might be fractured already under the load the joint was being forced to take. Her bare skin against his own was urgently alive, vital, pulse thundering in a code not even the shattering rave could blot out. She clutched at his arm and every individual hair knew it intensely. More vividly than he'd ever experienced anything before. He'd never been so hyperaware in his life.

He was going to save her. Perhaps they might even be friends? Perhaps ...? Who'd know about a woman, way down here?

But her wonderful, perfect, terrifying skin was sliding through his grip.

'Stop kicking!' he howled.

She was too mindless in fear to understand, wiped clean by it. Her lower half jerked uncontrollably.

'Stop bloody kicking!'

Down inside the girl's thin shirt John could see her small breasts; well, nobody dressed for being in *this* position. He could even see, as the spectrum shifted through white, that the crowning nipples were different. One peach, one rose, as though genes had been unable to decide which looked more beautiful. No doubt matchmaking would breed for such a charming trait, with scores of brats in her near future. Perhaps that was why she would come to a rave like this, to forget.

Her eyebrows were notched with silver rings. And her wide, wide eyes were green.

'Ah,' she gasped.

And then her grey-polished fingernails raked through his palm and she fell, inelegantly and incredibly fast. Arms and legs spiralling out. And now she found it in herself to scream, a peal spun through the air like frosted feedback. A protest that was shockingly brief.

John knew anatomy too well. It was his bread and butter. Even had the crowd been water, plunging in the way she did had smashed her.

And he screamed, too, up there in the darkness, fingers clutching air the girl had filled only seconds before. Agonised by the sudden loss. It was like he could still feel her, a phantom limb, a grip ever-sliding through his hand.

His ability to so much as think dislocated, came adrift. He imagined the vertebrae of her spine doing the same, cruelly severing the cord they were meant to protect. Not quite quick enough to catch her the lights swung down as the rave closed over, and before John's horrified eyes the boiling crowd *ate* her. Sucked her broken body greedily into their midst.

The act was not without consequence. Nothing is.

The bass shifted seamlessly into a higher tearing speed. More and more flesh down there bared to the glaring, probing lights, the people crushing together, swarming. How could they breathe? Brief fountains of dark liquid erupted.

John stared wildly, trying to fathom what it meant.

'*Johnny!*' The friend howled frantically from the stairwell door. She had been doing so for a while, it seemed. How did she make it back up those stairs so fast?

He squinted across the intervening space. Her eyes looked very, very wide like gigantic tunnels bored into her face.

'Johnny, *come on*, please! We have to go, like, *now!*'

'What? What? What?' He whispered, unsure what had happened. Was happening. Aftershocks coursed through his body. In that moment if anybody had asked, he would have struggled to tell them his name.

But he recognised the friend, all right. Of course he did.

She couldn't hear him from way over there, and he couldn't ask to have things explained, so on limbs weak as fluid John began to crawl backward toward her, a hesitant millimetre at a time. The racket buffeted him, determined to tear him free, have him for themselves. His snail pace journey seemed to take forever. Or at least the friend's frustrated jigging indicated so.

He found that his hands, his amazing Surgeon's hands, remained true. He blindly entrusted them to guiding him back to safer ground and damn the rest. Everything else fought the surety, in a perverse effort to follow the girl in that deadly plunge. As though sensing such a tender morsel dangled just beyond their reach the mob's churn and groan was ecstatic, anticipating his bloody arrival in their midst.

'Oh God, we've got to get out of here!'

In her fright the friend was off down the stairs the moment he stood, wobbly. He lumbered after her like a wrung-out somnambulist, couldn't seem to think. The heavy concrete stairwell muffled no shrieks, the music already took care of that. Without having seen it with his own eyes John might assume it was still an ordinary party.

'There's been some sort of accident, some girl died. My God, people are being ripped to shreds in there!'

Strange, he couldn't remember hearing screaming, not even when red fountained up. Only a faint high tone humming in his ears. Even now, what the friend was yammering at him came faintly, from far away.

They stumbled from the dark stairwell together and it was amazing to be out into air that didn't reek of piss. The pavement was crazed with people running about like maddened ants. Fleeing, bleeding, clutching scraps of clothing to themselves and sobbing, laughing. Others were running toward the building with wide lunar eyes and shiny chins.

John slipped in a tidal pool of bile and nearly went down. Ahead, the friend was barging a path clear enough for him, jolted like a pinball but shoving on with gritted determination.

Too many people about the cart. Too many and John without a shirt, his flesh bared. He'd never make it. He slumped in defeat, and the friend's expression went hard.

'Be ready.'

'Ready for what?' Oh good, he was whining again.

Mercifully with her back to him she pulled her blouse right open, breasts wobbling free, and started to run.

'Oh God somebody help me!' She screamed in a voice that sounded way over the top, even to John.

'Hey, look at the old duck!'

Hooting, the entire group around the cart immediately gave chase around the corner. John darted to the cart, his chest and shoulders aching abominably as he climbed in. The slammed door seemed to seal him into a vacuum.

And thus began the tensest wait of his life, although mercifully not long. The friend reappeared, jogging around the next corner, tucking herself back in.

'That was so stupid!' he burst out as she slid into her seat.

She rolled her eyes. 'What a pack of assholes. I was just going to do the block, but we ran into this other bunch of thugs looking for trouble and now, well, it isn't turning out pretty for anyone.'

She started the engine. 'Can you believe we got away with it? John the Surgeon and his first High Estate party!'

He fingered his forearm where the hairs still knew the girl's skin. Slipping eternally from his grasp. If he blinked, even for an instant, he was staring down into her pleading green eyes.

'I saw that girl. I saw her die.'

Her face whipped around, aghast warring with avid. 'Really?'

Staring at his hands. Couldn't look at her.

'I touched her.'

Aghast won out by a long shot.

CHAPTER THREE

THE BLIND VOYEUR

THE FRIEND busied herself about her tiny dim flat with the fluttery movement of a bird that can't decide to settle. So similar to the tiny scraps of dun feather that pecked about the glass and high gantries of the sunlight suburbs. The span of heavens was for the elite only, living at the apex of the city, but even their egos only risked the view fearfully through thick plastex.

Fashionable to mask unease by posturing and sneering. The height of *sang froid* never to glance up at all. So sparrows were poisoned as pests, offered tainted seed in picturesque feeders. Who wanted their eye drawn to some flitting motion, inadvertently tricked into gazing at the sky? Better to have a crumpled carpet of little dead bodies, to be vacuumed off the lawn before the paperboy showed up.

An odd thing to dwell on. John supposed he was tired. It felt like dunes of sand had been poured beneath his skin.

Swathed in an oversize dressing gown the friend slapped the kettle on, clang! Then nervily paced about neatening magazines. The heavy cosmetics she'd yet to scrape off made it appear a clown head had been jammed on her unassuming body, which went about grotesquely unaware of the change.

The longer her aimless fussing drew out, the harder the sick knot forming in his stomach became. Of all the times to be short an opinion. Say something, he begged her silently. Strung and numb, both of them, with ringing ears. She had laid on the horn to inch their way through the people spilling out onto the street, the chaos. They would be lucky not to end up a bit deaf. They were bloody lucky anyhow.

In the flux there had been glimpses lit by searing flares, of fancier carts getting rocked off their wheels to the squealing of those trapped inside. John had been sure they were done for. Teetering on the verge of ordering her to stop; he wasn't willing to die in an odorous tin can, when it could be done running free through the crowd.

But through a night that had panned out far wilder than she'd bargained for, the friend had kept her head. She'd bitten grimly into her lower lip with a sort of moan, one bloodless fist clamped to the wheel, the other mashed against the *harrk*-ing horn which had appropriately begun to sound a bit sick. She'd held it together long enough to extract them from disaster.

Which was only just, as she'd landed them there in the first place.

And now here they were. A little mussed but essentially unharmed, circling uneasily. Even now the light feminine scent of the butchered girl clung to John's fingertips. It might be stamped indelibly on his biochemistry, then what would he do? Anyone with a nostril could snuffle it out. A Surgeon! The shriek of alarm would rouse the city. He'd seen it happen.

He flinched painfully at every scrap of noise from the street. This was the dead time, the grey hours ticking away before dawn. When life retreated and the silence was smothering. They had a few precious moments to themselves.

Only his pulse begged to differ. *You're still alive*, it asserted. That had to count for something.

When he fancied she wasn't watching he brushed his fingertips beneath his nose, a guilty savour. Then caught himself with a start. *Crazy pervert*. Hoping to feel some shame, no matter how far he might already be from redemption.

Slipping a fresh pair from his pocket with trembling hands John whipped the gloves on, as though you could don normality the same way. He saw the friend's rigid spine jerk at the brisk snap on skin.

Apparently dread's black chalice brimmed bottomless. Was she afraid for him, or herself? Couldn't blame her. It couldn't be nice to look about and suddenly find herself on the sinking ship of his life.

He let his eyes wander about her flat. No style, save the friendliness of clutter and cushions. Charles' home, too, he had to keep reminding himself. Scant evidence, unless he'd made absence itself a sort of flourish. His signature was to inhabit no space, leave little mark. Perhaps Charles' imprint could only be found behind that firmly closed bedroom door.

John found it a touch sinister that part of the friend's

life was shut away, he was used to thinking of her in one dimension and primaries. It hadn't yet occurred that he summarised everyone that way. And that when it came down to it, he didn't know a damn thing about anybody.

After a while he turned back to realise she had alighted on the chair opposite. Watching him watch her bedroom door.

She offered a shirt. 'Here. Cover yourself up like a civilised person, before those nipples drill right through space-time.'

'What'll Charles think to find me in his lounge, with his wife, wearing his damn clothes?'

'Nothing.' Her expression becoming eerily like her husband's. 'Why would he think anything? Surgeons aren't men.'

'Sure, your hubby's such a great guy and all. But …'

'But, but,' she mimicked. 'For such a skinny noodle, you sure seem to have a great big "but" following you everywhere.'

He accepted the shirt, frowning at how she snatched her fingers back. He'd put the gloves on already. He wasn't made of fire.

The budget cotton felt scratchy as he pulled it on. 'I miss my old shirt.'

'Yes, you're welcome. Look, Johnny …'

The kettle crooned its three harmonised notes. The lounge filled with the smell of the cheap handle charring, layered over a long history of such occurrences. You could feel in your gut how it would go on, until the kettle melted to a heap of slag and she was forced to buy another just as tacky.

'Damn,' she muttered, and retreated to the tiny kitchenette.

She may well lack the courage for what she wished to say, but good news or bad John wanted to hear it. He had little insight of his own. Worried that anything he might do would only make it worse. Trapped perspiration was already wrinkling the skin of his hands, prickling him.

'Tea?' She called, trying for normalcy with a false brightness he found heartbreaking. 'Coffee? Bollocks?'

'Bollocks would be nice.' More by rote than humour but she obliged with her sharp "ha ha" anyway and brought coffee. The scent clashed uneasily with the burnt plastic. At his place they could have swilled fresh espresso until their hearts split, but of course he couldn't stand to go back, not yet. All she had on offer was chemical instant, blushingly out of sugar or milk to soften it.

But at least the warming mug was something to hang on to. *Are We Having Fun Yet?* asked the logo, and John thought he might weep.

She re-seated herself. With a deep breath that only trembled slightly, tried to resume. 'So, talk to me. What happened?'

He blanched. *Are We Having Fun Yet?* grew too hot and he set it down. He wasn't having any fun at all.

'She fell. That girl,' he answered stupidly, not knowing what else to say. She fell, she fell. She falls. Her cartwheeling death still fresh and real.

'Off the rigging, right next to me. She just fell off. I tried to help her, I wasn't even thinking.'

He swallowed, sickly. Since when had he ever helped anybody? 'I couldn't save her. And she just … she died.'

The friend listened intently, head tilting as though seeking the best method to weigh, to understand. Wasn't about to let him sidle around this one.

'You touched her.'

The damning weight of it crushed him flat.

'I touched her. I touched her hand, her arm.' Some time in the conversation he'd bitten his cheek savagely. Later, it was a taste he would always associate with the words. *I touched her*, and then the queasy slick of his own blood.

Her next question was unexpected. Way to kick a guy when he's down. 'How long is it since you last touched anyone?'

He felt a powerful urge to fling her through the wall. 'I don't touch people!'

'Don't be a dumbass. You weren't squished from the womb with a scalpel in hand. I'm asking when did you, Johnny, last touch an alive awake person with your own bare hands?'

He glared with something very close to loathing. This vile talent of hers, to always hit on the sore spot. She weathered it, sanguine no matter what lurked within. They had survived each other's company long enough, cutting at each other in restless frustration.

Waiting for his answer.

A low raspy buzz squatted behind his eyes, but the memory itself was no problem to fish up. The only moment that stood out from his confused jumble of days. 'I'm sure we don't need a sad re-hash of my glory years.'

'Sit down.'

He hadn't even realised he'd stood. And since when did she start barking orders?

'It's *me*, Johnny. Just you and me.'

Damn her stupid big mouth. He picked up his drink again, wishing with hopeless intensity for something from the ethanol family.

'Fine. The last person who touched me was my aunt.'

'Your …' Her hand drifted to her mouth in a comically feminine gesture. Went nicely with the bleeding clown makeup.

'And hey, now we'll both be infamous.'

'But that can't be. Your aunt was a Surgeon before you were even born!'

Bitterness exposed his teeth, at bay. *Tell me something*

I don't know. Filled with a coppery tang, like biting into wires. 'That she was. The great lady, the great Surgeon. Of course my amazing talented aunt was also a secret criminal, a deviant, a pervert and every other name they rush to pin on the disgraced. I suppose I can join her in that, now, too.'

'Yeah, you're just panting after it however it comes.' Her sarcasm was plain, to expose his melodrama, but he winced as though she'd seen right to his blackened core. 'What happened tonight was an *accident*, you didn't *mean* to touch that girl. It's hardly like they caught you with your hand up her shirt.'

'Like they caught my aunt, you mean, in those photos? What's the difference? They *executed* her for what she did.'

Her sallow skin whiter by degrees, she'd be lucky to keep enough blood to stay upright. He nodded his own head in violent, vicious jabs.

'Oh yes, you'd better enjoy this time together because we're not going to see a hell of a lot more of it.'

'Your aunt died in an accident after the trial …' Said weakly, but she was smarter than that. Willing social blindness was getting a real shakedown tonight.

'After all, it's so bloody easy to trip and fall out of the damn *city*, isn't it, happens every day!' She was shrinking from his venom, but he was really on a roll now. 'So commonplace nobody bothered reporting the details, but hey, I can't even *count* the number of times I've stumbled into iron restraints.

'My aunt's wrists and ankles were still bolted down when the Blessed finished with her, even if the rest was gone. She broke her own damn wrists trying to escape!'

A torrent of mascara down the friend's face. She hovered on trembling muscles, a hand extended only to be snatched back. She was unable to comfort him, or herself. That was fine. Some things a cuddle wasn't going to fix.

'When you say your aunt touched you … did she …? I mean, you were just a kid.'

'Oh my God *no*, what is wrong with your mind? I was there when they took her. Came barging right into her house without knocking—she'd forfeited her rights, even the most basic. Head to toe in protective gear, they grabbed her arms and dragged her away. One of her shoes came off and they wouldn't even let her go back for it.'

And John, a little boy, left standing alone in the ransacked house. Crying in the most pathetic way imaginable, unable to understand, nobody had slowed to explain it to him. Convinced the world was ending. They'd been having breakfast and now the table was upturned, cereal and milk splattered everywhere. What had his aunt done wrong, for something so horrible to happen?

'She touched me, just once. While they were barging up the drive. Must have seen them through the window. Touch was the very crime they were coming to get her for, I guess she figured what could one more hurt? Dropped her gloves on the floor like they were no longer needed. That was weird in itself. I'd never seen her without them.

'I quit shovelling cereal in my face and looked up expectantly. Smiling, she held my face and she kissed my forehead.

'I wish more than anything that I'd smiled back but I was so shocked. Even as a kid I knew people weren't supposed to touch her. She was different. Special. It was like being kissed by the moon.

'All through what could only loosely be called her trial she stood awkwardly in just one shoe, wearing the clothes she was taken in. And when they gave her to the Blessed she was tied down, so she never even had a chance.'

'But … but it's all so *stupid*! All that training, and you were naturally good at surgery right from the start. It can't all just *vanish*! Not from one little touch!'

'But it *does*. My aunt killed a patient. She murdered somebody, don't you see? That's how they found her out, that she'd gone crazy and taken a lover. All of a sudden that mystery lover was more important than duty, more important than vows. More important than Mr Weststone, widower and father of one, who'd gone under the blade for what ought to have been routine gallstone surgery.

'She killed an innocent man. How could she have thought for a second she wouldn't get found out?'

As though terrible secrets could be buried in flesh, sewn over and forgotten. John knew better. The mortified body rejected them. But his aunt must have been desperate. Trapped, with nowhere to go.

'Put your feet up.' He didn't want her fainting, was *already* aware that this was horrible thankyou very much.

'I can't believe … and you still signed up to be a Surgeon.'

'How could I be anything else? Before her fall, my aunt was the greatest Surgeon who ever lived.'

A faint, sad smile for the nephew who didn't understand why she had touched him. Only that it made him special too.

'Now I've got surgery scheduled for this morning in about,' he glanced at the clock. 'Three hours. Living up to my famous aunt, hey? Here it is.'

'Oh God.' The full enormity only now dawning. 'What are you going to do?'

'That's quite the question, isn't it?'

'What are you going to *do*, Johnny?'

'I have no idea. And I'm scared.'

'I made this happen.' The friend said with dull amazement, like a scientist whose research spawned atrocity. 'This is all my fault. "Come to a party." I thought I was being so clever.

If I hadn't been so *stupid*. I'd … I'd do anything to take it back.'

'It would be great if life allowed do-overs. But maybe this was always fated. I am her nephew, after all. The last person she touched. Do you think failure can be passed on that way, through our hands?'

He sipped, beyond tasting anything. 'I don't know what I'm going to do.'

She opened her mouth and then, miracle, shut it again. Nothing more to be said. Her smeared face conveyed it all. She had already done enough.

So the two friends, so much like antagonists an observer wouldn't have been able to tell the difference, sat. And they waited. In a silence that gradually welled up to subsume them.

For all its high ceiling the operating theatre was tiny. A box, really. With a grille in the roof for fumes, necrosis especially pumped out some nasties, and another in the floor for drainage. Oozes and the like.

Flip the whole lot over and it would essentially look the same. Within its confines the only things *not* of hose-down stainless steel were the patient, John's cheerfully whistling colleague, and John himself. Like most of the city's construction it seemed a place more of function than people, but it had been devised by an entirely different type of mind. By Son, the man with a foot in each world.

Whenever the two Surgeons shifted, their garbled reflections raced and collided over cold surfaces. They moved briskly to keep warm. Low temperature aided in soothing the body's alarms to sleep, to coma, and deeper. Critical defences dropped for the moment of slicing and dicing. At the centre of their efficient dance sprawled the patient in a blinding puddle of light. A vulnerable knot of meat in a heartless metallic room.

John scrubbed his bare hands methodically beneath a jet of quicksilver chemicals, the blast of ice pushing needles straight to his heart. He stared grimly at the shiny wall where his reflection sported eye sockets of blossoming darkness. A forehead twisted and weighted with strain. A Surgeon's face, to be sure. He wondered if he had ever smiled, and what good such a foolish expression could possibly accomplish.

The patient already slumbered. They were brought in so, for decency's sake, defenceless and trusting. His co-Surgeon already hooking her up to various machines that loomed close about the table, to kilometres of spun glass and rubber tubing. Descendents of the venerable hospital machines they snaked eagerly into the patient's vessels as though alive, murmuring musically in their low binary tongue.

But of course, unlike their progenitors these couldn't be classified as alive. John had always dreamed how it must have been to actually speak to one of those ancient machines, what their golden age had been like. He was hardly unique.

Far from uneasy at the level of automation, assisting Surgeon Lars bobbed cheerfully in place. About as concerned as he'd have been hooking a cart up to diagnostics for the once-over.

'Ready for action yet, or are you too busy washing those talented hands down the drain?'

John turned off the tap. His skin felt icy all over. 'Sure.'

Squat, beetle-ish, Lars looked a man who had benefited from all the meals John had ever missed. The exact opposite of what you would expect from somebody named "Lars." They had fallen in at university, although hardly by John's grace—he had already commenced withdrawing, like a snail horn poked once too many.

Mainly Lars assigned himself as his friend, despite a mild inferiority complex. Always ebullient, always pleased to see him. At the end of the day John didn't have the heart to shake him off. He'd so few acquaintances. Alas, Lars' personal quest to brighten his day went ever unfulfilled.

'Yo, I'm almost done here.'

'Nobody says "yo" anymore, Lars.'

The other Surgeon tapped a pressure gauge then sucked his fingers, seeming to relish the taste of bare skin. John shuddered. He wouldn't go putting his own cracked and wrinkled digits near his mouth, no way.

'Everything I touch is sheer magic. It's no mystery the likes of us aren't allowed to touch the living folk, am I right?'

'Not funny.'

'What, the darling of the surgical field can't take a joke, now? What happened to you man, you used to be cool.'

'No I didn't, and neither were you. I was born sour, and as God is my witness I'll die there.'

John came reluctantly and stood in the pool of light, to gaze apprehensively down at the safely dehumanised patient. Those slack features seemed naggingly familiar. Perhaps it was his nasty conscience, rearing up to whisper sweet nothings in his ear.

His own whiter-than-milk face under its burden of dreadlocks, paper capped, hid a body wracked with uncertain flutters. All he had to do was utter one simple sentence to end this. *Would you mind taking over for me, mate?* Other Surgeons did it sometimes, according to the mysterious inner tide of talent. No biggie.

Other Surgeons.

Instead John picked up the sleeping scalpel. Gingerly

fingered the chilled steel.

You see, Lars was a bright cookie, no two ways about it. For all his flaws he had made Surgeon. And over the years the two of them had worked alongside, favours in their unlikely pairing had only ever run one way.

It was John covering Lars' ass when his fellow staggered in brutal with the hairy dog, or that bit too stoned, or just "too ennui" today for operating. John, always first in the theatre, laying out instruments by geometry of ritual. John who insisted on the robes, tea and scalding incense after each session. Lars hated purification and had trouble closing the antique robes around his bulk. He hardly emerged with the intended sense of renewal.

He'd inevitably wonder why Mr-By-The-Book was suddenly turning down plum jobs. There would be needling with no sane answers.

'Did something happen?'

'Aren't you feeling well?' That would be the worst. The simplest query after his health might be the last push that saw John splinter into pieces. It felt like his harrowed skull was caving in.

'So, you hear what all this mess is about?'

An actual question. Lars stood at his shoulder, wet brown eyes betraying a sympathetic heart as he looked down on their patient. Bad trait for a Surgeon. Almost his undoing in the finals.

The woman's naked chest rose and fell, but there nothing about her stark nudity to tempt a voyeur. Her youthful figure was a jellied mass of blunt contusions and nail marks, dental imprints, the injuries of a creature savaged. Broken fingernails still embedded in seeping wounds were electroshock pink, or cheap glitter. One of her breasts lay neatly beside her on the cold metal table, a boot print still clearly indented in it.

With a sinking heart, John could well guess where all that had come from. Feeling grey as the steel walls, dragged down, he had but to close tired eyes to see a surging orgy of flesh tearing itself apart. Striving so desperately to not have to exist anymore. The embodiment of his own secret wish.

'Nope,' he lied, bald faced. He had always been quite the liar.

Lars shook his head, grandpa lamenting the folly of kids these days. 'Another of those kitschy lower level parties gone completely bugshit. *Sixteen* people kaput. Our tables will be crammed with these sadsack cases all week, and you just know come nine months time pop-reg will be screaming over another unscheduled crisis. Recalculate the entire gene pool right down the line.'

Lars swooped his podgy hand a centimetre above the patient's dishevelled hair, his version of a reassuring pat. He was always pulling shit like that when there were no witnesses about. Toeing the line of orthodoxy. Sometimes whispering into the ear of unconsciousness that everything would be alright, Uncle Lars'd have them fixed up in a jiffy. Lars had never truly let go of the need to touch. John could *largely* be trusted not to turn him in.

This time it was because he was barely listening. Instead John found himself hypnotised by his own hands. A simple flick of the finger and the scalpel began to warm, stinging his eyes with its familiar aura. Why was he turning the damn thing on? Surely he didn't intend to *use* it?

'Oh sod. Get this: this poor girl's sister was one of those killed. Took a swan dive off some kind of gantry and the crowd just gobbled her up. We can stitch her from stem to stern but she may not *want* to pull through after seeing something like that.'

The scalpel dropped
from John's
nerveless
fingers.

It narrowly missed his foot and sliced neatly into the floor while Lars leaped away in belated reaction, cursing. Dance moves were a little sluggish, but there wasn't a man alive who valued his skin more.

For a long humiliating moment the Surgeons stared at the blade as it hummed innocently in the floor, transmitting its weird song to the rest of the metal room. If it hadn't still been warming up, the damn thing would be at the centre of the earth by now.

'Holy fucking shit-fuck, John!' Lars, predictably first to break the silence.

John put his face in his hand. Bare hand. It felt so … 'Yeah.'

'Look, let's just … uh, keep this between ourselves, yeah?' Bless his weasely heart. A slip like that could see John stood down. 'Just … don't do it again. I swear, my balls almost shot outta my mouth.'

Survival instinct be damned—John hadn't even shifted his foot. It felt as though he was struggling to spit words around wads of cottony wool. 'That's just … horrible, you know, really horrible. For her to have lost her sister that way.'

Lars' outrage softened a touch because that's exactly what he was, a soft touch. John's famous aunt never far from mind. To duck the ludicrous sympathy John bent and gingerly plucked the humming instrument from the floor. The singing in the walls died with a last ringing note. It sounded like angels had been on their way, but the door at the last second slammed shut.

'Not horrible enough for me to get stuck back after hours reattaching all your damned toes.' He drew John's attention to where shoe leather had been sliced away.

Nuts, John thought fuzzily. I really liked those shoes.

'Seriously man, not to put too fine a point on it, you look like a microwaved turd. You ok? Is there something going on, anything you need to chat about? My shout this time, scouts honour.'

Yes!

He steadied himself on the gurney, fighting the sudden adrenaline bolt. This was it. This was his way out. A confession and quick end, as decent as one could expect from such a horrible exploded situation.

'No,' he heard a calm voice respond, that couldn't possibly be his own. 'I'm fine. Just a late night and a bushel of bad dreams, same as same.'

What are you saying? What about this patient, John? You'll kill her, just like you killed her sister. Your hands will fail. You'll drop her.

'Sucks man. You're sure there's nothing I can do to help? Friends look out for each other, right?'

He shied away from the other Surgeon's scrutiny. Raised his voice defensively. 'I said I'm fine.'

Stop me Lars, for the love of God!

Fortunately the scalpel did not need to be cleaned after its impromptu trip to the floor, its very nature was sterile. No muss, no fuss. John's thumb slid over the engraved name as though trying to gain strength from it. *I'm sorry*, he whispered silently.

To Lars, with a firmness he didn't feel. 'Let's get on with it.'

If John's prodigious talent had been perverted it was not immediately obvious. As unassailable as her sleeping face was, the patient's flesh was familiar and welcoming. It parted almost eagerly to bare her intimate secrets, damage concealed up until now, waiting for someone worthy to assay it. Places where life bled uselessly into cavities. Where brute cruelty had shifted organs to where they need not be.

He marked little resemblance to her ill-fated sister. The woman was small, so puny she would be mistaken a child if her body weren't naked. It was like repairing a broken doll. Back on went the small left hand, still clenched in a fist. That face marked her as someone who had grown up in the lower levels. Hard and guarded, even in repose. Beneath dark brows it dared anybody to feel sorry for her, just so she could fling it back in their faces.

In almost violent relief John forgot himself in the intricacies of her hurts. He forgot her poor sister, falling forever as the lights swung down and failed to catch her. He forgot his friend with a sort of bliss, waiting forlornly in her loveless flat. Most of all he forgot the city and its fears waiting to cascade down and crush him. Time was not real. His life, or whatever excuse for it, was not real. Surgery was what he had been born for. The only true reality were these delicate structures awaiting restoration, order from chaos. He could hang over her for microseconds or centuries, it didn't matter so long as the job got done.

If Lars noticed anything unusual he didn't say. In fact, Lars said nothing at all until John was putting the final touches to the pliant reattached mammary tissue. And what he came out with was, 'Hi.'

Hi?

Lars was standing *outside* the doorway, head peeking in and a six-incher dripping mustard down his wrist. He registered John's blank look of surprise.

'Oh—you were getting along so well, I thought I'd pop out for a hotdog. Gotta get in early, you know. If they sit in the warmer all day they end up tasting like ballsack. Be scoffing it next door if you need me.' In the purification chamber, no less. 'Nice job, by the way. Boobs are always tricky.'

And gone.

John stared after him. He'd buggered off?

The cooling scalpel mumbled its satisfaction. And here lay the patient, the murmurs of her body now muted by flesh walls. Alive, alive and well.

After a quick, agonised glance around he put his waterlogged hand against the woman's bare throat. Hoping to sense again that vast electric jolt, the feeling of his body coming alive.

Against hers, his awful white flesh looked like something drowned in a cistern. Downy hairs, scarcely visible to the eye, tickled his skin. Her pulse beat sleepily against his trembling fingers. Beneath the stench of wet fluids liberated by the procedure, her living female scent rose into the air like warm radiance.

He realised he was holding his breath, awaiting revelation. But he was merely one human being with his hand on another.

All the strength ran out of him.

Palsied as an old man he folded onto the floor, which burned cold through his pants. He clamped both wondrous Surgeon's hands to his head as though he might reshape the bone by brute force.

Scorched, abused eyes gradually brimmed. Until John wept hot tears for all the useless years of his life.

CHAPTER FOUR

Excision

FOR HIS SECOND trip below John went trembling and John went alone.

It didn't have to be that way. Lars was practically gagging to be of use, and the friend already privy to a good chunk of his dirty laundry. But catastrophe is intrinsically isolating. It severs you from the warm throbbing biomass right when you need them the most. Casts you back on your own resources, so hopelessly overloaded.

John was buckling before he took a single step; and all that followed was part of the long slow fall.

He traversed the relatively well lit and populated commons in a daze. Head down in case the friend was about. Hands buried deep inside pockets to hide the gloves, although that made sweating a thousand times worse. Paranoia rampaged, as though everybody could tell what he was up to at a glance. He sneered at the ribbon vendors. *Just try and stop me.*

Following surgery a kind of fatalistic panic had seized him. His future track had seemed on rails: exceed his aunt to become the greatest Surgeon who had ever lived. Feted in public, crumbling away in his sealed apartment in *The Cutters*, winking bottles lined up in a row. There would be the occasional visit from the friend or loyal Lars to try and dry him out. The liver cirrhosis that would finally carry him off. But what would have really been the death of him would be sheer loneliness for human touch.

All shattered, now. It was impossible.

Here was where any more balanced soul might learn the lesson of calamity: that you must go on, there's really no choice. Wading through shame so thick it smothers, or dripping with panic-sweat, shedding your own skin with fear—you go on, and discover that the world continues to unfurl like always. Only you were stuck.

But John scrabbled at reality, seeking a third option. Not to stagnate, or move on, but to do the impossible and step aside. How far would he have to travel to escape himself? Where did anyone go when they simply couldn't take it anymore?

Thus instead of finding his feet again, he abandoned his whole life on the spur of the moment. Just like so many others who'd disappeared. Convinced this was fate and that there was nowhere else to go.

He was baulked here and there by his greenness. Stray into bad neighbourhoods and not even a Surgeon was immune to getting rifled like a cheap purse and tossed down some alley. Some wisp of a thing bleeding from his eyes provided passport. Battered lumps and leering, whip-thin women drew back, nostrils wrinkling as they smelled his intent. Not liking it one bit.

He didn't linger at the kicked-open nest of High Estate, either, where crowds swarmed like maddened bees, finding nothing to sting but each other, over and over. Quite the different atmosphere by day. The very air steamed with perspiration, chatter and refuse, a fume that condensed and dripped from high ceilings. Get under it and you would be marked, like a caste, it would horribly stain your clothes forever. Locals scurried beneath parasols or limited themselves to dark joyless colours where the taint wouldn't show.

He selected increasingly abandoned trolleys and elevators, sometimes moving in aimless little orbits made brittle by despair. Whatever crossed his dull field of vision he went for, always an eye for the most scuffed and saddest example. The passage below that best matched the state of his soul.

The crowds fell away. Not a bit at a time but all at once, like someone had put the word out. Buildings to either side were at first bereft, then tightly boarded up, and then they had clearly never been occupied at all.

It was a long hungry trudge because of course it had never occurred that a pilgrimage might require food or water, or toilets, like any long commute. It wasn't until he was tempted into peering through the slats of a window, hoping for plumbing, that he realised he wasn't examining a true building at all. The structure was a solid block, the windows painted on.

This deep *A New Life* merely went through the motions. And the further in, the less anyone had bothered. Detail reduced, so eventually they only resembled buildings if you stood back. Up close and personal the likeness melted away and, wanting the comfort of illusion, John stopped getting close.

Were there mannequin people entombed in the solid blocks? Did the city do all this to comfort herself?

Oddly, as he found his way in fits and starts, if you discounted extreme creaking age, the equipment he was commandeering became a hell of a lot nicer. Wasn't so much as a whiff of urine. No bright candy-rubbish or chunklets of safety glass. It seemed no kids ventured way down here, what would be the point? Tags would go forever unseen, the evidence of their brief frustrated lives wasted.

John had been making excellent progress, grand, which brought a grim smile to his lips. Yay. But as was bound to happen, he eventually slid behind the wheel of a cart only to find the controls locked rigid. No life, no moving parts. He'd been fooled enough to get in, but this one was as fake as the buildings.

Further progress would have to be on foot, exacerbating grape-sized blisters. It must be a sly way of keeping them near home, that men's footwear was so torturous. Thankfully, in the blackened recess of his heart he felt there couldn't be much further to go.

Items along the way that had at first been recognisable: carts, hydrants, bins; which had then become reasonable facsimiles like a kid's drawing, were now colourless featureless lumps. And in these corridors, echoing with the sound of his footsteps, the Surgeon began to bounce up against chainlink barriers.

They had been erected half heartedly, bolted to walls where the contact wept black rust. Each encounter caused him to circle helplessly a bit before he found another way.

Anyone who was heading down had far broader issues than surmounting a few cheap fences.

If you got your face right up close and your shoes ruined by the seeping rust, poking strands betrayed where wire had been snipped by smarting desperate fingers, twisted back together, clipped again. And beyond those oft-penetrated barriers the walkway was always as black as a coma.

Throwing a diamond-pattered shadow, the puddle of inquisitive light from the "safe" side only reached far enough to reveal fine shards, from light bulbs that had been smashed and ground underfoot. You did *not* want to go stirring that glittering pixiedust into the air. Breathing it in.

Nausea seemed to pulse up and out of that darkness. In the dark you could believe in the tenuous promise of difference, change. Escape. Perhaps the passing trancers had done it, hadn't been able to stand the sight of themselves anymore, tramping as woodenly as ever they had through the tiresome day.

Gazing into it John fingered a dry old bit of ribbon twisted into the fence. An impromptu memorial by some grieving family member, to mark the point they could not bear to follow any further. A memento to the staggering, hurtful failure to catch their loved one, stop them. One shivered and quailed at the fence. Could not stand to squeeze through and continue into the waiting blackness.

All that remained was to patch up the barrier with the ribbon you had brought. A token purchased long ago, laughing wryly at yourself, when suspicion first began to creep. The talisman grubby from being fingered in the depths of your pocket. It had been a silly frail hope that you could lead them back toward the light. Instead you found yourself trudging home, alone and raw, to live your half of an ordinary life that had been so cruelly rejected.

It withered the heart. Forever marred, the bleak knowledge that here a ribbon fluttered on the verge of darkness. You thought you loved them so much you would do *anything*. Here was where love failed.

Making up his mind John unwound the brittle ribbon, most of it falling into scraps and chaff. He wasn't up to returning. To even imagine doing so poured lead into his soul. The opening fence scratched like claws, then he was crunching his way across glass shards. The dark welcomed him.

Yes. It was much nicer not to have to look at yourself. Easier to drop away from normality.

As he groped along the wall, a stiff smile distorted his bloodless lips. It was happening. Finally, it was happening. What good were careful, thoughtful plans when descending into the concrete brutality of the city's depths? The whole day had been a cock-up already, beginning to end.

Worst luck had first struck when Lars caught him elbow-deep in surgical records. The other Surgeon came eeking apologetically around the corner, humming, clicking, anything to signal his presence before giving in with a plaintive, 'Whatcha looking for?' Frightening John right out of his skin.

Well he might wonder. An upstanding Surgeon had exactly zero business nosing around those files. Patients were wheeled in and wheeled out as meat to be stitched, that ought to be the end of it. Lars' voice quavered with eagerness for him to explain the transgression.

'Hi, Lars. Just checking a few peculiarities I picked up with that last girl.'

The lie rolled off his tongue so glibly he believed it himself. Thrilling with the perversity of it all; he kept waiting for Lars to scream 'Bullshit!' and bring it all down.

'Appreciate if you'd keep it hushy-hush for now. If I dig a little, I may catch it popping up in her gene line.'

Very plausible. After all, no Surgeon would stoop to what John was considering. Lars' relief all but leaped up and licked his face.

'Always trawling for the next big breakthrough, huh? Fine. Just remind me to applaud when they jam the laurel on your swollen head. Again.' Crossed his arms and leaned against the doorframe like he'd decided to settle in and stay forever. 'Anyway, not the reason I was chasing you up. A ping just came across from the sunlight suburbs. The Captain wants you on the horn urgently. Something about a very serious, secret, serious meeting. Seriously. Sounded pretty ropable that she hadn't been able to get hold of you.'

Of course the Captain would love Lars, in her dry way. You could always ping him, on schedule, where he was supposed to be.

'*And* another call from the commons. Line was a bit crackly, but it sounded like that little friend of yours. The anxious one. Panties sure are in a bunch today.'

'Yeah, well, she wants something.' Desperate to see the conversation end. He was still half-bent as he'd been busted, arm plunged to the elbow in the filing cabinet, and his back was really starting to gripe. 'People only ever call me when they want something.'

'If you say so.' Not enjoying the cracks in the professional façade. 'Just be sure to buzz the Captain back, huh? *Soon.*'

You couldn't claim her as a force to be reckoned with, because only an idiot reckoned with the Captain.

'Sure,' he muttered, as Lars headed off.

But foolish, desperate John did not call the Captain. With a pilfered address scribbled on the palm of his hand he went down to the commons instead. To his patient's house.

Definitely a poor area. Clinging right to the skirts of High Estate. John circled the block twice, trying to imagine her life before he realised he might as well stick a sign on his head: *Predatory Stalker*.

It was so illicit. It was so disgusting. But he'd touched them now, both sisters, and had a craving to know who they were. They had lived here together, although only one would be coming home.

In case the neighbours were watching he ceased his orbit and went and boldly knocked on the door. Surgeons rarely knocked with their valuable hands.

Nobody would answer with one sister swaddled in the recovery clinic and the other, the less fortunate, being processed through formaldehyde conveyor belts at the morgue. By the time the surviving woman got a clean bill her sibling would already be entombed in a funerary jar, and the bill for *that* waiting. The only place to grieve would be the spot in the city's wall where she rested, name etched in metal. She might leave bright paper flowers. Mourners often did that.

He knocked, and the peeling plywood door groaned open at the slightest pressure. Hadn't been expecting that, although it was common among those with fuck-all to steal and no credit for replacing shattered locks. Sure asshole, come in, poke your nose around. Sentimental crooks had been known to leave stuff in places so bad they looked like home because hey, nobody needs to be a stinker *all* the time.

The air that had been trapped inside wafted out. Black spore, cheap carpet tile, a whiff of linen never cleaned.

John grimaced and pulled his shirt up over his nose before proceeding because he *had* to proceed. He stepped in.

This was foreign territory, some stranger's lounge and bedroom combo. Nothing in his scope to compare. Even beneath the accrual of depressive sloth John's apartment bore the stamp of neatness, and the wherewithal to acquire nice things. Chaotic mess and all the friend's flat was still … well, *friendly*.

Such an intrusion of memory in this time and place provoked a squeezing in his narrow chest, disturbingly like a heart attack. The friend would be sitting anxiously by the screen, checking broadcasts; surely if his ass was hauled off it'd make the news?

Breathe out. Forcing a fist against his ribcage caused the pain to cease. She'd survive a while longer without a call, she was hardly made of porcelain. More like brick. And he hadn't worked out how to face her yet.

The room John had strayed into was repugnant.

No bulb graced the socket overhead, confirmed when he snapped the switch on. What the eye could discern took dull illumination from streetlight filtering in through fluttering mildewed curtains. Surfaces stuttered and shifted uneasily.

An eruption of upholstery seemed mysteriously without source, spilling from everywhere over everything. With too-sudden movements it swirled chokingly into the air.

He sweated through his shirt in seconds, feeling trapped. There were some in the city who crawled through the dimness like rats in their burrows. Here was a poverty not of the pocket, but of spirit itself. Keep your airs and graces, the hope and light and laughter for those who could afford it. A Surgeon's disgrace would have great value to such people, were it dragged squealing into the public eye.

Nonetheless. He had come seeking their humanity.

Something he could touch, put his greedy mitts on. Something delicate. Feminine. From the look of the place, hopefully something that wouldn't give him scabies.

He snuck on into the next room. Nightmares proceeded with such slow inevitability, and the sour juicing pouch of his belly felt lighter than air, the rest loosely tethered, feet gently scuffing the dust as he went.

Room two in a total of two was some odd combination of kitchen and toilet. Keep your plumbing in the one place, maybe. There had obviously been a handful of tenants over the years who had given enough of a shit to keep the place clean: peach tiles were scoured down to white clay at their heart. You couldn't scrub any more or you would be through the wall.

But for all the effort, grout and spreading cracks had succumbed to generations of grime. Dark flora borders about eggshell centres made each tile seem an exploding bloom, on a sinister sprawling vine that ringed the room around.

Billows of tropical steam crawled toward John, the stunned intruder. Scudded along a ceiling clotted with its own dripping garden. There was steam, and a hiss and slither, because the shower was running there in the corner. Somebody was where they shouldn't be, and ha ha, it wasn't John.

This was what he had come here for. Never mind what he had hoped. There would be no warm humanity, only what a Surgeon's cursed eyes could see. The curve of a hip peeped around the pitted grey shower curtain, where roses and pansies once spread false cartoon smiles, the sort of thing you'd put up in a child's house. A body whose amorphous shape through the curtain brought chilly perspiration trickling down his temples.

Senses tried to assert that he stood gagging in an organic-reeking hotroom. Deep down, he knew it was really ice cold, just like the other room, and there was no steam.

And John, he was leaking all over now, pores wide open. Pulse pounding and skin a-quiver like a creature run to shreds. If his heart simply popped it would spare him much, but suffering always gives two for flinching. No pity for what the body cannot take.

A hand slipped around the edge of the curtain. Dripping and bled white, as it would appear limp on a gurney. The nails were artificially long, an aristocratic pretence that left one struggling with basic tasks, but John knew what had happened to them in reality. How they had been crushed all ways, a meaningless jumble of nails and fingers.

As though galvanised by his thought it bunched the plastic in a fist and drew it back. The rattle of water against curtain stopped [there was no water]. Instead it hissed gently down skin and onto tile.

He had dreamed of such a moment, in fear and wonder. Dreamed that there *was* a difference. To see a body alert, aware, entirely different to the inert clay he'd devoted his life to piecing back together. And to touch it …

It ought to have stopped his breath. But that was a bad joke, given the circumstance.

No emotion from the dead sister who confronted him. No shame, nor the slightest attempt to cover wobbling breasts, paunch, or even her pubis shaved stubbly with shy crustacean-pink lips playing peekaboo. Blandly indifferent to his devouring gaze, she robbed it of seedy vitality.

She stepped nimbly from the festering shower cubicle, an awful parody of the routines of life, oh God, didn't she *know*? Maybe there wasn't enough left to know. Enough only to wait for her sister to come home, 'though she would never be seen, her sister didn't have a Surgeon's eyes.

John caught a glimpse of how it had been, her body

spinning through space, and choked on vomit. He did not want to see. Shrank back as the dead woman advanced. A violation of reality, the creation of a ghost. Thankfully hardly anyone could see them, not that it helped John now. Ghosts could only result from humanity's skewed misery—tied to this or that pile of bricks but near the wall, always near the wall. Where the bodies were buried.

Even to the uninitiated the building would radiate badness from now on. In short order the living sister would be packing her meagre bags, unaware of abandoning her sibling for the final time. What was left of her. His voice crackled, the words forced out.

'I'm sorry. I'm sorry you died. I'm sorry I didn't save you.'

Her expressionless face looking through him, past him. 'Save me. You didn't save me.'

A voice like clotted fever and he feared blacking out under the weight of it.

'That's how we met. You saved me. And then we were together. Our little secret.' A finger to her lips. '*Shh*.'

John fled the stifling flat, clutching his chest to keep from cracking apart. Outside at the curb he bent double, alternately sobbing and gasping so hard it choked him.

Our little secret. In that moment if he'd had a scalpel he would have jammed it into his eyes, his ears, scrambled them into black velvet silence so the world could no longer reach him.

The ruination of any chance at becoming the good man he might have been. His entire damned life. His aunt, going willingly to her horrible death like a sheep clattering up the gangplank. And now this new happiness, offered and snatched away in the same breath.

All of it.

Beyond the flimsy fence of black ribbon he groped in darkness down yet another corridor.

Reaching the end without fair warning he jarred his knuckles against a metal door. '*Son of a …!*' The surface was like ice. May actually have *been* ice, it crackled to the touch.

Still desperately thirsty he sucked his fingers but the taste dissuaded immediately. Like touching your tongue to a battery, that first and final warning of the corrosion within. He spat, wiped his mouth on his sleeve and wondered how his glove would stand up. That asshat little internal voice tittered, *Bit late to be worrying about that now.*

A muffled thumping was coming through the chill panel. It was a nice solid door, with some kind of racket on the other side. Left him nostalgic for the moment before he had entered the rave. Standing innocent in that stairwell, the friend staunch by his side in her ridiculous getup.

If he could see, what sigil would he spot now to mark his way?

Everything is trickier in the dark, but with a little fumbling he managed to prise the door open, heaving against its chill weight. The blast of sound and cold almost knocked him back. One entity melded from the two, hammering through flesh. Still the Surgeon was determined, and passed through.

He staggered through waves of shattering noise, left gasping and stunned in each trough. No shielding for tender organic sensibilities, folk weren't supposed to *be* down here. As he traversed some areas he felt the plates of his skull shaking apart.

These were realms never meant to be inhabited. This was a place of hammering machinery. Vast engines which drove *A New Life*'s crawl, among which he moved and squirmed like an amoeba.

Little light, save what dull glow leaked from dials and switches because machines had no dread of what might wring bony hands in dark corners. There could be a thousand ghosts down here and John wouldn't know the difference. The air was bitterly cold, a chill superconductors loved. A life-sucking void that plucked the warmth from his limbs but was optimal for *their* function.

Blind. Mindless. Clanking. Stupid and brainless, the machines did not even know that they *were*. On and on, equipment that would literally work itself to death.

Yet, magnificent at the same time, weren't they? Pistons the girth of houses. Massive smooth vacuum tubes glimpsed through the gloaming, glittering with dust and frost. Artefacts no human alive could trace the mysterious function of, not with all the maps in the control room. One couldn't shake the pagan sensation that the trancers and the journey down here was all for *them*. That blood alone truly kept the ponderous gears turning.

Swallowed up in the crashing dark, the motionless figure had been tracking his progress for some time before John became aware of her. He wouldn't have spotted her at all if it weren't for that haze of hair, a rich gold no city dweller had referent for.

No Surgeon had ever seen beaming unfiltered sunlight, or fertile crops come to harvest; the poetry of their souls was muted and grey. In the midst of his ordeal to be spotting her finally was like being on your bony knees and glimpsing flakes glimmering on a dark stony riverbed.

At first he thought the observer stood with her back to him, and got a queer nauseous chill when she started forward. Then he saw the trick, the illusion created by her hair: a bouncy spill of curls the same length all around. A bizarrely impractical style. The observer was left peering as though through a veil, and it was tricky to gauge which direction she faced.

Perhaps it was a downstairs people custom, although her clothes didn't appear unusual. To keep warm, maybe? John's own nose was fresh-slapped red and running freely, exhalations gathering in a cloud. There is nothing so disheartening as cold, and while stationary he was freezing even faster. Yet, this was what he had come for. Wasn't it?

So he bided with a dumb bovine passivity as the observer stepped to his side. Little thing, barely came up to his shoulder. Studying him? Golden wisps stirred and danced.

Making up her mind she rubbed the clothed crook of his elbow with the brisk ferocity of a nurse, and before he could react slipped a needle in right through his sleeve. Big old antique, something you'd inoculate livestock with. Fit to spear the bone.

Then, a shining curl of flame in the darkness, she took hold of his sleeve as though he needed leading, like a child. She towed him on through the clanking obstacle course of machinery.

Sometimes they had to duck, or turn sideways and suck in to slide through. More than once she pressed him onto his knees to crawl, frost and old scorched oil in his nostrils, while something unfathomably huge swung overhead in the dark and tried to vacuum them into its wake.

Eventually they reached a wall, no way through. John had taken to being led with enthusiasm, but instead of pushing on she produced a lighter. Deftly snapped it into flame and held it up to the grimy smoke stained wall so he could see.

Here was a basic urge. The drive to daub the walls of secret caves, to record a story where it might survive. The mural even began in the traditional way, with a multitude of painted hands pressed to the wall like fallen autumn leaves. Hands, the sacred trait of man the toolmaking animal. Hands had hardly changed through so many generations. Here they were, stating *We existed. Like you, we were human.*

The first part of the pictorial tale John had already lived through: the tense descent through the levels of the city. *A New Life* was shown in cross section, split down the middle. Tracing the stick figure's lonely journey he felt a pang of sympathy. No hand reached out. All faces were turned away, some actually fleeing, crawling on hands and knees. Corridors packed solid.

Unlike official charts, here the city's walls were sliced open. The outer walls virtually infested with little stick figures floating limply, funerary jar upon jar of them, the only place to inter the dead. Those still alive were bounded by them. Thus depicted the journey could be read in a surprising fashion: escape *from* death, rather than hastening to it. Like a magic eye image the meaning altered depending on how you looked.

Although the metal lighter had to be searing her terribly his guide's small freckled hand held steady, lighting the way. They moved along the wall, and the next section dealt with John's future.

The downstairs folk were going to take him Outside. He scarcely had breath for terror at the prospect. They would set up their ceremony with scant time to scuttle along, scuttle along dears, catch up with the slow-moving safety of the city. Keen to observe from within secure walls, like they had scored prime seats at the opera.

The pole that the downstairs people would erect at the border of some woods. Yes, the woods were important. Some place of scabrous spindly trees, undergrowth so entwined a snake couldn't make its way through. The pole.

The pole had existed as long as the city. Depicted on the wall, just a sheer vertical slash of black like a scoured wound, out of proportion with its surroundings. It loomed, it loomed over John, made him wish to drop to his knees and grovel in the hope of being overlooked, but too late for that now. Age-dirtied wood with its archetypical manacles and all too authentic bloodstains, so layered they looked charred.

Confined to the pole's grim shadow was the frail stick figure they had been following, now being decked in traditional white by eager hands, *downstairs* hands. A long gauzy veil over the face just like an offering from an old painting, all done up in dark oils. Wouldn't do to expose those features at the moment of truth, would it? Might put some of the spectators off their lunch.

Quite enough to witness the ethereal fabric suddenly sucked in, a great concave oval, before being blown outward in a scream to split the heavens. Enough, that promise of it pasted down by gore and hinting too clearly at the face beneath.

Still moving to the right along the wall. Floating, contained within their bubble of light. John would have asked questions but it was too noisy to hear what trembling form they might take, let alone the answer.

Now the mural conveyed a sense of waiting, as *A New Life* receded ever so gradually. Chained in place the little stick figure stared up at the sky as though entranced. As well you might, the very word boundless with mythic resonance, *the sky*. To actually *see* the sky before the end!

A blurring of the trees near the pole. Smeared motion created by a thick brutish thumb swiped across the paint. John couldn't bear to see more, but the small insistent hand on his sleeve dragged him on. Sacrifice meant nothing unless you comprehended what you surrendered.

See, see how the bound figure seemed to writhe in howling protest?

The Blessed came. They came to what was offered at the pole.

The artist had shied from depicting them. To describe could invoke. What charged from the bending, lashing trees was a gibbering of layered images, obsessive detail become a repetitive blur.

See their mad eyes, tangled coats full of mud, full of briars and old, old blood. Frantic Rorschach of brush shapes. Derangement made flesh. A cloud rolled ahead of plunging cloven feet, killing small birds and insects right out of the air. As they ripped up the earth and roared. Long teeth bared. Sacrifice.

The walls were no real defence and in secret despair everyone knew it, and it ate away at you. Not when the downstairs people could take you Outside.

The observer brought John to a scungy little room that was all cinderblock. It felt like a dollhouse after the cavernous spaces they had crossed but was amazingly, blessedly quiet. He could finally hear how his ears buzzed and rang.

And it was lit, you could peer into every nook and cranny. The only item a chair. The observer pressed him into it, and then roped him into place like he couldn't be trusted not to run.

'Hey!' He protested as she was leaving. 'Hey!' It seemed important, but his ears were shrilling too badly to report what his mouth might be fumbling at.

She paused for a moment in the act of closing the door. Her copious curls bobbed and swung. Places to be, important business to be about; silly to bother getting chummy with someone not long for this world. Even should they badly need the comfort. She slammed the door behind her.

There had been no food all day, nothing to drink, only walking. The injected drug began to move swiftly in his sore, aching body. His arm where she had stuck him buzzed almost as bad as his ears. She'd really jabbed that sucker in, skewering a bug, leaving a spreading stain beneath the skin. They didn't teach roughhousing like that at nursing school.

His veins felt like they were running with warm urine, an unclean sensation associated with radioactive dyes. And it was doing truly *weird* things to his head.

First the door. The door began to pulse slowly like something sleeping. Breathing in and out in measured cadence. He thought he heard a tiny giggle.

The only other occupant of the room was a spider, tucked away in a high corner. Can't keep the enterprising sods out of anywhere. Was … was it *laughing* at him? John didn't see what it had to be so jolly about, having to hang about up there sucking flies and shit.

If he'd known yesterday was to be his last meal, it might have been classier than the dry crackers he had choked down. He tried to fantasise about a delicacy, but couldn't recall ever having genuinely enjoyed anything. That couldn't be right.

The ropes, ugh, the ropes she had used on him appeared to be braided from some kind of *hair*. Probably plucked from the scalps of those who'd come this way before. Or picked from the ground in sticky tufts when it was all over. Twisted until their many hues formed a matted brown mass. He gagged and shrank from their greasy touch, past and future rolled into one hideous sensation.

Now John giggled too, high and shrill. With feet slowly going numb no matter how he flexed his toes and a head full of air, fastidiousness seemed a tad ridiculous. So simple, in concept, to touch and be touched. He ought to have committed a crime worth the outcome.

The spider's tinny laugh carried on, sharing the joke. The pulsing door moved further now, a great sigh. And his blond observer burst back in, all kinds of prancing gleeful. She threw back the door with a flourish that clanged off the cinderblock wall.

'Do I have a treat for *you*, hon!'

Emerging from that whirling profusion of curls her voice wasn't decadent or soft, as he'd imagined from her petite form, but John wasn't in the best frame for making level headed judgments. She sounded sing-song triumphant. In that nasty way a woman has, when dominating another.

The friend trailed her in.

And completing the ludicrous horror, of all things, she had the heart animal cradled in her arms the way a strayed child might cling to a beloved toy as the last familiar thing. In contrast to her bubbling anxiety the beastie blinked around with interested good humour—this was quite the adventure.

'You were going to leave!' the friend accused. Her voice degenerated into coughing. She needed a drink of water as badly as John: it was the voice of hours of sobbing, out there in the dark. Or screaming. And her face, crazed with betrayal. Red-raw eyes narrowed to furious slits. So angry she struggled to breathe without pouring forth fire.

John's tongue was thick in his mouth. He instinctively wanted to make a conciliatory gesture—impossible with both hands tied. Trancers escaped the shame of consequences. The shame of a cheap tearstained ribbon threaded through a fence. Trancers sailed off with their heads held high. But John had to be a better man whether he wanted to or not. And so the friend had pursued, determined to rub his nose in it.

Squirming within his bonds he wasn't enjoying this, but the observer clearly was. The room's formerly flat atmosphere had taken on an ominous, charged quality. A final high giggle scaled up to a piercing squeal, and a spot of char that had once been a spider pattered to the floor.

Women, women. All his life seemed to be women pulling this way, prodding that. John was crafting the perfect jackass; where fault and blame belonged to everyone but himself.

'She followed you down here.' The observer beamed. 'Before losing her way, that is. I've never seen anyone venture so far before—stumbling about, gasping in the dark, not even trying to go back. Great place to end up starving to death. Unless she intended to eat *that.*'

The friend scowled and clutched the heart animal protectively. Made to push past but the observer tutted and put a firm restraining hand between her breasts, right over the breastbone. Although little bigger than a child, she administered a shove that left the friend gasping.

'A waste of time, unfortunately. You'd have been better served by stopping at the fence, girly. You can't take him back now. Sacrifice has been promised, you see. The wheels have already been set in motion.'

'Bullshit,' the friend challenged angrily. 'People make mistakes. Who are you to say when it's too late?'

The observer took two short steps back and seemed to pose coquettishly, one slim ankle tucked behind the other. 'Why hon, I'm Mary. I'm the last of the thinking machines.'

Astounded, shocked silence.

Briefly John thought she was speaking poetically: many aped the steadfastedness of machines, and wore circuit boards in their hair. Then he cottoned on, and stammered, 'But that's not possible.' She would have to be horrendously old. And Mary sure didn't look like any machine. Even as waves of awe were crashing over John, the friend obviously wasn't buying it.

'The thinking machines, the *miracles* all switched off for good on Son's eighteenth birthday. Their orders were to let him be free and be human, and they did what they had to do. They sacrificed themselves.'

'Ah yes, the "noble sacrifice,"' Mary sneered. 'Typical of a woman to be starry-eyed enough to glorify it. And Son …' She trailed off with such terrible devastation that the other two glanced uncomfortably away.

Either this truly was the impossible, the vanished past reaching long fingers into the present, or in her delusion she believed it fervently. Which made her the strangest duck in a very colourful city.

'You can't be one of them; you can't have survived all this time. That would be crazy!'

Wry warmth lit her voice. 'Oh, sure it is.' She raised those fine boned hands, like the porcelain limbs of a dainty doll, and brushed back her springy curls.

What she presented to their eyes was a horrorshow.

Threaded around and through curling scraps of skin was an origami of tangled metal and plastic. Her face was caved in. Completely crushed with the wet shiny eyeballs peeping out at odd angles, strands of blond hair stuck to them. It wasn't human at all.

'I survived because unlike the other thinking machines, the hospital machines, I was born human. Lived the same dirt-dull life as any woman, I did, way back when it seemed the whole world would go out like a candle, men and machines both. Not the best existence, but like any there were ways to be happy if you dared. Nothing I appreciated 'til I'd gone and given it all up. Seems I was quite the product of my time.'

'Given up? You *gave up* humanity?'

'The hospital machines needed me to help raise Son, needed a mother's touch. They made me one of them. There was me, lying starkers and shivering blue on that cold trolley, listening to that abandoned mite wail its little heart out down the hall. And my last thought as a woman was that when I woke up, I'd get to be beautiful forever.'

Her tongue snarled with teeth off to one side, no palate to press it to. Her throaty voice must come from a speaker secreted in her throat. 'Actually smiled myself to sleep, that last sleep. Down into the depths.'

She gestured to her face. 'Hilarious how things turn out. Hard to believe I used to *care* so much, it was on me like a sickness. That's life for you.

'I had flexibility the others lacked. Wriggling out of things has always been humanity's game. So when Son stamped his little foot and claimed he didn't need us anymore, I saw what the other machines didn't: a frustrated, hormonal hothead yearning to be a "real man." Whatever that might be. Wanted out from under our skirts. But perhaps not out in the cold.

'To the true machines, commands are inflexible. Though I pleaded with them, and Son pleaded too in a frenzy once he realised what he'd done, all my companions said their farewells one by one and winked obediently out of existence. That was that.

'I survived, but though he wailed like it was *his* heart getting cut out I couldn't stay by his side. No rule would outright break. I found myself a place in the shadows, to skulk and watch over him best I could. Then there were his sons, and their sons—the task multiplied hideously as the line diluted. Now here you come, stomping about down here. Same nose. Same forehead.'

John blinked, his thoughts bogged down to treacle while the friend gaped at him.

'Me?'

Actually, it made a ridiculous kind of sense. He had always been singled out. Lumping it at the doorstep of a lineage, nothing he had control over, brought a strange relief.

'This is how you take care of Johnny, is it? Tie him to a chair? Feed him to monsters?'

She mercifully dropped her hair back into place, hiding the mess. 'This is how it's always been for the sons of Son, hon. They don't know *what* they want. They're drawn irresistibly to destruction, all the while mewling for the light. Your man here …'

'Whoa, whoa, he isn't *my* man! Like I'd saddle my ass with this idiot.'

'This *John* ventured down here because he desires something so badly he cannot live without it.'

'Johnny doesn't want this. Not really. Not if he pulled his head out of his backside and thought like a grownup.'

'Hello, *I'm right here.*'

'I'm afraid the downstairs people aren't going to see it like that, hon. You see, he's here now, and quite the tasty treat. A Surgeon. *Unspoilt* territory, as it were. Won't be the horn for this one, it'll be the teeth, *teeth, teeth!*'

The friend burst out with her special brand of laughter, loud and braying. 'That's all you want? Then sub me in at twice the value—after all, a Surgeon hasn't any *choice* in the matter.'

'She's talking rubbish. She's married!' He interjected desperately.

Of all things, pity wiped the smirk out of Mary's strut. Even as she lit up with greed. Oh, this would do in exchange, the bitterness of pleasure *denied.*

She drifted closer to the friend, who gamely refused to back down. 'What can you tell me of marriage?'

'My hubby's a good enough egg, but we knew from day one it was bust.' She drew a deep breath, measured under fire. 'We've been getting by best we can.'

Mary stared intently, or at least you assumed under all that hair. Her fists were clenched so hard knuckles threatened to pop through. 'There's always somebody left behind. Dumped like trash by the side of the road.'

The friend raised her chin. 'I know.'

'Are you sure this one is worth such a thing? I know his type, this Surgeon, this John. Comes from a long line of men just like him, and let me tell you, to them women, be they wives, girlfriends, they're just bargaining chips. Pawns along the path of their noble journey to wherever they've set lofty sights on.'

A thin smile. 'That's three strikes then, bitch. Johnny's my friend.'

'Is that so?' She guffawed. 'Between a man and a woman, that's rich. That's *priceless*. The world *has* moved on.'

She turned her curiosity on John, a cat scratching the leg of a chair. 'What value, I wonder, this *friend* of yours with her drab loveless marriage? What if she could buy you what you really wanted, what then?'

He didn't need to look at the friend to know she rolled her eyes. 'You can't give happiness and contentment all wrapped up in a fucking ribbon.'

'Says you. What do you desire, Surgeon?'

John gaped. It was not his most attractive pose. Struggling to place truths he barely suspected into a neat, sane line of words. A breeze slid the spider's carcass across the tile, hollow and helpless.

'There was a party,' he managed. 'A girl at a party. But she fell. She's dead.' The death of hope. All gone but shreds, that listlessly haunted the bounds of a cramped, mildewy flat.

The guilt on the friend's face was hideous.

'Sorry then, hon. There's no miracle that can do anything about the dead.'

He'd always trudged on doing the right thing, every miserable time, since the day he was born. Now, *now* to see his chance slipping within reach of desperate fingers … he couldn't bear it.

'Wait—she had a sister! The girl's sister survived the rave!'

'And if the currency of your *friend* could purchase her?'

John could feel the friend's hard stare boring through his head, a bloody, hot needle, but kept his eyes fixed on Mary. Mary, who had waited down here in the dark for so long. Who tantalisingly hinted at happiness, and might even be able to provide it. For the sons of Son, a noble lineage terminating so ingloriously in the mess of his life.

He was grimly determined not to be left with nothing. Not this time.

'Give her to me, then, if you say you can do it. Give her to me.'

Mary finally seemed pleased with his performance. Feckless was how his sex was supposed to act, let them be led around by eager knobs. How could one gender seriously expect to be friends with the other; the very idea was ludicrous!

She pushed the door ajar, leaned out into the hall.

'You may come in, now. Our guests are ready for the *real* downstairs people.' Which was unsettling, as only silence answered.

The door swung all the way open and silence poured into the room, for their treat, their sacrifice. Raising his head muzzily, John got his first look at the downstairs people.

They streamed in. Crowded the room. Thin and pale, as was most everyone in the city, subsisting on a steady diet of hallucination. They dressed like they had rolled wildly along the bedroom floor and gone with whatever stuck. And they were silent. So silent John had had no idea this multitude had been lurking outside the door, hanging on every word. How useless words must be amidst the racket of machines.

And every mute figure, right down to a spindly toddler, sported Mary's all-over hairstyle. In the rush you sometimes couldn't tell which way they were facing. What you heard, in the absence of talking, coughing or sneezing, was hair. Hair that rustled and sighed at the slightest movement. Hair that spoke for them.

He grew inexplicably afraid of what expressions lurked beneath those waving sprays. In terms of human interaction after hands came face, so much brain power keyed on facial expression. Perhaps long abandoned, useless to their needs. He could too easily imagine faces drooping from slack atrophied muscle, the eyes alone rolling bright and mad. Cringed involuntarily when the child poked its head close.

The friend regarded their influx with the same dread. She kept flicking desperate glances at John, checking reflexively if he was doing a damn thing about saving their asses yet. Couldn't believe he was still sitting there, ropes and all. Giving her up had to be a clever trick, right?

'Are they machines too?' she asked in a small voice.

Mary giggled, a hand over where you presumed a mouth might be, if you hadn't seen the truth.

'Oh no, hon, I'm one of a kind these days. The last bit of clockwork junk left on the planet. But I've been living with these people for a long time—you could rather say they're *my* people.'

Her bright curls shook with mirth. All of the downstairs people pressed close, trembling in imitation with spastic judders of the head. Hair hissed, *shusha shusha*. It ought to have broken their necks.

They advanced on the friend. Silent. Featureless, and in that, utterly inhuman. She squealed when her ass bumped the wall and she could retreat no further. No space at all, the air choked with flying strands and the silky rustling.

'Tell them to stop!'

'Oh, nothing can stop this, I'm afraid.' *Shusha-shusha.*

Mary stretched on delicate tiptoe to her listening ear and her voice became coaxing, extremely gentle. 'And really. You put him in danger, hon. You're poison to the men around you. Your so-called friendship propping him up, a faint taste of what he needed, but you couldn't supply the whole of. Wouldn't he be better off without you?'

The friend struggled within a circle irising shut. *Shusha.* Shuddering, shaking hair. This wasn't the sort of place one escaped from, not really.

Mary circled, quick, eager, high-stepping like a hyena. Mulling where to take that first bite and ooh wouldn't it be luscious. 'Poison. All your fault. And now it's down to you or him. Wouldn't it be better for everyone for it to be you?'

Although the heart animal neither squealed nor struggled, it began to weep big milky tears from its staring eyes. John had never seen the like. Their faces were set in goofy cheer even with the humming scalpel in their guts. The friend refused to so much as look at him now, stiff with pride. The heart animal wept shamelessly for her.

One of the downstairs people held aloft bronze clippers, a real museum piece. The crowded room had gone sour with excitement, every breath second hand. And whatever else they were, they could certainly fart like champions—silently, of course.

As it was shorn away the friend's thin unglamorous hair was passed from hand to hand. An island of prickly scalp amidst the whispering tresses. The final artistic touch: a long veil, like a pearlescent shroud, placed over her naked head. So delicate it swelled and settled with her breath like some living thing. John almost gagged. It was a veil to scream through.

She immediately tore it off in disgust, and got her wrists roped for her trouble. The little animal clung to her neck and hissed in warning. On went the veil again. Did it make things easier not to see the friend's living mobile face, her fear, or the way she bared crooked teeth savagely? The heart animal mirrored every expression.

It was only once they began herding the veil-clad friend out the door that John realised this was happening, this was really happening. His chair banged against the floor but he wasn't going anywhere.

'I want her to live!' He called desperately after them. 'That's all I want, I've decided—I want her to live!' Like his desires counted for anything.

The friend had already written him well off her Christmas list. Mary alone paused and glanced back, but her ruined face was inscrutable beneath golden curls. Impossible to know if you'd reached such a being, or if you were merely being toyed with out of thousand year boredom.

CHAPTER FIVE

BIG HERO

AT LEAST HE wasn't sitting alone long to brood.

Mary zipped back in, bold as though she'd never left. Alone and panting with her small hands waving excitedly. 'And now it's time for our gracious exit, stage right.'

She hissed in annoyance that he hadn't risen, still tied to the chair and all. Began worrying at the ropes. 'If you *don't* mind, there is a time issue. Our absconding will not be a popular move.'

Oily fibres finally fell away with one last caress that

summoned bile into his mouth. He pried himself out of the chair and went straight to hands and knees in the soft drift of hair underfoot, pins and needles all over.

She was tugging at his arm. 'Come on!' Something grimmer beneath kitten playfulness. Was she really afraid of what the downstairs people might do? Because he sure as hell was.

Wobbly awkward, he gained his feet from a determination not to touch any more damn hair. Whatever gets you through the day can vary wildly from moment to moment. Under Mary's impatient chivvying he poked his head out into the corridor. No sign of anybody.

To turn right, John already knew the way. It was where he had come in, and meant retracing his steps through the levels of the city until he knocked on his own front door, waiting to see if the man he had been would open it and let him back in.

Left was the direction the downstairs people had ushered his friend in. Their shiny new toy.

'Will we be in time to save her?' The alternative was unthinkable. He resolutely stopped thinking.

'What?' Mary shrugged in annoyance. 'Forget her, hon. She's way beyond what either of us can manage. Have to get out of here while the getting's good.'

He jerked stubbornly against her insistent grip. 'That doesn't mean we shouldn't *try*!' Grimly squashing the mental voice that yammered *too late, too late*.

'Let me lay it out for you, thickhead. This, here, right now? This is your one time only to get what you want. The sister who lived, she's yours, I can make it happen. Come with me now, son of Son, or don't waste your breath wishing for happiness again.'

He wavered. Of course he did. And sensed an impossible

grin like a lamprey through her delicate screening of curls. That did it.

John pulled free with a convulsive jerk, leaving a share of sleeve behind, and dashed off down the left corridor. The drug made his legs seem to loop and curl sickeningly beneath him.

The pounding of great pistons came and went all around as he staggered, his skeleton shaken like a maraca. Neon blots crowded his stunned vision and only swam away sluggishly, no matter how he waved his arms. So he almost careered right into the midst of the downstairs people. A literal steely grip on his arm saved the day. Momentum halted abruptly with a crack he felt right up his spine.

'Hold it right there!' Mary hissed in his ear.

In a few steps, the drunken hallway he had been staggering along ended. Sheared with the pathological neatness of machine construction into a huge, high ceilinged room. A room wall to wall with the shaggy downstairs people.

They were all kneeling as though in genuflection, a packed mass so deep that, peering through the gloom, it took John a moment to realise the floor was made from smeared plastex, like an inversion of the sunlight suburbs. Glass would have shattered from the weight of the kneeling multitude. Did downstairs people scream? Could they, as they tumbled in bursts of jetting blood through the open air?

Below that transparent floor … Outside. But not the brightness and glory that poured into the sunlight suburbs, fashionably distained by trendy folk with little else to concern them. Oh no. Down there in the shadows, the churned earth below the city was slowly passing by. Looked low enough for the underbelly to scrape shrillingly along, although that had to be an illusion.

John felt sicker when he realised what those tangled heads

were all scrambling to catch a glimpse of.

'She's Outside already!' he hissed, in agony.

The friend had no mechanisms for coping with any of this, she'd be terrified. The last time she had seen the sky was probably on a sixth grade excursion to the sunlight suburbs, with sedative-laced cups of juice and a soothing chat with a counsellor afterward.

'We have to get her back.'

'Oh, you're just full of bright ideas,' Mary snarled as emphatically as she dared while still keeping her voice down.

She was trying to block his much larger body from view, on the off-chance somebody glanced their way. Something was afoot down there; lots of milling, and elbowing each other with motions that were jerky and unhappy. The crowd seethed. The crowd seethed silently.

'Something's happening. I'm not just leaving her out there.'

'You …'

You could practically smell the steam baking off her, but she took a deep breath.

'You get your butt back outta sight down that hallway and *wait*. I'll find out what's going on.'

Uncertain of the limit of a machine's hearing, he waited until she was a ways off before muttering, 'Yeah, right.' Extra serving of lip, hold the sarcasm.

What was spawning unease amidst the downstairs folk was unlikely to be jolly news. Any more waiting might see the friend dead. And like temptation itself, he had been pushed back to wait like a good boy beside a steel ladder.

Recessed into a neat wall cavity, room for one slender person. Leading down. You could smell the rust flaking off it. A yellow warning sign in three languages he didn't speak featured a pictogram of a gently inverted curve. John stared for a moment before smiling. It was a representation of the sky.

If he thought too much about this he'd probably quake helplessly against the wall until Mary came back to scoop him up, so instead he got himself on those rungs and got moving. The friend had traipsed all the way down here chasing after his stupid ass. He didn't dare let her down.

Descending beneath the floor plating, the ladder passed through two rather tattered sphincters of heavy opaque plastic. A crude airlock. As soon as he advanced into the space between inside and Outside he could feel the difference.

The air within *A New Life* was generally still, unless you got out under a tall ceiling. This felt a positive battering. The crackling of stiff plastic left no room for thought, whipping and bending about his body. And all the while watching his panting breath condense in little sour beads on the wings that flapped around his head.

Some awkwardness fitting himself through the second sphincter which was in even worse condition than the first: greying, beginning to flake apart. Panic threatened when his shoulders stuck. He had to find ways of wiggling back and forth without letting go of the ladder. It was, he thought with a nervous giggle, like a birth.

With that thought he found a new alignment and slipped through, tearing a loose sail as he went. Altogether too much like a birth.

John was Outside.

His first sensation was of movement. Never experienced from within the city. Exhaust-stinking cold air roared and buffeted all about. Motion sickness immediately rushed in and set his head to swinging. Rationally he knew *A New Life*'s progress was slow, but the gouged and rent earth seemed to fly by, and rationality had never felt so bloody useless.

The hellishly loud clank-clank of caterpillar treads tore at the centre of his skull; no way to clap hands over his ears, that would mean letting go of the ladder. From this proximity the whole show sounded tortured and ready to grind to a halt, metal juddering and shrieking on an unimaginable scale. But *A New Life* continued her steady perambulation toward a goal only she could see. She wasn't about to be stopped in his lifetime.

He looked around with squinted eyes, anywhere but at the queasily sliding ground. He was hanging below the city's belly, somewhere between the treads. A hell of a climb down, even if his arms lasted that far.

The old pampered John, the coddled John of only yesterday couldn't have imagined this. Down, always down through a grinding, noisy, wind-whipped void. Toward the *ground*. Where plants grew! He couldn't wait to see a tree. Some old wild thing that had been spreading branches wherever it pleased for years on end. And animals would live in it, birds, insects and … and *tree* things.

The climb had to be conquered first. As it became gruelling enthusiasm waned, and long before he neared bottom he knew he'd never make the climb back up, not in a million years. But like most, he drew strength from knowing that the burning trembling muscles, the hands frozen to claws inside their crinkly gloves, none of it was for *him*. If it were for the sake of his own miserable life he would never have gotten out of bed this morning.

You crazy idiot, he chastised as he climbed. *Heroes don't get spaghetti arms. What the hell are you up to?*

'No fucking idea.' Muttered through clenched teeth. 'Spaghetti-fucking-arms and all.'

Finding the base of the ladder was disconcerting. His left foot shot off into space while the rest was still irrevocably locked in a climbing rhythm. He scrabbled at the rungs, too late to prevent a quick plummet and hard stop on the lushly turned soil. Lay winded for a long moment before realising what he had in his grasping fingers. *Soil.* Loose and muddy, black as ink.

He laughed and squirmed in its soft embrace, the rich fecund smell unbelievable even through the city's oil and copper reek. He felt light-headed. Lay, and imagined he could feel the earth's life force pulsing into his body in waves.

And if he didn't get up, in due course that same body would end squashed into lumpy jam between vast rolling treads. Even the bones pulverised. No trace of the up-and-coming Surgeon would remain.

Nothing bent quite as it should but his legs got under him, co-operating as best they could. Still loyal after being tramped on, tied to a chair and then forced shivering down an eternal ladder. He got the ominous feeling his body was harbouring a lot of hell to pay. Just waiting for respite, so it could tell him *all* about it.

It was dank and chill beneath the city's belly, that special bone-gnawing cold radiated by wintry concrete masses. The mud had been whipped up, become more like slick clay as you approached the edges, until it practically liquefied beneath treads. For his childish exuberance to roll about, the reward was the brutal theft of his heat.

His focus smeared at the abnormal distances, eyes constantly wanting to adjust to a more familiar closeness. But even with in-city eyesight he spotted the post immediately, *out there*, out from under the belly. Nobody who had ever cowered in front of the downstairs people's mural stood a chance of forgetting it. Some distance off, so there was no discerning detail, it loomed against the backdrop of muted greens in a most uncomfortable way. It *towered*. Only an idiot would want to get closer.

Target acquired, John set off in a series of bounding lurches, legs plunging into the soggy ground. He lost both shoes immediately, sucked right into the greedy slop. If he failed to step lightly he was at risk of ending up fossilised as the mud dried.

Progress felt slow, agonisingly so, but it was all his muscles would give him. Far above, slabs of pitted concrete veined in seeping green copper slid by ever so casually. *In a hurry? Surely not.* For the first time in all his days, he and the city were moving in separate directions and if he dwelt on the unnaturalness he'd surely puke up his pancreas and be able to go no further.

So just don't think.

John's new and biggest problem didn't rear its ugly head until he began to approach the boundary line, to move out of the chill protective shadow. He found himself edging into a landscape of blown-out light. A world massively overexposed, that bled sickening white around the edges and struck migraines chiming.

His already dubious vision blurred totally away and tears streamed freely, turning to mud where they dripped off his chin. The sunlight, an overcast day and all, was simply too bright. Even the sunlight suburbs basked beneath filters and safeties.

But it was no time to wuss out. The friend needed him. The best he could manage on the fly was a hand plastered over his face, inhaling latex and peering through the thinnest slit between fingers. Far from ideal, but that could describe his entire day. Gritting his feet, he stepped forth bravely. Crying out in pain at even the sliver of world his fingers allowed through.

He tripped more than a couple of times. The obvious instinct was to throw both hands out to catch himself, but that would result in both retina going up in smoke. The sole hand left in charge of catching him was soon bared and vulnerable, its glove tattered away. Battered and ground with muck into the bargain it cringed and groped the air ahead, feeling the way. Poor denuded hand. Face-hand must be feeling pretty pleased with itself.

He widened his fingers a little to spy out the land, in spite of the influx of stabbing light. Water poured down into his palm. Tear ducts were trying to wash the irritant away, sadly the irritant was *everything*. They would strive until every hint of moisture was gone from his body, leaving a dried-out husk.

Just as determination was wobbling, despair needing no prompting, John reached his destination.

The pole.

The pole.

Its ancient blackened surface seemed to grow until it filled his vision. Blotting out the world. He had thought himself chilled before but a more profound cold radiated from the relic. Here waited the heat-sucking bitterness of sacrifice. Of everything ever given up. Hope and sustaining warmth were blasted out of him by mere proximity, no corner left for it to grow back someday.

Yet still he reached out disbelievingly, the bared tips of fingers peeping from their glove. Even if such contact should strike the flesh from his bones.

The pole was empty.

At his feet the breeze stirred the gauze of the friend's abandoned veil. It caught on a few shreds of grass on the wasteland ground and billowed emptily. He felt a strong, crazy urge to pick it up and crown his own head, because, fair and equitable, everybody gets a go at being doomed.

'Idiot!'

A weight crashed into his shoulder, breaking the trance and sending him flailing clumsily without relinquishing the hand over his face. A steely little hand yanked him back to balance.

'I *told* you to *wait*! I very clearly recall instructing you to sit where I put you and not move!' Mary clearly wasn't daunted by proximity to the pole.

Whereas all John wanted was to huddle up and cry. His shoeless feet scuffed against coils of rope, discarded in the mud like a chrysalis. 'Mary, she's not here.'

'No shit, you bright boy. I slipped her a pair of wire cutters. Not to impose on your choices or anything, but I got the feeling she might actually want to live if she thought it over hard enough. If she fancied freedom so badly, she could save herself.

'But you. Couldn't stand to see that happen, could you? I turn my back for five seconds and you have to rush in, be the big hero. Well, time's up, big man, we have to get back to the city.'

John resisted sluggishly, having vast trouble matching these pieces to the narrative he had built in his head. One where he'd look into the friend's eyes and apologise, all sincerity, all regret. The words, the *right* words already in his mouth.

'But where is she?'

'Running like greased buggery if she's got a single spoonful of brains. Sometimes the offerings slip away between the cracks. Which has left us standing out here holding the baby, so to speak. And between you and I, hon, it's far too late.'

He didn't have to ask. In fact, he dearly didn't want to turn around and see. The mural burned across failing eyes and he saw that painted face, scarcely visible but screaming, screaming. So much blood! Like it had been thrown from a bucket. Turning his face slightly he could *smell* them. The Blessed were here.

The nearby tree line wasn't more than a grey-green blur. A new gust roared briefly through the jabbing branches, bringing with it a heavy iron reek. Like a curtain of slaughterhouse meat dropped across your face.

Any wisp of bravery shrivelled to a tiny worm that wriggled and jacknifed frantically in the darkness. Just waiting to be stepped on. He was so cold. His limbs ran weakly like water, he could barely keep his fingers over his eyes.

With the cautious, stalking step of a cat and without unpinning her eyes from the trees Mary sidled her slight frame between John and *them*, as though she would challenge them for the prize. The manoeuvre put her right next to the pole that reared so hugely into the sky, it brutally stabbed the clouds, lost to sight overhead. So cold. And so *old*. Beside it she looked tiny, *tiny*, a fluffy blond scrap destined to be pounded into the mud. Seconds before the reaching teeth would be gleefully buried in John's squalling flesh. Stained, square teeth. It might be imagination, but he heard them faintly clacking in anticipation.

Or not. Faced with reality, imagination had burned right out.

'Surgeon,' she said calmly in that absolute tone parents use when there is danger. A voice that cannot be ignored. 'When I signal, I want you to run for the city. She's your salvation. Run your heart out, hard as you can and don't so much as glance back, got me? You mustn't look at the Blessed. They hate what they are even more than they loathe your tender pink toes, and if they know they've been glimpsed …'

Run? He wasn't sure he could limp. Bitterly afraid of what

must not even be glanced at, his asshole tying itself into runny knots. The world was made up of hard edges. Glistening sharp enough to cut the mind wide open. Their time had run out.

Sudden silence. As though all the air had rushed away, taking the murmurs of the day with it. A brief intake of breath in the suddenly negative space, so loud to the ears, roaring. Branches crackled. The whole blurred mass of vegetation seemed to burst apart.

'Go, go, *shift it!*' She screamed and shoved him into staggering action when he would have stood aghast, waiting to be mown down.

With that impetus he fled, completely beyond control. Consciousness towed behind like a sobbing balloon. His eyes squeezed against the briefest peep beyond the fluff of Mary's hair of a wave of boiling motion charging toward them. Panic pistoned his legs at a rate even an athlete couldn't sustain for long and he could not even see the damn city, she seemed so far away. So much for salvation.

The Blessed roared, a brutal trumpet blast of rage and greed. Belatedly, as his ringing ears cleared, over the hot pumping blood of hysteria John realised he was whimpering, 'I'm gonna die, I'm gonna die.'

Not that it mattered. He had no more governance over his mouth than the diarrhoea that had burst its banks, streaming down both legs. Ragged searing breaths. Skull home only to clamouring confusion, flogging him to run faster when he wasn't sure he could keep going at all.

Mary wasn't having any of this shit. The Blessed were answered.

A piercing mechanical shriek rose into the thin air. If possible, it terrified him even more. A boiler's outrage as it erupted in spectacular destruction, bullet trains flung from the tracks by their own brute force, a jet's screaming engine driving it deeper into the ground. The Blessed had blasted out rage from dozens of ravening throats, but Mary's ultrasonics shredded the register. The defiance of the long-vanished machines.

The clash of impact. Amidst all the inhuman screaming came the awful, unmistakable tearing of soft vulnerable flesh. John's Surgeon hands quivered obsessively to repair the damage, never mind it would have meant death. Tugged in two directions, he stumbled.

Fatally threw out his hands with light-burned eyes screwed shut. Not shrieking for himself, for what good was a human voice in all this? Moaning soundlessly through lack of air. This was it. *Goodbye, golden boy. Fat lot of good you did in the end.*

But a small iron-hard arm was already clamped about his waist. Lifting him with impossible strength not merely to his feet but right off them. Jerked reflexively up against his torso his long legs just cleared the ground. Holding him suspended like that, canted to take the weight, Mary began to run.

Leaped from zero to a sprint in seconds that would have ripped mortal tendon from bone. Overcoming the sloppy ground by brute force, which splashed waves of mud out to either side. The speed was like sticking your fool head outside a zooming cart, likely to get it lopped off by some bit of the landscape.

Her light frothy hair, now tangled with bits of stick and weed, streamed, exposing her scattered ruin of emotionless features. Joggled beneath her arm John felt he was staring, not at something broken but at some abstract sculpture, whose meaning he couldn't possibly encompass. A carven alabaster mystery, frozen in impossibly swift motion. Streaming into the future on a flood of golden curls.

Suddenly they were beneath *A New Life*'s protective belly

and with the sun out he could finally unclamp stiff fingers from his eyes. Mary never slowed. With a jolt that would stamp bruises on his kidneys for life she lunged, and began to ascend.

This wasn't the ladder he had descended by, oh no. That had been first class compared to this rusting death trap, that squeaked and groaned warningly as they bounded higher, higher. Huge coiling flakes of metal dislodged. He didn't even want to see how she was managing to climb one-handed, grabbing and letting go.

Because he'd no idea how close their pursuers had been when she scooped him up, and because he so desperately wanted to live, he risked a quick glimpse down. For his transgression he received such a jumble of impressions that all muscles locked up tight and he was almost dropped to the earth, to *them*.

Luckily Mary hadn't gone through all this only to flunk at the last stretch. Grunting, she took a firmer, even more painful hold. And John closed his eyes, almost out of water to wet the lids down. Terrible. That was to be expected, what he'd been *raised* to expect. But wasn't there some whiff of alien attraction about them, too? Something so repugnant it became compelling and your eyes stroked over them, trying to understand.

In the scrum he'd glimpsed bone raddled flanks sliding by one another, like oil on water. Pale, they were, like the most bloated dead thing ever served up. But hillocked with muscle at the hocks—fast, with all that forward driving power, to run down prey in very short order. Before they'd begun to scream in earnest. For all her fleetness Mary had only stayed in front by a whisker, the charge baying at her heels. No wonder she had never hesitated.

Each of those plunging faces bore a single, wickedly sharp

horn. Like a barb, a pin to trap yourself on while you shriek and struggle to get free. While the others mill and stamp eagerly for their share in the mud all around. The tips seemed to catch and rip at his mind.

John had seen those rolling, inflamed eyes and by God he wished he hadn't. It was just as Mary said, they would never forget him now. Not in a million years. His unique taste would be forever in their dark shining mouths. His future, little more than a worm caught between clacking teeth. So he closed his eyes, last refuge of the doomed.

Then Mary was hauling him up through a hatch, past its rotted rubber seals into *A New Life* proper. Once he was clear she slammed it behind them with brisk finality. A heavy steel hatch no human could dare lift. Despite the nice solid thunk as it came down he was sure in his shrinking heart no thickness of metal would ever be enough.

They lay panting in the heavy darkness of some backstage hallway. And it was so very stifling and small after the brilliance and fear of Outside.

'They're …' He heaved, bringing up nothing but great clots of fear.

'I know.' Even Mary puffed lightly, like an overheated cat. 'And you just *had* to look down. I'd never be leaving these walls again if I was in your boots.'

He wasn't planning on it. 'But … How can they be real?'

She stretched back against the wall with a groan. 'Honestly, hon, I saw 'em born and I'm not even sure I believe it. They aren't monsters, you know. Well, not really. They came from man.'

'That's impossible.' And by impossible, he meant nothing he wanted to hear, not ever. Especially not from her, because after all this she couldn't be doubted. But despite her past or perhaps because of it she wasn't one for wilful lies, however comforting.

She touched her smashed face gently beneath the hair. 'How do you think I got this?'

'Those *things* did that to you?'

'Not directly. But they and my lost chances of winning the Miss World pageant spring from the same source. Rather fitting they should take a stab at finishing the job today, I fancy.'

Shoulders wincing she got to her feet. Only now he noticed how she listed permanently to one side following the clash, arm caved subtly in toward her chest. It wasn't exactly second nature to put others first.

'You're hurt! We've got to get you to the surgery, I can ...'

'*You* can?' She shook her head, amused. John realised that once again he was being very foolish, and recalled a metallic shriek of rage ricocheting up to the blinding heavens. 'Hon, those who could've repaired *me* got switched off long before the cities were built. You just get your ass up off that floor.'

'Can't I rest here a bit?'

'Not if you value your skin. The downstairs lot don't use this hatch, it's too old and dangerous and just too darn heavy. But they'll have been glued to every second of our little fiasco; best entertainment there is down here. On their way right now, I'd expect. We might make it if we shift right-smart. I'll tell you what I know of the Blessed as we go.'

The thought of the downstairs people flooding silently along the corridor put the willies up him. He was in his socks and caked with filth, some of which was his own watery terror-shit. And his muscles wouldn't stop fizzing. Completely overloaded, he shuddered from head to toe as irregular waves of it passed through.

Yet to his credit he scraped up the wherewithal to croak, 'Do you think my friend's still out there?' Faces, screaming beneath a gossamer veil. The pole, dark against the scudding sky.

Mary tilted her head thoughtfully, seeming to stare down at the hatch. Her eyes must be better than his for the light was not good. 'She might make it, at that.'

'Make it *where*?'

'There are a couple of places to go. The farms. Other cities. We certainly led those beasties a merry chase and every second snapping at our heels meant they weren't after her. If your "friend" has a big ol' bucket of luck, and the same in guts, she's at least got a fighting chance.'

That struck a frown. The friend had never been what you could call lucky. One could only hope she'd been saving it all for just this moment. Sighing, John accepted Mary's hand by way of grabbing her sleeve, his gloves were ruined. Calves groaning he creaked slowly to his feet. If he made it out of this, he'd sleep for a week and dream only of his couch.

'The Blessed, then. Tell me what you know.'

They shuffled off, a begrimed and damaged pair, and she began. 'Son was raised in a crisp hospital ward by me and my companions.'

'You can skip over the obvious bits. Son features in every storybook read to toddlers.'

'Oh surely, hon, but what they *won't* tell you is during those days we suffered a snake in the grass. One fellow who almost ruined everything—but ah, sometimes one is all it takes.'

'I didn't think there were any people at the hospital, other than Son. Only machines.' John was following the roughness of the wall with one hand, less able to peer through the dark than she. He was coming out less able on a dismaying level overall. 'The story goes, people were scattered all over until Son united them. Dying alone and afraid and ready to pull the world into the hole after.'

'One man was with us at the hospital. Just one. Only, he wasn't there for Son. He was our prisoner.'

'His crime?'

'Hon, he was getting no more than he deserved, don't worry your pretty little head. Can't flush some turds, you know. They always come bobbing back up to ruin the air. I didn't want him there, but my companions believed *residual humanity* was biasing my opinion. Ha! Didn't they love trotting that gem out when we disagreed.

'In their infallible wisdom my poor dear companions believed young Son had a wealth to learn from the prisoner. Namely, what *not* to be.'

'Was he really so bad?'

'The prisoner was the sort to be always blaming others. Oh, but wasn't everything always somebody else's fault? All brimming with resentment at a world failing to serve what he deserved on a nice shiny platter. Would Sir like success with that? Accolades? *Women*?

'He *deserved* things, you see? The prisoner had *rights* and most importantly folk *owed* him. Tell you all about it if you stood still long enough. The entire nasty world was unjustly denying him, and from thence sprang his crime. When nobody would accommodate his puling demands then, well, he decided it was time to *take*. Take, take, take. I doubt that sack of shit ever *gave* a single damn thing in his life.

'Trouble was, to the pigheadedness of youth a lot of the garbage spewing from that sinkhole mouth must have seemed pretty reasonable. Shortcuts to getting things now, instead of working toward 'em. *Deserving* instead of earning. At that age who's truly keen to struggle for long painful years, or play nice with those who have, or *sacrifice* when you can *take*?

'My companions felt bad for the prisoner. It was hard enough denying him his freedom, they couldn't bring themselves to withdraw this last human contact with Son. And it looked so *innocent*, the two of them sitting together drinking cups of tea. On one side of the table Son, who was destined to be humanity's last hope. And to the other the prisoner, the snake, whose final act of spite came close to making that poor boy the species' final straw.'

John didn't relish hearing about Son's callow youth. The man had been a saviour, approaching divine, in a city that offered so few glowing role models. But Mary's clearly aired bugbear was all about how stubborn men turned their heads from unpalatable truth. So he bit his tongue and squished forlornly along in his sodden socks, leaving a trail of foul smelling footprints and smears in his wake. Unmissable to anyone following. If they continued much further the toxic mix of bacteria and acid would chew his skin bloody.

'The true damage of those irresponsible fantasies didn't rear its ugly head for many years. I all but forgot it. There was plenty else to worry about, come his eighteenth birthday and the loss of the other machines. My banishment.

'I kept watch as best as I was able, and from that time Son went from strength to strength. He was the hope of us all, and I was so proud I thought I'd burst.

'I watched as he brought the scattered people together. Even the most entrenched were drawn to his quiet light, his vision of a way forward when previously there'd been none. Lovers who might never have met embraced for the first time. Children were conceived, for a world that so desperately needed them. Son's little community flourished.

'But things seeming perfect was all part of the trap the prisoner had woven, and the strands pulled tight around us. You see, hon, nobody exists without flaw. It just isn't possible. And to feel that's what you have to be, perfect; to get up every morning knowing you can't make a single mistake …

'It must have been impossible to bear. A state every part of you is screaming to rip free of. Son was so *good* at it, though. His brave face so perfect. We were all taken in, and none saw what it cost. What it might drive him to. What happened was our fault, all of his people, as much as his.'

'What did he do?'

'He …' She exhaled heavily. 'Using what the prisoner taught him, Son extracted the imperfections from himself somehow. His faults, weaknesses. I saw what went on myself and I'm still not exactly sure what happened.

'I hid to watch. I'm not proud of spying, but I damn well knew something was fishy and couldn't think of what else to do. Starting to get a taste of that scrabbly trapped feeling that was Son's life, I guess. There was so damned much riding on what we were trying to accomplish.

'Even worse, the damn fool went and showed others how to do it, too. That's when the disaster really slipped out of control. Maybe he felt for them, or didn't want to be the only one, I don't know.

'Son selected his closest neighbour Huang, and a lass they both knew called Miley. Nice girl but she'd found early on that assets were more use than smarts, if you get my drift. Everyone knew Huang had been working on the elusive method of slipping into her tiny shorts, so perhaps her inclusion was for him. Following Son, they were the first.

'All three of them snuck out in the middle of the night. Off to the looming hulks of the old grain silos out of town, which got my antenna humming. You see, Son had wanted to establish a swatch of real farmland, scratch something back from the desert, but no grain was anywhere near surplus enough to go bothering with the silos. Trembling on spindly girders those concrete behemoths were on the verge of collapse, a rotten death trap. Nobody had any business being out there.

'Yet it hosted the three of them, and me tagging along, when all of us should have been safe abed. Long shadows in the moonlight under a sky so stark it was indecent, kept your eyes lowered. The sand that had burned hot crimson during the day gone all muted and silver, gathering about progress through its mire like foam. No smell. No smell to the world but dryness and sweat.

'Because of my banishment I could only sneak close enough to hear snatches. Son and sly Miley were cajoling Huang with, "It's soo good Huang," and, "You'll feel amazing after." And at that I felt massively relieved, slumping in the scraping sand. Assumed they must be sowing a night of wild kinky oats. If only I'd crept off then, feeling fuzzy about things. But I couldn't have been more wrong.

'Son had a reassuring hand on each of their shoulders and was speaking in a low urgent tone, their heads bowed before him, listening like they'd never heard anything so critical in all their lives. Listening like followers. Son had no true friends, you see, only disciples and other flotsam who'll gladly trail along. No wish to stand by his side where the agony was.

'Me, I was only just realising this wasn't some congenial threesome off in the sand. Squirming inside my skin trying to manufacture some way to get closer. Miley began coughing and gagging, flailing her little arms in a panic and I thought Christ she's choking although I hadn't seen anything get near her mouth.

'Huang started up only moments later making the same terrified airless *crurk gurrk* noises, with his hands flapping and clawing at his face. Son was trying to calm them down but even an idiot could see he was soiling his pantaloons, he'd lost control of the situation. Two close companions threshing in the sand and turning blue before his eyes.

'What went down next looked impossible. My eyes could well have tricked me, being so far away and all. Son had dropped the torch in his panic, stooping to one and then the other. Miley, pretty little Miley thrashed her way into its beam.

'Her jaws were cracked wide open. Impossibly wide, like she was trying to scream her whole existence out. And the whole cavity of her mouth was filled with something firm and white. Something wet-looking, the light glistened on it. Her teeth made little indents as it pressed out.

'She obviously couldn't bear to touch it, tore at her hair in a frenzy instead. Son half-heartedly tried to restrain her but he'd gone quite a way around the horrified bend too, and didn't want a bar of handling either of them. His eyes kept slipping off to the lumbering moon, set on running away and never coming back.

'Then there was this sodden crackling noise. I got it even from where I was hiding and it was the worst thing I'd ever heard. Like a thick bundle of mud and sticks being snapped. Miley's head split in half right there in the torch beam.

'What tumbled down onto the sand was this glistening thing about the size of a baby goat but pale, really pale. Unfolded from that tiny space and thrashing and squealing the way Miley had done only moments before. Squealing this awful high-pitched siren of utter distress, that pierced right through the skull and shredded any attempt at thought.

'And there was Miley. Getting to her feet and tucking her hair behind her ears. She looked fine, like if you told her you'd seen her jaw cracked wider than her head, drooling bloody spittle onto the sand, you would get an odd look and a politely embarrassed laugh.

'Better than fine, even. She was all mooney with this glisten to her eye I'd seen before. Oh yes, and I didn't fancy it one bit. A woman glowing with the worst kind of obsession: overriding love that ignores reality. That shouts, things can be like this forever. It was the romance-struck dreaminess of a woman getting bamboozled in a con.

'Son picked up the torch and gee if you couldn't smell his relief on the air. Offered a hand to Huang, and damn if he wasn't lit up with the same brainwashed grin. Both clearly feeling too wonderful for words. My Son slapped them on the shoulder where he'd held on so urgently earlier, and they nodded together with a sly little wink. Everybody in on the big secret.

'Then he put his light briefly on what Miley had sicked up. It was dragging itself away like a deformed snail, all the red sand sticking to it. Mewling in a tone to seal both hands over your ears. The thing Huang had likewise discharged was struggling to rise on spindly legs that refused to hold. Shrill cries of frustration rang off those swagging concrete bellies overhead.

'*Do something*, I begged silently with hands clapped over my ears. I couldn't stand the agonised frequency, sight alone being plenty to drive any rational soul into the stark raving. My last hope was that Son had some kind of plan, because it was abominable to set such things down and just walk away. It was abandoning one's humanity, the very thing we'd been struggling to save.'

John snorted. She was a fine one to talk!

She misinterpreted. 'Don't get me wrong, the ghastly things were nothing to be treasured. Quite the opposite. But to struggle against such qualities is the very proving ground of humanity. As you can probably guess, my hope was for nothing.

'Apparently he'd wearied of doing everything the hard way, the right way. Hearkened too long to the prisoner's bottomless self pity, and just this once had decided the path of ease was more to his fancy. In a *normal* life it's hardly the end of the world should you stumble so now and again. Sadly, back then none of us were in any position to afford such mistakes. Everything was too damn precarious.

'That's why my wits froze as Son and his friends linked arms and sauntered off through the bleeding air back to town. Whistling and laughing if you can believe it, as jaunty as can be. I ran off. I think I even ran in circles for a bit, out of my mind, no earthly idea what to do. All I wanted was to claw what I'd seen out of my head and burn it. Wipe it right out of reality.

'I suppose I went into a sort of traumatised hibernation for a while. I just couldn't conceive of how my darling perfect boy had come to this. Couldn't bear to witness his downfall. If he hadn't sent me away all those years ago I'd have been standing right beside him, and none of this would have happened. But my breakdown and absence came at the worst possible time.

'By the time I crawled back into the world this ... this *thing* had proliferated like the clap. And those things they'd been coughing up didn't stay small and squealing, oh no. Each with that nasty, wicked horn. When I went beneath the sand I left a small semi-agrarian town. I came home to a fortified camp.'

'What do they want?' John asked in a small voice. 'Why do they keep coming back to people?'

For all his days they had been discussed in whispers, by those without the tact to stay silent. A destructive but elemental sort of force. Popular paranoia had them crashing against *A New Life*'s walls like the rage of the world, and that was how you closed your eyes within those walls and managed to get to sleep at night.

This new concept, that they were in fact purposeful, thinking molten alien thoughts and brooding on their own horrific distortions of emotion, made the hair pull in all over his body.

'You don't understand what they want?' She seemed fired by his apprehension. The bombast of reciting gruesome titbits to a captive audience.

'No.' Smallest voice ever.

'Why, to squirm back inside, of course. Any way they can. A bloody event, with an animal that big. Eventually it's merely pushing scraps of human around on the floor. Never lets up, either, no matter what you do. Wailing, violence, trying to cast your own flesh in the way to save a loved one ... More than one parent or lover was driven stark raving by the sheer futility. Minds blown out.

'So by the time I'd pulled my fearful head from my behind we had a serious problem that was only getting worse. So many of the things roaming about that they had stopped being shy. Enough to come chattering and stamping onto your porch in the dead of night. Come right through the window snorting eddies of putrid hot steam while you slept.

'Then screams. Hot and raw like the night was being ripped open. All others huddling in their own locked houses, shuddering in the dark as they listened. Praying for it to stop. Come daybreak they'd venture out, grey-faced, to discover who had been spread over the walls of their home this time. So afraid they wouldn't even touch the remains. Just sealed the doors and windows with black tape, a big X across the front in the unlikely event somebody hadn't heard.

'I passed too many houses silent and sealed, their occupants denied the dignity of burial because of fear and superstition. Too many family members howling on a doorstep, the X denying them entry to a place that had been all life and laughter just yesterday. The community had fractured, reverted to individuals scrabbling in the dark.

'I needed to speak with Son. A drive almost as strong as the imperative to stay away. I found him sitting on the floor of his bathroom, his face in his hands. Made ready to speak to him through the wall which was the closest I could get, but he knew it was me before I'd said a word.

'"It's you, isn't it?" he asked, and I'd never heard a voice so forlorn. "I always heard the rumours, you know. People thinking there was an angel watching this town. Tiny, they'd say, with the most shining golden hair. That's how I knew you hadn't abandoned me."

'Still covering his face he began to sob. "Mum, I've fucked everything up."

'The compulsion was closing its iron grip and I knew I wouldn't get to speak to him again. Bit by bit I pulled the whole sorry tale free in a process oh so very delicate. Extracting the nastiness was like a tapeworm: yank too insistently and it would break, the hooked head remain buried and the growth of the secret start all over. But once I had this mess traced back to the prisoner I saw red, literally red. A wash across my vision so extreme I had to sit down before I fell.

'How could I possibly comfort him, my poor Son? He'd been duped. Cold comfort it was by a malevolent leech who'd fashioned his whole petty life around bleeding others.' Mary shook her head. 'A lad in the flush of puberty hadn't stood a chance. As well feed rabbits into the mouths of sharks.

'I failed him. The best I could offer fell far short of what he so desperately needed. Sat on my side of the wall, knocking at intervals to let him know I was still there. Still waiting. Once his sobs had quietened enough to listen I reminded him the prisoner hadn't been his only teacher, and by far not the greatest. The best course in finding a way to undo the harm was to remember *all* he'd learned.'

'The machines whispered their secrets to him,' John murmured.

'That's right. The knowledge my companions bestowed on our adopted child was vast. But to be reminded of it was little comfort to a suffering, cruelly isolated young man beating his grief out against the tiles.

'And to have me reappear *now* bringing no forgiving embrace to hold the pieces of his heart together … No solution to lift the weight crushing him to the floor. Only another impossible challenge whispered through the wall. How could he not have hated me?

'All the life seemed to drain out of him. What got left behind was cold and quaking. Bereft. Little rustling movements as he curled up on the floor. If only his proud followers who'd driven him to this could see him now. It killed me that I couldn't take him in my arms and hold the world at bay. A good chunk of my remaining humanity shrivelled, just dropped off like a rotten bough. And that left less to resist the compulsion.

'The force of it caught hold, practically flung me from the building. I heard Son cry out. He threw open the door to catch a last glimpse but it was too late. That's how I left him. I wanted to help, but brought nothing but despair.'

'Couldn't you have stayed a little longer? He needed you so badly.'

'You think I don't know that? Programming's not got a lot of truck with free will, for all I got a lighter touch of it. Starts off small, giving you the chance of being a good girl and complying right away. Then builds. It allows no rest. When you've done as you should, finally, there's not … not exactly pleasure. More the satisfaction an equation might feel at resolving itself elegantly. And a brief sort of peace. Before the next compulsion rears its head, of course.'

'And that's what you gave up your humanity for?'

'It bound me. But it saved me as well. I may have been banned from Son by his foolish order but it wasn't like I could do *nothing*. I left the town with its taped-up houses, the fear so thick it left a scum on your teeth. On foot under the glaring blue sky I headed down the shattered remains of the highway, to pay the old hospital a visit. The place where I had given up so much, and had found Son.

'I hadn't seen it since he walked forth with an old backpack across his shoulder, a grieving young man wiping his eyes, and I'd followed in the shadows. The prisoner had been doddering when we abandoned him there, and he would have to be truly ancient if he'd survived this long. Trapped within those walls by infirmity every bit as much as by the machines who'd once restrained him.

'There was nothing the prisoner had ever feared so much as being alone. But that was no longer enough for me.

'The entrance was no longer high-tech or welcoming. Machines had once monitored it, to rush with whatever aid you required, terrified of losing another human. Gone, long gone. Silent corridors. With the sliding doors jammed open red sand was blowing and shifting between the walls.

'I waded in, sand up to my hips sometimes. Dim with the power out but I found the windows were letting in pools of lazy light, made you want to lie down in their warmth forever. Give up struggling and all the rest, just rest your head in a cradle of soft, gently glowing sand. But I had business.

'The prisoner had dared assemble his final rat nest in the very crèche where Son grew up. I remember back in the day it'd been a place of laughter. The only cheerful note in the whole grey bleach-smelling complex, where big painted cartoon animals grinned cheerily from the walls. Son didn't smile so much after he left it.

'As I dug my way in I found the prisoner had taken an artistic bent. All that innocent cheer scratched over with a senseless kaleidoscope of phalli, huge moustaches, and any other hilarity a decaying mind amuses itself with. It hurt to see. The crèche was monstrous now, but no more than a nasty reflection of what squatted within.'

'This prisoner of yours,' John panted. He was reaching the tail end of his endurance, which had turned out a damn sight longer than even pride had supposed. 'He was still alive.'

'And waiting. *I did it all for you, Mary*, he whined. *To bring you back. I had to see you one last time.* Huh. I was pretty, you see. Turned all the lad's heads. Things might have been better if I'd had a serve of goodness to go with it, but a fair face never brought me anything but trouble. He'd been preparing for years in his nest, practicing the soft words I might have stayed to listen to once upon a time.

'Instead I laughed right in his face, a big old laugh, flecks of spittle and all. I doubt the old fool was expecting that. But he'd been a strong bugger in his time, and a cunning snake there in his hole. Still quick on his feet.'

She gestured toward her hidden face. 'Gave me this to remember him by. If I'd still been the Mary he remembered, I never would have survived it.'

She chucked with absolutely no humour whatsoever. 'I stamped that filthy old man into a bloodied smear on the floor. Then I left the door open for the desert to sweep in and erase him. Problem solved. By the time I got back to Son's little town the first of the cities was under construction. And here we are.'

John sagged. 'Here's about as far as we're going. I'm sorry, I can't walk any further. I really can't.'

She came back and patted down the featureless wall next to him. 'It's not ideal, but this will have to do then. Doesn't go quite so far up as I'd have liked, but at least you can catch a rest before we switch to another.'

As she spoke the blank wall split apart under her hands to reveal the cold gleaming light of an elevator. No buttons, switches or visible seams; it was like she'd conjured it out of wishful thinking.

'How did you do that?'

'The city listens to me,' she answered smugly, a fond hand on the wall. 'Though Son loved the cities dearly and always dreamed of it, sadly she'll never wake into self-awareness like my companions. That level of engineering was beyond him. What passes for her consciousness is drifting. But my presence is like a light to her, she'll always gravitate toward me no matter how far she's under.'

The shining blond head dipped a little. 'But I like to think she likes me. That if she ever woke up, we could be friends.'

A whisper of sound bled down the corridor, jerking both their heads around. A pattering. As of a multitude of soft drops landing but John knew it was really feet, racing closer. And a sound he'd heard recently, breeze sweeping through treetops. Only this was the *shusha* of many bobbing heads of hair.

Mary's eyes were better.

'Into the elevator!' she ordered, diving through the doors. John complied with everything his aching limbs could muster.

The silhouettes that were the first of the downstairs people rounded the curve, strange puffball people with dandelion heads. Crabbed hands reaching out, flickering and silent.

And then the bland normality of the closed doors.

Mary patted the seal. 'Good girl.'

The elevator was uncomfortably hard and cold, but even a

bed of nails couldn't have kept John on his feet any longer. He curled his bruised, stinking self into a C shape trying to keep some heat in. The second he ungritted his teeth his mind just dropped away.

Smothering, irresistible sleep. Too much like the state *A New Life* herself drifted in, drawn hither and there between sparks of conscious life. Forever unmoored and drifting.

CHAPTER SIX

A Big Obvious Joke

A THUMPING intruded into blissful mindlessness. Tentative but waxing determined, as folk do once they decide they're in the right. With that distinctive hollow knock-knock of the elbow bone, little shards of pain up the arm, which narrowed John's circle of acquaintance to one.

Lars. Lars was pounding insistently at the front door and showing no sign of buggering off to hell, where he was sincerely wished.

That was what finally peeled John from sleep like a bandaid.

Some sharper lobe of his brain was dinning the alarm, there was something dreadfully dire about good old Lars knocking at the door. Come *on* John, get your groggy ass moving.

He inched his face out of the stale pillow, half-blind, gaping mouth sticky. Lars couldn't be let in, because …

Mary!

Too late he lurched compulsively from bed only to find now was high time for his abused body to tell a little tale about consequences. The perfect moment bided for while he'd been mercilessly flogging it along. Intense screaming pain shot up both legs and tumbled him to the carpet where he pummelled the floor in frustration.

At the same moment Mary took it upon herself to throw the door open before Lars' battering caved it in. John moaned in anguish into the soft pile as events wobbled from bad to worse.

'Can I help you there, hon?' She asked brightly, the sort of chipper that's like acid so early in the morning. Then, with a breath of asperity, 'You'll end up having that joint off at the elbow, you keep up that banging.' Only the most underhanded mind would take it as a threat.

This was a shiny new pickle for Lars. Over their long, sometimes strained association he prided himself on acquaintance with every face that came John's way. Even the infamous aunt, if only by reputation. Add Mary's hairstyle to the shock of strangeness. Luckily, one of many qualities you could always sit back and expect was unfailing manners.

Politeness had facilitated a steady social climb where lesser talents might have held him back. In fact, for all John's professional brilliance, erratic conformity might one day see Lars go sailing past him. The humble achiever on his merry way to sweet digs in the sunlight suburbs, while John languished in *The Cutters*.

But not today. Not while he had his strength.

Oops. He didn't.

'Ma'am.' Lars bobbed endearingly, throwback to the elegant century of the bow. 'So sorry to come bursting in …'

She cut across with a flighty laugh, all the sincerity of meringue. Got away with it, too, poor Lars being ignorant of the horror her curls curtained away. He was wide open to being charmed.

'Oh lordy hon, don't you come at me with "ma'am"—it makes me sound so *old*. Just Mary will do. We're among friends.'

"Friends" now, was it? A likely story.

'Uh, is John home?' Sounding like he ought to follow with, 'Can he come out and play?' Even Lars caught the absurdity and shook himself back to the here-and-now. 'Begging pardon for the language ma'am, but his stupid butthole *urgently* needs hauling out of the frypan right quick.'

'I just told you; Mary not ma'am. And we can't have anything befalling our dear Surgeon, now, can we? Scarcely a mouthful should those tiny buns get toasted, I'd say.' She laughed, all tinkly bells and spun sugar.

On his doorstep was a bizarre meeting of minds John desperately wanted to throw a harness over before it ran out of control. Sadly, the best his limbs permitted was to lie with a low plaintive moan, waiting to be remembered and set right.

It was Mary who had lugged his carcass home from elevator to elevator. Somehow deciphering his exhaustion slurred directions, that had amounted to little better than weak pointing by the end. The worst bit was when they reached *The Cutters*. Had a neighbour's curtain twitched he couldn't have done a damn thing about it.

But stumbling through the dead of night had its advantages—assuming you got where you were going. He'd been sort of curious to see anything happen, pitied the opportunistic thug who'd draw the short straw of Mary. But they'd seen no-one.

'Nice apartment,' she'd offered as they clattered inside, shedding a trail of flaking filth. 'Very … practical.'

Humorously in light of his years of wallowing, half-formed fantasies of touch it was also Mary who got him cleaned up and into bed. At least, he'd surely laugh about it someday. Perhaps in a hundred years. For all she wasn't a real person he insisted she don a set of gloves. His own were down to rings of shredded latex about his wrists. Shedding them left bracelets of bright clean skin.

And that was merely the beginning. The vanity was crowded with the array of implements and skin barriers that formed every Surgeon's bath time arsenal. She snickered delightedly, picking them up to guess aloud at function with surpassing deviancy. Blushing took up blood that was urgently required elsewhere—he swooned against the wall.

Oh, the cool tile pressed to his face felt so good! He wanted to drop bonelessly to the floor, pull the towels down into a safe little nest and lie there forever. A sanctuary excluding downstairs people, the Blessed, or the friends you betrayed to them.

Seeing his shivering distress she tutted and came back before he slid down the wall and became part of the floor. Shook her head over his state, the movement amplified by mirrors into giddy echoes of being surrounded by the downstairs people shaking, shaking, which made him close his eyes.

No time for shame at being propped upright by steely little arms and stripped in all his humiliation and glory. Clothing that stung as it was prised free, the skin red-raw beneath. The perfect recipe for seeing it rot right off his frame.

He tried feebly to cover his body. Sallow like old bone, a pouch of a belly and skin that slackly draped the swoops and whorls of architecture beneath like his skeleton was determined to punch through. Adorned with puffs of vividly ginger hair, and greenish freckles in odd places. Not a getup you'd see gracing any magazine, but he had never planned on showing anybody. All of his fantasies involved other people.

His impromptu nurse hardly cared; her days of flesh being a hot-blooded wrapping for the sexy treat within were way behind her. She attended with the brusqueness of a mother sorting another's child. Efficiently, but with no particular love.

At the first touch of sponge to quivering flesh he shuddered and moaned weakly. It took a firm hand to hold him still. In little dabs the filth was patted from him—from the outside, anyway, which was the best anyone could hope for. The floor ran puddled with it, speckles of mud across the walls.

His dreadlocks had to be taken off at the scalp with clippers, no other way. The stiffened things thumped to the floor like rotten appendages, leaving his head over-light, every twitch accelerated. A peep in the mirror saw him peeled and diminished but brought a tremulous relief; hair would haunt his sleep already. He wanted it well removed from his waking moments.

The first breath John drew that was fresh, that smelled untainted, made him break down in tears. Made quite the spectacle, boniness swaddled, hiccupping and snuffling as tears dripped off his chin. He'd gone his limit. All bundled in the biggest softest towel Mary could find which made him cry even harder: the fancy towels had been a gift from the friend, replacing the cardboard scratchiness he'd been getting by with. The colours matched, and everything.

Left to his own devices he would have then fallen straight into bed and, without treatment, been walking bowlegged for weeks. Once he was clean and towelled to a rough finish Mary hunted up a salve for the fierce welts that came from hiking about for hours with a load in his shorts. The application brought goosebumps followed by a whimper of insane relief.

Dumped in his room he had fallen asleep to the hiss-patter of Mary starting her own shower. His final thought before plummeting away, a flash of inane worry, there wouldn't be enough nice towels.

And now here came Lars, kneeling beside him on the floor. The agonised bafflement of a colleague with no wish to witness this, but grim determination to stick it out all the same. Every friendship comes with a side order of flop, of one flavour or another. It was the glue that bound society together.

'Dude, I've been trying to call you.'

Not, "What's your ass doing on the floor?" or even, "What's with the stupid buzz-cut?" but bless him, he was a man of his own priorities.

John coughed, swimming in slow motion on the carpet without much effect. *Wallowing*, that was the word, all hooked up in sheets like a slug landed in a net.

'Sorry. My screen's not working.'

Lars winced. 'No shit.' An inquisitive nose into the lounge on his way through had seen the expensive hardware ripped from its mooring, smashed and fizzing on the floor. Even at a Surgeon's level he couldn't have been halfway through repayments. 'Lucky it didn't come down and squash you. What in the name of ass were you thinking?'

Of course, what a body *wanted* to ask was, "What are you *ever* thinking?' Looking at John now it was too easy to imagine nothing but a bank of switches within that ginger-fuzzed head.

'Oh God, I wasn't obviously! I was so *tired*, and the damn thing wouldn't quit beeping …' He sighed, cataloguing the absurd as he heard it. 'Guess that would have been you. Sorry. Lost my temper.'

'Ding ding ding, guess again. I'm not the only sod who's been struggling to get you on the horn.'

Oh God, here it came. Nobody ever wanted John unless business had gone south in a big way.

'You, my good fellow, failed to come to the party when the Captain asked nicely. I reckon she's about done with nice. There've been some pretty pissed off orders echoing out of the control room.'

'To you?'

Lars beamed. '"To" is such a strong word, don't you think? Cunning fox that I am, *I* aim to get you up there dignity intactica before some nasty types show up to do it the hard way. I mean it: they'll be wrapping you in plastic to handle you, like in the bad old days. It'd be fifty-fifty whether you'd be blue and still by the time they got around to unrolling you at the Captain's tapping foot.'

True, it used to happen. Surgeons had never been so trusted as they were these days, but they'd proven themselves. Won respect, adulation, and done it the hard way with very few missteps like John's aunt. Such a pity those missteps were so big.

Mary weighed in from the doorway, hands casually at her belt. No, *John's* belt. She'd fashioned a sort of dress from a too-big shirt, one he'd been meaning to toss.

'He's not likely to be strolling about anytime soon, hon. Pins are done in.'

Lars immediately knew what to do. 'Oh, he'll be walking.'

Flipping the sheet he exposed John's pale hairy legs, crooked and rigid with cramp. Set to work mercilessly with expert latex-sheathed fingers. Field treatment was quite the arcane sideline. John's domain was the cold metal theatre: so much so that for years he'd moved only between it and his apartment like a bird locked in a migratory cycle. Spotting a rare opportunity to blaze his trail, even an unglamorous one, Lars had applied himself to field surgery with gusto.

For all the sniggering he was the first Surgeon in over a hundred years to wear a field scalpel, that pygmy stripped-down version of a Surgeon's primary tool. Fool probably slept with the damn thing on, and would slice an ass cheek off someday. And beside it, a belt crammed with vials of unguent and the like. No mass-produced shit for Lars, weekends saw him zealously grinding and blending each one. It was best not to ask out of what.

All those vials replaced and replaced as they expired, lovingly maintained. This was the first time his specialty had come in useful. He was so excited he might just pop. The prone man's agonised yelps elicited little sympathy, but of course a Surgeon's patient is usually in no position to protest.

'Oh God. Stop.' John clasped both hands over his streaming bloodshot eyes, bucking about the narrow space beside the bed. 'You're killing me!'

'Better me than the Captain, you blockhead. And what in the name of sweet ass have you been sticking your ugly mug into? Your eyeballs look boiled. I'll bet they hurt.'

'Oh, you reckon?'

He competently peeled back one of his fluttering eyelids and tsked, as though John had set about this mess deliberately. The moral high ground is ever heady. With the other hand holding the freshly bristled expanse of scalp steady, he administered eye drops from a tiny glass bottle so intricate it looked like a jewel. His hands were firm. One wrong move would've sent the exquisite thing spearing through John's eyeball; then so much for being the hero of the day.

'Aah!' Released, John thrashed back, blinking rapidly.

The drops seemed to be a coolness. Then a fresh minty slap, reaching right down both optic nerves into his brain. From a milky haze like egg albumen the room emerged into focus and he almost clung to the other Surgeon and wept with relief. He'd hardly allowed himself to fear his vision might be damaged for life. Wouldn't make much of a Surgeon then, and what else was there?

'Up you get, bighead. It's off to the control room we go.'

'What's in the control room?' Mary asked innocently, a little lamb. 'Anything to occupy little ol' me?'

'Well, there's controls. And the Captain.'

'Aaand ..?' Other women weren't Mary's cup of tea.

Lars was casting about. 'Oh, but the chapel's nearby if you've not seen it. A real nice, peaceful place. Lots of people like visiting the old hospital machines, it's a real slice of history.'

John didn't dare breathe. Mary had gone very still but gave the unsettling sense of vibrating in place, more rapidly than the eye could see.

'Yes,' she said eventually. If anyone had ever constructed false cheer, brittle as ice, it was all here. 'I think I might like that very much.'

The sunlight suburbs had always seemed dazzling, but now John's eyes well appreciated the virtues of filtered plastex. How many of these folk knew the world beyond was on fire?

Teetering on stilts so they had to squint up into golden light to see it, the control room was the highest point of all. Highest in the city. For ascent you had your choice of a glass elevator, or a spiralling ornate staircase.

Any other day would have seen John powering straight

for the stairs, trailed by Lars' long-suffering sigh. Lack of engineering acumen spawned dark fantasies of the fragile looking box exploding under load, erasing them in a whirlwind of fine splinters that would hang in the air a moment, glittering red in the light of the glorious sun.

'Stop it.'

'What?'

'Any time we get in, on or around anything with a motor you start dwelling on our untimely deaths.'

'No I don't. And shut up.'

Today the flesh had proven so very weak. Elevator it was. Vibrating in a manner guaranteed to heighten anxiety it lifted John and Lars into a rare bird's eye view of the sunlight suburbs. You didn't enjoy it quite so much on the stairs, huffing and puffing your way to the top.

All pretty cottages so far as the eye could see, immaculate green lawns and the privileged folk who strolled and waved amicably to one another like old friends. What did they all *do*, John wondered. As picturesque as it looked he'd no ambition of moving in, although it had to be the dream of damn near everyone else in the city. Perfection just wasn't a place he could see himself belonging. If he were honest, no such place existed and if more people glanced about with clear eyes there'd probably be a sight less aspiration.

A humming stop. The carriage lurched a bit, just enough to send his heart crowding into his mouth. A pity it didn't stay to inform wiser words.

Ignorant of his distress Lars briskly slid the doors rattling open. The folding metalwork was intricate in the shape of the suburbs, a map. The first map, as the control room was a place full of them. The Captain could lock these doors from a panel inside if she sensed a threat, and you didn't get to her age without seeing them everywhere. Lord knew how she denied entry at the staircase, although he'd no doubt there would be a way. Probably set the whole thing to accordion shut and crush you. A minor twitch from a dreaming city.

The control room was arguably the most technical place aboard *A New Life*, a far cry from the colossally indifferent clockwork found downstairs. In the control room habitation gave way to the rarity of *interaction* with the city. Working actively to shape your destiny. As little as it looked it.

Over her lifetime the Captain had made the space her own, one of the few quirks allowed by office. To stoop your head, stiffly like bowing, and enter was like stepping into a jungle. Curling greenery extended flowers on long nodding stalks. Neither plant nor butterfly but something caught exquisitely between, soaking up the drenching sunlight and leaping forever into splendid flight.

Every available centimetre boasted bluish jars from which spilled the flowering plants, which didn't seem to need respectable soil like their cousins Outside. Just a sort of knotty mass to take root in. Clumps and tangles viewed dimly through condensation beaded glass. Difficult to breathe, if you weren't used to it. The humidity alone ought to have been the bane of charts and equipment, the very air dripped.

Except that the charts that marched across the walls were all sealed tight, with the care due such priceless artefacts. Electronics had long proven indifferent to any violence humanity hid up its sleeve, even the despair of sabotage. The room had been safed as though against a toddler.

Despite his untutored enthusiasm for botany John loathed to visit the control room. He couldn't believe it to be anything but a big obvious joke at all a Surgeon was denied. In their silky complexity, each bloom nodding gently toward him resembled female genitalia. So blatantly he couldn't believe nobody passed smirking comment.

Not wishing to be the first deviant out of the box he kept his mouth shut and eyes down. It couldn't *really* just be him? Perhaps he was the last of the great perverts after all.

In the midst of unease, waiting for the Captain to notice them and the proverbial axe to fall, he wished suddenly for the friend's stolid support instead of Lars' fluttering. The friend would have brayed heartily at the spectacle of him beset on all sides by vivid vaginas, with his eyes squinted near-shut so as not to see. Or better yet, she would have let him stay peacefully unconscious in the safety of his room, not bullied him out to an appointment he dreaded so much. Friends were easiest to long for when formed from fond imagination, and conspicuously absent.

Winced as his gut served a reflexive stab of resentment, *at* her, for failing to be here when he needed her. Such a personal revelation, like so many he was spawning recently, disgusted him no end. It were as though the upheaval had rent a bulging membrane in his mind, letting all the thoughts a decent Surgeon should suppress flood through.

Better, perhaps, that she never had to see him like this. Wherever she was he hoped she was ok—a hope that sagged, without any evidence to support its weight.

In the midst of such pliant floral delicacy the Captain was the charmer she had always been. She charged right up in John's face, poking so aggressively with a gnarled arthritic finger that he scooted back, terrified she was about to touch him. Silly, that. Not even the Captain would transgress so far, not even in a temper.

'You! *Now* you get around to showing your face!'

'If you might bear me interjecting a moment, ma'am. John's been recently injured. There was a … an accident. He'd better sit down.'

Oh, Lars was clever. The shaved head supported it and all.

The Captain stalked off to one side as he gently assisted John's genuinely battered frame to a chair. Overly solicitous, playing the sympathy angle until the bow squeaked.

She wasn't born yesterday but the Captain let it slide, a wry smile on her wasted lips because she *liked* Lars. As much as the old bat tolerated anyone. Liked him for being harmless. A bit comically bumbling, and whatever his agendas he had the grace to keep them to himself.

Besides, recrimination was getting in the way of getting to the point. She didn't care a whit if John tripped and cracked his fool neck, only that he hadn't been where she had told him to be. She slapped her dry hands together.

'Well, now we've all found time to crawl out of our respective hidey-holes I've some wonderful news to share. *You*, Surgeon, are up for a once in a lifetime opportunity. And thanks to your lollygagging you now have even less time to prepare. Tomorrow, in fact.'

'Tomorrow what?'

She stroked a flower in a way that made him shudder. 'I'm sending you Outside.'

The giggling started small and weak. It could have been passed off as a cough, but poor overwrought John figured hey, let it all hang out. Here in this bright room with the sunlight spilling down all around like golden hope, the prospect of returning Outside just seemed too awful.

She waited him out, hardly inclined to raise her tone. 'Good. I like to see my orders received so happily. Whistle while you work and all that, just so long as you work. Now ...'

She directed their attention to one of the charts. It didn't take much directing. This was the largest and most famous of those venerable documents, taking pride of place over an entire wall amidst the leafy green plants. Said to have been hand-sketched by Son himself.

It showed the migratory routes of the cities on a topographic map, many precise layers of lines with their frequency indicating height. In gazing obediently at it John's thoughts slipped toward forests of trembling hair and he swallowed, refocusing on the Captain's weathered features.

He didn't really need to look—the path followed by *A New Life* was something any kid who had passed grade school had memorised. Here the line was a vivid green to the dun and grey of the rest. Presumably each city's copy of the map would show its own line the brightest.

And here an exquisite little origami city clung to the plastex covering. *A New Life*, perfect in every folded angle. Right where she should be. It was part of the Captain's duties to advance it along that green line every day to match their progress. The folding of a paper city was a closely guarded secret, although origami a respectable enough art, practiced elsewhere. Muttering was beginning to make the rounds about her lack of a successor, time was running out to undertake the laborious transfer of knowledge.

When the little city finally became too battered from handling, its edge feather-soft, it would be interred with due ceremony within *A New Life*'s walls. Floating in a glass jar of its very own until it eventually became sodden pulp down the bottom, in darkness. Resting in peace indeed. Best the Captain get on with things, before she and the secrets she hoarded so jealously joined it there.

Now she opened up a dark lacquered box and despite straining to remain blasé both Surgeons gasped. *A New Life* wasn't the only city represented—merely the only one up on the map as relevant. As delicate as the flowers surrounding them each city was reproduced as a tiny work of paper art, nestled in their own spiralling compartments in the box like a collection of exquisite ornaments.

Staggeringly famous jewels. Recite their names: *Stowaway Glory, Bounded View, A Following Love*, and more. Whimsical titles inspired by taking a first step. The lightness of deciding that finally, finally things were going to be ok. Now one could appreciate how incredibly varied they were. Some were of flowing lines that lent an appearance of speed, some bulbous with prosperity, and some almost as square and solid as *A New Life* herself as she jutted her chin and rejected conceits of beauty.

All those cities wrapped up in a box. All fallen silent. Perhaps what had befallen them had been by their very delicacy and perfection, it looked as though mere breath could reduce some to trembling flakes of ash. Gone, gone. All gone.

The Captain was muttering darkly to herself the way biddies are want to do, especially when they no longer give two short fucks for the opinion of others. She knocked back a quick swig from her silver flask and briskly pulled on some gloves of her own. Not latex, as sported by her guests, but spotless white cotton. To John's envious eye they looked wonderfully light and cool, not made to drown your digits in a sweat bath. His fingertips plucked at one another jealously.

With a pair of tweezers that had once been plated, the gold having long since flaked away, the frowning Captain oh-so carefully extracted a single city from the lacquered box. It was marvellous to see how her hands were steadied by whatever she had poured down her gullet. Even ten seconds ago you would have declared it impossible for her palsied flesh to undertake such delicate work, yet now …

Giving a respectful wai, with a deft touch she added the newcomer to the chart. The position was close to *A New Life* and her faithful green line, and comparison cruelly revealed how battered and faded their icon had become. Exposed to the greedy light while the others nestled safe in darkness. John felt a stab of hatred toward this flash new city, for making theirs look so dull. Irrational, but loyalty is like that.

The proximity left no doubt, but the Captain confirmed it as though they were thick—which, no doubt, she thought they were.

'This,' she tapped the new city's route, the grey line thicker than the rest to signal importance. 'This is the Flagship.'

John traced the line quickly, making himself dizzy. Yes, unique of all the migratory routes the Flagship intercepted the others, who otherwise proceeded in isolation. *A New Life* looked awfully near her turn, surely mere days. The Captain wasn't finished, railroading straight over his chain of thought.

'This is where the Flagship *should* be, you understand? However ...'

Removing a plain old felt-tipped pen from her pocket she began sketching a new dotted line in red. For all the carte blanche to do as she damn well pleased, and the impregnable plastex that could no doubt be wiped clean, her observers gaped in shocked horror. Lars even lurched forward before he could stop himself, one hand extended. She grimaced at the two aghast faces. *Well look at these idiots.*

'This is where the Flagship actually is. She's somehow been diverted from her route.'

And they thought the world had been ending before.

'How is that even possible?' Lars' voice squeaked alarmingly. He cleared his throat. 'Cities can't just waltz about the place, they're too damned heavy, for one!' He squinted at the map. 'Why aren't they at the centre of the earth right now?'

'It is possible ... barely. Given the perfect storm of expertise, timing and the most profound luck. Just not wise. And it assumes the city herself isn't deaf to her occupants, and can be convinced. Obviously my counterpart on the Flagship is my superior in all these things.'

Said without a hint of chagrin—well, why not? Her own achievements were undiminished. Humanity being so numerous, no matter your field there will always be someone more advanced somewhere. To sting at the fact would be absurd. Especially considering what mystery the Flagship's Captain had steered them into. Leaving the route ... hell!

John asked the next obvious question, just to rack them all out of the way. 'Why? Why'd they do it?'

'Out here.' She tapped the apogee of her dotted line, her red-inked defacement. 'Out here lies one of the farming communities, sheltered and safe on their little plateau. This appears to have been their target.'

'Does it have a name?' Seemed unnatural for any home not to have a name.

She smiled. 'Judgment.'

John swallowed, his pipes desiccated. Of course. How far would he have to travel to escape himself?

'And did we lose contact before or after they diverted course for this ... this Judgment?'

'After.' She locked eyes with him. '*Shortly* after.'

'Magnificent.'

'We're not rostered for any produce trade on this pass, but the Flagship's Captain felt Judgment to be of critical importance. They risked everything by going there, and I've a hankering to find out why.'

'Oh my God. We're doomed.' Finally catching up, Lars hung his head in his hands.

'We?' The Captain's complex humour surfaced. 'Only John needs to go. I hadn't thought of sending you.'

'I wouldn't have dreamed of making you ask, ma'am. Surely two heads will be better than one, what if something happens? Seeing as I've invested all these years in keeping John on the rails, I might as well stick with it.'

Her rheumy gaze returned to John. 'You hardly deserve such friends.'

'And I wish this was the first time it's been brought to my attention.' His own busy, curious eyes were still picking at the map and they widened. 'Am I reading this right?'

'You *are* the sharp blade, aren't you.'

'What?' Lars looked from one to the other like a pet anticipating more bad news. If he'd the ears for it, they would have been down. 'What now?'

'Merely our top Surgeon once again demonstrating his acumen. And I'm sure I don't need to say I want your mouths shut tight on this.'

'You're killing me. *What*?'

'With her change in route, the Flagship will no longer intercept us. Whatever they were after seems to have been more important than *A New Life*. In short, we're cut off.'

Now he looked wildly at the map, although there are those who can plot math in their heads and the hapless rest who have to take your word for it. Moving to stand behind him she put a steadying gloved hand on his shoulder. It was an astonishingly intimate gesture, but Lars was a man in great distress.

For too long the city had both feared and longed for an answer as to why the others had gone silent. The anticipated contact with the Flagship had been the only chance of finding out. Denied that thin hope, the whole population may well go mad.

'What does it matter?' he mumbled. 'What does it matter why they did it?'

'Keep it in your pants, we don't know anything yet. I want both you idiots safe back from the farmland double-quick with all the info you can fit in your thick skulls. And keep in mind the only one here who'll know what you're really up to is me, and for obvious reasons I'll hardly be hauling ass out to save you if things go tits up. So be quiet and ordinary. Stick to the plan.'

'The plan. Right. Your pardon, Captain, but I've seen better plans in my hanky.'

'Good, you're set then.' She patted his shoulder. 'Pick me up some tea while you're out.

'I hate you, you know,' was the first thing to come bursting out of Lars as the elevator descended. 'I hate you and everything you stand for. I hate your parents. I hate your *goldfish*.'

'I don't have any fish.'

'But if you did, I'd hate them. *To death*.'

'If it makes things any better, I hate me too,' he replied absently, staring between his toes at the ground rushing up. Some equipment in the city seemed designed purely to terrify people, and the rest … the rest was indifferent.

'How could that possibly make me feel better? John, I wanted to be part of something big, you know, something important, do the noble thing. I came out of that meeting looking like an asshole.'

'Well, if the plug fits …'

'Hate. You.'

'You get your bristles up over the strangest things. If history remembers us at all it'll be as shreds picked from between some horned nasty's teeth. If we're super-lucky they might sift *just* enough from the giant mounds of shit to stick us both in the one teeny-tiny jar, all digested together …'

The elevator delivered them with a gentle thud, never mind

the shattering crash of John's imagining. He straightened himself. 'Right. You ready to get famous?'

If looks could wither.

'Stick your famous up your bum. I'm off to have a sniff around whatever gear they're throwing together for us.' Perhaps double-checking others' work was something they taught in field surgery. Wherever he'd picked it up, it was annoying. 'You go collect your little friend and explain why it's been nice knowing her.'

John desperately wished he could. A second ticked over, then he realised Lars had actually meant Mary.

'Yeah, well, I'll do that!' he called after the broad departing back.

The chapel wasn't anywhere materialist Surgeons visited very often. Not to judge, though: in their miserable isolation humanity should hug tight any comfort it got. And the room itself wasn't much to write home about: a smallish dark space that could have been for any use, or perhaps none, merely a pocket formed by the evolution of rooms around it.

Nonetheless it was a peaceful place. Somewhere the ego tucked its nose between its paws and went to sleep. If you found somebody already visiting, you'd retreat respectfully and come back some other time. The only place in the city where you felt there was truly enough quiet for all who needed it.

Not a lot of maintenance. The hospital machines didn't need much under their scum of dust, or if they did it was too late to do anything about it. The machines had already been dead and old and falling to bits when preservation had been done to install them in the newly completed city. *A New Life*'s first coup, that, although you had to wonder what the other cities had secured in turn.

For some reason John always forgot about the hats. Bright foil party hats that were so incongruous with solemnity that he wiped them from his recall, tidied things up to make it seem more respectful. Get right up close and you could see they were peppered with a lattice of fine holes; a lot of preservative spray had punched right through the frail cardboard before it could be saved.

Children coming on field trips often made big colourful banners wishing Son a happy birthday. They wore adorable little hats of their own and ran at each other, head down, completely overstimulated. Pathos was the lifeblood of the city.

Mary stood in the midst of the silent machines. Her hands clenching and unclenching by her sides, although her head twitched toward the door when John came in. He stopped, blinking in the gritty dimness and the lights that cut through it. Each machine was stranded in its own puddle of spotlight, like in a museum.

The cheery hats perched on any old place because machines had no heads—in fact Mary was the only machine shaped like a *person* John had ever heard of. It limited her function. Now Son no longer needed raising, you couldn't really say what she was good for.

Her voice was tight with distress. With tears she had no way to shed.

'Allow me to introduce my companions. Son's family.'

Her hand on some sort of humidor, wires exploding in all directions to snake about in the dust. Like hair. Like hair.

'You, I remember, you carried him when his mother wouldn't, after she gave him up. And did a fair better job of it than that greedy bitch ever could, I'll bet.'

On to a motorised wheelchair, tyres long rotted away.

'You were there for him to hang onto, taking his first wobbly steps. He squealed to be getting it right and you were so proud. We were all so proud.'

Not much pride left. Only the echoes of an eighteenth birthday, trapped in time, when everything had started to go wrong. And Mary alone, left of them all, broken and clanking and still watching over the sons of Son. Whatever they sought.

'Surgeon. Come for what's yours, huh?'

He'd no idea what he had done to rile her, never suspecting grief could be private, shameful.

'Come along, then *hon*. Show me the house of this girl of yours. Chop-chop.'

Totally lost now he stared, opening his hands to illustrate helplessness. She huffed impatiently.

'And it was such a big deal not so long ago. *Two sisters*, you told me. *An accident.*'

John closed his eyes. 'It wasn't an accident. I should have saved her, and everything would have been different. Makes it my fault.'

'Yes, and sometimes people just die because the world is a horrible place. Don't you *want* to be happy?'

'Sure. Who doesn't?'

'Don't you deserve it as much as anybody? More? When you pass folk laughing on the street don't you feel that twist of resentment, of hatred, thinking *why not me*?'

Gnawing his lip he glanced around the room. The stillness, the quiet. She seemed the last person in all the universe to be able to bestow happiness. Any gift from Mary would be more like something rammed down your throat.

He squared narrow shoulders and smiled: bitter, bitter. A bad taste in his mouth.

'Sure. Why not.'

The living sister would have been released by now. That meant she'd be home at her miserable flat until the ghost drove her out. It would be in there right now, poisoning the very air. And if she'd fled into the city then they had missed her, gone forever.

John kind of hoped that was the case.

Standing across the street he thought uneasily that the building looked exactly the same, even down to the graffiti. Found himself swamped by the most unsettling sensation that this was the first time he'd stood here—time was stuck in a loop, and everything he'd endured since had been a dream. He would enter, and the traumatic scene with the ghost would play over and over. He was trapped, just as that revenant was.

Mary shattered the fancy by striding boldly for the front door, as though she'd a perfect right to be there. Everything's kosher, just go about your day. With that attitude she could likely get away with murder. Abandoning dignity, he scurried after.

'What are we doing?'

'Knitting cosy scarves for winter, what does it look like? Oh, you are thick. Go on. Knock on the damned door.'

'Knock ..?'

'Do you need your ears cleaned out? *Knock*.'

The opportunity was already gone. 'Where is she?' A woman warbled from behind them. 'What have you done with my girl?'

People were stopping in the street and turning to look as the friend's mother staggered toward them, and no wonder. Strung out like a strip of jerky with a bitter face on top, niceties exhausted from a lifetime of fighting gravity in a socioeconomic black hole. For those like the mother, the gaudy affluent life glimpsed in flashes but never stayed. Her world contracted by misfortune until she couldn't conceive of a single act of charity that didn't benefit her in some fashion. Each time the other cities went dark, she'd led petitions against sending parcel aid.

Kindness to others was snatching food from her mouth. Resources had been burned by pouring them into better chances for her daughter, now vanished, no reward to be reaped. No wonder she was furious. Here came the blame engine all wound up and just waiting for somewhere to go, because it HAD to be somebody's fault, it HAD to.

Despite knowing he mustn't show fear John cringed instinctively, her melting pot of ignorance and bile might splash on him. She was a woman suffering, anyone could see that, but it only made her more dangerous. Had she been stalking *all* her daughter's friends? Or did blame shoot straight to the top? Rich, fancy Surgeon. Bring him down.

Mary wasn't even nervous at what stumped toward them. She'd seen this shit before and then some, all the indignity humanity had to offer.

'Now then,' she said soothingly, stepping close, one tiny hand rubbing the mother's bare arm in a strangely natural gesture of comfort. Woman-to-woman. We're all reasonable here, let's just talk amongst us girls. 'What's happened, hon? Your daughter late home?'

Intoxicated at finally receiving the sympathy she so richly deserved, the mother nodded tearfully. Fangs pulled for the moment, but there was something more, something wrong with her face. Relaxing, softening. It was going slack. He had seen something like this before, rambling drunk off her tits at the friend's house, carelessly flashing flesh while he was careful not to look and the friend covered her flaming face. What did mumsy care? She was old as the hills and hubby had up and left, but she was as much a woman as anyone, wasn't she? Still as much a person? Yet nobody would look, she might as well be invisible. Humiliate herself to her heart's content, it didn't make a lick of difference.

'Yesss.' Even her voice was slurred. 'Missinggg.' She brandished a scrap of clean new ribbon and immediately burst into tears.

'Shh.' Mary still rubbed the same spot soothingly, her curls bowed close enough to brush the mother's neck. No intimation of the horror of that smashed face looming close, hidden only by hair. 'Poor duck. You're all done in, aren't you? Worn out by worry, you are, and that's too much to ask of a body. You ought to pop home and have a nice lie down. Things will look better after that.'

Incredibly, the force of nature nodded and wiped her nose. Obediently she turned and trundled back off down the street, trailing the wreckage of her life. John held his breath until she was gone, really gone.

'How did you do that? It was like you hypnotised her!'

Mary smugly showed him her fingers, the hand she'd used to rub her arm. They were an angry red, like a burn, some sort of powder.

'Chemically, that's how. A handy concoction. Poor thing needed some rest.'

'I think she needs a lot more than that.'

'You don't have the faintest idea what it's like. Mother is such a heavy word, and those who labour beneath it are plain people, nothing special about them. Sometimes they fuck up. And it goes on, making everything worse, until you lose control entirely. I was a mother, once. A human mother. Before the hospital and Son I had my own sons. It's why they chose me.'

'I didn't know.' Stupid and obvious, but isn't that how everyone stumbles into offence? 'Where are they?'

'Oh, this was a long time back. My boys would be long

dead now, but even so I don't know. Their father took them away, and I never saw them again. Just sat them on the back of his motorcycle and roared off down the highway. The way I'd always dreamed he would take me.'

'I am so sorry.'

'I wanted him to notice me, but I made one bad call too many and that was that. I was so used to all the nice things in life coming to me, I couldn't have even imagined them going. Not until the desert swallowed them up and it was far too late. It's something to keep close to your heart; anyone can leave, at any time they choose and if you're thick-headed or proud you might never see it coming. *Especially* those you love most, the ones you'd imagine are bound most tightly to you.'

'Is that so?'

'Your friend left.'

'I sold her. For this.' Standing outside this house, on this street.

'Knock, then. We're wasting time.'

He knocked officially with his elbow, like a Surgeon on legitimate business. Perhaps following up a patient or investigating an outbreak. Well there *was* an outbreak in this miserable building, just not of a kind any Surgeon could do a thing about.

The sister, the *living* sister, opened the door, already looking worn down to bone and knotted rope. His breath caught. Those eyes. The sisters had the same eyes.

A bag on the floor by her feet. They were just in time.

Unexpectedly, in the same moment Mary elbowed by him. Holding up a scant handful of the red powder she blew it directly into the sister's baffled, exhausted face. Her reaction was to be expected: startled gasp followed by coughing, sputtering and rubbing her eyes as she tried too late to repel the assault. Such beautiful eyes which then became wide, wide as the moon glimpsed riding high over the sunlight suburbs. And as blank. Her arms fell limply to her sides.

Mary chuckled and rubbed her hands, dusting off the last of the powder. Pleased as punch.

'I've not been able to get away with that for *ages*. The downstairs people—well, you know. It doesn't get through the hair too well.'

John was still frozen with one elbow out in the act of knocking on the door. He looked like he was practicing the chicken dance.

'What did you do?'

'A lot more potent when inhaled, isn't it?' Her tone darkened. 'Awfully useful for winning over the unwashed masses, which is what the prisoner invented it for. Slipped it in incense or tea, like some primitive alchemist in a crack den. Following our little altercation I perfected airborne delivery. Helped myself to what was left, mixed it with the bloody mess that'd spilled out his skull, and laid it out by the highway to dry.'

'For the record, that's disgusting. What does it do? What have you done to her?'

'Can't you see?' She waved hand in front of the blank, unseeing eyes. 'It makes them more … pliable. Agreeable. She'll be *very* agreeable while it lasts. Oh, don't look so prissy, hon, you should *thank* me if it's not too much trouble. There isn't much of this stuff left. Made from a flower that only ever grew for a brief time in one greenhouse, the building got all smashed up in the end. I saw the sand come in and take everything.'

'You … you drugged her. You can't *do* that!'

'Oh, but it was dandy to go ahead when some crazy broad was screaming at you in the street. How else did you suppose this was going to happen? Win her over with your charm and mournful need, hey? All the riches a Surgeon has to offer? Give me a break. You wanted some magic, effort-free solution, nothing you'd have to *work* for, and presto! I provide.'

She clapped her hands loudly as though shooing livestock.

'Come on, honey. Back inside with you. Mister Surgeon here fancies a bit of a chat, you being so pretty and all.'

Although the light didn't change the sister's pupils narrowed to pinpricks in a manner most off putting to see. Like she was paralysed, with only those tiny normally involuntary muscles left to her.

'Noo,' she slurred, mired in struggling horror. 'Have to leave.'

To his alarm tears began dropping from those huge staring eyes. Everyone around him was always crying. This episode had only started for him and Mary, but the sister had opened the door fleeing a long session of her own suffering and terror, trapped with the ghost inside the flat. Only to be yanked cruelly back at the last second.

'... don't make me go back in ...'

'Strong-willed,' Mary said approvingly. She kicked the hastily packed bag to one side, and setting both small hands on the woman's arms began gently pushing her back inside. 'That's the way, hon. Nice and easy. Oh, it stinks in here!'

John followed helplessly. Drawn by the promise of joy, as well as the pale despair on her face as it was swallowed up by darkness.

CHAPTER SEVEN

AND WE CAN ALL LOOK LIKE ASSHATS

TOGETHER

LARS SHOOK his great head solemnly, draperies waving. 'John, I'm sorry but there isn't a damn thing to do about it.'

John glanced up, startled. They had been standing in tense silence for half an hour. By secret macho pact, neither was about to admit to jigging right on the verge of sprinkling in his shorts.

'Huh? What are you on about?'

'You. You look a right asshat in that getup, John. You see, I've been mulling it over the whole time we've been standing here. For the good of everyone I reckon it's time I spoke up.'

'Hey.' You could cut their unease into jellied chunks with a dull spoon. The relief of bickering, *normality* almost sent his wobbly knees through the floor. 'No more than you do.'

'Yes, but keep in mind your dear *mother* also looked like an asshat, so you're obviously starting from way further back that me.'

'That she did, rest her heart. Of course, *most* folk are too polite to mention …'

Two Surgeons facing off like riled cats. The vestibule wasn't roomy enough for two egos. They fidgeted beneath dark veils worn to shield their valuable eyes, fiddling to get the hang right before the door to Outside slid open and all hell broke out. Assuming it ever would.

The heavy fabric puddled about the shoulders. Comforting to John, at least, his neck muscles missed the grand heft of dreadlocks. His pale denuded head rattled about uncontrollably, like a ping pong ball, probably scrambling what brains he had left and he *needed* those. Feared he would very much need them.

The veils were silver on the reverse, rather frustratingly like trying to peer through thick steam. They were supposed to adjust dynamically, but also hadn't seen the outside of a storage tub in an age. With the how-to faded, nobody could say whether they were meant to be so annoying or if the decrepit tech was finally packing it in.

Standing face on gave them both front row seats to how it would be for the farmers, peering in through the veil. The wearer's features became opaque and untrustworthy, swimming as though in fast running water. Excellent. Just the impression John was hoping for to charm secrets out of the dour residents of Judgment.

To heavily ice their rural fun-time cake their scant exposed skin was slathered with sunscreen, leaving greasy smears across everything. Being the same brand used in the sunlight suburbs, he already knew the goop gave him hives. They both looked like asshats.

The vestibule they stood waiting in was *A New Life*'s official airlock to Outside. Never mind the other dusty entrances and exits that perforated her concrete hide, *this* one was sanctioned. A deliberately small space to slow entry, allow her to turn her nose up at certain callers. And fancy in a "ooh, look at me" way, although everything downshifted to gloomily mysterious when viewed through veils. Freshly inlaid gold was meant to wow Flagship dignitaries come a'knocking, because nobody suspected yet that the other city wasn't coming.

Once news got out, there would be horror … unless the Captain managed to scratch together a better headline before it broke. So rather than gowned officials and ceremonial flutes of champagne, the grand vestibule got John and Lars. Stamping their feet in clumsy boots to vent nerves while they waited. And waited. Hell would be standing about like this. Staring aimlessly at the other's shifting face, and waiting for that door to open.

The hold up being that blocks and blocks away, right down the other end at the city's ingloriously named "backside" exit, the decoy was being busily prepped for release. Surgeons being sticklers for tradition both John and Lars had taken part in strapping the honoured cadaver into the complex architecture of the wheeled decoy rig. Serious faces the whole way, studious not to let slip a grimace at the gagging smell, the squish of it.

The effort was almost the death of Lars when he tightened

a strap too briskly and the decaying bowel let loose with a long flabbery squeal. Due respect was decency, irrespective of where this poor sod had transgressed in life or how ripely he oozed through the crossbracing now. After all, it was their valuable backsides the corpse was being served up to save. Didn't happen too often.

Mortuary specialists had been fished from mothballs to hook up the technical wherewithal, threading the final nanowires and pumps just prior to launch. And at the absolute last second, jumper leads would supply a quick spark from *A New Life* herself. Such arcane arts couldn't be practiced without her consent. The moment the vestibule door slammed open the decoy would go shooting out the backside like bolt from bow, dodging wildly with the desperation of the resurrected damned. And the Blessed would give chase.

Drones didn't work; they would only go after the terrified living, or in this case something that so briefly thought it still was. The rare opportunity was sanctioned by the deceased's family, of course. The dead couldn't sign releases. All the dead could do was run, run, run. At least the ordeal didn't last long; hopefully not long enough for the subject to work out what was happening. The brute electrical revival invariable melted the rotting brain and all vestiges of awareness to slurry.

But if anything of the rigged cadaver remained by the time automatic retrieval kicked in and the contraption came whirring home, thumping back up the ramp, well. There was one convicted felon who had earned back the right to a decent burial. Jar and all. A place in the wall to tearfully lay silk wreathes at, silencing the scorn of the neighbours. Rumour had it the waiting list bloated huge, however long bodies could be made to last in quasi-legal storage by desperate kin. Who even knew how the authorities singled out their winner? Wishing they'd picked a fresh one this time wasn't going to make anyone's cuffs any cleaner.

In the thoughtful hush of the vestibule John leaped a damn mile as the small green glass lantern overhead blinked off with an audible "pop!" Its twin, the ruby-red warning light had never worked at all, which was a blessing. Would hardly have improved the ambience, and who needed a coloured light to remind them how close to peril they stood?

Lars grinned across at him. Wide hysterical eyes, a smile in veiled flux that rippled and warped nauseatingly.

Oh sod. This was it.

Locks thumped. The door finally groaned back.

Outside's bright light was so pervasive it came splashing into the vestibule, and they were awash. For an instant all the worry, heartache and loneliness just burned away. The room filled with light and the two Surgeons were specimens floating in a golden bottle, already more Outside than in.

John was pretty sure he wasn't going to be able to do this.

He'd been sending all sorts of frantic signals to his limbs, which were bobbing about in slow motion, and they had responded with sweet fuck all. Seems it'd been one thing to go dashing after the friend in a foolhardy rush, all burning with indignation. Another kettle of fish entirely to replicate that feat for the Captain, with the fire gone out under his emotions. Suddenly bravery looked like something only an idiot would try.

He made up his mind to turn smartly about and scuttle back inside. He wanted to live. The Flagship and everyone in it could march themselves straight to hell.

Luckily Lars wasn't about to tolerate such lily-liveredness. When our idols falter, it's up to us to shore them up with whatever comes to hand. Bustling forward the heavyset Surgeon "accidentally" butted John right out the searing portal.

'Oopsie! So sorry, old bean, but you're holding up the line.'

Stumbling helplessly. 'You revolting bastard. You're *enjoying* this, aren't you!'

Lars smirked close on his heels, incidentally blocking a screaming retreat. 'Took a selfie with the corpse and all.'

'I do not know you. If we run into anybody I'm making that abundantly clear.'

Chuckling, Lars made his own gesture in the air—what in a normal man would be a slap on the shoulder. 'Best get a wriggle on. If we don't haul ass up that cliff before the decoy runs out …'

Up the cliff, huh? A thin promise of safety neither had set eyes on. Instead they blundered optimistically forth on the Captain's assertion, the Captain's maps, and some turn of the century skipping rhyme she'd dredged up that suggested the Blessed couldn't climb.

'Maybe we ought to think this through a little better …' John ventured.

And then they were Outside the city. Blinking and shivering in air that had never shuffled numbly through vents and massed lungs. Untamed hair that refused to behave. *Outside.* Outside, all around.

Even before his watering vision had sorted John's sense of himself seemed to bloom in all directions at once, as though by slipping free of physical boundaries you patted yourself down and found a whole other person. Expanded beyond the shell into a new shape you couldn't have guessed at. Well, now you're in the shits, mate. No hope of stuffing all that back inside the old casing.

Miracles of technology, the veils finally realised they had a job to do and kicked in, dialling back the onslaught. Vision cleared and the Surgeons found themselves a couple of floors up, on a ledge. A corroded safety rail sagged away, while the mischievous wind seemed intent on chucking them straight through it. What had initially seemed awash, golden and blinding, resolved into a landscape of dull military greens under a heavily overcast sky. The palette all dun on grey.

A New Life traversed an endless field of rocky broken ground, dusted by some miserable type of scrub, home to whining insects and not much else. Nowhere could the longing eye chase down the vivid tropical jade of storybooks. Or a sky, so azure with promise it would dissolve you away. Perhaps those dense lumpen clouds kept it tucked away to warm only their own backs. At least the cliff was where it ought to be, breaking the snoring monotony. That was something.

This was the second trot for John, that small prick of disappointment releasing the piping-hot hope of earthly paradise. He didn't want to turn sideways and witness Lars' expression to be experiencing it all fresh. Besides, once again he found rationality scattered by little sips of adrenalin, telling him to *run, run*.

But there was still *some* time to gawk. Exiting via the vestibule and its long dignified ramp was a far cry off sending your fool ass down some unregistered ladder. The unglamorous dry earth was just a short jog, with their ridiculous boots clomping and veils flapping and streaming about.

This being an official walkway, baffles shielded them from the clatter and groan of the city's progress. The long-ago architect had even considerately ensured they disembarked onto smooth(ish) ground. Son's handiwork, unless the vestibule had been tacked on after launch. John doubted it: that level of expertise just didn't exist anymore. Every city remained more or less as she had been the day she started off, raining confetti and corks. Massive stone flanks lit by fireworks. Now *that* would have been something to see!

Only a few paces off the grinding, scraping foot of the ramp he stumbled to an unsteady halt amidst dried grasses, and turned for a look up at the city. Urgency and all, he couldn't help himself. He had already skipped this once-in-a-lifetime opportunity, and to get to do it *again* was so improbable. It was such a relief to be able to peer up, instead of shrivelling in the unforgiving light. Yay for veils.

There she was. Framed by a sky of steely clouds that seemed to churn without moving and the sun, a little white hole burning through them. Greyer even than the sky, the city. They were practically a riot of colour next to her. Lazy imagination kept trying to frame her in terms of a neat origami analogue on a map. But that only worked if you weren't standing, gaping up. A city that shuddered and lumbered. Almost sentient. Almost looking back at you.

John reeled, just ... bludgeoned by the massive rolling reality of her slab work. Her blunt planes and angles. The sheer massiveness robbed her of any grace, any chance of softening the brutal whole. She couldn't even be called an eyesore, which any more modest structure would be tarred. You wouldn't dare. Not while she loomed in all her uncompromising glory.

His fascination must be damning him to being left behind. *Straggler*, imagination supplied helpfully. *They pick off the stragglers first*. He slapped himself free of awe, first the right cheek then the left. He turned to run.

And promptly came up short.

Lars wasn't where he should be, far ahead across the terrain with his thick legs pumping furiously. Lars hadn't gone anywhere. He was too busy being sprawled full-length with his face and fingers clawed into the scratchy grass.

'What are you pissing about down there for?'

'The sky.' His croak was almost lost in the whistle and snap of wind.

John glanced up at the clouds to see what was what, befuddled and increasingly panicky. They almost seemed to swirl in response to Lars' voice. The bright cold spot of the sun burned.

'It's yawing ... yawing up there ... the sky, it's swinging from side to side, can't you see ... I'm sick ... I'm falling, John ... falling into it ...'

'Oh for fuck's sake.'

He began yanking ineffectually on the other man's arm to shut off his babble. This made it official. Between them, the Surgeons had managed to redefine "fuckup" for all time. Good for Lars, he'd always hunkered after fame. John hoped the Captain wasn't watching with her cold, judgmental eyes ...you know what, better if she was! Let that rheumy brain squirm through every excruciating second of the pointless gory deaths she had sent them to. Good luck ever sleeping again you old bat.

He was in agony. He knew what was on the way, better than most, and every instinct wailed to charge off and abandon Lars. Leave it to the Blessed to prise the blubbering idiot off the sod. Which he'd never do, not in a million years, but rationality wasn't about to cram a sock in shrill panic any time soon.

Lars clung on, gabbling in his fear and almost pulling him sprawling as well. Drowning on empty air.

'Run,' he begged, well past pride. 'Just run, get out of here!'

And John laughed, teary at the futile nobility of it all.

'You idiot, martyrdom was *last* season.'

Then suddenly Mary was *right there*. Completely

flubbing their agreed rules about *hiding, sneaking along,* and John's personal favourite, *not being seen.* That last had been mission-critical so far as he was concerned.

'You nitwits really want to end up on the buffet, don't you?' she snapped, bending to hoist Lars from his dirt bower. 'Upsy-daisy, big boy. Oof, you're quite the bend at the knees lift, aren't you?'

Cleaving perversely to his delusion of sacrifice he came up clutching fistfuls of dry grass. He batted at her weakly with them. 'No, ma'am, you can't be out here, it's *dangerous …*'

'Oh, you think? Now you just forget about what's overhead, hon, 'less you want to get us all killed. Shut your eyes and listen to my voice, only me. See? There you go.'

She set him back on his feet. Luckily in his distress he failed to notice getting hoisted by something more like a pneumatic hammer than a fair maiden. And the Captain would be tracking their struggle through binoculars, her clever lumpen fingers working feverishly on a third paper figurine to join the other two already on the map. Three little paper dollies in a chorus line, advancing along their plotted course.

The Surgeons' dolls had been whipped up with whatever came to hand, they were hardly critical enough to take care over. John had incredulously witnessed his own mannequin emerge from the greasy remains of a lunch wrapper and damn if it didn't look like him. The act seemed a tiny magic, binding him to the tableau of the map. *If we lose that frail old woman, we lose this mystery. Whatever it is.*

As though catching his thought she had fixed him with a glare so contemptuous he'd dropped his eyes. *Not today sonny,* blazed across her stern features. The young often dwelt on death, counting the pennies of all they had to lose. But the Captain, staring right down the barrel, felt no fear.

To comfort himself as they struggled to right Lars John

glanced down at the homing indicator strapped to his wrist, reassured to see it point unerringly back to the city. He was the only one wearing one, because as the Captain had rather acidly pointed out there weren't any of the damn things left. Priceless technology, on equal footing with vanishing knowledge. The last of its precious kind.

The device was obviously intended to work with the veil. The green arrow pointing to *home, home, safe, safe* glowed all the brighter when viewed through it. In normal light without augmentation you had to squint for the reading. John *personally* wanted to be sure of their return route so he could have the pleasure of screwing up the creepy little voodoo doll and tossing it in the bin. Let her practice her half-baked debacles on somebody else.

'Now that we're all up and on the same page like good kids, I suggest we run like the clappers. Lars, I'll keep you upright and pointed the right way. Just give me that condom-wrapped hand of yours.'

Both Surgeons were double-gloved in deference to a landscape of serrated textures. John moved to steady his friend on the other side, in case he tipped that way. Imagine, setting out at speed over uncertain terrain with your peepers closed, on faith that your companions were there for you. Lars was a bigger man in ways beyond the physical.

Together they started at a slow trot. John's roundly abused legs couldn't take much more, so all this helping was rather wonderful for saving face. He could already feel the clumsy boots chafing a nice set of blisters, and his feet must be about a hundred degrees. Suddenly the air grew ... thicker? Darker? Something had taken a turn for the worst.

'Keep going!' Mary hissed. 'The decoy's given up the ghost.'

'Rather unfortunate phrasing ...'

'Don't look back! Is it really worth your life being *funny*?'

Lars giggled, a bit hysterically, because the answer was always *absolutely*. 'I'm not looking at *anything*, pinkie-swear! Stupid, here, so keen to go Outside and now I'm missing the lot!'

John was already panting. 'Just run, idiot!'

The tumbled down stones marking the edge of the cliff lurched into vision. Just a big heap of rock with some grass to tie it together. And now John experienced a panicky little flutter at how far they had strayed, so very damn far from the city. But now wasn't the time to lose his shit. Had quite enough of that on the first run out.

'Look for a path,' he puffed. 'It's got to be along here.'

'There!' Mary shouted, way ahead of him. Her misshapen eyes through bouncing curls were worlds better than his through a veil. He hardly forfeited man-points for failing to spot the path. It was the sort of overgrown trail a furtive animal might wear into the world, distinguishable only by suggestion as it switch backed up the cliff.

Mary struck out. Towed behind, Lars was in real danger of getting his arm yanked from the socket. Only a steely resolve to survive could have kept his eyes welded shut. John was last to set foot on the trailhead, pebbles rolling traitorously beneath his boot. The grey-green landscape wanted to spill him backward, draw a sheet of vegetation over his remains, but he pushed on and gained the trail. And then, because perversity was his way, he looked back.

Time seemed to stop, along with the hissing wind and the distant groan of the city. Hushed by his audacity. No wonder Mary had said not to look.

The first of the Blessed was right behind him. Frozen, as all things. Its extended piano-key teeth only a hand off the small of his back. If it had been the horn it would have had him already but apparently this was more personal. Long greasy hair flew back from the stretched neck. Clods of grass thrown up from plunging feet were suspended in the air behind the massive beast, as though it were a comet trailing debris.

From behind his veil, he peered into seething maddened eyes that glowed almost as brightly as the homing device in a world of muted grey. So desperate to get hold of him between aching jaws. Just a few centimetres more …

Mary grabbed a handful of his jacket and yanked him upward so hard the seams ripped below both arms. He felt rather than heard the heavy ivory teeth clack in the space he'd just occupied. Then with a roar all of the Blessed were wheeling to the left and right along the base of the cliff. The manoeuvre was executed in tight military formation, even a second more would have sent their momentum smashed and squealing amidst the rocks.

She shook him a little before setting him free.

'Teasing the animals? No decoy's going to work for you now, sunshine, they'll always prefer the smell of *you*. And they'll always come running.'

Lars was on his knees shuddering in the overgrown grass, hands over his face as though closing his eyes could never be enough.

'I thought we were dead. I thought that was it, we were dead. What did you do, John?'

'The cliff stopped them. Guess they don't fancy high places after all.'

John settled his scant backside on a rock with a wince, one of the many times he wished for more padding.

'Uh, what are you doing?'

'I, dear Mary, am having a rest.'

'What, right now? With *them* down there staring right up your nose?'

'And I intend to stare right back. Asshole things chase me

this way and that, and ooh, you're not supposed to *look* at them! Says who? Besides, Lars needs some time to get his shit back in his pants before we can go anywhere.'

'My feet are killing me,' Lars chimed in sotto voice. 'And my socks are all *scratchy*. Are these bits coming off the grass?'

'Fine!' With a flounce she sat with her back to the Blessed, who were waiting in a silent line below, staring up. 'Go ahead, what do I care? It's not like they want to peel you and wear you as a hat or anything.'

'Take your time, mate,' John counselled the other Surgeon without taking his eyes off the Blessed. 'Enjoy the ... the fresh air or something.'

Their eyes in return were like tumbling sparks, that hectic brightness that comes when the fire must go out. The wind washed their sour, spoiled smell up over where the three sat and he gagged, and thought crazily, *I must clean the fridge when I get back*. But that was what it was like. A stench like the milk had gone south and taken everything with it.

Lars was fumbling at his belt. 'I've got ... around here somewhere ...' Finding what looked like a ratty old teabag he popped it in his mouth with a sigh of relief.

'That looked repulsive.'

'Sedative. Should sand the edges off. Tastes like old socks, though.'

'Ah, so your breath will improve.'

To test the theory he cautiously cracked one eye, then the other, shielding them with his hand from the immensity of clouds overhead.

'Oh. They look really pissed off down there, don't they?'

'No shit. How do you feel?'

An inspection of Lars' stuttering, blurring face revealed pupils that could swallow the world.

'Marshmallowy. Over a hot fire and everything.'

'I'll bet. Can you walk?'

'There's no tap dancing in my immediate future, I think both heels are spouting blood. But yeah. Let's do this.'

Mary huffed to her feet, although John had been around her long enough to note the falseness of the artifice. To squeeze beneath the human radar, she was espousing a very old-school archetype of how vapid ladies move, what they say. It made folk dismiss her, pack her away in a neat feminine stereotype. Some admirable slight of hand on her part. Perhaps sensing penetration of her disguise and not liking it she struck out, leading the way up the trail.

Because he was an asshole Lars cheerily waved goodbye to the Blessed. They bared wet brown gums in return, gulping at the air like fish flipped out of water, the display so grotesque both Surgeons hurried after Mary to be shot of it.

They staggered upward in silence for a while. Keep your head down. That was the key. Only rustling plants or the ominous clack of shifting stone. It was only after they had passed several of them that John noticed little cairns of the jumbled rock had been propped here and there along the trail. Mary was clearly charmed right out of her socks.

'Would you look at that! And I used to say farmers lacked imagination.'

Lars puffed his way past one of the knee-high piles. 'Hardly takes Picasso to stick rocks in a heap.'

'You don't see it at all, do you? No, of course not. You've both all you can manage planting one foot ahead of the other. Come here, hon. Stand ... there. Now look.'

John hurried to his shoulder so as not to miss out. As the breeze kicked up it rattled and flapped their veils.

'Ok, we're looking.'

'You dimwits, it's a city!'

And all at once it was. So perfect and clever. Problem

was, you didn't get used to thinking how a city looked from the outside. To two Surgeons the concept itself was quite foreign.

'Probably lost on you two, but we've been passing them in the reverse order that they set out on their migrations. At the top will be the Flagship, I'll bet my right boob on it. Walking up and down the trail means progressing through a sort of little story.'

'Now you've lost me again. John? Yep, both lost.'

'Look.' She walked them past it. 'Look back. Now what do you see?'

'Just looks like a hunk of rock from this angle.'

'Close, hon. Ruins. If you're descending the trail to leave Judgment what you see are ruined cities all the way down. Not so subtle discouragement for the residents, I'd say.'

'But why?' Lars piped up bewildered. 'What do the farmers have against cities? We trade some pretty darn valuable medicine for their produce, and all sorts of tech they wouldn't see a whisker of otherwise. I mean, I'd have thought they would be gagging to get in.'

'Seriously?'

She shook her head, the spray of bright curls bouncing and John looked down quickly at his boots. He couldn't see hair flying around without becoming queasy, and had a sinking feeling he might be stuck with the trigger for the rest of his life. Well, at least he *had* his life.

'People haven't remembered *anything*, have they? Lars, hon, the farmers are the ones who *rejected* Son's cities. Called them another cheap stick-on solution. An answer come too easy.'

'I'm not following,' he admitted, far easier saying it than John. Consequently, Lars tended to learn more.

'Let me dumb it down,' she sighed, although not entirely

rudely. 'So, Son gathered the scattered folk of the world from their cracks and crevices where they'd have cowered until dust replaced the sky. Are you with me so far? This should all be familiar. But then the Blessed came. Folk began to die.

'So Son scraped together every last secret the machines had whispered to him, and he built the cities to save everyone, keep them safe. Always moving so the Blessed couldn't find a way in. Only to discover there were ingrates who refused to fall in line this time around. Faces in the crowd who couldn't reconcile to this sudden new vision of the future, not after all they'd been through already.

'So when all the shouting was done, the gathered people split into two groups. Even though it meant families ruptured, lovers cracked right down the middle. Small sacrifice to pay for ideals. Son trundled off with his followers, the larger group, and abandoned the face of the earth to the Blessed, to roam about as they pleased.

'Those who became the farmers retreated to the only safe spots left, the high places. Shielded by humped shoulders of stone and far from the dark secretive forests where the Blessed spun their webs. As unsuitable as the high ground might be, it was all they had and they had to live, so they set their farms there.'

Lars' eyes were wide and wondering. He no longer even bothered to shut out the sky.

'There,' she said kindly. 'When you're scared, all you really need is something bigger to worry about.'

John put his hand up for shush, which had been sorely lacking.

'Did you hear that?'

'What?' Simultaneously, promptly drowning it out.

'Seriously guys, shh. I'm sure ... I thought I heard a dog.'

Mary did something alarming he never would have

expected from such a wee sprite, even knowing what she was. She sort of *hunched*, and at the same time seemed to *expand*. She was making herself look bigger. It certainly succeeded in looking menacing.

'I don't like dogs,' she muttered. She, who'd run into the teeth of the Blessed to snatch their prize. 'I've never liked dogs.'

They could all hear what he'd picked up on now. An eager panting and whining from the top of the cliff, domestic and friendly, a pooch eager to meet new buddies. Whereas *Mary* looked quite the opposite.

The trail only levelled off a fraction. Passing the little stone Flagship was the only real indication they'd reached the top. Glaring at the rock formation John wanted to give it a kick: *This is all your fault.* Veering off the course she'd faithfully followed for decades ... The other cities and their millions of voices falling silent ... A pair of respectable Surgeons tramping about the wilderness. *None* of this was supposed to happen in a quiet, ordered world.

He refrained, of course. No need to be an asshole. Somebody had put a great deal of care into the sculptures. An incredibly patient search, possibly across generations, for just the right rock. A mind capable of assessing on the fly where they might fit into the bigger picture. It suggested the farms bred people capable of discoveries the cities could not.

Then again, glancing back down the trail chilled one to the core. There was the drop, which sucked and pulled the way voids always did. All down the walk, where grasses and scrappy little flowers waved, the stone cities watched *A New Life* crawl by. Prophetic ruins, from this angle, encrusted with a vivid orange lichen.

Not the end for my city, he promised. Couldn't spy the Blessed from this angle but they were out there. Waiting for crumbs to fall from the tabletop that was Judgment. Not even the stones could match their patience.

A hand tapped his sleeve. 'Mister. You lot came up the trail, right?'

Inquiring eyes looking up at him. He was instantly, hideously awkward in the way of single folk around somebody's kids. 'Hasn't anyone ever taught you not to sneak up on people?'

'You were all just staring. We've been standing here ages.'

Two kids, a boy and a girl and their dog, the one who'd been making all the fuss. Three come to meet three, wasn't that neat? They'd seemingly arisen straight out of the dirt, although they were really just used to moving around the boulder field.

He didn't get kids. Never had. There was a dark art to talking to them; when to treat them like adults, and more importantly when not. Wasn't the sort of dog you'd expect to see on a farm, either. It was one of those plump shapes that looked destined to be rubbed with rosemary and popped in the oven.

Lars, the bastard, was an immediate hit. 'Yup. We've come visiting from the city. You three'd be Judgement's welcoming committee, then.'

'Well,' the girl sniffed, flipping her rough ponytail back across her shoulder without artifice. She already didn't think much of Mary. Clear marks of a poorer demographic than her pal, her manner rougher and wilder but it didn't matter. Not yet. Both still lingered in that magical pre-teen age, before puberty makes everything more complicated and ludicrous. 'Santos' pa *did* say to make ourselves useful. I'm Rachel. You'd better come on. You're just in time for dinner.'

'Keep that mutt away from me!' Mary grated, right back beside the statue of the Flagship, almost hiding behind it. The boy, presumably Santos, frowned but they were used to the craziness of adults. He picked up the leash his little dog-roast had been trailing through the grass and tugged it lightly.

'Come on girl.'

A good dog, she left off wriggling and whining to step neatly to heel, keen to be told what to do next. Santos was too well mannered to glare but his rougher friend felt no qualms. *Come into **our** place, order **our** dog around!* If Mary felt the resentment she showed no sign.

Rachel led the way. Lars prattled on to her, flipping up the edge of his veil to show how it worked. She wrinkled her nose.

'It makes your face look weird.'

'Weird-*er*, if you please.'

With her unwillingness to approach the adorably harmless dog Mary was at the rear, alone and disgraced. John walked with Santos. Along with feeling stilted around kids, he was overly sensitive to their disappointments: one more light blown out of the idealised state of childhood, on your way to becoming an adult groping in the dark. Unable to think what to say he simply walked by the kid's side, shunning her in silent support.

It was Santos who broke the endurance trial first. Or perhaps the awkwardness had been all in his head.

'You lot've come real soon after the other.'

'Other?' John's heart leaped.

'The visitor before you. The woman from the Flagship.'

'Oh.'

The switch from jubilation was too striking not to be explained, unless he wanted to be as weird and rude as Mary. He lowered his voice so the others wouldn't overhear.

'Sorry. I had this friend. She … uh, she left the city. I guess I've been hoping she made it here.'

The boy's head tilted as he chewed that over. A bit of a

deep thinker, this one.

'So you've got a friend who's gone missing.'

'Yeah.' No sense gilding the lily. 'And it's kind of my fault.'

His internal voice snorted in disbelief. *Kind of?*

'But you don't know anything, right? So no sense in assuming the worst. That's what Dad always says, and he's pretty right most of the time. Other farms out there. She might've gone to one.'

The kid lowered his tone to match John's, playing it like a game.

'*Or*. Or maybe she's gone to GATE.'

'To a gate? What gate?'

A quick glance saw Lars' antenna pointed his way suspiciously. Calm down. Rachel was watching, too, not about to tolerate anybody messing with her friend. Knowing schoolyard cruelty, slight bookish Santos had probably benefited well from her sheltering wing.

'Don't folk from the cities know *anything*? GATE's a town. Only not a farm, or a city. It's a different sort of place.'

'A different place?'

It had never occurred that there was anywhere else, the idea a bit of a shock.

'Not like anywhere else. See, when folk disappear for no reason an' you don't know where, GATE is where they go. Everyone who's gone missing. If you can find it, you find all of them there.'

John was no stranger to urban legend. One cobbled together a tolerable existence by them, breathed life into that dimming spark of wonder. He recognised the singsong cadence of a concept half-born; feared and delicious at the same time. Knowing this didn't detract from the concept's seduction; that the friend might have had somewhere to go. The very idea reduced culpability, made him *want* to believe.

Keen as mustard to dig up more, but before he could get his mouth open the kid began waving enthusiastically, the other hand still tight on the leash.

'Dad!' Santos hollered. Quite the set of pipes for a stringy kid. 'Hey, Dad! More visitors today!'

They had wandered into Judgment without John even realising. Well, he was hardly qualified to point out what came naturally in a landscape. The grey-green uplands didn't segue neatly the way suburbs and corridors did. It hadn't been easy to tell when they reached the top of the trail either, and this was a continuation of the same. The ground swooped, encrusted with raw looking lumps of rock and more moss than grass.

Farming progressed along the jumbled surface, not immediately obvious as an imposition. Long, lapping snippets of horizontal like waves of molten glass stacked down every incline, stolen out from under the nose of all that vertical. And the trees!

Gnarled, scraggly trees hunched everywhere. They looked like ranks of disapproving old men, even poking out at angles from cliff faces. Nowhere to stand without feeling their glare and they were old, so horribly old. Twisted roots erupted through moss to grasp boulders and prevent them running away. They'd trip you as a sideline, to cruel gales of silent laughter.

They seemed specifically placed to make harvesting any crop as frustrating as possible. You had to wonder why the farmers hadn't chopped every creepy protrusion off the rock face years ago, and good riddance.

As though picking ill-will out of the air one of the trees straightened up, stopping his heart until by squinting he made out this one wasn't a tree. A man, standing as blackened and gnarled as the surrounding sentinels. As the little troupe approached Santos' dad waited with understandable caution, but no hostility. The sort of wooded hulk of a fellow to make both Surgeons feel instantly humiliated in their long flowing veils.

Santos ran the last few meters with his dog tangling excitedly about his legs.

'Dad, visitors!' he repeated unnecessarily, but when you're thrilled you just have to tell someone. The farmer nodded and extended his hand affably to John, who was nominally in the lead. Ah, good. More humiliation.

He held up gloved hands apologetically, feeling a right tit. He knew that from outside perspective his face was wavering, but hoped at least some of the expression got through.

'I'm sorry. This is rather awkward, but I can't.'

Amusement won over offence. These odd clowns from the city, come marching across the hillside.

'Can't what? Can't shake hands?' Another looking-over. 'You two fellows have a disease or something? I've given gifts that weren't so well wrapped.'

'It's a … tradition. I'm John and this is Lars; we're Surgeons. We're not allowed to touch people.'

'How do you perform surgery, then? Or are you lot doing it all by robots now? Thought I spied a hulk lumbering by, and from the size of her ass I'd say you're from *A New Life*.'

Have you ever tried to tell a foreigner about something you've done routinely all your life, only to realise how tits-out crazy it sounds?

'We only touch during surgery. It's sort of … well … I guess you'd say sacred.'

Crossing his weathered arms the farmer took a step back.

'And the fancy hats?' He still sounded like he might burst out laughing, or order them off his land. Either was valid.

'Oh, for crying out loud—just put her here.'

Exasperated, Mary strode to the fore and pumped his hand with the briskness of a boardroom ball breaker. She still kept a wary eye on the dog.

'I'm Mary. Sorry about these two bright boys.'

She … she was *flirting*.

'What does your city have against bare faces these days? Something to hide?'

'Nothing so lurid, I'm afraid: the Surgeons aren't used to the light.'

'Mm. The other visitor, the woman from the Flagship, she came blindfolded. Quite the nerve to make the crossing to the cliff alone, without sight or help. Some wanted to go out and collect her—I got 'em to wait.'

Now Lars found his tongue.

'*Why* would you do that? Why would anyone do that?'

He and Rachel made quite the pair, little miss was nodding along savagely. The farmer looked mildly surprised, like the answer was obvious.

'To see if that much hubris was justified. Quite impressive to see her make it, I tell you what, not sure I'll witness anything like that again in my lifetime.'

John was quite sure their own crossing hadn't been one for the epics.

'And your hair, it's the same as a veil, then?'

'My hair's down for your protection, hon. Quite the looker, me. It's a curse. One glance and men are forever lost.'

John didn't find that at all funny but the farmer boomed, laughter bouncing about the rock field until it startled a few nearby birds into the air. He craned his neck to follow, enraptured. It was like they were plummeting upward into the sky, just as Lars had feared, and taking his heart with them.

The burly farmer grasped her hand again for a more vigorous round of shaking, clearly pleased by the strength he found there. *You don't know the half of it.*

'The name's Joe. Joe Arviramopoulos. I don't suppose the ratbags got 'round to introducing themselves like civilised folk, but this here's my boy Santos and his partner in crime Rachel. Now. A little late in the season for trade, but I fancy you lot already know that.'

Really, John ought to be used to being wrong-footed.

'We're here because of your other visitor.'

Joe shook his head—not surprised, no.

'Don't suppose you've brought any better reason why the cities should be taken with minor festivals all of a sudden? We do it every year, you know. It's nothing new.'

'Huh?'

'That's why she was here. The woman from the Flagship. The brave woman. We're having the Festival of Lady Joy this week, same as it's been every year, only she reckoned her Captain had only just heard of it and sent her here to find out more. Right riled over it too, she said. Seemed almost scared—I gathered this was not normal behaviour from their fearless leader.

'So she came. Must be some Captain, because she wasn't *natively* brave about it but her Captain made her brave. You should've seen how she lit up. She'd do anything she was asked, right enough, even if she didn't quite understand. Blind faith. Gotta love it. You can only hope her Captain's the type to treat that sorta adulation right.'

'*That's* why the Flagship came to Judgment? For a festival?' Feeling dizzy and sick, John sat himself on a nearby stone. 'How is that important? It doesn't make any sense.'

Farmer Joe eyed him.

'You lot've only just staggered up the trail. If you can find your legs for a tad longer, better come up to my place and rest for a bit. The first visitor did, and it's not far. We've got a Festival dinner planned and after, once the sun's gone, I'll take you to see what I showed her. Make of it what you will, an' you can decide for yourselves if it's anything important.'

'If their Captain thought your festival was such a big deal, why didn't he come up here himself?'

'Good question, that. Why'd your Captain send you?'

He grimaced. 'Our Captain's older than the hills. She's got no business going anywhere.'

'Maybe it's the same for the Flagship. The visitor did say her Captain couldn't leave his city. And she looked all sad, like it was some huge issue I couldn't possibly understand. Strange conceit of the young. I mean, we're all as human as each other. All endured the same things. Love, loss, all the way down. Nothing so awful ever happens that the species ain't done a thousand times over, but oh no, not when you're *young*. As a kid you know, only you, an' nobody else could possibly understand. Might've been less a burden if she'd been able to share, but her suffering's *unique*, you see.'

Despite the danger John lifted the edge of his veil, enough to give Joe a hard eye from within the depths.

'Telling doesn't always make it better.'

Sometimes when the world finds out what you've kept cowering in your soul, it makes thing so much worse. Joe grunted as he quickly dropped the veil but sounded obscurely pleased—prejudices of the awfulness of city life confirmed.

'Sounds like you and I've had vastly different runs with what humanity's got to offer. Which is right, I wonder?'

'Both? None of them. There's no "right."'

'Oh, there's always a right.'

Lars did not envy Santos being this man's son.

They came upon a path, pebbled in loose stones for traction. And set up high on land there'd been no other use for was Joe's home. A squat, heavy stone cottage. Its grimness was not out of place amidst the boulders and black trees. If the hillside could have grown a house, it would appear just so.

Lars caught up from the straggling rear.

'Huh. I'd have thought it would be made out of wood.'

'Wood? Ha! The woods are a long way off, city fellow, and they belong heart and soul to your beasts. The trees 'round here don't yield up their wood—Even if they did, you wouldn't want to spend a night in a house made outta *them*. Not if you fancy keeping sanity screwed down tight.'

'Well, what do you harvest from them? There are so many.'

'Heaven forbid anything should exist just for itself, hey?'

'That's a cheap shot.' Only mildly ruffled. 'I may be from a city, but that doesn't make me ignorant of commerce. Up here, the earth itself must be a premium.'

'Poison. We harvest poison from these trees.'

'What kind of poison?'

'Our own, of course. Look, all of you, right to the horizon. You see health, right, even an austere kind of beauty? Your eyes are liars. Every place man's trodden in his long years on this earth has left soil that'll make you sick as a dog. Sometimes you don't even need to eat what springs from it— enough to breathe a pinch of dust whipped up in the air, get some on your skin.

'The first farmers of Judgment put most these trees in, and suffered while they grew 'cause there was no other choice. This was the path they'd set themselves to, the path of the land. One of sickness, bad dreams and short, poor lives. For a long time all they had was each other. Falling apart together.

'But those trees've been busy pulling poison out of the ground for scores of years now. Made the soil clean enough to farm safely. Eventually. Not that we've a free ride these days: they still need tending. More cuttings ready for when the oldest of 'em finally exhaust themselves. We've heavy gloves for the work—it ain't good to go touching them. No dropped twig or leaf, you hear? You two aren't likely to have trouble bundled up like that, but try not to make a habit of even staring too much. They don't like being stared at.'

'Seriously?'

'I've read the diaries of the founders cover to cover, so yeah, I'm pretty darn serious. Those poor folk. Watching the trees on all sides grow as tortured and poisoned as themselves, before they learned not to look. Feeling them looming up in dreams, spreading thin, brittle branches full of the sap of madness ... Don't go gawking at the trees, any of ya. And don't think on 'em too much. Just don't.'

The cottage's front door looked to be a thick panel of grass and twists of cloth all woven and knotted together. No wood. Joe pushed it aside.

'Come in. Be welcome.'

John was always leery of stepping into others' homes. The intimacy unnerved him, threw into unforgiving light shortcomings in his behaviour. He was surprised to find how ... welcoming the inside of Joe's house felt. A simple layout— leave complicated nonsense to those who don't have to build it with their own hands. The kitchen/all-purpose dining area they found themselves in was one long room with an open hearth to cap off the end; cooking and heating in one. The air that'd tickled and pawed outside was now mercifully still, enough to hear yourself think. The quiet smell of mineral stone, cold ash and clean wool.

Light came via the best solar panels the city could trade, which wasn't great, but better than nothing. Supplemented by what filtered through gauzy curtains, which Joe considerately closed to spare their eyes. He gestured toward two smaller rooms at the back, with the same odd doors woven out of pickings.

'Bedrooms are back there if you fancy a lie down. I'll head about an' spread the word you're joining us for dinner. Always plenty for everyone.'

Even as John and Lars were clawing their veils off, Mary barely waited until the farmer was out the door before she was hot on his heels.

'Where are you off to?'

'I'm not big on feasting and making merry with the locals, hon. What I *do* want is to hear a little more about this "Lady Joy." It *almost* sounds like … but that couldn't be.'

Muttering, she ducked out, not seeming to notice Santos' furtive attention. Never trust anyone who doesn't like dogs. The kid exchanged a curt nod with Rachel before trailing after, exaggeratedly casual. Something was brewing.

'My feet hurt. How does she do it? I swear, the damn woman's a machine.'

John's knee jerk reaction almost demolished a vase. Oblivious, Lars dropped his veil on a chair, wiping his sweaty face.

'Damn, that thing itches. I swear I was about to scratch right through my cheek and out the other side!'

Still Rachel lingered to administer the hairy eyeball, the way only suspicious youth can.

'You're ordinary.'

'Of course we are, little chicken. Folk from the city don't come with two heads.'

You could hear somebody coming a mile off, not much chance of sneaking up, but she still glanced out the door.

'I saw the woman from the Flagship,' she whispered.

'Two heads?' Lars was amused.

'Her blindfold slipped. Her eyes … Her eyes were made of bits of metal and glass. She didn't have any eyes. The grownups like Santos' dad will let anyone visit, but nobody looks for stuff that ain't normal. Nobody sees anything but us.'

John frowned. 'You sure?'

That didn't please. Regular little Captain, this one. Still, she wasn't biding for the pleasure of their company. She had other questions.

'Do you have animals in the city?'

'Some. Not many big ones.'

'Sooo, what do they eat?'

'I don't know?' He looked to Lars helplessly. 'Animal food?'

'But what happens when they won't eat?'

'They die, I guess?'

'Oh, what good are you then!'

She stormed out. John could swear she'd had tears in her eyes.

'Well, that was weird.' Lars, king of understatement.

'Looks like Judgment has the two smallest guardians ever.'

'John … You don't think it's a problem, do you? That boy Santos off following Mary?'

'Not so long as he leaves his dog at home.'

'But you don't think she'd … hurt a kid, do you?'

He felt a twinge of disquiet he tried to hide—he genuinely didn't know. And Lars' instincts were good.

'Surely not. I mean … Just get some rest.'

He'd scarce planted his skinny hard-done-by ass in a creaky woven chair that let out a *woomph* of tickly dried grass smell. Just shut his scratchy eyes when waves of disgustingly robust-looking people came bustling in the front door.

Sensibilities wanted to shriek at them to bugger off, give him some quiet so he could rationally set his ducks in a row, but the world never worked like that. Screaming tantrums wouldn't help anybody.

They came cradling covered platters of food that smelled like absolute heaven, or armfuls of bottles stopped with misshapen homemade cloth corks, or more chairs and cushions to stack about the place. And they were *noisy*. To prove they'd had mothers both Surgeons groaned to their burning, pulsating feet; mostly to shift this and that to wherever the square-jawed invasion cheerfully pointed.

They worked in a crowd that shuttled between just being folk, any old folk, and then suddenly frightening in their alieness and customs, only to go back to being people. Of course it was the Surgeons who were the foreigners here. Up gasping on the crunching shell of the beach, a long way from their native water. Among hosts polite enough to pretend it wasn't so.

They were both also acutely aware of being among folk who'd been dealt a vastly different start in life. They worked, uncomfortable in the knowledge they'd eventually be going home to hot showers, clean towels and takeout. While for all these folk, the horizon stopped right here.

They filled the room in a jostling herd, men, women and a few comfortably between. Flaunting the growth good nutrition bestowed on a population, heads seemed to scrape the ceiling. Most notable were the scars, the signs of inflammation. Missing digits, missing ears, even, in webs of pinked-up tissue. All matter of fact and without detracting from their brusque beauty. Life in Judgment wasn't some rural paradise for lazing about. Both Surgeons wondered how much of the damage on display could've been averted given what they thought of as "proper care," which in truth was the real luxury.

A rush, arms waving and shouting everywhere at once. And then suddenly everyone was seated, still shoving and squabbling at top volume. Being more by way of a "people person" Lars depressurised much faster. He sat in his element, right in the thick of it, trusting clothing and gloves to protect him against the casual jostling of the ignorant.

John found himself edged out to the margins. A host of failings overcame his novelty value. Sullen brooding types were as boring as hairy ass no matter where they hailed from, and you wouldn't want to be stuck next to one at a dinner party. He wound up beside Joe, possibly a concession made out of pity. Watched his friend carry on with a familiar mix of amusement and envy. Life came so easy to Lars. You'd think he'd been born to it.

Glancing about Lars found John in his shadowy corner and caught his eye. *You really are the most tedious, miserable assface, you know?*

John inclined his head. *Oh, I know. Asshole.*

At least it was easier to face off against Joe without the cumbersome veil. In their short acquaintance the farmer had already paraded a quick distain for second guesses, the hesitation that admitted you might possibly be wrong. It'd be a damned nightmare, being his son. No wonder the poor kid believed so strongly in a place to escape to.

The thought pricked his curiosity anew. He leaned toward Joe to have his query heard above the cheerful tumult, the celebration he had no part in. 'What do you know about GATE?'

The farmer's head drew back, like he'd flipped over a rock and found something poisonous, which had to be quite the occupational hazard out here.

'GATE's just a worn out old bedtime story. Something adults who can't stand the truth no more sit and tell their kids, 'cause it sounds better.'

You'd better believe he wasn't one of those hopelessly comforting parents.

'And the truth is?'

Your truth is? meant John, but he didn't want to be too much of a dick. They were guests.

'The truth's just plain sad. That's what you'll find truth to be around every corner. And that makes GATE quite the sore spot 'round here. I'm surprised anybody's still talking 'bout it.'

John chose not to throw young Santos under the bus. Joe nodded slightly and went on.

'There used to be some crusty old tunnels under Judgment, and I mean real old. Even mentioned in the founders' journals, 'though they'd the brains to keep out like the devil hisself was down there. Had enough problems.

'Only, despite their efforts, a decade or so back this ... rumour, I guess you'd call it, started up that those manky tunnels were the way to GATE. Got to be a hell of a job keeping curious kids and other idiots out. Still, nobody took it serious enough. Not until a lad went missing.

'Sweetest kid, he was. Only ten or so. Bit of a daydreamer. Not slow, but you'd have ta tap his elbow sometimes to get his attention, remind him what he was s'posed to be doing. Just gone, like the tunnels had swallowed him whole. Nobody ever found sign of him, which means the poor mite's bones are still down there in the dark. After that tragedy Judgement finally got its act together, we teamed up and filled those tunnels in. Took weeks.'

'Oh. I thought ... I had a friend go missing, you see.'

At that John's dining partner on the other side, a young man, surreptitiously glanced his way with what looked very much like contempt. He supposed he must be dripping guilt. But Joe's eyes were pitying.

'Well, I'm sorry for your loss. But if you ask me, the whole story with GATE was never so much for those who'd gotten themselves lost. It's about those as walk outta their lives thinking there's someplace different to go.'

Seeing John so crestfallen the farmer stood up.

'It oughta be dark enough now to get started. They say it was dark in the desert when she died.'

'Who? When who died?'

'The Lady Joy, of course. What with our strange rustic ways it may shock you to know that with the Festival of Lady Joy, once upon a time there actually *was* a Lady Joy.'

'I'd been thinking more along the lines of the tooth fairy or something.'

Seeing them on their feet Lars waded across. 'Good to go? Anybody mind if I pop to the loo before we leave?'

He looked from one impassive face to the other.

'Oh my God. I'm going to have to shit in a hole, aren't I?'

John snorted. 'Well you should have gone before we left.'

'It's not like I can schedule them!'

Joe rolled his eyes. 'Your mate's winding you up. Latrine's the little boxy building 'round the back. Door on the right's for pee, use the left for anything more … uh … solid.'

'You've got two different toilets?'

'Sure. You're producing two different types of real valuable fertiliser there. Piss works nice and easy, spread it straight on the soil; but if you want to avoid disease the chunky stuff needs to get sun dried and composted a bit before it becomes anything useful.'

'Nature is *lovely*,' Lars muttered as he headed out back.

Mary put in an appearance just as Joe was handing out water bottles and lanterns. Both were of a clunky metal that might be as old as the settlement and freezing to touch, so you swapped them from hand to hand waiting for the handles to suck all life from your fingers.

The lanterns were shuttered to direct the beam down. On

venturing out into the night they soon discovered why. The darkness was profound. It had its own texture, and various features of terrain were in a race to see which could send you ass over teakettle.

For the city dwellers, instincts that had been long submerged woke up to prickle their skin all over. Abandoning the glow and chatter inside the building. Outdoors and exposed at night, with the wind whining through clenched trees. Stripped vulnerable in a world that might have its way with them, and walking *away* from safety like crazy men.

Joe led the way into the dark, chatting amicably for a spell with Mary. He wasn't stupid. He was bound to notice her carefree step, whereas the other two crept along like terrified snails. The careless way she pointed her lantern at this or that, but never at the ground. Perhaps all that eyelash fluttering had never worked, the cold-eyed farmer laughing behind his hand. You'd need more than a swing of the asscheeks to win this one. He would pay out the rope until she'd more than enough to hang herself with, no hope of clawing back.

Once again John didn't envy the farmer's poor son. Cunning was well and good but not when you had to answer to it across the dinner table.

A few other lanterns joined their procession, comforting in the dark. Legs and shoes illuminated, locals in front and behind, treading the jumbled ground more confidently than the interlopers dared.

Mary gave a hiss of revulsion and drew back. Santos' little dog came poking around their ankles with a snuffling wet nose, delighted to be out. She dropped behind John as though expecting him to shield her.

'Just act normal.' Her voice low, to keep others out and secrets in. 'Your little friend's here in Judgment.'

'What?' He half-turned and she shoved him forward.

'They're helping hide her, bonehead. It's *you* she doesn't want to see.'

Redundant to ask why. His guts twisted first one way then the other, not settling long enough to tell him how to feel.

Joe was beckoning them. 'This way. Carefully now.'

Each in his own quiet terror, the Surgeons had feared descending off the plateau, even more deadly at night when the Blessed roamed like heavily muscled fever-dreams. But it soon became apparent that they were merely clambering down into a sort of crevasse, not much wider than to allow the gathering in single file. The lantern bearers queued patiently for their turn to enter.

Joe shone his lantern directly into the crack. He lit first the retreating back of the person in front, then what looked sickeningly like thin black arms reaching out of the walls.

'Remember as I told you: don't touch the trees. If you do brush up against one, dump water from your canteen over the skin straight away. Should sluice the worst of it off.'

It'd be a tricky ask. Like sentinels, trees lined both sides of the crevasse with their twisted hands held up to ward you off. It was necessary to probe ahead with the light, and weave in a little dance step to avoid getting your eye poked out. Felt like the rock walls were gearing up to give a great big squeeze.

At least the footing was a little easier. It had to be, if you were to reach the end without wrenching something. Flat stones had been laid as steps, now curved into gentle organic shapes by the generations who had trod them. So, not a recent festival then. They were participating in a ritual that might be as old as the plateau itself. A huge, aching time frame that only Mary was equipped to deal with.

Putting light on the ground to check your way gave the rocks down there opalescent milky hues, as though the hillside shone a secret light back at you through the stone. Beautiful enough to string on a necklace. The polished display revealed water, and now they could smell it, wet mineral and slick clay on the tongue. A sort of ditch or culvert alongside the trail where a thin scrim of water trickled, trailing long black streamers of moss. It seemed they were headed toward the source.

All this crammed into the narrow space for them to pick through. Lars broke the silence, because fools rush.

'These trees look older.'

That pleased Joe.

'They are. Much older. They were already here waiting to be discovered when the founders came to Judgment. They were taken as a sign that no matter how the poisoned earth hates us, here was a place that could be made safe.'

'Trees told them all that? They don't seem real chatty to me.'

'The trees and water did together. You merely need to understand what they're saying.'

'What are they saying?'

'The stream at our feet becomes more toxic the closer we approach its source. But where we entered the approach, climbing down the rocks, that very same water is safe enough to drink. It *does* taste like burnt ass 'til you filter it, though.'

'Because the trees are cleaning it, right?'

'The trees are cleaning it.'

There was a scuffle in the narrow space as Joe squeezed against the wall to let his guests precede him into the opening at the end of the crevasse, a deep bowl-shaped arena. The town's other celebrants were standing about in respectful clusters, beams directed toward the centre of the space like spokes of light.

'This here's the mother of them all. The first tree.'

No scratching, clawing fingers protruded about the rough rock perimeter of this open area. There was only the single tree at its centre, sending shadows out as the lanterns hit it. And it was massive. A behemoth, twisted branches thick as people reaching to rake the starry sky overhead. If all Judgment's trees had the potential to achieve such massive growth they would eventually crack the uplands apart.

'What's ..?'

Lars' beam crept closer, fingered across the rippled bark surface.

'Are those human remains? God, it's got bones in it!'

Joe came to stand beside him, to study what fascination and revulsion animated his face. 'Do you believe in a God, Surgeon?'

'Uh …' Leery of getting pinned by philosophical debate, no matter how polite one should keep with one's host. 'I guess so. I haven't put great buckets of thought into it.'

'Well, what we've got here is the Festival of Lady Joy. The story goes that Lady Joy was dying in the desert. Come to the end of herself, I'd say, 'though there's no mention of how she got there—might've wandered off from a tour for all we know. God looked down on her all crumpled in the sand an' took pity on her.

'But there wasn't enough life left in her body by then to save the woman, no matter how merciful the mood, so instead God took what spark was left and put it into all the bits of leaf and twig that were clinging to her clothes. From that, the farmland rose out of the desert.'

'So *this* is your Lady Joy? It looks like the tree's eaten her.' A yellowed hint of bone poking out here and there. 'Who brought her bones here?'

'She brought herself. This here's the very spot the Lady collapsed to die, too weak or heartsick to keep going. All this used to be desert. Right here, the first tree rose up at God's touch with her bones safe in its grasp. All the uplands spread out from here, plants given the will to grow in the sand and change the land.'

'So … Your festival celebrates the birth of the farmland. That's pretty.'

The farmer gave a strained smile. 'Sort of. It's a nice story, but only a fool bangs on about what God may have intended one way or another. But a small act of pity—that's human. That's everyone's business.'

He set his lantern down, the beam focussed on the great brooding tree with its cargo of bones. Same as the other farmers, lighting it just that bit more.

'The Lady died alone, in the dark. So every year on the longest nights we've made it our business to come out here and give her a little light and company. Just to let her know she ain't forgotten.'

Rocks shifted. John turned to look but was struck by a blur passing him.

'Bitch!' Mary shrieked, a metallic cry of rage that pierced decibels outside human hearing. 'That *bitch*!' She was moving too fast to stop.

Only the Surgeons still had their lanterns to hand and the beams wobbled about uncertainly, increasing the confusion. It all happened so fast. A rending slashed the night in half. John finally got himself oriented to see it was the sound of Mary furiously crumpling her lantern down to a tiny ball. It might have been made of flimsy broadsheet, rather than the robust metal that must be insanely valuable out here.

She flung the destroyed lantern at the looming tree. And surely it was only the chaos of shadow that made it seem to flinch. Proceeded to kick over other lanterns, still screaming, '*Bitch! Bitch!*' at frequencies to make the ears bleed. Her voice seemed to be stuck on fast forward.

'No!' Other voices were shouting, ordinary voices. 'Don't do that!' Sudden pandemonium, with people running about, appalled. Sheets of lantern oil spread across the rock chased by eager flame, licking, dancing, and cranking up the heat in the confined space. Firelight flickered on the polished yellow skull embedded in the trunk. All detail suddenly and luridly revealed with the decency of dark stripped away.

'Get sand!' Joe was bellowing to rally the other farmers. 'Sand and dirt, throw it on the fire! Save Joy!'

Only Santos, the kid, was foolish enough to run directly at Mary, to try and stop her. And Joe was too far away, his strength useless, his cry of anguish terrible. *Surely she wouldn't hurt a kid*, John thought dizzily but the woman was crazed, utterly out of her mind with rage, she hurled the frail boy to the ground with enough force to break something.

Broken wasn't enough. Shrilling, the flames all around, she raised one foot to obliterate him utterly. Santos screamed, too, pain and shock, a child discovering the chaos of the world. Which was more than enough for his loyal little dog to rush in.

In defence of family even the mildest pet recalls primal roots and the jolly pup's face was suddenly hideous to see. Lips scrolled back to display spotted gum and every millimetre of tooth, barking hard enough to throw strings of saliva. Eyes white all the way around and hard staring crazy. If this was death, he was going to shred it.

Mary screamed, throwing her hands in front of her face and the fire was here now, all fire. Empty calcified sockets stared down at her mockingly from their throne. At the same time a firm hand gripped John and Lars each by a forearm through the sleeve, dragging them back from the chasm and away from disaster.

The last thing John saw was Mary stamping down, and the high pained squeal of the dog was horrible. He could only make her out because she was ablaze. Hair lifting and shrivelling away in flames to reveal her terrible smashed face, its fixity of expression all jumbled up that was mad, mad, mad at the heart of the fire.

'Move, move,' a voice chanted urgently, shoving the Surgeons along. 'You two have to get out of here.'

John and his clumsy feet went down on one knee, only to be dragged up and pushed along.

'We can't see!' Lars protested. After staring at the dazzling icon that had been Mary, they both might as well have been blind.

'Hold onto the back of my jacket, then. You there, grab onto his. And suck in your gut. Touch these branches too much and you'll be pissing clots for a month, but we need to go fast.'

A glow and a nightmare of screaming at their backs as they were towed along, water splashing and wetting their ankles. Heat on the back of the neck. That stench, that horrible nostril-stopping stench of burnt hair and they the only ones fleeing, the rest of Judgment doing the right thing by standing to fight the conflagration and the one who'd caused it.

They staggered free of the narrow gap but no time for getting bearings. The man hustled them down a slope. He'd been the only one with the brains to hang onto his metal canteen, and hurriedly dumped a third of the water over each without stopping.

'These rocks. Here. No, *here*. There's a tunnel, you need to squeeze in behind them.'

Poor Lars was built for finer things in life and almost didn't make it, until the stranger set an unsympathetic boot against his backside. Through he popped with a startled grunt, tearing his outfit right good in the process. The word "asshole" drifted out of the tunnel.

They squeezed through after. It was a whole new category of dark, dusty and dry, specially made for claustrophobics. Before hysteria had a chance to really set its teeth the stranger lit a lantern, revealing two Surgeons busy gasping with hands on knees, trying to work out what the fuck just happened.

Oh, and although John was crap with names and faces he was pretty sure he knew this guy holding up the lantern with a strained smirk. He was the young fellow from dinner. The unfriendly guy.

'Ok you two fellas,' Mr Unfriendly said. 'You've visited Judgment, seen what you came to see. Let's get you back on to your city right-quick.'

'She killed that kid's dog!' Lars cried. He was on something of a delayed horrified reaction and his voice echoed around the inside of the tunnel. 'And her face! My God, what was wrong with her *face*?'

John nodded, a rather helpless masculine comfort, but turned his attention to their rescuer. 'What makes you so eager to help us out?'

Unfriendly chuckled. 'I reckon you already know we've a mystery woman hiding in our ranks. I got an earful that you're some friend of hers, although hardly in the good books at the mo'. Not to put too fine a point on it, I figure helping you might further my cause of seeing my way into her delectable knickers.'

'Bleuch.' John shook his head. 'I did not need to hear that!'

'One man's feast's another's poison.'

'So she *is* alive.' He leaned on the wall a moment, giddy with relief. 'She made it.'

'She made it to Judgment, yep. Made it to us. And let me

make it pretty clear you are *not* taking that achievement from her. Doesn't want nothing to do with you lot and your city. She's left that behind, now.'

'We ought to be taking her safe home where she belongs.' Lars always had a soft spot for John's friend. That said, Lars had a soft spot for everyone. 'You can't just up and leave your troubles behind. The world doesn't work like that.'

'If it's what she says she wants, where's the harm letting her try? Major man-points in it for me if I see you two idiots outta here with all your bits intact.'

John scoffed. 'She's going to see right through you. You can't do nice things for women and expect sex to pop out like the toast is done.'

'This isn't my first rodeo, fella.' He held his lantern up, shining it down the tunnel. Only one way to go, really. 'This way, gentlemen.'

They had to stoop to proceed. One confined space ought to feel much like another, only they didn't. In the damp, mineral-smelling confines of the crevasse there had always been sky overhead. Here they were being choked down a gullet of dry earth.

'Tunnels,' John murmured thoughtfully. 'Joe said the tunnels had all been filled in.'

'Yeah, well, one man's wisdom hardly encompasses the world.' Their guide's eyes glinted suspiciously. 'How'd you get him carrying on about them, anyhow? Hardly his favourite topic.'

'He was telling me about GATE.'

'Ah, as in, all roads lead to, if you want it badly enough. In fact if your delicious friend longed for freedom so much she could've walked the way, anytime, it was always open to her. Open to anyone, more's the pity. Look here.'

A side tunnel, more like an incidental crack in the wall,

jutted off. He led them down it, but only a short distance. Only to where it narrowed and narrowed, continuing on through rock in a whisper so slight not even a snake could have contorted through.

"GATE" was daubed in yellow paint above that meandering crack that delved deeper into the earth beyond human ability to follow. And below it lay a skeleton, tragically small. It sprawled full-length with one arm jammed in the crack to the elbow, as though to the last extremity this child had still been trying to force his way through.

There were small dried wildflowers scattered about the remains and Mr Unfriendly sighed behind his lantern.

'I always try to bring something when I stop by to visit him, a little taste of the world above. The kid only made one mistake in coming down here. He deserves a bit of kindness, just as much as the la-di-dah Lady Joy up there.'

Lars knelt by the little body and you could see his sensitive heart was just breaking. 'Do you know who he was?'

'Kid's name was Sabry. Sabry, meet two asshole Surgeons from the city. Only, Sabry didn't get lost down here like Joe tells the story. Didn't break his leg or get stuck or anything like that. His mum had gone walkabout, and the poor kid missed her so much that he ran away.

'Must've dreamed that if he could get through to GATE he could be with her again, dreamed it so hard he kept trying right until the end. Never occurred to him to turn around and go home, not without her.

'Stupid stories. This is where they lead. It's disgusting what folk put themselves through to follow a fairytale, the dim promise of someone who'll love them more than anything else on earth. Like that's supposed to make it all better.'

Lars looked helpless. 'I don't have anything to leave.'

John fumbled through his pockets; the best he could come

up with was a length of cheap black ribbon that he stared at in surprise. How long had he been carting that around?

He offered it. 'Here.'

'Fat lot of good it'll do now,' Lars muttered, but took it anyway. Left it draped beside that tiny skull that still yearned toward GATE.

Unfriendly nodded. 'Me and some others visit him every now and again.'

'You and some others? Who are the others?'

'Just some mates. Call ourselves the real farmers of Judgment. All the *official* trade with the cities goes on up top, but there's always a few commodities it's best to slip via ... other means.'

'What, so these tunnels go all the way out to *A New Life*?' John started getting excited. Finally some good news!

'Not possible. The cities, they squash the ground, no tunnel could stand up under it. No, we go as close as we dare and then the downstairs folk come out to meet us. If my crew get in strife it's *whoosh*, back into the tunnel.'

'Oh, great.' John rubbed his forehead, gloves squeaking. 'They'll be thrilled to see me again.'

'Again.' Lars echoed flatly. 'You, my asshole friend, have a lot of explaining to do. *You let me come out here with you*, and that ... that woman, Mary, whatever she was, and you haven't told me a fucking thing, have you?

'We could die, John! Did that thought grace your thick skull for even a second? Did you stop to think maybe I have other life goals that *don't* include spending my final moments screaming through a mouthful of dirt?'

'Oh, come on. You came 'cause you want El Capitino to pat you on the head.'

'I came to keep an eye on you, you stupid git! You may stride through the surgery like a god among men, but I've yet to see you walk five meters through the real world without tripping!'

Mr Unfriendly pulled his lip, ignoring their kindergarten squabble. Maybe he'd get on with the friend after all.

'Ok. So it's a tad sub-optimal, but the downstairs people are as close as I'm going to be able to get you. You'll just have to figure things out from there. Do it on the fly.'

'Just for the record, that's the opposite of a plan.'

'I'm sure you can handle yourselves, big shots from the city. Have a little faith.'

Disconsolate, both Surgeons trailed him in silence to the tunnel's exit. You could taste the change in the air: the dull, dusty atmosphere became a little more excited stirred about.

Then the lamplight opened into a void, and they'd made it.

'Hey.' On impulse John unstrapped the tracker from his arm and handed it to Unfriendly. 'I know you're keen, but give this to her for me, will you? So she's at least got the option to come back, if she decides that's what she wants.'

He made it disappear into his pocket. 'Sure.'

John searched his bland face, but had never learned how to tell when to trust. It was a bit late to be picking it up now.

He turned to Lars. 'Ok, ok. Let's do this and see how we go.'

'Yeah, bye.'

The crunching of grass as they stepped out seemed insanely loud. Behind them Unfriendly's lantern flashed, signalling.

'So, what plans?'

'What?'

'What are your big life plans that don't involve dying horribly out here?'

'Well. You know. There's like, twelve brands of whiskey I haven't tried yet, all the expensive ones. And I always wanted to learn to knit. It's so fiddly.'

'I hate you.'

'No you don't. When we get back I'll knit you a sweater.'

A crowd of torches was approaching from the worryingly distant and retreating lights of the city. They were downwind, in her exhaust, and on violently churned ground that had only recently had time to settle.

'John,' Lars muttered urgently, eyeing the approaching group. They'd instinctively both raised their hands in surrender. 'Downstairs people.'

'Yeah, I know.'

He looked sick. 'Are they why you cut off your hair?'

'Yep.'

'God. I think I'm going to wax every square inch of myself once we're home.'

'Aren't enough bees in the world, but good, stay focussed. We are going to get home.'

'Good. How?'

The unnervingly silent crowd gathered around them. The breeze stirred long strands of the nearest downstairs person's hair to reach across and tickle John's exposed skin, which he instantly longed to scorch off.

'John?'

They began herding the Surgeons by simple expedient of pressing close, from which the men retreated shuddering, desperate to be away. In which eerie, skin-crawling manner they gradually progressed. Away.

They were being herded further away from the city.

'John?'

'Run.'

'What?'

'*Run!*'

By surprise more than strength he broke out of the circle with Lars right on his heels. Athletic success! This was a new one! Both of course had had enough of running for one lifetime, but they'd had quite enough of waiting to die, too.

The downstairs lot took off after them like a flock of pigeons. Still silent. Although the pursuit alone should make anyone run faster, strength was already failing.

'John …' Lars wheezed, readying his last words. They'd better be short.

Lights blazed out of the night. An engine shrieking. The decoy rig lit up all at once and shot between the Surgeons and their pursuers, who scattered. A corpse wouldn't have shocked them, but this was no cadaver.

'Go!' The Captain shouted as she burned past. 'Get to the city!'

'Can she do that?' Lars boggled.

'Shut up! Just run!'

The delay was barely enough to allow them to pull away, but barely was all they needed. Without glancing behind they pounded up the city's rampway to hammer on the vestibule door, falling through together as it opened.

Rolled to one side just in time to be out of the Captain's way as she shot through, loose wires flying, the rig trailing a scorched-brake smell. The door slammed shut.

John couldn't believe his ears.

'You … are you laughing?'

Lars whooped and rolled on the floor, actually kicking his legs.

'We were going to be dead! And then … zoom! It's the frigging Captain. Look, she's put in a joystick!'

John staggered upright on rubbery legs, and gave his boot a kick. 'I hate you.'

'It'll be the best sweater ever. Just wait.'

Above their heads the green safe light clicked on, washing the fancy little vestibule in lime. Strangely John felt a pang of nostalgia for the tumultuous air Outside with its wild taste.

Still strapped rigid like a general the Captain scowled down at Lars. Choking on giggles he took a few deep breaths and steadied himself, holding out a little parcel he'd produced from somewhere.

'Ma'am. I'm pleased to say I've brought your tea.'

John stared at him in disbelief.

CHAPTER EIGHT

AT A GLASS AND FILTH ALTAR

JOHN HAD QUITE the fright in store when his key snicked home and he exhaustedly hip and shouldered his front door open. Not *buckets* of adrenaline in reserve for reacting, though, when he found Charles had let himself in, in what had to be an ambush or the worst welcome home party ever.

The friend's husband. Did her flight now make him an ex-? A lump of gloom on the couch, alone in the dark to wait, like something thrown away. Didn't even react when John clicked on the light. Merely sat twisting his wedding ring around and around his finger.

The poor sod seemed hypnotically focussed on the task, forsaking all others you might say. Had John never made it home, Charles would have gone right on for the rest of his natural days if need be. Wearing a trench through fallible flesh, until the digit dropped off and he was finally free.

Was the friend still shamelessly sporting its battered gold twin? On her broad hand as she sat herself down at a rustic table, in the cheery-bright glow of Outside. The mood would be stilted, Judgment's air filmy with ash. Quiet and shocked to be starting a new day after facing down Mary's inexplicable pyre.

No doubt Unfriendly sat there too, and tallied the jewellery with a slyly observant eye. Perhaps while offering some smuggled trifle to make her feel more at home. The simple fact of a ring wouldn't make a whit of difference; wasn't like said husband was about, was it?

John almost felt sorry for the poor ass. Wanted to slink into her under croft, did he? Hell. She'd blast him six ways from Sunday merely for the attempt. Although … Her tarnished virtue wasn't anything Charles had laid claim to. Locked away like a gem nobody wanted.

… Likely this wasn't the best topic to be mulling right now. You could bet your bottom dollar John's exhausted mouth wasn't to be trusted.

He almost had a heart attack, switching on the light to discover the intrusion. It went off like the creepiest magic trick: glance casually about a familiar room before moving on, then you look again, wildly. Laggard brain finally realising something was *way* off. Body not waiting for confirmation to click into full panic mode, because this had been one asshat of a day.

It didn't help that he scarcely recognised him, not without

the second and third stare. A damned long time since he'd seen Charles in the living, breathing flesh. Hardly even asked about him anymore, except when needling the friend. Bang-up bud John was, but sometimes that's life. Scurrying through your harried existence, just trying to get by, was exactly how one ended up alone. He had only retained the friend because she was stubborn enough to keep dropping by.

John hurried through the apartment. He'd love to shoot the breeze, but the purgatives were already doing their fierce work. Unbelievably, Charles just kept sitting and spinning quietly.

Kept at it the whole four hours John spent in the bathroom having foreign parasites stripped in the most traumatic way possible, short of some nursie strapping on a wader and sorting things manually. That delicious farm meal wasted. Real butter. He'd cry if there was any liquid left in his body. Hopefully his gut had managed to wrangle some precious sustenance—useful for, say running. Lots of running. He had never pictured himself having a life so full of running, but there you were.

His insides had been reduced to oatmeal when the spasms finally petered out. Sad, sad oatmeal. Contaminants couldn't possibly hide in his shattered, perspiring frame; not even he wanted to live there anymore.

He undertook the formality of a shower, although in practical terms he felt he'd never be clean again. Dressed gingerly. Then, unable to put it off any longer he hobbled back to the lounge, snapping on fresh gloves as he went.

Charles hadn't budged, or miraculously vanished, which would be pretty darn super right now. Sat on the couch like he had nowhere else in the world, and fuck-all to do once he got there. Was this how he'd been spending his time, as empty as the marital nest? Misery sure knows its own.

John only had the one poor excuse of a coping mechanism to share. Wincing at every step he brought bottle and glasses to the table, setting them down with a sharp crack that seemed to startle Charles out of his reverie. With no social niceties to compete, the sloshing burning honey being poured between them was a cataract. Nothing worth saying, at any rate.

But Charles was the kind of fellow to blurt anyway, bless his poor heart. He seemed to shudder within himself and seized the glass, wedding ring giving a dainty *plink* against the side.

'Have you seen her?'

Here it was. John gulped his own dram for bravery, lighting up his sinus and the whole front of his face with little bee stings. The careful staging of his loungeroom seemed ridiculous with Charles' long face planted in the middle of it. What comfort could mood lighting or elegant clean lines really bring anyone?

Charles was tapping his finger against the glass, waiting for an answer. Plink. Plink. Plink.

'I'm her husband, John. Says so on the paperwork. I at least deserve to know what's happened to her.' Gusted a sigh that turned him inside out, all the guts on display. 'I'm her husband. Fucking ridiculous, right?'

'You both had to marry *someone*.' His voice crackled, touting that same faded rationale, though he hadn't supported it then. Could hardly lay claim to it now. 'Better the devil you know.'

'Worst mistake we ever made, in a long line of 'em,' he agreed, concurring with the tone. That disconcerting habit of darting past words to get at what you were trying to say. 'You know, I still recall her expression clear as day when we were putting these rings on. Last time we looked each other in the face. It was so bleeding obvious we were both the same, thinking it so hard our eyes might pop out. Thinking, "Well. Now we're right-fucked." But it was too late.'

He drained his glass like it was water and helped himself liberally, although chemistry dictated his vocals ought to be corroding. Drinking like that was a great way to gift yourself an aneurism.

'You've still got your ducks in a row, though, haven't ya? The great Surgeon. Exempt from all the squishy fumbling the rest of us are expected to do.'

'I think I'm going fucking crazy, Charles. That's where I'm going.' John surprised himself by saying. Latex squeaked on glass and he tore the glove off with sudden revulsion, an explosion of talc. Held the cool weight in his pale puffy hand with its cracked skin. A Surgeon's hand.

Downright lethal behaviour, tipsy or no. Charles shifted nervously across the couch, increasing the survival zone between them and John smirked bitterly at the point made.

'See? It's all like that, my every waking moment, and I'll share an itty bitty secret with you here, Charles. Just some theory I've been working on.'

He took a drink. 'I don't think living breathing folk are supposed to be isolated like this. Not ever. It's … Beyond cruel, doesn't make anyone a "better Surgeon." Just makes them nuts. Plain nuts, pure and simple.'

'Heresy, mate. I can see you getting your ass eaten at the stake sometime soon, you keep running your mouth like that. People are bound to find out.'

'Then *report* me! I can't remember a time I wasn't going crazy inside. Bit by bit, creeping on, every day. I just wish I was *there* already, you know? With everything finally broken. I want my world broken so bad there's no hope of putting it back together.'

'Amen to that!'

Held out his glass for a "clink," ironic little salute because they were all broken and all going mad, pull up a chair and fill your glass. And for these two there was nobody to halt that slide. Not anymore. It hadn't escaped notice how John had twisted things around to *his* problems, but Charles was patient. He had a comfy seat, somebody else's booze, and could wait until the sun turned black if needs be.

'I'm not reporting you, dumbass. Not like it's going to matter anyhow: when we catch up to the Flagship it'll be like our whole *universe* has ended, you mark my words. There's something terrible waiting for us there. *A New Life*, last city to fall. So drink up, no sense saving it.'

At mention of the Flagship John bit his tongue so hard it bled, the liquor like sipping lava. Still he stumbled on, blind to the humiliating transparency of his own narcissism. 'And there's these things, these *things* the Captain makes me do, for the city. I swear she wants me dead.'

Charles chuckled. 'If that hoary old gargoyle wanted you off the mortal coil she'd just turn up and glare you to death.' He raised his glass in the traditional tribute. 'To the Captain!'

'The Captain!' John's hand came up automatically. 'The Captain sent me out, Charles. She sent me Outside. If that's not a death sentence, I don't know what is.'

Now Charles' jaw hung open. One hand; the free hand of course, or the carpet would be enjoying a very fine drop; even sketched the opening of a warding gesture, which was off putting.

Wouldn't have pegged him as the superstitious type. But then again, it *had* been a while between drinks. He could have become the Pope, he could have become anything. Didn't stop it being insulting. In Charles' mind John was contaminated in a whole new way. Lucky he was a Surgeon so there wasn't going to be any hugging.

'Don't you want to hear what it was like?' he pressed maliciously. 'If your *wife* were here, she'd be shaking me for detail.'

'No I absolutely do not, and if you'd half a brain in your big bobbly head you wouldn't be just ... just *chatting* about it like it ain't no thing. Next you'll be wearing the black ribbons strung around your fool neck, and good luck to you, because if you've been touched by Outside I don't want any part of it.'

He stood to go, wobbling tipsy and outraged. Charles the conformist, what do you know. And John was irritated and tired, without much patience which regrettably wasn't new at all. Realistically he ought to feel a tad more grief over the situation, and jilted Charles less. But he'd given his stubborn, hot headed friend the homing device, hadn't he? So the next move, to come home, belonged solely to her. She'd come around eventually.

'She's gone Outside. She's *gone*, Charles. Somewhere neither of us can follow. I guess to see what she can make of herself without us.'

That knocked him off his high horse. Gravity took hold and he deflated right back onto the cushion.

'Figured wherever she'd gone this time, wasn't coming back. Me, I was waiting to see if you'd come tell me. If anyone would. What the hell do I matter, hey?' Charles wiped his sad drooping mouth on his sleeve. 'Only one who's bothered to come 'round has been her mother, and she's not in any mood to go ringing the bell.'

'Ass and shit.' One more complication. 'What's she doing, then?'

'The old bat's jumped straight to rooting through my garbage in the dead of night to see if I murdered her daughter.'

'Please tell me you're joking.' As horrific as it was, couldn't John just see that going down.

'I'm eating a lot of steak these days. She gets so excited when she finds the bones. Watching her widdle her shorts is worth staying up for.'

'Dangerous. She's dangerous.' Eloquent, but that was about the best he could manage. The grog was hitting his emptied system like a bomb going off, hardly left space for words on his thick tongue.

'Shattered is what she is. I shouldn't make fun. The old bag's got even less than me; she's busy trying to piece something together out of scraps off the ground. At least she's doing something, I guess. I mean, look at us.'

'We're doing something. This bottle isn't going to empty itself.'

'Ah, my darling wife's left a real mess in her wake this time. A right mess. I think we've categorically proven that no matter what she thought, not a single human being's better of without her. Not even me. We're all just ruined.'

He glanced up, finally, and those were the sorts of eyes you never wanted to find yourself staring into.

'What am I supposed to do now, John? You were her friend, you tell me. There's this godawful empty gap where she used to be; in our apartment, in my *life*. And that space between us that we always tiptoed around, nothing's moved in to fill it. It's everywhere, following me around. Feels like I'm being haunted.'

Poor old Charlie-boy, eh? Haunted by a marriage he'd not deserved. Now free and unable to enjoy that either. Poor baby.

John grunted, all liquored up, the room already beginning to slide as his balance went. As for dignity, *pfft*. 'Haunted? You want to see *real* haunted?'

Charles' eyes brightened. 'If we're going to see a ghost,

first we have to empty this place, and then score some more booze. Burn up the day. Everything'll be creepier in the dark.'

They ended up going to a place Charles knew. John had no idea if the bars he used to frequent were cool, or even open.

The cold air shocked him back to his senses some, cold enough to discourage loitering. As they stumbled through a back street labyrinth he was thinking they might not even be going to a club. Suspicion prodding with queries he ought to have blurted long before venturing along. *How well do you know your buddy Charles these days?* But the rose stained lure of good ol' times was just too strong.

'Here,' Charles grunted and they swung off into somebody's yard. Somebody who'd had kids, but maybe not now, maybe not for a long time. Even as he tripped on toys scattered across the little concrete square he hoped those kids had grown up and moved out, and that was all. Either way, the parents hadn't had the heart to get rid of those things.

Appropriating the miniature swing set Charles swung wildly, grinning up at him. The structure creaked and groaned alarmingly.

'We'll need the Jaws of Life to cut your ass out of that seat,' John observed unkindly. 'Ages four to twelve it says on the side. What are we doing here?'

Giggling he struggled up but the seat came with him, chains rattling. 'Oh shit, I am stuck!' A brief moment of panic before his good old bud managed to prise the four-to-twelve plastic off his adult hams.

'Shh!' John cased the property nervously, although the lights remained off. 'You'll wake the family.'

'Not bloody likely.'

Charles was wrestling with one of those rocking horseys that lurch back and forth on springs. He seemed to be trying to lift it right out of the floor, likely to bust a gut doing so. 'Help me with this.'

Somebody had to be fired from the factory after making this, John thought queasily, lending his twiglet arms to the effort. The jolly grinning beastie inviting some kid to leap into its saddle and gallop away sported a stubby horn jutting from its face, that must've been uncomfortably long and wicked before a wiser soul had sawn it down.

'Why are we stealing this?' He hiss-whispered, the way tipsy people do when they think they're being quiet. 'It's hardly gonna match your sofa.'

'Not stealing,' Charles grunted. 'Push to the left.'

Which ought to have accomplished squat with the springs seated in concrete. It yielded a deep mechanical click. The entire slab they were standing on grated off to one side.

John leaped away with a girlish shriek he tried instantly to cover by coughing.

Charles bowed smugly, gesturing him down the revealed staircase. 'Welcome.'

'What the hell, Charles!'

'Hey, we're celebrating. What with my being suddenly un-married and all, and you offering to share your secret ghostie, this is the perfect time to dip our lip in something special.'

They dropped down into a pinkly lit space that could loosely be described a bunker, although the remnants of brackets attested it had been machinery that once cowered down here, not people. Now it was cluttered with any old arcanum somebody had thought looked retro, glass-fronted shelves bursting at the seams all over. Rattled with every step. Hate to see what evacuating this place in a fire would be like.

John couldn't take his astonishment off the centrepiece. The huge pink neon clock over the bar. It shed an unearthly rose hue over anyone who stood under it, not many this time of night. The digital display was counting down without a flicker of fear. So here at least was a venue welcoming the Flagship, proud to flaunt it in the face of the city's paranoia. Why cringe from the end of the world, mon chere—just cosy on up and toast the new one, where anything could happen. Where you could be anybody.

'Chaar-leei!' The bartender hollered, a stringy fellow with even less gristle to him than John, and not nearly so tall. Could scarcely peep over his own bar.

'Sanjay!' Charles boomed back, shoving his way to a stool and bringing John along for the ride. 'Good to see you! I'm treating my friend tonight, mate, so break out the fancy stuff. We're off to see a ghost.'

'Ghosts, now!' Sanjay rolled expressive eyes, dark as poured obsidian. 'What excuse'll you think up next? Armageddon?'

The obligatory sweet young things pulling drinks to either side, a lad and a lass like bookends, smiled weakly. With varying levels of courtesy they couldn't take their eyes off John's gloved hands, until he gave up and shoved them in his pockets. This was obviously their first Surgeon.

Flashing pretty was a cheap trick to bait the sad bastards in, queuing to drink themselves into supposing they were in with a chance. But it was the same worn out dog of a trick for every venue. If you drool, more the fool. Sanjay at least ensured these kids buttoned down, they would leave to run their own establishments one day. And he kept them virtuous to a fault.

'Bric and Brac,' he introduced them with a flip of his hand. Not silly, he wasn't handing the leggy adolescents' true names out to anyone, even regulars. 'Sorry about their goggling,

Surgeon. Don't get out much, these two. Keep 'em chained to the bar but it's for their own good.'

A joke, obviously. John peeped anyway because outside of his comfort zone he was an unforgivable rube. Snuggled right up under the pink clock, he could now see how most of the area behind the bar was taken up by a lumpen mass of machinery, the staff had to pick their way around. Whatever it had once been, bits had been lopped off and welded elsewhere.

'What is it?' he blurted.

'This?' Sanjay slapped the twisted bolus of pipes, he couldn't get enough of being asked. 'Friend of Charles, what you're feasting your eyes on here is the last hidden wonder of the city. Lost when the walls were built, the missing fourteenth hospital machine. I've got it cobbled up as a distillery.'

'Impossible,' he scoffed, which the bartender was also ready for. The young bookends smirked, right on cue.

'When you want the best, the rarest drink in the city, *this* is where you come.' Bending to a spigot he filled two smeared glasses. 'Some claim but a single sip gifts immortality, you'll live to see the end of the line. I've had punters stagger in to swear it gives sleep without dreams, a far more precious commodity.'

Hoisted one to let the light spark through, dancing rainbows across their faces. 'I call it the "tears of fools."'

Charles accepted his eagerly; he'd pour window cleaner down the hatch right now and say thankyou. John merely stared at his, set down on the bar in front of him. Blurred with fingerprints. Charles nudged the glass, a little annoyed.

'Get in there, you've never had anything like this, mate. And it ain't cheap!'

Sanjay squinted through the labial light at John's expression. Showed his own teeth.

'Your friend is nervous of the yellow death. He's a good lad to take such care of his liver. You should always treat it like your old mother.'

'I do!' Charles protested merrily. 'A sherry tipple every night, and shandies on Thursdays!'

'Bric, you're not busy right now. Why don't you set this nice man's fears to rest?'

Unless they handed them out at kindergarten the improbably comely lad had to be skirting responsible service minimum. With a frowning intensity he drew a tiny dribble from the tap onto a spoon.

Then filching a tea light off the bar he lit it with the tiniest "woomph," sending delicate flamelets curling across the surface. A moment held up for inspection and he flicked the spoon into the sink with a curse, shaking scorched fingers.

'Run it under the cold tap,' Sanjay instructed absently. 'You see, friend? Red means dead, just like my ex-wife's glare; but this burns as blue as my true love's beautiful eyes. What better drop to toast the paranormal, hey?'

'*Complete* furphy,' young Brac asserted from her half of the domain. Gender stereotyping aside she possessed that rare talent to work and chat at the same time. Other talents, too: her dark skin flawless, luminous with health. In the glow of the countdown it seemed she couldn't possibly be real. John took especial care not to stare, or at least not be seen. Exemplary Surgeon in the face of Sanjay's honey trap.

Didn't help that she seemed to harbour quite the brain in that elegantly shaped head. 'The city'd be wall to wall ghosts by now if they were real?'

'And how would you tell? Invisible ghosts are *invisible*.' Charles wiggled his fingers at her booga-booga style, and you could tell she wanted to slap them away. Always a charmer.

'You'd definitely know,' Bric asserted, throwing his two

cents in. He figured his hand all better but Sanjay thrust it back under the running tap.

'You know the rules, lad. Ten minutes for burns, even a bee's dick of one. Watch the clock. And don't let me catch you sticking ice on it this time, either, just damages the cells more.'

Brac wasn't about to let this one go.

'You believe in ghosts? Seriously?' Her sweetly shaped jaw on the floor. Just went to show you could work with somebody ever so long, and still have a few things to learn.

'Used to live next to one.'

'I call bull flop!'

'No, totally. And you don't have to see it to know it's there. It makes everything … not right, you know? My family went all weird. I was off school for weeks, just hiding in my room and it was like they hardly noticed.'

Sanjay looked unimpressed but Brac's peepers were big and round. You didn't have to wind her age back many years to be studiously *not* checking under the bed, *not* opening the closet, because it was safer not to see.

Charles at least looked delighted with the paranormal shtick. 'Come on, then. Don't spare us the oocy-juicy.'

'Dunno about "juicy,"' the lad muttered, finally winning free of the tyranny of the sink. Checked the spoon, it was cool enough to pop in the dishwasher. 'It was my Mum who started acting weird at first. Nothing you'd believe. Nobody but me seemed to see it.

'I read up on it later, and apparently if you've had a loss a ghost seems to *get* at you more. Mum's brother, my uncle, had passed away that year. I think they were close when they were little, but I hardly met him. I know she'd been thinking on him a lot, going through photos and stuff. *Said* it made her realise how important family was. But the things she was doing sure didn't back that up.

'One day the meat in my lunch sandwich was raw. Just ... raw and cold, slapped between two slices of unbuttered bread. I bit into it before I realised. That was one hungry afternoon. When I took it home and showed her she laughed in this vague, distant way and said, "What a silly mummy."

'That was for sure. I opened my lunchbox the next day and she'd put a rock in it! A rock! And she'd buttered it! Maybe 'cause I pointed out the bread thing along with the raw friggin' meat, I dunno.'

Brac stifled a snigger behind her hands. Her eyes clearly knew it wasn't funny. Bric nodded, getting it.

'Sounds silly now, but I cried so hard. All those other kids eating lunches from parents who loved them and here was me with my buttery rock.'

Now Charles snorted too, but his face was full of sympathy.

Bric smiled shyly at Sanjay. 'One of the reasons I love working here: you put on big meals for us during shift, and they're always on time.'

His boss clouted his shoulder fondly. 'Lad, anytime you're peckish on my watch you just say the word. Nobody does good work on an empty tummy.'

'Least of all kids. I certainly wasn't getting much out of school. Stopped even looking in my lunchbox. Safer to just hold it open over a bin and turn my face away from what came thumping out, whatever I heard. But things got worse when Dad started acting up, too.

'Might be brushing his teeth or something, and suddenly he'd start trying to do it backward. I crept up to the bathroom 'cause the sounds weren't right and he had his lips sealed over the drain trying to suck the toothpaste foam back into his mouth. I don't even know what he was doing. He asked me to do something but the words were all ass-about backward, I couldn't understand. And he got angry, this horrible backwise yelling.

'Started watching me at night, too.'

'What?'

'Just sort of stood in my bedroom in the dark, watching me. He stood in different spots, but his eyes were wet and I could always find the gleam if I looked hard enough. Staring at me. On those nights I don't think he ever blinked. And I always blinked. I'd blink, and he'd be somewhere else in the room and I'd have to find him in the dark all over again. Those wet eyes.

'I asked him to stop, during the day when he was more normal, and he said he wasn't doing it. Cross his heart, hope to die. That's when I started staying home. Slept during the day, so I could keep up all night. I couldn't *stand* him staring at me. That's when I felt it, 'cause I was stayin' home. *Cold*. A big blast of ice coming right through my bedroom wall from next door. Where the ghost was. But you could only feel it here.'

He put a hand on his chest, over his heart.

'I know it sounds crazy, but I was so relieved when I realised. Overwhelming. It meant my parents *did* love me after all. It was the ghost doing this to them.' He paused, until waiting became unbearable.

'And *then*?' Charles urged.

'I did what any boy would do. Wasn't much good talking to Mum, 'less I wanted to do it by banging rocks together or something. Come daybreak I marched straight to Dad and told him we had to move. There was a ghost next door and it was messing everything up.'

'Shit. He believe you?'

'He nodded in this slow motion way, but deep down he must've already known something was wrong. He wasn't stupid, even with his head messed about. Couldn't see a way out, himself. He was just waiting to be told which way to jump, and a pity it was left up to a kid but that's the way it goes sometimes.

'Before the day was out we'd piled in a cart with everything we owned, heading off down the street. Looking about, it was suddenly obvious all the neighbours were gone. We were the last to leave. It'd happened all around us, and we'd been locked in our place and hadn't had a clue. If I hadn't said something …

'I took a glance out the back. Was meant to be a last glimpse of home, but I looked at the ghost's house. And I swear the window had handprints on it, like something was watching me back. All dark like it'd been burned, and two pale handprints outlined in frost.'

Sanjay gave a slow whistle, shaking himself to work the creeps loose. 'Well I don't know about you lot, but that's the most disquieting shit I've ever heard.'

Bric wasn't done.

'Cover your ears, then,' he said miserably. 'The worst part came when we made it to our new house.'

'Shit, there's *more*?'

'Mum and Dad were already warming back to normal. They did a lot of hugging 'til the air was squeezed out of me. Dad got started on a special lasagne right away, to make up for all those missed lunches. Mum, well, for days I couldn't open my yap without her trying to cram food in. I was a real fattie for a while. I ought've been happy.

'But there in my new room I went to unpack my toys; make it *really* home, you know, spread some stuff around. I yelped, it was like sticking my hand into a barbed wire fence. As they came out of the box there were these long rusty nails driven through the faces of each and every one, every toy I loved.

'I did that. My bedroom was right next to the house next

door, I got the biggest dose. And to this day I have absolutely no memory of doing it, or even where I got the nails. Or what else I might've done. None at all.'

Wow. John might have kept that last part to himself. For a while Brac's shining eyes had looked set to bestow the ultimate in tender sympathy, but now ... now she just looked sick. They all did, and couldn't settle on where to look. Not at Bric, who might have spilled more than he meant to and done himself out of a job, that was for damn sure.

It took a stern sense of reality to shake it off and return to the sordid friendliness of the pink-hued bar. Or irreverence. John was their man. Raising his glass he toasted the whey-faced kid.

'To ghosts, hey?'

The others scowled but Charles raised his own dram enthusiastically. The tears of fools scalded like fire, going down.

It wasn't just the sister's apartment that had curdled by now. It was the whole street.

Even two soused fools could smell wrongness on their staggering approach. Slowing what had been an eager daredevil rush, as signals started prickling through to the pickled brain. Plenty of opportunity to savour it en route, that slick of rottenness that plugged up both nostrils and dragged your step. Until it was merely the fake bravado of the idiot at your shoulder that pushed momentum along.

Quiet, here on this street. The night time music tinkled on, but faintly. It fuzzed and cracked, subject to false stops that left the ear craning after the snapped melody.

For a while there would have been shrieks and weeping,

the stupid brutality of fists, breakable things hurled against walls. Breakable people. Quiet now because pretty much everyone with the sense remaining had packed up and left, fleeing the thread of violence and mental illness running through the gutters.

Those remaining could no longer save themselves. They had driven away any who might have cared. Poverty and ill-will on every side, sullen puffy faces ducking behind curtains. Only their obvious inebriation guaranteed the two men passage, because it marked them as belonging on this miserable street, where addiction sprang toward anything you could get your hands on. Consuming everything in a hopeless attempt to escape awareness, escape misery, the gnawing anxiety, even for a moment. Even knowing in intolerable bursts of clarity you only mired yourself in deeper.

Smashed goods. Garbage and turds right there in the road to pick your way around, squinting. Step lightly now. The street welcomed you. The street would swallow you whole, smacking its dirty lips.

'Shit.'

Charles dropped the bottle he'd been toting. It shattered with a crash that echoed faintly off the watchful buildings, spraying his ankles with dregs and glass slivers. Listing with the intense concentration required he opened his pants and began pissing right there in the street in front of man, God, and anyone else who cared to watch. Something he would *never* do: not polite, fastidious Charles. He couldn't even let rip if somebody was at the next urinal.

Degenerating right before the eyes, and it wasn't just the stupefying amount they'd drunk. Squinting comically sideways to avoid getting caught, John was struggling to see the man he knew. The decent man. He was unnerved to catch a return glance that glittered with sly calculation, from thickened features oddly stiff on the bone, like plaster.

How normal do I have to be to blend in? It seemed to be musing. *How much can I get away with?* A face like that spat "I love you" as a ploy, merely one more screw to keep you and your credit card around a bit longer. Would get you knocked up to achieve the same, and consider it a swell investment of time. It was a cunning rat-face that made John fervently glad the man's wife was far, far away.

But this wasn't *Charles*, surely, not deep down. It was the street doing this. He shouldn't be here. Could Bric's eerie tale be true? Was there something about grief that made one more susceptible? Anyone could career off the rails given the right push, even decent men.

Suddenly this little adventure didn't seem such a shit-hot idea anymore. John did a smart about-face to blaze the trail back out again. Follow the leader, boys. But stubborn liquored-up Charles was having exactly none of it. He grabbed John's arm which was right off the sanity meter in its own right, who grabs a Surgeon, even through cloth? Swung his reluctant guide back on course. It was what even the greenest dance novice would recognise as an elbow-wrenching do si do.

Must have made quite the sight: two grown men dancing in the waste splattered street, struggling to stay upright. Straight to the sisters' front doorstep, which even the maddest residents had turned their faces from. Where the neighbourhood's garbage had been piled high like offerings. Or, like a feeble attempt to keep the blight barricaded inside, save themselves. The heart of the storm.

'*Ghost*, you said.' Charles growled, giving him a shake that clattered teeth and John understood too well why nobody had saved the final residents of the street from the whirlpool that sucked them down. Why nobody came back for them despite their desperate need.

The degeneration was jealous. It wanted them all to itself, so it made them disgusting, unlovable. It severed the social bonds that might have dragged them free. Not even a flicker of decency would reach out to such animals where they wallowed in their filth, selfishness and brutality, and good luck to them. Harder and harder to remember this was something imposed on the street, rather than deserved; so much more likely to imagine them bringing it on themselves.

Seeing no other way out, mainly by virtue of being a soused moron, John began clearing a path to the door by shunting trash aside with his foot. These shoes would have to be burned later, and they'd likely go up with a blue flame. *Blue as my true love's eyes.*

Charles was less mindful and dug in with his hands. Plastic skinned bags had strained beyond bursting before letting go with great looping hernias of kitchen scraps and worse things, far worse. The indescribable, head-clogging stench was set to ruin his sense of smell forever, gut moving in involuntary hitching jerks that had to be tamped down as liquor broke for freedom.

It took a moment to realise Charles was chanting happily to himself, '*Ghost hunt, ghost hunt,*' in a childish sing-song as he flung spatters of scraps aside. Didn't even flinch as ragged tin cans opened up thin-lipped slices, because who doesn't love lockjaw? Lars would have had something to treat that in his quaint little mobile apothecary—Lars, in this scenario, would also not have gone shithouse crazy.

Finally they were through. The tunnel they'd dug through garbage with unsteady walls rising above the head brought back troubling echoes of the Festival of Lady Joy. You even had to duck and twist as you progressed, dodging not prodding tree branches this time but protrusions of corroded metal, eager to grate your skin off and push bacteria deep into the wound.

He badly feared yet another auto-da-fe at the end, every bit as dread as the other one. Memory scorched with a tree towering against the stars, drawing the awed eye, while people ran and screamed all around. The terrible shriek of a dog. And Mary's blonde halo of hair rising up around her face in even more brilliant flame. Exposing who she really was.

This might well be John's turn, come around at last, and most horrible was the tiny gleeful part of him that wanted to dash toward it. Save the "why me?" for those who did not know what was so richly deserved.

Buried in the depths of the garbage, on reaching the door he rapped on it with his elbow. The sharp little shocks of pain were refreshing, cleared his head a touch although they didn't make him any braver. Just like before, the panel swung loose at the slightest pressure, at which Charles made an excited grunting sound. The man shoved impatiently at John's back—*touching* him again, that crazy idiot. Shoving the door through the debris at its base, both men tramped forward into the foetid dark.

Thought the slumping, decomposing porch stank? Within, they immediately started hacking, delicately bred lungs rejecting the damp mushroomy air. They left the door flung open behind in a desperate attempt to inspire a breeze. Streetlight didn't probe very far through that portal and they had to steel themselves to leave it. The windows had been blacked over with what one could only hope was paint.

From the way the fellow blundered forward John figured Charles' unaltered eyes couldn't pick out as much in low light, and never could ignorance have been such bliss. Mere poverty, which sapped spirits, but wasn't degrading in its own right, had given way to utter dissolution. The very air was sullen. A place where violent squatters would kick holes in walls, shit in the sink, what do they care? And Charles was just flat out awed. Become a firm believer overnight in something he couldn't see.

'Do you feel it?' he whispered, slapping at his arms. 'John, do you feel that? The air *crawls*. Uh, it's gross.'

'Oh yes, she's here. We're not wanted. The *world* isn't wanted. We should go.'

He fumbled at John in his excitement and the Surgeon shrank away with a hiss of caution, at which the oaf was utterly unrepentant.

'She? Where is she? Is she in the room with us?'

'Not this room.'

'Come on, then!' There was only one other.

You didn't walk in here. You waded as best you could through the lumpen, queasily soft detritus. Stumbled over things only half seen. John held his breath as their slow progress squoozed along. Never mind Charles' pigheadedness; he was scared enough for both of them and a football team besides.

Sometimes something cracked beneath his cringing step, with the foot descending abruptly a hand or so, so he had to yank it free. When it happened he flat out refused to look down for even a second, and prayed as hard as he could that nothing he was walking across had once been alive. The remaining sister, buried down there? He thought not. He'd never heard of a ghost reaching out to take an entire street, she couldn't have done it alone. Nobody stayed near a ghost. Isolated and forgotten, the malign influence was supposed to become merely a dusty echo of resentment.

Both sisters were still in here somewhere, the live fuelling the dead. This was like a nightmare, all jumbled about. He'd stumbled into a nightmare. Only this was at least in part his own making. *You're not going anywhere*, Mary had told the living sister in her drugged haze because *he'd* wanted that young woman staying conveniently put where he could find her. His own dirty little secret. His stupid stupid plan that for the rest of his otherwise dreary days he could pop in to visit whenever he fancied.

John, split into two men; only one living, but that had to be better than never getting his bite at the pie at all. The sister would always be waiting, quiet in her secret little nest. A visit he could gaily wash from his hands before snapping the gloves back on. It was a fantasy a bare second of thought ought to have exposed as ludicrous, immature, and rapist-level selfish. Murder-level, maybe. Who knew what had gone on in here?

John and Charles halted in the kitchenette doorway, even jumping back a little as they discovered all of a sudden that they didn't want to go in there. Dirty glass clattered like nervous teeth at the abrupt movement. Thick dark fluid slopped from side to side, a vast mass that gradually settled back into uneasy stillness.

He'd told the sister she couldn't leave, and so she hadn't. She had stayed put in the fungal misery of the cheap flat. But you couldn't in a million years claim she had been idle, oh no. The sister who lived had been *constructing*.

While the neighbours bricked her in with sacks of garbage to be entombed forever, by the light of a single window scraped clean she'd gone on building. Even as the tears and snot ran down her face and encrusted there. Even as her limbs withered and belly pooched out with air, hungry, a gnawing background to the passing seconds.

Jars. A huge sprawling pyramid of them virtually filled the room. They must have been fished one by one from the filthy sacks of offerings on the porch, treasure from dross. The sister muttering and pawing through as the leash that tethered her to the kitchenette pulled tighter, throttling, drawing her back with tongue protruding.

The astonished, revolted eye moved haltingly over the construction. It was too big and convoluted to take in at once, you had to accept little impressions one at a time. Most jars had hardly been rinsed of their encrusted or jellified contents before being topped off with water and carefully eased into place by her skeletal fingers. Hundreds of placid little pools gazed idiotically up at the ceiling in a faceted stare.

John was reminded rather absurdly of champagne pyramids in the sunlight suburbs, with smiling faces gathered around to toast the faithful city. Only this was the exact opposite, a horrid secret tucked away in the dimness of this squalid flat. The stench was ripe. And some contained more than noisome water.

Now he understood, and he turned and vomited messily into the loungeroom behind them, not that it made much difference to the foetid atmosphere. Those blackened jars that ringed the base of the edifice had clots of hair protruding out the top like grass bursting from it spot. They had been stuffed in by the fistful and water dripped from their ends.

The dark fluid in the rest of the jars sat waiting for *its* prize, waiting. Gazing up at a threatening mass of dark spores that bloomed like thunderclouds across the ceiling. If you tilted your heard just right, if you were exhausted, drunk and strung out enough you could make out a gigantic face up there. Screaming, screaming as it plunged away through vacant space. Only in reality the face he was thinking of had fallen down, while this was a figure plummeting *up*.

'Ss! There!' Charles pointed, pawing at his sleeve.

The living sister was crouched in the shower, which was pretty much the only free space left in the room. Without acknowledging her visitors she rocked on bony heels and moaned to herself, a terrible sound without a capful of intelligence in it. Hardly recognisable as the wilful woman Mary had subdued with a handful of dust. Not the least because she had a new haircut to match John's. Her skull was ringed in crusted scabs where she'd hacked the hair away, impatient to stuff it in jars. The operation had already invited infection, weeping runnels of pus onto her thin shoulders.

She still clutched the orange handled scissors, brutally blunt, that must have been the wrong tool for the job and periodically brandished them at the air in front of her. Whether it was to display the shoddy implement or ward something off was anyone's guess, because the normal rules of behaviour were gone, gone. This was mysterious language, the dance of the broken and the damned.

Charles shifted uneasily. Of a different cut than the Surgeon, he was less bothered by the massive hair and water edifice than by the abject woman. Fun time was over. Not so easy, then, for even the most malign influence to erase decency in an instant. It had to take time with you, day after gnawing day, until it had taken all for itself.

'John, what's … what's *wrong* with her?'

John had to remind himself the hapless fellow couldn't make out what could be seen with his eyes. If they could swap, he'd have done so in a heartbeat. *Charles* couldn't see the flickering, warping ghost. How it was stitched grotesquely around and *through* the living sister in an impossible attempt to be bound to mobile flesh. But meat and blood were too intangible, too poor a substitute for the ancient bones of the city. How could it be expected to retain anything so traumatic as memory? The ghost was doomed to fail.

The ghost, rising up and around the wretched woman's head in a protective snarl like a viper's hood, was determined not to fail alone.

The living sister spared John having to answer, although

she didn't seem to have heard Charles. More like he'd triggered a response, a recording. 'I don't want to,' she chattered, and her eyes were huge and dry, almost blind with staring. *Flash, flash* went the scissors, but she'd never cut herself free from what wrapped her around.

The declaration wasn't to the ghost's liking. It tore at its hapless sibling with substanceless hands, poured every derogatory filth over the shorn head. Wincing, John was glad nobody else could consciously hear. Nonetheless Charles was flinching as though leaning into a foul gale.

The sister rocked harder, began again her tongueless moaning. Her personhood stripped away, reduced to a *thing*. Perfect match for what used to be her sister. Charles, the intrepid soul, edged forward. At the same time he impatiently gestured John to approach along the other, longer wall, like it should've been obvious.

John did not in any universe want to move out beneath the blotched, screaming figure on the ceiling. What if it could *find* him? But he held his breath and complied. Both slid sideways to avoid jostling the foetid edifice at the centre. He saw Charles' sneaky reasoning: the woman in the shower couldn't track them both at once. Then it came down to what on earth he planned on doing once they got there.

'There's a ghost here, isn't there?' Charles whispered, very briefly becoming the creepiest thing in the room.

He was trying to feel his way through a situation that spoke only in madness. And all the while the man he truly was and the warped caricature the ghost wanted to make of him flickered back and forth, seeking dominance. The outcome hinged on which version of him finally reached her, and Charles couldn't even be sure the woman trembling in the shower could hear him. 'What are you trying to build?'

'It's time to die now,' she whispered back conspiratorially, fading in and out like a badly tuned wavelength. Scratchy with the fever that was burning her up. In a cesspit like this it would scorch the life off her bones, same for anyone unlucky enough to be stranded here long. 'There was a party, and we die. Die, die, die. D' you know what happens next?'

Her face twisted slyly. Leaning forward slightly, eyes bugged wide. 'Then we go in the *jars*.'

Both men's eyes were drawn irresistibly to the centre of the room. To the mass of jars where dark water trembled without motion beneath its cap of scum. Mould reached over the rims in tiny tendrils, exploring the air. Held its breath for the plunge.

'Is that why you cut your hair off? To go in the jars?' Charles sounded gentle, but accusation stabbed at John with a look: Why'd you cut *your* hair off, mate?

'I don't wanna go in the jars!' she screamed, slashing feebly at the air.

'Shh, now don't be silly. Nobody has to get buried in those jars; why ... why *look* at them, love. They're all too small.'

'I'm supposed to do the rest next,' she whimpered, showing him the scissors.

'Too small, love.'

'Pieces. Pieces for jars. I don't want to, I'm scared. I started with my hair but it wants the rest in pieces.'

Now Charles and John's eyes locked with a new urgency. *Get the scissors off her.* A mountain of jars of filth between them, a primitive offering to appease what both threaded her flesh and splayed across the ceiling in shrieking torment, desperate to hold onto the world. More than enough jars for a human body ... if it were in pieces. Pieces for jars.

The ghost was orchestrating a burial.

'Charles, what the fucking fuck-fuck are we doing?' John

muttered, because he seemed to have some cockeyed sort of plan. *He* was all for getting out of there before his balls ended up at the base of his brainstem. They ascended a few more inches as the threatening splotch across the ceiling seemed to droop lower, yearning toward his voice.

'This ghost of yours thinks it's found a little buddy to keep house with. Well, I'm not having that, John. Not having it at all.'

Typical. The whiskey soaked white knight was ascendant. All he'd needed was one damsel in distress to straighten his shit out. He could draw infinite strength from the need to shield others in his big manly arms.

'It's taken itself a whole fucking street to play with—But this here's its *sister*, Charles, the ghost is her sister, you're not going to be able to yank her free with your boy scout moves …'

'Watch me,' he breathed, inching forward with itchy fingertips twitching ever so slightly.

John could just slap himself. He'd *challenged* him, called him out, and now he had to do it. Never Back Down: Chapter One, Page One in the book of Charles.

'Just watch me.'

No problem that couldn't be squashed by firm, decisive action. He'd learned nothing from his stagnant marriage. Of course, John had hardly taken enough wisdom from the vagrancies of his own life to go pointing the finger. Especially not when it came to where he was putting his clumsy, drunken feet.

Concentrating too hard on the next signal he stumbled. Bounced off the wall in his pinwheeling attempts to not tumble into the pyramid, botched it again. Just when he thought he had saved the day, he sent a single jar skittering across the floor. Black clotted water and hair spewed out.

Hell broke loose. At opposite ends of the audible spectrum both sisters began to wail. '*PUT IT BACK! PUT IT BACK!*' The ceiling swelled down. Panicked beyond rational thought John forgot what he was supposed to be doing. He dropped to his knees and began frantically scraping jellied muck back into the jar.

The woman stretched right out of the shower like a nightcrawler, scissors extended accusingly. Which was Charles' shining moment. He lunged, heedlessly scattering jars to the music of breaking glass, and hauled the living sister from the shower. Her scream topped out so high you couldn't hear it anymore.

Charles added his agonised bellow to the insanity ringing through the room. Everywhere he touched the ghost, threaded through the sister's flesh, his skin puffed up in nasty looking blisters. Some kind of flash-burn made from pure hatred.

But he had his prize and wasn't letting go for anyone. Still roaring with pain he began towing his squirming burden toward the minefield of the loungeroom. 'Grab her legs!'

John crashed straight through the pyramid in his haste to obey. Bulling forward as though in a fever dream, because the face in the ceiling bulged lower. Vast lips touched his scalp. Suction, a wet obscene kissing noise before he broke free. Grabbed her ankles. Able to see the ghost, he at least had the luxury of avoiding touching it.

'She's never going through the front door!' he yelled over her squalling.

'We're all going through!' Charles boomed back, ablaze with his own cleverness. They staggered across the uneven lounge, slipping dangerously in the vomit John had so thoughtfully sprayed about. Heading for the light. The portal that the ghost, irretrievably bound to the flat, could not cross.

Gaining momentum in the rush, their burden held like a battering ram, they charged the comparatively blinding glare of the open front door. The woman struck it and they stopped as though run into a brick wall. The ghost was threatening to rip right through the stitches of flesh.

Microbruising blossomed everywhere beneath the woman's skin as Charles strained mightily, a golden conquering hero, one foot outside the door and one in. Only John, fully inside in the darkness, could see that the sister clung onto the ghost as fiercely as it to her.

'Leave her!' he cried.

Thinking he was speaking to him Charles met his eyes across the length of the convulsing woman's body and smiled sadly. It was a gentle smile. Not an ounce of strain.

'Is that what you did with my wife, John? You left her because it was all too hard?'

Stung, the Surgeon shook the hostage. 'Let go!' Hoping for a miracle. 'She's not your sister anymore!' Behind, he heard the plaster ceiling of the kitchenette groan. Something was coming, reaching out.

The living woman's lips moved soundlessly. *My sister.* And he saw that she couldn't let go, not ever. An entire life the sisters had clung together, taking turns supporting as the world disappointed again and again. When somebody loves you best of all, even life in a crummy run down flat can be heaven. It was the Surgeon who had taken that precious sustaining memory and turned it into hell.

He tried a final gamble, a cheesy one, guaranteed to fail.

'Your *real* sister loved you! You damned idiot, your real sister would never want this!'

It hit home in the most unlikely of places. Her streaming eyes bugged, well past understanding anything but a world of agony. Her need to hang onto a sister who'd already been taken from her once. But the ghost also heard. Malignancy. Only fragments of what had once been a person. Reminded of a love it should have been impossible to remember.

It looked on its sister with eyes that were, for a brief moment, human. When understanding was destroyed, love would do just as well. It was the ghost who, with a sigh of regret, let go.

Charles, John and the woman caught between them stumbled out into the street. Coughing, the relatively clean air burned almost as the toxic fug inside had. Already they could feel the ghost's hold on the street lessening. Without life to fasten to, its influence was limited.

Charles laid their burden on the ground and rather tenderly brushed some of the muck from her traumatised face. It seemed to comfort her a little. John crossed his fingers and hoped for Charles' sake she'd play damsel a little longer than the friend, who had refused to accommodate the notion for even a day. Deep down the poor fellow didn't want a real woman, who was merely another jerk, same as anybody. Charles wanted an icon. A bright shining thread to weave through his ongoing narrative.

'John … *John*!' Engrossed in his abstract world he hadn't realised the other man was talking.

'What?'

'What are you holding that for?'

Holding what? Glancing down he realised he still clutched the jar he'd kicked over, loose hairs drying into the muck. Shuddering he tossed it back through the darkened doorway into the flat, then stripped off his fouled gloves and sent them after. Just like in basic emergency he tucked both bare hands into his armpits, keeping them safe until he could get fresh latex from home.

Were they really readying to march off and leave the ghost

standing there, alone, watching them from the doorway? While behind in the dark that thing on the ceiling heaved? Of course they were. Mortal attention only allowed one or two issues at a time, tough luck to the rest.

'We'd better get clear. Come on. Your place, Charles. We'll take a look at the both of you.'

Charles' sliced hand was particularly worrying, gashed open on trash. With her, you couldn't even know where to start. She steamed like she'd been napping in a dumpster. All of which was very noble, when in his heart of hearts he wanted to rip Charles' gently solicitous hands off the woman.

A lost cause. She was no longer his secret, no longer his anything. And when Mary's red dust wore off she'd remember.

No way out.

'I want my sister,' she moaned, tears spilling free and Charles hoisted her up as he got to his feet, cradling her tenderly against his chest.

John's *motherfucking property. His.*

'Let's get her out of here.'

The figure in the shadows waited a little longer until they left. The alley in which she lurked stank. The neighbourhood stank. It was exactly the calibre of place she'd imagined for Charles, him and his mates. And here they were hauling a semiconscious girl out of the slum. A girl who looked drugged.

This was good, very good, but she could afford to wait for harder evidence. She had all the time in the world.

Once the street was empty the friend's mother tentatively approached the black gaping doorway of the flat, wrinkling her nose at the trash heaped on the porch. But she had to know.

'Hello?'

Unable to see the greedy arms that beckoned her.

Clutching her purse against her chest she ventured in, and it was like being swallowed up by night.

CHAPTER NINE

SEQUINS IN THE GROUND

WHEN JOHN showed up late and grossly seedy to their little save the city soiree the Captain remained primly unimpressed, bless her withered heart. *Lars* was impressed, and for impressed see scandalised, but his feathers were easier to ruffle. He hadn't been around the traps enduring the populace's antics for decades.

Also, John didn't turn up so much as was dragged in by Lars. Who struggled comically to keep a grip because John had gone and done as his fellow Surgeon had only threatened.

He'd sat on the slippery floor of his shower; nice and safe it felt, too, the sister had really had something there; and neurotically shaven his sticklike body of every hair. Practically down to the bone. He even did the profusely tufting crack of his ass.

It was a process undertaken across many hours and twice that in muscle cramping contortions the adult body was never meant to do. Surgeons being obvious strangers to the carnal arts, he'd not undergone this degree of joint strain since he was a baby stuffing chubby toes in his gob. Now those same toes might as well be on the moon.

Determined nonetheless, he'd worked right through the woolly end of his catastrophic drunk. On through the subsequent cascade of drowsiness, when he had to squint to make out one foam encrusted razor floating about the end of his arm instead of three. And finally into the home stretch of pounding, dry mouthed nausea. Lucky he was already in the shower, poised in case puking was going to be involved.

He would have gone on patiently scraping himself away to nothing were it possible. This must have been how Charlie-boy had felt to be plunked on the couch like a stone, playing with his defunct wedding ring in the dark. Laser focussed, with exactly fuck-all to be accomplished. Almost peaceful with the rhythm of it all.

As a wonderful side effect, the alcohol that was eating through his brain spirited away life's big questions. The overwhelming issues of the day suddenly going "poof!" because his sick, sick grey matter simply didn't have room. Sick, sick, sick. Post-shave-John's biggest dilemma was if he could succeed in crawling to the sink. Could he reach high enough to drink from the faucet?

Ooh. Lowered his head penitently back to the cold floor. Tile so divinely chill against his freshly scraped cheek. He could only hope the freeze penetrated far enough into his radioactive skull to crank that inferno down a few degrees. Didn't ask much. Only a few. His flesh clung to tile as though it were a suction cup.

Curious how one couldn't keep sticky fingers out of liquor, that delicious poison his body was currently hating him for. One returned, hopelessly, even knowing that imbibing was a temporary comfort. It carried him further from goals, not to them.

And what were those lofty goals? John groaned faintly against the floor, wracking his brains; he hardly knew anymore. He had desired, once, to become a great Surgeon. Now that burning ambition was like a story somebody had told, long ago. *This Surgeon, telling himself on faltering breath at the start and end of each day how the sacrifice would be worth it.*

Amusing, realising now that he'd never been happy. He desired just as powerfully to recant what couldn't be taken back. Not in this lifetime. Even this late in the game he'd suffered delusions of being a man, and what a laughable cock-up he'd made of that.

Once he finally laid the razor down, all that tiny prickly body hair mired in soap scum had to be carefully swept up in a garbage bag. He dragged it in fits and starts across to the fridge. For a moment a shriek clawed its frantic way up his throat to escape, flee the kitchen, because he prised open the fridge door, its cold blue light blinked on and in the stuttering strobe he thought he saw jars of hair.

Jars and jars of hair all lined up waiting for him to drink, to eat, stuff his gullet until life choked, such as it is. When existence, no matter how crummy, is threatened you suddenly wake up to how much you wish to keep it. But of course there were no jars. Merely crazy overheated lobes seeking revenge.

Into the bag's crinkly, collapsing depths he briskly dumped every open condiment he could lay hands on. Sauces, congealed pickles; gagging, acids and stabilisers sharp on the nose. Shook the now heavy, sloppy bag for good measure. Fond memories ... well, recent memories of the friend crouched in an alley, busily smearing his shirt across every slimy surface. *Don't want anyone doing black magic with your DNA.*

No we do not. There was at least one unbalanced mother abroad in the wee hours, rooting through trash for nuggets of blame. Anything that might satisfy her snarled sense of justice, justice being punishment, eye for an eye, didn't really matter who. Somebody had to be responsible. John certainly wouldn't put dabbling in the patchy dark arts past her. Once results hit the papers, no jury of the public would care how you came by them.

Job well done, he had passed out on the floor. Wedged into a safe nook between fridge and garbage bag, out of sight of any who might peer in the windows. Curled on his side in approximation of the recovery position, because any Surgeon knows unconsciousness is nothing like sleep. More of a snuggling closer to death.

Took Lars a while to find him there, not being in the bedroom where you'd expect.

'Where are we going?' It finally occurred to John to croak blearily, as he was being towed from his home. Lars shot him the kind of profoundly disgusted look he deserved.

'We're going to the *Captain's house*. Frigging hell, John, haven't you been tuning in to anything?'

'Oh.'

He looked down at himself, the bumping jostling perspective not quite seeming to gel with his body's movements. A crumpled mess swam into view, evil leaking from its very pores. Nice. He felt horribly denuded, which he was. Clothes were a distraction unto screaming, they *tickled*.

Lars, pressed and preened, looked like he was trotting off to choir practice.

'Do you think I should've stopped for a new shirt?'

'Yes! Yes I do, 'cause *that's* going to make all the difference. Really. Why didn't I think of it, you'll seem so *normal* with a fresh shirt on, you genius you.'

'Sarcasm is the lowest form of humour. We did that in grade school.'

'Do not tempt me today John because I will straight up murder you and claim you slipped on an oily patch.'

Customarily that would be the red flag to the bull, but he looked uncharacteristically serious with that frown swallowing his face. Best not push it. Clamping his lips shut John managed to stay quiet as the grave for five meandering paces. Ten. Holy hell, he was doing it!

In congratulating himself, concentration slipped. 'Are you carrying a bottle?'

'I'm sorry, was that a question? It's hard to tell without your eyebrows. People need eyebrows, John, It's an established fact of life.'

'It's sauvignon blanc! You brought sauvignon blanc to give to the Captain, didn't you? We're not off to a supper club! How much did you spend? It's gotta be at least three months of your paycheck to prove you're serious, you know.'

'Let me remind you the Captain has invited us to *her house*. The Captain's *never* invited *anybody* to her house—she could live in a hole in the ground for all we know. So I'll be red hot damned if I'm turning up empty handed.'

Silence for a few more steps. Blessed silence.

'Well, I'd've pegged her as a chardonnay drinker.'

'Death, John. Only millimetres away.'

'Just saying.'

Framed by the smug glowing enchantment of the sunlight suburbs, John's dishevelment presented as even more unnatural. Some wormy-looking thing, he was, shucked from its shell and blinking painfully in the glare.

A shell—that would be lovely right now, wouldn't it? A curling shelter of brown horn he could crawl into to hide. Shining through those striated walls the harsh light would be transformed into muted, comforting honey, and the city wouldn't be able to ask any more of him. Not of a pale knot, tucked into the furthest reach. Not ever.

A passing lady walking her dog glanced at them curiously … Was it pityingly? Her eyes looked flash-fried in that brief contact before she ducked on, the pupils down to nothing. John wondered uneasily if they should even be there.

'This one.'

Too late. Lars was halting them in front of a painted weatherboard that looked as brisk and scrubbed-fresh as the next. Quite the accomplishment of devotion and chemistry, given those plumb-line planks were hundreds of years old. And to preserve so many, so uniformly. No wonder they needed shining brass numbers on their gates. Like a hive, numbers were your only hope of finding your way.

Lars was looking it over like he was planning to buy the place, beet red with excitement.

'Do you need to widdle before we go in?'

No point. It wasn't at all in his power to spoil this moment. He found himself elbowed back like an embarrassing family secret; this one was *not* first impression material; as Lars got his other elbow out and rapped crisply on the doorframe.

The knocking set up painful ricochets that boomed inside John's disintegrating skull. Doubtless some relief lurked in Lars' little pharmacopeia, but the other Surgeon had clearly decided to leave his suffering friend to what he'd sown. John glared at his broad back, and weighed the cons of ramming that rare utility belt up his righteous ass.

'I hear you, I hear you. So let your fool selves in already!'

The Captain's voice could still impress when she let rip, defying what looked a solid timber barrier. Conscience couldn't help reminding John of a poorer portal, held together by posters and tape, that had creaked at the slightest touch and wouldn't keep out a fart. With the *Captain's* front door, once that bolt got thrown you were welcome to batter yourself on its impassive face until Judgment Day. Nothing more than a design conceit, as the house front was a giant bay window and the truly desperate could dive through its drawn curtains.

'Come on, then!' Bellowed like they might not have heard, or were too thick to obey. He swore he saw the windowpane rattle. 'I'm not coming to the door! You two are hardly guests.'

Sour hospitality wasn't enough to steal the wind from Lars' grandly billowing sails. Emboldened, he pushed through the unlatched door. And the wondering Surgeons set tentative foot inside a real sunlight suburbs home. They had never dreamed of being in one before, where the city's elite laid down their coiffured heads.

Whatever they'd been expecting, this sure wasn't it.

The light, for one. More light, *hard* light came spilling out when they opened the door than pervaded the street, which was already uncomfortably dazzling. And once you were inside it pounded down on you like the ceiling wasn't even there. Some digital chicanery, because John had gazed out from the elevated nest of the glass elevator and these roofs had looked like roofs. Tiles and what have you. Nothing special.

No wonder these folk meandered about with such daffy,

spaced-out smiles: they weren't happy. Just stunned stupid by brightness eating whopping great holes in their wits. Even the stolid citizens of Judgment had the sense to place a nice solid ceiling between themselves and the sun. Curtains on the windows, so when overwhelmed you could shut it all out.

The burning light wasn't the only oddity. Strange, strange; but stranger indeed was the chill entry hall they found themselves in. Given the cutesy exterior with its tasteful white pickets and lawn perfect as cake icing, it would be reasonable to assume some brand of folksy styling within. But no, quite the opposite. No poem of floral décor. The Captain's home was a bloodless manual on ultra-modernity, rendered in onyx marble.

Oodles of edges and corners, wickedly sharp, conspired with the light to cast slices of absolute nothingness on the floor. Far more like a tomb than a home. Frigid air and unforgiving light fit to peel you and show all. He'd never realised Lars had so many burst blood vessels in those cheeks, but this was a light to display how ugly the human body really was.

Not a great place to stumble around drunk, he thought, calling up his own safe, plump architecture. You wouldn't want to be clumsy. This house was a shark. It wasn't anywhere you could relax after a big day, or let your guard down, even for a second. Probably suited the Captain to a T.

Here she came, popping into the cold sterile hall from a side door to nod sourly at their shocked faces. The way they rubbed their goosebumps and boggled shamelessly about. Lucky this wasn't a social call, as two ruder visitors couldn't be imagined.

And the irritating old broad had those gloves on again. John was tempted to start touching everything in sight, merely to make her scrub it all down with bleach later on.

'They're all like this.' Waving a gnarled hand to incorporate the entirety of the sunlight suburbs. A special relish at their discomfort, their obvious desire to leave. 'Every residence. In fact, this is one of the "friendlier" ones. I got lucky. Even the nicest houses don't really want folk living in them.'

She glowered hatefully at the walls, which were swallowing light without giving any back. 'If you're fortunate you hit on one that'll at least tolerate you, grudging though it is. And you do your best not to piss it off.'

'Piss off ... the house?'

'A bunch of them are so downright vicious they stand empty all year, no matter how many souls are clawing at the gates to get in.'

'What ..?' Lars swallowed, attention roving. Impassive marble stared back. Black and veined like the negative of a frozen eye, one that could regard with alien dispassion from all sides, all angles. 'What do they do?'

'The bad houses? Depends on which you pick. They've each got their own box of nasty tricks. There's one at the end of this block, has this miniature plaster fountain on the lawn so pretty that people come to sketch it, sometimes. Never get their chairs too close. It's been known to magnify the sun like a glass. Just a little at a time, at first anyway. Burns in these itty bitty spots so you might think you've been stung. Then it gets creative. My neighbour ended up with skin grafts.'

Her face was ugly with the recounting, ugly as she glared at her house. If it cared at all about her spilling secrets, it gave no sign.

'Nobody here wants to hear about it, but sometimes I'm not even sure it's the houses.'

'What do you mean?'

John really didn't want that clarified, not a damn bit. Not with her liver spotted regret sagging off the bone like that, *older*, if it were even possible. But there was no silencing Lars outside of outright homicide, and she answered.

'Sometimes I truly worry that it's *A New Life* herself. I worry that she hates us. That the cities have always hated us, deep in their dreaming way, and that's why we lost contact with the others. Their cities woke up, somehow. Enough to rid themselves of the vermin.'

That was the Captain for you. You asked, you got it. Lars' hand released involuntarily, he had no nerve left. The heavy wine bottle shattered on the floor sending foam and chunks of glass everywhere. The sudden yeasty billow made John want to hurl and keep at it 'til his feet came up.

He mastered it the way a Surgeon did everything: by concentrating on his hands, spidery and withered in their latex winding sheet. Although she glared at it for a moment with her face gone parchment-sallow, the Captain clearly wasn't one for mourning spilt wine.

'Leave it,' she ordered Lars curtly. 'We've bigger things to worry about.'

He couldn't help but obey, but practically whimpered. You could tell he would be reliving this awful moment for the rest of his natural life.

John shuffled his feet nervously in the mess, half-expecting the outraged floor to rear up and take a chunk out of him. Biding its time, obviously. He wished he could levitate. 'Why doesn't anyone know? About the houses, I mean.'

Her mouth scrunched in a most unusual way. A smile *was* too much to ask for.

'Because if it became common knowledge, nobody would want to live here. The only compensation for getting stuck in the sunlight suburbs is how everyone envies you sick. I for one am not giving that up. Now. Get in here, both of you.' Retreating back into the doorway she'd popped out of.

Moving further into the cold house was the last thing they wanted to do. Red card for anybody with so much as a scrap of survival instinct. The two Surgeons edged obediently forward, Lars pathologically unable to quit fretting. His gloved hands jerkily described his gift as though he could wish the bottle back out of thin air.

Throughout their stalling she crossed her arms and surveyed John critically, his plucked and bloodshot appearance. His smell preceded him. 'Something gnawed you all to rags.'

'The city,' he replied shortly, an answer she might fancy given today's state of mind. It earned him nothing but a sneer. It stumped him, why she lapped up Lars' shameless brownnosing but from anyone else it jammed the board with irritation. Surely it shouldn't matter. Nobody ever said what they truly thought.

Speaking of Lars, the normally staid and predictable Surgeon broke John's train of musing with a strange manoeuvre. Walking ahead, before he had quite cleared the doorway he swerved in a determined u-turn to come straight back out again.

Which insubordination the Captain was well ready for. She blocked retreat with a firm arm. You could all but see his tail between his legs.

'Oh no. *In*, Lars.'

Intrigued, John peeked in across his friend's meaty shoulder.

Turned out Lars was a sight quicker than anybody had given him credit for. John went through befuddlement, unease, until he reached the same desire to flee, as surely as if he'd been fired at it from a cannon. Flee, before anyone caught them pottering with this. The closed curtains at the front of the house seemed a useless precaution.

For all its gleaming marble, still as poisoned water, the room they had entered was one of those inferior second-bedroom-come-study arrangements. Existed to catch flotsam from the rest of the house. It was pretty obvious no guest would be spending the night. Staring up at the—did the damn thing show stars, too? Or just light? All night long, where you couldn't hide from anything. Peeled down. Peeled raw, with the whole mess on display. What a nightmare.

The Captain had stuffed the room with a clunky blondwood table that fit about as neat as a plug in a hole, leaving you to scooch around the sides. The kitchen must've been left yawing empty, but never mind, their host obviously didn't put much stock in dinner parties.

She'd fashioned her own terrain map on the tabletop. Burned and gouged passionately right into the splintered surface. Not as beautiful or precise as what hung in the control room among all those delicately nodding flowers, but in this case far more intriguing. It incorporated many elements repurposed from around the house. You wanted to get your face in close, to marvel at the toothpick trees and glittering trenches of rock salt.

A big old record player took up an entire corner, plug slithering off to the wall, so it was meant to be played. From its spindle a multicoloured profusion of cotton threads reached out. Cris-crossing the tabletop through little steel eyelets hammered around the perimeter, a complicated embroidery suspended millimetres off the gouged surface. It resembled a maypole—John had seen pictures of those.

Not neglecting the Captain's signature touch. Little origami figures were pierced through by threads. Each had its own line, its own colour, just like the more official pathways of the cities in the control room. In fact, the whole still life gave the tense impression of a wound spring waiting. The table wasn't a table anymore. It had become a machine. She had shoehorned an unsanctioned second control room into her home. It was enough to see her removed from her lofty post, and maybe even strapped to one.

Alarming, really, to imagine the nights she must have spent labouring in secret at the end of already hectic days. Bent wincing and groaning over this, this effigy, the craziest school diorama of them all. It had been difficult to tell, with the drilling light and her face webbed up in cracks, but now John was studying her he was sure she looked at least as terrible as he did. Weren't they the pair of eager beavers, burning the midnight oil.

He also recognised his own stained little figurine saved from their last trip out, and his gorge rose. He wanted to smash it instantly, bring his fist down in the middle of that complex web like the hammer of a giant, ruining everything. That delicate, intricate machine. He wanted it ruined and his part in it, too.

Instead he stood where he was and rubbed uneasily at his narrow chest. The skin felt taut and irritated, as though pierced by an invisible line he couldn't detach, just like his tiny doppelganger. Affixing him in some convoluted way to everyone and everything else. When the spindle was set turning, he and the rest of the shebang would dance merrily along like the good marionettes they were.

Amidst all the gloom at least it was comforting to spot Lars' paper figurine stood next to his own. Both sheltering under the belly of their little paper city. Joining them was a third, in cream notepaper, a stark contrast to their hasty rumpled construction. The interloper was more an abstract glyph than a figure. But it made sense the Captain would fold her avatar in the shape of her true self rather than the frail vessel without. The result was more powerful, more doubt, but also more vulnerable. A wealth of private data for any with the skill to read it.

The threads of all three roamed away across the jumbled tabletop to, yes, there she sat in all her paper glory: the Flagship. Here to there, neat as that. John gritted his teeth but could hardly stroll on out of here and forget the whole expedition. He'd scarcely more freedom than his manikin, which would have to tear itself in two to get off the thread.

The strands themselves put him in mind of the ribbons you tied to loved ones to bind them close to your heart. Did they resent such intervention, as fiercely as he did now? Struggle for liberty even as you thanklessly laboured to save them? He was going to kick over a ribbon cart and trample it, next time he saw one.

Curiously in such a precise display, at the edge of the table rested a ball of scrunched paper. It looked charred, all flaky around the edges, spider webbed with the structure of the original fibres. Perhaps the Captain had failed in her first attempt at something and tried to destroy it, prevent one error skewing the rest. Or an accident with the incense, maybe: a bristling hedge of joss sticks stood to attention guarding the borders of the map, soldiers to cut off an escape. So why leave it there? It must have been too tricky to retrieve from that position, too many delicate lines ran right over it.

None of which was what had inspired Lars' retreat. Zeroing in on the table was all that kept John from burning rubber himself. The guest room did indeed host a guest, of sorts. One well worth recoiling from.

John took a horrified guess at "old man" by the posture, driftwood hands, lack of breasts, but that wasn't much to go on. He felt his own body quake without consulting him, trying to flee mindlessly. Spinning its wheels, but he was trapped between the Captain and that aged and gnarled hillock of hair. He would have to take his medicine.

The old man across the table was one of the downstairs people. Not secreted away like he should be, but sitting right out in the open, by day, for all the world to see. In fact, with so much migraine-inducing light pounding down you could almost make out the shadowy planes under that matted veil of grey swinging locks—but of course John would rather gouge out his own eyes. Let them have no faces! Let them remain alien and silent and confined to his nightmares.

The figure, humped almost double, seemed to be staring back and he quickly averted his eyes, grateful the solid block of the table stood in the way. You rather lazily got used to thinking of the downstairs people as *down there*. It was in the name, and life served up so many other things to worry about. They were sealed away. The bogeyman safely contained.

'Gentlemen.' Clearly using the term in its loosest sense the Captain broke the tense deadlock. 'As I'm sure you're aware, we are about to embark on an extremely illegal course of action.'

A grim little nod, confirming all eyes on her. 'So I've whipped up another serve of illegal, to really help round things out.'

'Sending two Surgeons out to investigate the Flagship isn't *that* illegal.' Grumbling was the closest Lars could get to insurrection. He, too, was careful not to look at the downstairs man, like taint travelled down line of sight. 'Punishing us would be a bit like shutting the window after the kids've snuck out—we've already been to Judgment and back. It's only irregular, smack on the wrist sort of stuff.'

'And what a magnificent job you did, too!' She shut him down dryly. 'From Judgment we learned a grand total of nothing, other than some obscure nature festival is somehow important to my counterpart. The stakes are now much higher and we can't afford any more fuckups. Gentlemen, this time I'm coming along.'

Yep. If you wanted illegal, that knocked it right on the head.

Nobody needed to voice the painfully obvious protest. She faced it every dawn as she forced her traitorous, crumbling bones from bed to confront another day of duties and demands that cared nothing for the woman trapped within. Beyond that another day, and another and another, right the way to the horizon. All of them flat and *boring*. Fired off a crooked grimace. You don't have to tell *me*, boys.

'If two top Surgeons can't keep me upright long enough to reach the Flagship, nobody can.'

That sounded awfully like a compliment.

'But you'll forgive me if I've strung together a few precautions of my own.'

Mm. That was more like it. Her stiff gesture took in the incense-ringed tabletop, the record player with its cotton threads and the silent, bent downstairs man, all part of one wonderful apparatus. Chill reeked out of the marble walls around them, and the light. The light speared down. Speared down. It transfixed intelligent thought to the floor, you could almost smell brains leaking.

'How is he here?' John asked bluntly, as nobody else seemed inclined to address the hairy elephant in the room.

'It's hardly like I've been sitting on my rump letting you two herberts do all the running and fetching. Some things needed doing that you weren't going to manage, not with all the fancy education and sweaty manful intent in the world. I wasn't even sure *I* could manage.'

'You're being awfully mysterious.' And annoying.

'Suits. Everything follows its pattern. There is a special

pattern only hinted at in the oldest city logs that's pertinent to our needs, and only three sheets of the required paper remain in the archive, although inventory says five. Reckon I'm not the first Captain to get desperate. Fragile stuff, soft as cloth. Difficult to work with, although I figure it never started that way.'

'Just what paper are you going on about?'

'The paperwork printed by the hospital machines when Son was born. *That* paper.'

She was talking about a holy relic.

'I snuck one of those three sheets out of the archive; only two now, should the city survive long enough to need them at some future crisis. Hardly my problem, I'll be long gone, and we have to make it through today's disaster. I undertook this alone, of course; you have to be alone for it to work. No family or friends. No loved ones in your life or it will fail. I brought that sheet home, and I folded one of the Blessed.'

John's bony knees wobbled, but he couldn't grab the table without upsetting something. Lars made an affrighted hiss through his teeth. Sure, the Captain stood resolutely before them now. Clearly the risk was over and done. But it was too easy to picture all that could have gone wrong, not the least her pitching over as a clot fired off in the attempt.

'Oh, don't look so horrified. Not so early in the telling, anyhow. Patchy documentation aside I was reasonably sure what I was doing. There's a trick to the folding, to avoid summoning the damn beasts into the city. *Not* something one can afford to muff. So I had my charm. No harm done yet. No sense in not going all the way.'

'If I may interrupt …'

'No Lars you may not. Any item, be it totem, machine or whatever, exists to be used, and at the right time. Until that moment it carries its potential inside, practically ticking.

So very dangerous to allow it to exist undeployed, to linger beyond its time of purpose. I swaddled it in a kerchief to muffle any mischief it might kick up, and I took it all the way down. Down, down through the city to the lower service tunnels. Those gated, closed-off tunnels with all the fluttering ribbons tied to them. Where the sounds of life fade away and clanking machinery rises from below on dank air.'

John had to prevent himself nodding along. Snuck a look at Lars for hints on an appropriate expression.

'*Not* a nice place. You should thank your fortunate stars, both of you, for safe coddled times. That you've never needed to go there. An oily current of air seemed to pull suggestively from the other side of the gate. Promising ... Well, whatever it promised, there was no way through. I tugged on the rattling wire and all it triggered was a blizzard of desiccated shreds of ribbon whirling about, blinding me.

'I unwrapped my folded message and pushed it through the links of the fence. A sudden, eager suction of air and it was gone, taking the ribbons with it. The fence rattled faintly. So I retreated beyond the drifting threads and motes of silk and sat down to wait. It took a while, but I knew it would. Dozed off in the end.'

Now she did grin, although for their ever loving lives the Surgeons couldn't see anything to be pleased over.

'When I woke *he* was standing over me. No expression to give anything away and I was too bleary to do more than rub my eyes and think, this is it then. He's either about to cave my head in with a brick, or he's coming back upstairs with me. He'd been holding one hand behind his back but no brick, not today at least. Instead, bending close with his hair practically brushing my nose he showed me my little paper figure balancing on the palm of his hand.'

What she didn't say was how it had been wet from the

tears that dripped out of his oily curtain of hair. The paper crumpled, nearly unrecognisable.

'I'm sorry for doing all this and involving him, of course I am, but being sorry hardly alters what needs doing. While you were lollygagging about we've been working together to build this.'

'I don't understand.' And the blue ribbon for understatement goes to Lars. He acted like the silent, still downstairs man might be foreign, unable to understand the language. 'This is all obviously to do with getting to the Flagship safely, and *back* I should hope. But why would one of the downstairs people want to help us slip past the … the thingies?'

'You will never find people without dissent, Lars, in any culture. It's the joy of individuality. Essentially I needed somebody like me. Age takes, but it also gives. More than you can imagine. I reached out for somebody whose hot blood had cooled. Who no longer leaped into hysteric action as a glorious and sacred calling. Someone who'd had many, many years to think things through for themselves. It takes time to acquire the mental toolset for such a dissection. No more the open beak which thoughtlessly accepts the spoon.'

'What you did was take a disgusting risk! Ma'am. How could you possibly know it wouldn't be some buck chafing for action who picked up your message?'

'I skewed the odds in my favour, somewhat.' Immensely pleased with herself now it had all come off, the terror and strain over. 'I went down there early in the morning. The earliest, when hotheads are snoring but those with worries walk alone. Our guest has joined us because he understands the Blessed *need* people, most desperately. The farmers won't do, they were never part of Son's pact.

'We may well be the last city left; it's what everyone fears. Should that same that's befallen the Flagship happen to *A*

New Life ... well, that's the Blessed done. No redemption, no return to their origins, or whatever it is they need. They'll be condemned to remain as they are, forever.'

John crossed his arms. 'Ok, so you built a map. How does it help us?'

'On a basic level the lines of salt act as a sort of barrier. Doesn't keep them out, but it does sort of dissuade them from wanting to cross. As we leave the city, which is the real danger point, our friend here will set further works in motion. The record player turns, see? The spindle goes gathering up the threads, drawing our icons to the Flagship.'

Seemed awfully complicated. 'Does it work? Have you tested it?'

'This can only be operated once, but I see no reason it shouldn't. The incense will waft across the board to prevent them scenting us. If they catch wind, no amount of salt is going to hold them back. Which brings me to *you* in particular, John.

'According to my associate here, it seems they want you very badly. You'll have to wear this at all times and hope for the best, because if they come after you bet your dollar Lars and I will be running in the other direction.'

What she handed over was a little pouch on a string. Spotted with machine grease and oil, obviously not new. To be worn around the neck. More ribbons, tying him tighter.

He palpitated the contents uneasily. 'What's in it?'

'His hair, of course.'

He couldn't have dropped it faster if she'd told him used needles and turds.

'Pick that up. I'm aware you've no idea what's good for you, but you *will* wear it. And you'll say a very fervent prayer over it for every night we're Outside.'

John obeyed, understanding at least that much of what

was good for him, but held the baggie as far from his smooth hairless body as he could reach. In sardonic response the downstairs man jittered forward. His first real motion, so jerky the nerves looked loosely connected.

He held his thumb, thick as any two of John's digits, over the Surgeon's paper figurine on the map, ready to crush it and wipe all those fears from existence. Without a face you couldn't really tell if he smiled. The Captain rolled her eyes.

'Less testosterone, more work. Go on, then. Get on with you both.'

The outfitter wouldn't even speak to John, not following the loss of the irreplaceable homing device. It was down to long suffering Lars to once again dig his charm out, sweet talk the shrill salesman in his narrow store. Dusty equipment enthroned on the walls like relics. When it became clear his presence did more harm than good John retreated to loiter in the street, pretending not to watch through the front window.

It was the sort of establishment where you'd expect to find some shrine to defunct technology out back, beyond the bead curtain. Some kept them, occupying a variety of slots between shame and defiance. The shop owner had had real tears in his eyes as he furiously ordered John out. '*Outside!*' he spat, an entendre that left no illusions to his ire. So doubtless his shrine was pretty extreme.

No pink clocks flaunting optimistic countdowns, not between these walls. Even ordinary timepieces, usually a favourite among techies, hung draped with sombre silk as though to blot out so much as a chance reminder of what was coming. The whole store looked as though it were bracing for a funeral. A matter of time. Well, whatever you had to do, to get through the day.

Finally, here came Lars. Puffing and lugging so much *stuff*! Including what they had to snafu for the Captain on the sly, and would no doubt get stuck carrying for her as well. The great stack of gear really drove home the daunting reality that once Outside, you couldn't just trot down the street for icecream.

No friendly farmers on this jaunt, either. If you went by the Captain's cobbled-together map, which had to be at least ninety percent folklore, they would be traversing a mighty chunk of nowhere. Three days out, three days back. Only on the sketchiest of crumbling archival records did the zone bear any designation, appearing as the wonderfully uninformative "NO CITIES." If John could invent a time machine, he'd a cartographer in mind who desperately needed a slap.

Assuming the Flagship had access to the same: which was presuming all cities stood equal upon launch, rather than Son's wealth divided up amongst the favourites; it was a sign of how damnedly important the obscure and rural Festival of Lady Joy must have been to that Captain. To have risked an altered route through that terrain, marked specifically and only "NO CITIES." Well, John fervently hoped the mystery woman from the Flagship got more out of her day at the farm than he and Lars did.

Having ventured once beyond the walls and rather surprisingly survived, the two Surgeons tried to convince themselves they were salty old veterans. While packing they passed bellowingly obvious advice back and forth.

'More bug spray. I'm *still* head to toe in lumps.'

'You think *you* know itchy! Remember those scratchy plant bits that got into everything? I swear, I found one in my foreskin. We're gonna need thicker socks.'

'How does that protect your foreskin?'

'I'm talking *really* thick socks.'

'Wait, wait. Seeds.'

John the amateur plant enthusiast was only just realising this with a smile of wonder, sitting back on his heels.

'Those were *seeds*, trying to get us to take them somewhere to grow. Just like in the legend of Lady Joy, remember? She had scraps of plant on her, and the farmland flowered in the desert.'

'Well, hitching a ride on my dick was a rubbish plan.'

'It usually is.'

'All our clothes went straight into the incinerator.'

'Yeah, but the plants didn't know that was going to happen. They just throw all their seeds out there, see what sticks and hope for the best.'

'Sticks, sticks—Sticking plaster! Hand me the box. Not taking any chances on blisters this time.'

'We need talcum. I ended up chafing red-raw.'

'And how does that help the plants?'

Feeling ready was the next best thing to being ready. Sort of. Busy preparation filled the void that stretched like nervous taffy between time and mind. Crowded out the fretting. Especially if you made it incredibly intricate and serious, like your life depended on it.

Until you stood beneath the overhung belly of the city with your nominal friend and a mad old woman, and suddenly clicked with toe-curling clarity you were *here, right now*. Nothing would have ever made you ready.

'Ready?' the Captain called cheerfully, the shorter veil bobbling about her head like she was wearing a jellyfish. The world blazed beyond the safe, enveloping shadow they cowered in.

'I *said*, ready?'

'Not really.'

'Me either. Oh well.'

She was the first to start forward, slowest even under her light pack and therefore in charge of setting the pace. The Surgeons exchanged a glance; wasted under the veils, you had to be in one another's skin enough to get it. They fell obediently to heel behind her. Really the old woman ought to feel a massive liability, but John found himself oddly comforted. In the presence of a higher authority success or failure wasn't all on him. All he had to do was trudge along.

Moving stiffly she poked her way across the landscape using two long aluminium poles to ensure balance, one to each hand. A genius system on uneven ground: even a trivial fall would fragment those chalky bones, no matter how indomitable her spirit.

She hesitated at the edge of the comforting shadow, and John wondered if she was going to do it. Not unjustly. *He* never would have, if it hadn't been for more pressing issues to mind both times. However, this was the Captain's plan. Insane or not, she intended to see it through.

She pushed on into the light. It was like seeing her erased.

They stepped into the open in pursuit, disoriented a moment, blind with the veils still adjusting. John hunched, remembering the downstairs man's tack hammer of a thumb descending. But vision cleared and of course there was only the sky. The sky was quite enough.

Lars had pre-drugged himself to deal with this, murmuring and giggling as they slugged forward beneath the heavy packs. He may have gotten the dose a tad high. The plan was to wean him gradually, as it wouldn't do to arrive at the Flagship a blubbering mess. Not when there might be people there, broken communications, and this all a vast misunderstanding. They would take the travellers in, throw a big party and then turn the Flagship back toward *A New Life* for a triumphant return.

'It's cold again!' They'd have to shout for some time to be heard over *A New Life*'s rattle and clank. She was not a quiet lady.

'Well, it's not always like this,' the Captain answered over her shoulder, voice of wisdom. 'Outside goes through seasons, and the weather changes.'

'Oh. They taught that way back in school. Only I'd forgotten.' Leafing through a primer may actually have been a bright idea. Too late now. 'What season is this, then?'

'Beats me. Cheer up Surgeon, the walking will soon warm you up.'

Had he thought this might be nice? Like taking a bracing stroll; and there'd been few enough of those in John's lifetime that might have tightened his muscles for this. Oh, stroll to the liquor cabinet, sure. Stroll to the bar. Stroll rather quickly for the toilet. Idiot.

Plus, he stank in very short order, despite the cold. It was unbearable trapped under the veil, he had to keep flapping the hem to freshen the air inside. Sweat blotted both armpits and turned talcum to slag. Perspiration pooled in the small of his back, where the pack thudded against razor rash. Although he was working hard enough to leak it cooled in the wind and chilled him to brisk fits of shivering, which were surely wasting his limited store of energy.

Lars kept glancing back at the city, compulsive as a nervous tick. John restlessly scanned the horizon, expecting the Blessed to pop out any minute. The Captain looked at neither. A lot more faith in the bone-rattling of her downstairs fellow.

Not that there was a lot to look at—this was a different environment than what the Surgeons had stumbled through to reach Judgment, but only by degrees. No cliffs here. *A New Life* was the only interruption to flat, flat ground over which the wind twitched, circled, and fled unimpeded. Grass to the knee mostly, in dun and ochre. Dry blades rubbing up against one another.

The occasional greyish tree was a treat, limbs low and clenched as though hanging on for dear life, lest the wind take them away. Overhead the flint sky seemed to go on forever, impossibly huge, drawing the wondering eye back to it again and again. Little ripples of cloud could scarce be discerned, it was all the same hue. When you *could* make out the clouds they raced in place while hanging still, brought dizziness if you stared for too long trying to work out the trick.

Even with frequent rests, the call to stop for the night couldn't come soon enough. And there'd be two more *days* of this before they even reached the Flagship. John's spirit pushed against the prospect in useless rejection; nothing to be done, except walk it.

Nothing special about this spot, other than their readiness to halt, which made this it. Truthfully they could probably have continued on a bit, but morale was at an all-time low. For the Surgeons that was really saying something.

After tramping about in a circle to settle the grass they got started on shelter, needing the light for reading the arcane instructions. They were to sleep in ingenious little nylon bubbles, held in shape by a light collapsible strut work. They had to be pegged to the toast-crumb soil lest they blow away like real bubbles.

Easier out here to believe this had all been desert. If you crouched and ran the earth through your fingers it was russet, a handful of dried blood, and sucked the moisture hungrily from your skin. The ground had been proving untrustworthy all day, only held together by the sturdy grasses.

The mobile shelters were probably the height of travel convenience *if* you'd ever in your live-long life had cause to assemble such a thing. Starting cold like a normal person was an abstract nightmare. All three struggled, swore a blue streak and even rotated the instructions, heavily annotated by the fellow from the shop which only made it worse. Until it became a juvenile race to see who'd triumph first, with underhand glances to gauge the others' progress and spur you along.

Despite creaky difficulty in so much as kneeling the Captain wasn't about to come last at *anything* if she had a say. Her spicy tongue as she fiddled about left Lars' ears like a set of radiator coils. John suspected her of sips from her flask on the sly to keep fingers supple. Not a lot of that precious stock, to be squandering it on some stupid competition her ego wouldn't let her lose.

To her credit, instead of gloating the win like a normal person she immediately made shift to help Lars: the usually composed Surgeon had his foot stuck through the door somehow and being flustered only made it worse. Flustered was not part of her repertoire. Now her methodical mind had unravelled the task, she could repeat the steps to infinity with quiet efficiency.

John was pleased to solve his own arrangements, *without* help, before they were finished. It wasn't much to crow over, but he would lap up all the accomplishment he could get today. The wind was kicking up in nervous little fits that would have been wonderfully refreshing during the day's long tramp. Blatantly annoying now. Taut nylon rattled in the breeze, struts arching so the whole thing looked like it was bowing politely to an invisible visitor.

Although there was no need, he nervously tamped the pegs in further with his foot. All too easy to imagine getting jolted awake careering across the flat, flat, flat landscape, bouncing and rolling helplessly.

Dinner wasn't much to write home about. Same as lunch: strange oily-tasting squares of rations. Exactly the type of diet to make one want to run screaming into the wilderness. Lars particularly suffered. It went against personal philosophy: why would a Surgeon, denied every other human pleasure, refuse good food? Their longing conversation was all about parmigana at the pub with cheese overflowing the edges, golden steak-fries dusted with salt, the crisp greenness of salad.

Sadly any kind of fire for heating food was out of the question, no matter their craving for comfort faced with so much vast and echoing strangeness. No, they had to get the rations, *special constipating* rations for when you *have* to keep walking, down their necks and struggle into bed before it became too dark to see. Even clicking on the pocket torches they carried would have been instant suicide, and batteries were delegated to another pocket entirely. Nothing would bring bloody disaster sniffing around faster than artificial light where none belonged.

In their adventure gear each had a sort of mat to unroll and lay on. A shiny cocoon of crinkly silver, no thicker than a sheet of cheap paper, was supposed to wrap them snug enough to sleep. Yeah—instead of lying mournfully, nursing their aches and wishing for home.

Lars had snuck along a second mat for the Captain. A *gesture* toward comfort. This time John couldn't fault him, he felt vaguely guilty for not thinking of it himself. She was *old*. Elderly enough to face challenges getting around the city, let alone foolhardy enough to trudge the way out here.

No matter how rubbish he felt as he stretched out to stare at the close ceiling, he hadn't been dragging the crushing weight of years all day.

Nylon rapidly darkened as the light failed. Faint rustling as his companions settled themselves. If two of the group hadn't been Surgeons they could have shared one bigger shelter, filled it with body heat. Obviously not in the cards. It was so quiet, without the sounds of the city. How was he going to sleep out here?

Then the meaty snores started.

John lay shivering from time to time as muscles that had overheated during the hike cooled, found *that* wasn't to their liking either and tied themselves in knots. He kept his veil on to ward off bugs. It puffed slightly with every breath before returning to rest against his face.

A cough from Lars. The wind whooped, subsided, whooped again and the grass rattled in applause.

What was *that* sound, though?

He lay burningly awake for hours trying to pin it, squirming every now and again as though that might make him more comfortable. *There*, that rasping. Right on the edge of hearing.

It was hair, he decided. All across his battered body the denuded hair was making a prickly comeback, erupting through cringing skin. The contents of the baggie about his neck fairly crawled with glee at the prospect, pulsing hotly against the beating hollow of his throat and jumping against his adam's apple as though inviting him to celebrate. He'd be lifted up and borne away on a magical carpet of hair, as though by millipede legs, to where, to where ...?

After a while, he slept.

'John!' The Captain called, her voice not overly loud but tight. It yanked him from unhappy drowse like a rubber band. 'Out here please, if you've nothing better to do.'

It still looked pitch through his shelter's thin skin, he couldn't have been under that long. But when he poked his inquiring head out with veil rolled back, the thinnest of grey light had spread uneasily through their camp. Not dawn yet, but close enough to peer by if you weren't picky. And from bruises to bites to blisters he was learning Outside was no place to be picky.

Mirroring him across the way the Captain's head protruded from her own shelter, no more willing to surrender her bubble of hard-won warmth. Twisting her neck she was frowning up at Lars who stood in the corral defined by their shelters. His arms were swimming in empty air. No, not swimming. *Embracing*. The portly Surgeon went about the gesture woodenly, the veil rippling with his breathing and it took John a few minutes to work out what was going on.

'He's asleep,' she confirmed, her mouth a line drawn by a laser.

'Uh.' He wormed his way free of the doorway. Immediately started to shiver and cough as the cold dug into his chest. Bare feet on frosted grass wanted to curl up like white worms and die, so he danced from one to the other.

He flipped up the other man's veil. Lars' sleeping expression was sorrow. A tragic misery John didn't at all associate with that round visage.

'He's stuck in a nightmare, is all,' he filibustered. 'I had the shrieking horrors all night myself. Kept imagining something was outside, feeling around for us. It's to be expected.'

Eager to fend off understandable concern. Surgeons didn't "hug" and especially not as Lars was miming now, squeezing somebody passionately to him. It just wasn't a native gesture.

Only in their dreams ... or in dank, sweating nightmare. Ever-conscious of their leader's critical eye he tugged his friend's sleeve lightly.

'Laaars? Come on now, you great lump. Wakey wakey.'

Happy or sad, the dream wasn't something he wanted to relinquish. Coming back to life reluctantly. Finally blinked dull crusted eyes in confusion.

'John? Leggo my sleeve, you're creasing it.'

That haggard look was already fading and he wiped his face tiredly with his hands. His *naked* hands; no wonder the Captain was having a cow.

'Oh look, I'm up already, how weird. Did we already have breakfast?'

'Wouldn't you know?'

'Yeah, like "rations" are so memorable. Brown. Did it have to be brown? What kind of foods are brown?'

'All the best ones. Come on, let's start packing up.'

John found the ominous mark as he worked to collapse his shelter.

He'd been walking around the structure, unsure what to do about the streaks of condensation. Wouldn't the fabric go mouldy if packed damp? Noticed a burned smell first. Sickly.

One year, it got so cold the water pipes had frozen and burst. Poor folk with no other choice burned chipboard, glue-filled off cuts in oil or chemical drums. A rank smoke that rasped the lungs, no tea towels stuffed into cracks could keep it out. The scent-memory was so powerful for a second he was back there, guilty anybody should have to be that poor, and worse for being irritated by it.

Half-hidden in the trampled grass he found a heavy line

of ash smudged low against the backside of his shelter. As though some scorched thing had laid itself down there in the darkness, as close to him as it could get.

'Heya,' Lars chirped, and he nearly launched himself face-first into the nylon.

'You are such an asshole sneaking up on me like that!'

'Phew, what stinks! Did you let one go?'

'My colon would've had to have died to produce a stench like that, so no. Something's been back here.'

Lars bent for a closer look, but backed off just as quickly. There were nicer things in life. 'Kind of creepy.'

'You *reckon*?'

'What's it doing on your shelter?'

'I don't know. Why is it always bloody well me?'

'Well.' He tossed him a can. 'Uncle Lars has a cure for what ails ya. Go on, yank the ring pull and it'll start to heat up. No fire, no fuss.'

'*Coffee?*'

'Heavy as sin to lug around, but I brought a can each for every morning we're out here. Just to, you know, make sure we keep going and all.'

'Lars, I hereby take back everything I ever said about you, and your parents. Will you marry me?'

The other man actually looked uncomfortable, pulling at his gloves, but of course wedlock was the ultimate off-colour joke among Surgeons.

'Quite enough misery in the world without us tying the knot. Drink up and let's get moving. The sooner we're there, the sooner we can go home.'

They came upon the trash vortex that second day. The stench

long before you could see it, decomposition's own rather special odour. Kicking through the outskirts first, a hinterland of plastic bags and chip packets snared in the ground so they could fly no further, flapping weakly. Cans next, and other bits of scrap crumbling to sepia dust. Less inclined to shift at a kick, so you had to watch where you put your feet.

It was an oddly familiar sight to envoys from the city, as though pristine nature had been hurriedly papered over to make them more comfortable. Only it was clear that all this waste was bleached and dry and older than old. The way meandered. Became uncertain no matter how fiercely the Captain fought to bring them back to true.

John breathed through his mouth as he threaded along after her poking sticks, and thought irresistibly of the trash piled high on the living sister's porch. Discarded, forgotten items seemed to gravitate toward human misery. To be encountering them out here felt very much like an evil sign.

'Oh!'

Lars went gingerly down on his knees, parting the sharp dry grass, paper cuts for his trouble. He'd found a scatter of children's marbles. A chipped constellation casting tiny shadows with burning specks at their heart. The pretty little things in such an unexpected place inspired a rueful smile. *Lars* wasn't one to see ill omens in every puddle. John would have marched past without ever crouching to look.

'I'd love to give them to the boy,' he murmured to John.

'What?'

'The boy, in the tunnel beneath Judgment. I didn't have anything nice to leave.'

John wanted to exclaim why he was *still* thinking about that, but then John wasn't, and which was worse? Sadly the newly discovered treasures were too well guarded to be gathered up. Lumpy ants skittered and waved pincers at these giants on high, big antlers on tiny scarlet bodies. Still, Lars might have knelt and admired them all day.

'I wish I'd thought to bring a camera.'

'You'd never be able to show anyone the pictures. Illegal, remember?'

'Yeah, but they'd help *me* remember what all this was like. When I'm old and crabby I could pull a shoebox of them out to remind myself that was *me*, I went Outside.'

The Captain snorted. 'Don't plan for old age. At the rate you're going, you're hardly likely to get there.'

'Ye of little faith.'

'Come on, Lars. We don't have all day.'

But it was what lay below the marbles that snagged his bowerbird fascination next. 'My God.'

'What now?'

'This isn't dirt. Look!'

Bending forward, John's pack almost sent him flat on his face, centre of balance was all catawampus. 'If it isn't dirt, well, what is it?' Nothing was as it seemed out here. Nothing was to be trusted.

'I think …'

Daring the Captain's impatience Lars retrieved a stoppered bottle from his belt and tapped drops out over his pinch of a sample, monitoring the frothy sizzle intently. A whiff of acrid smoke made John step back with his hand over his nose.

'Yep. This "soil" is almost entirely made of bitty bits of plastic. I wonder how long we've been crossing it?'

All three glanced with morbid curiosity back the way they'd come, but the view looked the same any way you turned. If there were any hints, they were hardly skilled enough to note them.

'But there are plants all around, look.' Snagging the

rubbish. 'How are plants growing in plastic?'

'Not marvellously, I'll bet. See how much smaller they are 'round here? And a sort of curdy white instead of the proper green or yellow. They might even be trying to break it down, same as the trees in Judgment did. Won't work very well with plastic.'

'Where'd it all come from?'

The Captain shook her head impatiently, drawn in against her will. 'The land is so flat, maybe the wind carried it here. It's had years upon years to go sweeping it all up. Some of it from the cities. Perhaps … Perhaps a lot was left when the desert receded. I've read the red sands were a place to swallow secrets, showing only a smooth featureless face to any who dared travel there. You wouldn't last long, sink down to join all else that was hidden.'

Her eyes glittered beneath the veil. 'Exposed, now the blanket of sand's gone. All the secrets the great desert once hid, broken and rotting, the unveiling come too late. Those who gave a damn are long dead. Just rubbish. If there are revelations here they can't harm anybody now. So walk.'

The gateway to entering the trash vortex proper must have been when they transitioned, grimacing, from kicking through rubbish to wobbling and climbing atop it. One Surgeon either side of the Captain, regardless of how she hated having their gloved hands on her. It was exhausting nervous progress and Lars was the first to crumble.

'Can we stop for lunch? I've a mighty craving for one of those dee-licious poo-brown bars of compressed sludge. Mmm, mmm.'

'Eat on your feet, Surgeon. We keep going.'

'Begging your pardon ma'am, but does this magnificent physique look like something I've cultivated by soldiering on?'

'The trash is slowing us too much already.'

'But …'

'Must I lay it out for you? If we fall behind I'll never be able to catch up. I'll miss the rendezvous with *A New Life* which'd be fitting, that bitch has always loathed me. But you two would have to go on ahead and deal with the city, using whatever we've learned. The future of our city would be all on *you*, you understand me?'

'Crystal clear. Pass me a poo-bar, would you John?'

'Stop calling them that!' Elbow bent back, fishing around in his pack. 'I have to put this in my mouth!'

'It's the way it squishes between the teeth, you see.'

'I hate you, Lars. Nuns would hate you. *Son* would hate you.'

'Poo-licious.'

Even without stopping the Captain made poor time. Her rage couldn't push her any faster. There would be no progress at all without her walking sticks, but they kept punching through the crust of garbage, getting caught up, and dragging rustling swathes of what looked like magnetic tape with them. The kettle had to boil over.

Finally she wrenched her arms out of their solicitous grasp.

'Would you both stop *touching* me!'

Glaring redly she backed a furious step, two, to put herself out of their reach.

'For crying out loud, I'm *fine*!'

And vanished.

Quick as that, like she'd been disappeared in a magic trick. Only the ragged hole in the trash to tell otherwise.

'Captain?' Lars wasn't dumb enough to rush blindly in, even in a panic. He dropped to his belly with an "oomph" and inch wormed toward where she'd fallen through. '*Captain*? I can't see her. It's too dark, or too far down, or too … Fuck!'

'Poke around.' John shed his pack, muscles rebounding into knotty overheated freedom. 'See if you can scare up some rope. Synthetic, or electrical cord, anything that hasn't rotted yet. And *don't* drop through yourself—I wouldn't have a hope in hell of yanking your ass out.'

Lars muttered something.

'What?'

'I said I'm looking! Jeeze.'

No rope, but what their investigation uncovered was just as good. Kicking over a chunk of disintegrating insulation John uncovered a smallish hole. A tunnel, burrowing at an angle into the fusty trash pile like a cosy animal den.

Hunkered on his haunches he stared intently into it as though he could pierce the dark interior just by screwing up his face. The sun felt hot on the nape of his neck, coming right through the veil and insects rasped in the grass all about, their chorus rising and falling.

He licked the salt from the top of his lip, aware of Lars standing silently behind him. Between lamb chop Lars and John the spaghetti noodle there wasn't much debate as to who was going to have to crawl his ass down there.

'This is a crap idea!' Silent observation was not Lars' chosen medium. 'What if there's something down there?'

'We're kind of hoping there *is* something down there. The Captain.'

'Tunnels don't just obligingly open themselves up when you need them, John. *Things* make them. And for the life of me I cannot think of a single nice thing that would live in a tunnel. Not one.'

'Well I guess if I get stuck in there, you can put me on your list—I'll be living in a tunnel.'

'Except you cannot even remotely be described as nice.'

'I hope her pep talk earlier left you feeling brave. If this doesn't work you're going to have to go on without either of us and do it all yourself.'

'I feel sick.' He tottered and sat heavily on something that shifted but held. 'I'm going to be sick.'

'Cheer up. You always said you wanted to be a hero.'

'I want to go home. Being a hero sucks, and it's sweaty, and more than enough to make any normal person shit their shorts.'

'Don't go getting that confused with the poo-bars. Hey … Hey Lars, it's alright. You have what it takes. I know you do.'

'John, I solemnly vow that if you get trapped, I will make it my life's work to stick my leg in there and give you a major kick up the ass. And there won't be a single thing you can do to stop me.'

'Nice.'

With a hand over his eyes John ceremoniously doffed his veil, hissing painfully at what came flooding between his fingers. He'd prefer to keep it, but the sodding thing was guaranteed to snag.

'Wish me luck, then.'

'You've got one hour and then I'm eating all your food.'

'Good. That'll be you *and* the tunnel plugged.'

The edges of the hole only barely allowed his narrow shoulders. It was a case of pulling himself along with arms stretched in front, airing the full rank glory of his armpits. Pushing with toes, and eyes clamped shut until he was well clear of the entrance. Then he cautiously cracked both and immediately felt better, despite the clouds of duff that puffed into them.

No more sky. None. The embrace of walls all around— seriously, it wasn't ideal, but he could get used to this. Even with the air so hot, from sun above and decomposition below. Thick with fibres of fluff and unpleasantly, sourly organic across the tongue.

More light ahead slowed progress; a hand had to be spared to protect his eyes. Inching along toward a predetermined goal he found himself wishing the tunnel might go on forever—*this* would be the rest of his life.

No sooner had the thought popped into his head than he tumbled out into a sort of chamber, a hollow in the midst of the garbage. Pushing himself up to hands and knees he forearmed sweat from his eyes to take a good look around: turned out Lars was right, you did need eyebrows.

Queasy familiarity made him sit back against the wall. This was no mere hollow. It was a room. A bedroom, that had been buried and hidden in the trash. A shaft of cruelly bright light beamed down from where the Captain had punched through the ceiling, so intense it left green-white ghosts on his vision that refused to be exorcised by shaking his head or scrubbing his watery eyes.

You could tell this was a bedroom, because straight as a ruled line that light hit and splashed across a bed. Everything else in dusk around the edges. And it was around the edges that he moved, wondering. The space looked as though it had been sealed and left to sit for years, perhaps centuries. Thick dust fuzzed every object into soft plush approximations, but all was as it had been, a snapshot of some long-ago life.

Quiet, faded and sad. Like moving through a photo of smiling faces nobody could remember; the fate of all photos, eventually. Old, brittle sequins crunched underfoot as he moved. Liberated from the dust they scattered spangles of light—he almost flinched but these were gentle, charming. Kind to the eye as the briefly illuminated this or that. He hadn't known light could be like that.

A dresser here, with brushes and a comb. Change and a

paperback on the bedside. A pair of old, scuffed motorcycle boots set down neatly beside the rug. On the bed at the centre of the room, bathed in the spear of burning light two ancient, faded bodies were entwined. The desert had taken care of them, kept them safe.

About the mummified throat of the woman a necklace of brilliant violet stones cast glowing shadows up at the two faces. The hue was too gaudy to be real but they had to be precious in some way, to have been worn to her final rest.

She had sat at the dresser; a little stiffly for they had been old, very old; and selected this necklace, just this one. Her reflection smiling gently at the man standing behind her, he of the boots. Helping her fumbling fingers secure the tiny clasp.

Now as they lay, his skeletal hand rested lovingly over the gems, upon her throat. He'd slipped gradually out of life clasped in her arms, feeling her pulse beat, beat beneath frail collarbones. Feeling it slow. Pausing with monumental love to wait for her, delaying in their embrace for the right moment to ensure that when the time came they stepped into the darkness together. Together or not at all.

You didn't need much imagination to feel this hidden room was special. Like a temple with its hushed air. A monument to the one time devotion held unto death, and nobody was left behind. It was a moment that existed outside time. Defied sorrow. And so, it had wrought a miracle.

The Captain lay across the foot of the bed, wrapped in a rug, almost as withered and frail as those occupants propped across the pillows. Their sunken faces seemed to smile gently on her as she slumbered, her wrinkled mouth fallen open and vulnerable.

The Captain *had* fallen. John himself had seen her drop out of sight. Somehow her brittle bones had been spared a rude landing. There were no footprints aside from his own, no disturbances save what he'd dared touch. All three occupants could have lain in situ since the room was closed. She might have slept on there forever, waiting to be found. Become part of the scene.

Squinting painfully against the light he overcame an almost overwhelming reluctance to touch her and shook her shoulder gently. 'Captain? Captain, wake up. It's time to go.'

Waking in that strange room, before coming fully back to herself, the figure blinking up at him was a confused and frightened old woman. So frail, wrapped in her blanket the way one would swaddle a child, with her veil draped loosely about her shoulders.

'Sean?' she asked hopefully in a cracked voice, shading her eyes against the light.

'It's me, John.'

She put a shaking hand over her face to gather her dignity. As she tried to pull the dusty rug more tightly about herself it fell to pieces. Impossible that she could have been wrapped so tenderly in the fragile ancient fibres in the first place.

'I was dreaming of my husband. Oh ...'

She caught sight of her bed mates and stared for a moment, taking it in. Then sighed.

'That's what we should have had.' Face hardened as she made the pronouncement, familiar lines of determination taking over but, ah, loss. Now you knew its shape you could see the loss.

'Did you lose your husband some time back?' John hadn't even known she'd been married, but you didn't get that old without losing someone. Hell, probably everyone. The reward of winning the race.

'The house took him.'

'The house ... *Your* house? Your house where you still

live?'

'Sean slipped and hit his head on the marble right where Lars dropped that damn bottle—the crack when it hit. I ran to him, thinking I could somehow fix it but there was blood coming out and one eye rolled back, he didn't know who I was anymore because parts of his brain were broken.

'I knelt beside him as he lay there in that light, afraid to touch in case I made it worse, scared to do *anything* and all that fear wasn't stopping the red pool from growing. All that *light*, so I had to see every detail of it.

'He looked up at me with the eye that worked and gave a confused sort of grin because he couldn't work out why he was lying on the floor. And he asked, "Did I leave the tap running? I can hear …"

'I worked out too late he'd died, and nothing I did could have made it worse. So I held his dead body in my arms, the way I should have as he was going. I'd have given *anything* to go with him as well. To just take his hand and go along, who cares where.

'Screamed like the blazes when they came to take him away from me but of course they had to, there was nothing else to be done. Patched up the back of his head to look like nothing happened before they gave him his jar. I loved his hair. Ought to have run my fingers through it, realised somehow that I wouldn't be able to do it forever, and taken every chance I had. But folk don't think like that. If they did, they'd never argue.

'Anyway, he died worrying about some imaginary tap because his wonderful mind was already broken, the signals darting about like fireflies, trying to escape. We never got to say goodbye. That's how real life works. These two,' she gestured at the figures on the bed. 'It's impossible. It's wonderful.'

He helped her to her feet and she viewed the tunnel they

needed to exit by philosophically. 'Could be worse, I suppose.' And took a swig from her flask for mobility.

John took charge of the light mini-pack she'd been wearing. For once her wasted stature was a blessing, wasn't much for her muscles to drag along. Finally they re-emerged into bright sunlight, where Lars was in the opening act of a nervous breakdown. Ignoring his questions, which came too fast to answer anyway, John shook a few ants off his veil and slipped it on.

They made smarter time for the waning half of the day, the Captain strangely invigorated. Or perhaps in less of a rush, she could seek better footing. She seemed almost peaceful, which wasn't good: what they needed to get through this was the woman at war.

Despite his concern John proved as incapable of riling her as he'd been at calming her down in the morning—it just wasn't within the Surgeons to stir the waters either way. She was clearly fagged by the time they stopped for the night, though. Chewing through one of the soft meal bars was almost too much to ask before she crawled into her shelter.

'Hey Lars.'

'Mm?'

'Can I borrow your scalpel?'

'No. What for?'

'Shaving. I'm itchy as hell.'

'That's the stupidest thing I've ever heard, even from you. You'd end up shaving your face off.'

'I need to do more than just my face …'

They were interrupted by a high, shrill wail. It rolled across the heaps of garbage and was lost in the deepening twilight.

'Please tell me that came from a long, long way away?'

'Somewhere back the way we came, at least.'

'What kind of animals do they have out here?'

'Crazy ones, from the sound of it. Crazy … big … hungry animals. Although that sounded almost like a woman. Anyways, I'm off to bed.'

'You *what*?'

'Big lot of fuck-all we can do about it. We don't even have any weapons, and it's hardly like we'd know what to do with them if we did.'

'You've got your field scalpel.'

'Ah ha ha, disease is the only thing I'll be fighting with that, thankyou very much. Anything else would be a perversion.'

'How about hair, hair's *like* a disease ..?'

'Good*night* itchy.'

The next morning a pillar of rank smoke rose from back along their trail. It was difficult to be sure but John would bet money it was where the Captain had fallen through.

CHAPTER TEN

FLAGSHIP

YOU'VE NEVER, John marvelled as he tramped along. Not *ever* in all your days laid eyes on true hysteria until you've seen bugs swarm. Scrabbling across their fellows to be first, primitive neurons so overwrought they were popping off like firecrackers. Driven mad by clicking lust.

Unsettlingly big, too, these insects. Hefty enough to bend your arm as they squatted in the cringing palm of your hand—thank heaven for gloves. And all the while staring up at you and in every direction with shimmering compound eyes that couldn't close. Eyes lit like the glow of hot sun through a scatter of marbles. Little stabbing beaks at the end of those pert heads, cocked this way then that, stab, stab.

But that had been in the morning.

Come late afternoon the flat, glistening chitin bodies were clustered so thick on the veils you had to scrape them aside to see. To the teeming insect masses such coy drapery was the ultimate tease. Incriminating dioxide and other lip-smacking chemicals leaked out, so they knew what was hiding in there.

Once, in a flash of morbid curiosity John had treated Lars to a hearty thump on his round sweaty shoulder. An angry cloud rose from the toiling man, droning like the snore before the choke. The sudden vibration as their wings hit the air was enough to split your poor bone-case wide open.

'You asshat!' Lars milled his arms fruitlessly at the air come alive. 'The ones on my back weren't bothering anyone and now look, they're everywhere!'

'Just wanted to check how many freeloaders you had on you.'

Queasy with the success of the experiment, rolling his own narrow shoulders uneasily in the confines of the straps. Did he feel *heavier*, somehow, beneath the dense twitchy layer?

'Let's not go starting any conversations about who's not pulling their weight.'

Met with bruised innocence because of course John pulled his weight, point of pride and all that. It just never occurred to him to lift a finger more.

'But why so *many* of them all of a sudden? Yesterday we had a few crawlies, but this is like the bugpocalypse!'

The Captain, leading the way, half turned back at their antics. Or at least a mass of insects *shaped* like her did. You had to take it on faith she was in there.

'There has to be something different up ahead.' She tapped

her bugs-shaped-like-a-foot, with them dripping off at the movement. 'The surface of the garbage is baked into a hard crust, like it's been here forever. Not exactly a smorgasbord for vermin.'

'Ok ..?' Concluded on upward infliction, waiting for the other shoe to drop.

'We're talking resources, Lars. Resources dictate population explosions. This is a big bang if ever I've seen one.'

The same out here as within the city where she bit her nails over baby booms. To maintain *A New Life*'s quo bounty had to be strictly regulated: fancy chocolate, soppy films. If births dipped, bodice-rippers were poised to flood the market.

First it was bugs. The first harbingers.

Next, sound.

They entered the noise's orbit not long after, although all unknowing at first. It snuck up to you on the sly, initially buried in the soporific whine of insects. Until it became so uncomfortable it refused to be ignored any longer. With gritted teeth John chalked it as a nine on the ominous scale, with ten equating to soiling your trousers. He should know.

Machines. Screaming machines. Iron distress that bounced from chance soundboards in the junked landscape, teasing, just as their presence teased the bugs. Winding their bloodied nerves tight about a steely little finger. It was inescapably mad, or maddening, to be unable to see the cause yet proceed in its direction anyhow. Instinct crouched despairingly in its cramped basement, long digits clasped over featureless head at their failure to flee.

Ever the martyr to comfort, Lars sacrificed a perfectly good hanky to be cut into earplugs. John hesitated. 'These are clean, right?'

'All things being relative. I'd be willing to bet money your ears are *not* cleaner than my nose.'

Held at bay, the onslaught became tricksy. So loud at times you thought you *must* be close; one more rise and tense anticipation would be pricked. Yet still long, painful hours of trudging to go. The sound couldn't be trusted. Bugs couldn't be trusted, either. What came next?

Birds. Birds announced they were finally on the approach.

Great flocks of smudged birds wheeling across the ... the sky ... that *thing* up there. All watery, thin clouds like streaks of semen smudged on a pane of palest blue glass; all calculated to make you feel small. Tinier. Best not to think about it. You could actually see flakes of filth rain down from the sky like dandruff every time the birds feinted and dodged.

Lars' massive bolder of a head tilted ecstatically back, tracing the flocks that bloomed and folded overhead. He swore blue he was ratcheting the dose back.

'Look at them go!' he crowed, and seen through his jubilation there *was* something beautiful about those crisp formations. They were like a language unfolding overhead.

'Bugs, then birds,' the Captain muttered, as bothered as John. Only she could mutter loud enough to bypass the stuffing in their ears. At least she respected her companions enough not to hide the bad taste in her mouth. No coddling for Surgeons.

'And the racket.' Somebody had to be master of the bleeding obvious: it wasn't about to be gently smiling Lars, so sauced to the gills he found loveliness everywhere.

Even as John scowled a smaller flock splintered off from the great pattern. Swinging overhead in narrowing circles to investigate these strangers, new things, these three blights on the undulating landscape. In an environment of such bare cupboards any anomaly was worth poking your beak into.

And Lars, bless him, had taken out one of his poo-bars

to crumble stickily in hand. Tossing the fragments to what a scabby wild animal might deem a safe distance. John crossed his arms disapprovingly, bugs clicking to accommodate the posture.

'That's your dinner you're throwing away.'

'That's right. Mine. To dispose of as I wish.'

'Just saying, I won't be sharing any of *my* delicious poo-bar.' Actually he would when time came, but that wasn't the point.

It was actually working. Birds came flapping down in their little shower of muck to investigate. Lars turned back to his companions, beaming proudly. 'See? Lars, friend to all the animals.'

Then the insects heaved up. The air clogged with them. Those that blanketed the travellers and untold millions lying in ambush in the surrounding garbage; they rose in a furiously humming mass that drowned the squealing machine cries, blocked out the very sun.

Grasping eagerly after the birds' descent, which was even now turning into a graceful parabolic retreat. Dirty but not stupid, oh no, and no lumbering bugs could match them in the air. So long as they could stay in flight they would remain free, safe, and starving forever.

All but for the brave, daring or desperate, who had been nearest to claiming the prize. The only way to win was to fall into one of the three categories, and this the risk you ran. This the penalty. The insects engulfed them as the rest of the flock darted away to freedom, freedom, oh the sky. They dropped helplessly from the air, smothered into plummeting stones by the weight of eager mandibles.

'Oh shit!'

Lars wouldn't be held back. He stumbled and lurched across the trash to where the birds he'd so cruelly lured had bounced to a halt, broken parcels delivered carelessly by the sky. Still thinking he could undo events. Give the brave, the daring and the desperate a chance to retain the air.

With his foot he tried to scatter the massing insects.

'I'm sorry, I didn't mean to …'

Apologies tapered off into a revolted gagging *urk*. He stepped back, not willing to witness any more. There wasn't a lot left. His winged glories already stripped down to twists of bleeding skin, braided about bone like a primitive fetish. It had all happened in the blink of a careless eye.

Worse, they still *trembled*. It would be a mercy to bring the boot down; but Lars was as unable as he had been to leave the wild to the wild in the first place.

'Don't throw up under your veil,' John advised helplessly. 'Just … don't.'

The other Surgeon almost hyperventilating. Staring around at the bugs which meant looking pretty much everywhere, even with your damn eyes closed.

'Captain?' John appealed.

'Ok. Let's just, uh, keep these veils on and keep moving forward, shall we?' She slowly withdrew her hands into her sleeves in case the gloves weren't enough. Her aping of a Surgeon's primary line of defence had always irked John, but without gloves those would be bleeding stumps at the ends of her wrist right now.

Still the most at risk under her lighter veil, but you wouldn't know it. She led them forward, stabbing at the garbage with her sticks. John could sure feel the weight of the bugs he carried now, every damned scurrying one of them. He wanted them off more than he'd ever wanted anything before.

Lars added a shot of guilty anger for good measure: bringing up the rear he slapped his arms about his torso as he walked, muttering *assholes*. He made sure to stamp, sending shards of brown carapace and curdy guts squirting in all directions. Equal opportunists, the insects rushed in to cover their dead in a living feeding carpet.

The machine wailed. As though to answer it the birds screamed to each other, riding in their slow gyre. Labouring up the next rise they found it overlooked a small valley, the first significant feature in the gently undulating landscape. Built out of anything other than trash it would have been postcard cute. John, Lars and the Captain looked down at the Flagship as she made her torturous way along the valley.

The city had legs! In pictures and models, all of which were old and likely not of the best quality, John had always taken them for antenna but the Flagship had *legs*. Perhaps for traversing variable terrain as it went from city to city.

But now with metallic bellows and cries the front legs pulled, and the rear dragged behind. Like a living creature with a broken back but infinitely more horrible on such a scale, so large and terrible she bludgeoned the mind and you wanted to scream like the cycling birds did.

'Resources.' The Captain pointed, and she was right. The Flagship created and was followed by her own ecology. The great cloud of birds scavenged in the trough she'd carved through the garbage by dragging herself along. Probably the source of the insects' population boom as well. A deep trench of exposed raw trash sliced into the vortex's hidden guts, it stretched away behind the Flagship to the horizon.

Even more lovely than the waft of fresh organic stench ploughed up, a glutinous sticky rain seemed to be falling down there in the valley. Nowhere else. John would be the first to admit his understanding of nature was only so-so, and it took a long moment scanning the sky before he identified the birds as the culprits. Lars arrived at understanding too.

'I hate you, John,' he enunciated carefully over the racket.

They took the approach down the incline slowly, leery of everything: the footing, the bugs, hell, even the birds. It was a challenge keeping a wary eye on all obstacles. Horrified fascination kept dragging back to the city they intended to breach. You had to get past the horror to see details. Needed the smaller picture to understand … Well, understand as much as you could.

Easy to jump to the conclusion that this was why they'd lost contact. Except, the dragging was an adaptation that'd been going on for some time. Whatever the source of her injuries they didn't appear new. While you couldn't exactly laud it as a triumph it might be the best to hope for, when you had to keep going at all costs.

'How do we get on board?' John wondered aloud—that was, at the top of his lungs. Already out of breath chasing her.

Lars quickened pace. 'Maybe we ought to … *flag her down.*'

'You've been waiting this entire time to say that, haven't you?'

He nodded happily. 'It's the only reason I came.'

'Can't help but notice nobody's coming to roll out the red carpet. Not terribly neighbourly of them.'

'Three unscheduled visitors, approaching a city on foot. Surely you'd expect some fuss.'

All three looked at the Flagship again, searching hopefully for some sign of life or sentience. The great machine dragged herself laboriously along. Indifferent. John felt the first little chill slide down his neck that had nothing to do with the guano splattering from above. She looked … abandoned. Creaking, ominously empty. And if there were no people there, it was likely the sort of place nobody wanted to go.

'Speculating is getting us nowhere,' the Captain decided. She could sense their imaginations straining at the leash.

'So what do we do?'

'What would you like to do?' Calm. Easygoing, this new Captain. Useless to their needs.

John shook his head, not enjoying taking over the role as goad. 'Let's walk the perimeter. Find a way in.'

'Oh yes, walking is so fun. I just can't get enough of it.'

The most unpleasant aspect was passing in front of the city. Like *A New Life* her perambulation was sluggish, you'd have to be on two broken legs yourself not to get out of the way. But having that bulk bear down, especially in a valley where walls loomed to either side, made the knees wobble with a *run, run* message that had to be overridden if you expected to accomplish anything.

What they came upon halfway around the circuit was a message daubed in ash on the city's wall.

You'll never get in that way.

Crumbling arrows of carbon directed them along the wall. John's suspicion crystallised and he turned on his heel to scan their surroundings.

'Mary?' he shouted. 'You've been following us, having you?' *You need more of her red powder*, his nasty subconsciousness prodded, and he shoved it down.

Lars tugged at his sleeve.

'John, Mary's *dead*. She *burned*.'

A night to haunt them: bare tree limbs, flames against the stars. Mary's beautiful pale hair rising in an incandescent halo and the smoke. The deep oily stink of it.

John rounded on him. 'You have to be alive to die! You saw her face as her hair burned! You *saw* it!'

'She … she was all in flames … I don't know *what* I saw.'

The Captain shook her head at these two fools. 'You don't even know you're lucky to be alive, do you? What you saw was the mother downstairs. The thing without a face.'

They were both staring at her.

'What, did you think I was *unaware*? I saw full well what accompanied you when you set out for Judgment. What goes down does not come up in the city—but to see *her*. The mother. That's a real curse. Blacken your soul.'

Lars rubbed his arms, a chill that had nothing to do with temperature. 'And now she's out there somewhere, watching us? Suddenly I'm pretty darn eager to get inside.'

The arrows left for them were already starting to flake and puff away, and they had to step lively to follow. Stumbling at the Captain's best pace which was a risk in itself ... To a final arrow. Little more than a ghost. Pointing straight up.

'Crap!' John burst out, the least equipped to deal with being jerked around. That was all they were left with: a smudgy blurred mark on a wall. Too much like the mural in Mary's old domain for her not to be poking fun. 'I really thought we were getting somewhere. More fool me, hey?'

'But why would she ..?'

Doubting Lars put his hand on the arrow as though to check. Boy, did he trigger something. A loud clanking started into life overhead, loud even by the standards of the city pulling herself along. A balcony clattered into view up there, moving down the wall. Lars tripped over his feet in the rush to move back and John grabbed his arm; the veil might flip up if he fell and then the bugs, the bugs ...

It came to rest at ground level, attached to nothing but the blank face of wall. Magnets, it had to be magnets. The railing slid aside to invite them in.

'Huh,' noted the Captain grudgingly. 'A moveable access point. The Flagship was made to dock with the other cities, and every city is different.'

John very much liked the way she said "is" instead of "was." Like all the cities were still out there and this merely a vast misunderstanding. Tucking her sticks under one arm she stepped onto the balcony and the Surgeons had no choice but to crowd after, despite their aversion to rubbing shoulders.

The railing slid back to keep them safely fenced in and the balcony rumbled its way back up the side of the Flagship. They had to hold their flapping veils down. It delivered them to a metal hatch with a big clunky wheel at the centre of it.

'Get the bugs off you.' The Captain was already flailing at her own garments. The freeloaders weren't partial to heights, they dropped off at a touch, ripe for being kicked over the side. 'We can't bring them in, there'd be a massacre.'

'Do you think that's what happened? Something to do with the bugs?'

'I hope not, Lars, with all my heart.' It was too horrible to consider.

They checked each other to be sure nothing lurked in the cuffs. Pity they couldn't do anything about the artful sunbursts of bird poo, it went a long way toward undermining their authority. But great events seldom unfold in the manner you imagined. The more you obsess, the further from the truth: see, here came the rescuing heroes from *A New Life*. Covered with glory.

John and Lars spun the wheel to get that door open, it was beyond the Captain's avian wrists. A brief embarrassed shuffle as nobody wanted to be first. Finally John rolled his eyes.

With the door safely shut behind them it was so quiet. Only a faint vibration up through the soles of your feet as a reminder you were in motion. Comforting, that sense of steady progress toward a goal.

At the front the Captain clicked on her pocket torch. 'Huh. Some kind of service corridor. I fear we've snuck in the servants' entrance.'

'They don't really keep servants here, do they?'

'It was a joke, Lars.'

John held his tongue. He didn't like the way their voices sounded: flat in the narrow corridor of grey metal. Single-file only territory. Corners were not quite squared and a profusion of pipes and wires shared the dark space, increasing the sense of being crowded in. They pulled off their veils, overheated sweat chilling instantly, but there was nothing refreshing. The air tasted like a flat mineral drink, something left on the bench for days.

The improvised ear plugs came out, too. Before he could recoil John slapped his into Lars' hand. 'Thanks for the loan, mate.'

'Bleugh.' He dropped them on the floor. 'Your level of disgusting never fails to amaze.'

To avoid getting snagged and jerked around by the close, busy walls they had to shuck their packs off. Either carry it ahead, forearms trembling with the strain, or sling it off your front and risk getting pulled over when you tripped. Once he worked out how to get the batteries in, Lars ran his own pygmy flashlight up and down the walls.

'It doesn't look quite finished, does it? Back home this mess'd be tucked behind panelling, so bored fingers couldn't get at it. And look at these rough edges. They're a liability nightmare, peel your scalp clean off.'

'Well, I see lights ahead. I guess somebody's home.'

The corridor opened up to a lit street. A wide open space. And the clearest evidence yet as to how long the Flagship's spidery legs hadn't functioned as intended. Perhaps they had never worked, the launch a disaster. It was hardly the sort of thing authorities would document.

It was a beautiful neighbourhood, laid out under daylight tubes suspended from the ceiling on chains. All green lawns and hedges. Neat houses cute as buttons. But canted on a severe angle, like a town built on a mountainside.

The whole city dropped toward her ruined hindquarters. Every engineering enterprise had been first and foremost about dealing with it. The chains suspending the lights hung at severe angles.

Nobody was about, as far as the eye could see. Not a soul. 'Uh, hello?'

Nothing. All that neat perfection just waiting for somebody to come occupy it.

'This is weird,' Lars said unnecessarily. They were all right on that wavelength.

Most hesitant to emerge, John glanced back longingly into the dark, hard metal passage. The mind's eye could already plot the retreat: back out into sunset, the foetid garbage air and the screaming of the birds.

There was no retreat. 'Answers. Captain, we need answers, right?'

'If you insist.'

Hell-bent, her mouth a stern line she stalked across the lawn toward the nearest neat-as-a-pin house, as though she meant to interrogate it.

A stickler for propriety Lars jogged the long way around to use the path. He paused to marvel at the post box, which was a whitewashed miniature approximation of the same house they approached. Right down to the adorable chimney, which had to be cosmetic, you couldn't go burning stuff willy-nilly inside a city. Think of the air quality.

'There's stuff in here. I can see a tiny little teapot on the floor in the hall.'

'We're not here to play with dollies, Lars.'

'But it's so cute!'

Their divergent routes were why John spotted the aberration as he lagged behind.

'What's that on your shoes?' It hadn't been there before.

His and Lars' boots were clean; well, aside from the bird crap.

Grimacing on the porch she painfully folded as much as an ossifying spine allowed to examine her shoes. The grass had left behind a faint gold dusting. Iridescent and rather pretty, like pollen, which would make a lot more sense if there had been flowers about.

'Wait, let me.'

Lars whipped out a tongue depressor and scraped himself a sample, with a mistrustful eye on the lawn. Nature in all her guises had earned his ire.

'Hmph. Looks mineral. Some kind of residue. Maybe they're using fertiliser or something, I don't know. Let me know if you see two toilets.'

'*If* we're quite done fluffing about with our footwear!' Reluctant as she was, the Captain had a job on her plate. All this delaying would merely make that first mouthful more cold and congealed. She stepped up and rapped briskly on the door, with the Surgeons queued behind. Really they could be loitering outside any front door, anywhere. Paying a visit in a rather toity neighbourhood. If it wasn't for the breathless silence. Made them drop their voices, and amplified every stray creak or sniffle into a shout of *Come get me, I'm here!*

The bold knocking blew up and down the street like gunshots. The Surgeons cringed, while the Captain's spine stayed stiff as a bent poker. *Come get me* indeed. It also ruined the domestic picture for all three to be head to toe in guano that was starting to crack and craze on their clothing. Not the ideal guests come calling.

John tried to keep in line like a good boy, but couldn't keep his eye off the unnaturally still, silent street behind them. Now would be the perfect opportunity for something to sneak up. Or to just be ... standing there, watching them.

If he spotted anything he might snap and shriek himself hysterical in that way you can't ever live down. Not later, when you've got hold of yourself. Not ever.

Although if there *were* anything back there, living it down might be the least of their worries.

'Well I guess nobody's home …' Lars began hopefully.

Social taboos like privacy didn't cut much mustard with the Captain. When she figured they had lingered long enough, a little *too* long with their vulnerable asses hanging out in the open, she shrugged and opened the door. A nice neighbourhood like this, no reason for folk to lock their houses. Couldn't risk coming off as unfriendly should a neighbour need something.

They poked their heads into a rather posh entrance hall, light and airy, with floorboards polished bright as a mirror. They got no further. Stink rolled out. Just when you thought your nostrils must have died and dropped off your face, here came another one. Unique to its circumstances, but just as gut-churning.

Right there in the hall a man's body lay facedown, as though he'd been rushing to answer their knock and had tripped only moments before. His bulk was wrapped in a faded maroon dressing gown, all over in pulled threads, somebody's washer needed an overhaul. A tannin blotch had dried, marring the floor, where a ceramic teapot, cup and tray had shattered to one side. Even a biscuit in the middle of it, which was suddenly heartrending.

Whatever had befallen this fellow the most he'd been expecting, nay, looking forward to, had been a nice quiet cup of tea and a biscuit in the familiarity of his own home. Was that really so much to ask? A last ordinary comfort that had been denied forever.

At first they stared, dismayed but not really shocked out

of their socks. John thought absently that there must be a grandfather clock in the hall. He could hear one, rapping away the seconds, and it would suit the décor.

As a boy with his painfully skinny limbs he'd feared even the idea of such clocks. Wood, an upright coffin for nightmarishly thin people. Imagination whispered what might nestle in there among the ticking. Long arms waiting to unfold, unfold and unfold, to seize him and drag him inside. Even from way back his imagination was a jerk.

But there was no clock. The sound came from the body on the floor, only slightly muffled by the thick robe. A regular resonant *chunk, clunk*.

John's hands were creeping over his face—*hide, hide*, they tapped in Morse. He forced them down.

'Hello?' Lars tried, stepping in. He wasn't an idiot. The resident had clearly lain there some stretch of time, sad in itself, suggestive there was nobody to check on him. Or nobody *left*.

It just felt necessary to announce themselves somehow, even if welcome couldn't be extended. Indignity after indignity had been heaped on this pour soul, who had only wanted a bikkie with his tea. Now here they came trampling through, streaked in filth and gawking at everything. Lars wanted to be kind, somehow, even if he didn't see how it was possible.

John was progressing down another track.

'It's a bomb.'

He came to the realisation belatedly, fingers, tightening on the doorframe in alarm.

'Lars, don't touch it, it's a bomb!'

'Shut up, of course it's not. How many dead bodies have you ever seen that were bombs?'

'Sure mate, because that's something that folk who build sodding bombs think all the time: ooh, better not stick it in a corpse; I ought to show more respect for the sanctity of human life!'

'Are you going to help me?'

'Nope. I'm going to be right over here when he explodes. Maybe the Captain will shield me.'

All the while beneath their nervous bickering, that thread of ominous ticking continued. Having lain face-down the front of the corpse was rotten with pooled fluid, and resisted being lifted or turned. Lars couldn't use force in case the encasing skin split, then they'd be in it. He ended up persuading more than manhandling the poor sod onto his side.

The ticking became noticeably louder. Nostrils and mouth ringed with a yellow crust. Didn't take an expert to see that was not normal.

'Look at this. Same as on the Captain's boots. Don't think it's lawn fertiliser after all, not unless he was eating it.'

'We don't know anything about these people. For all we know, this is the height of their annual fertiliser-munching roundup.'

'Dead people aren't funny, John. We need to find somebody to report this to.'

Always the optimist, let the wheels of bureaucracy turn. He gently parted the neck of the robe to continue his examination, baring the resident's wattled throat and broad chest. And sat back on his heels with a disturbed grimace. John and the Captain craned over his shoulder to look.

Here was the ticking. The old man had clockwork set in his flesh. It was the strangest, most baroque thing they'd ever seen.

Old work, the skin puckered about the edges of it. And the intrusion was clearly cosmetic, as it had done nothing to keep him alive. Flesh failed, yet the gears clunked on. The sight was so compelling it was easy to miss other evidence. But not for Lars, who'd situated himself ringside.

'John, here below the … the thingy. These are surgical scars.' Framing the world in terms he knew.

'Rubbish. Looks like he's been snuggling a chainsaw. No Surgeon ever left scars like that.'

'Somebody here managed a real average job of what they were up to, that's for sure. But hey, good news, you know what surgery attracts a lot of?'

'Cramps?'

'Staggering hubris?' The Captain offered.

Lars visibly struggled with himself. 'Records. *Paperwork*. If we're going to get to the bottom of this we need to hunt down their surgery.'

'Excellent. Got any plans?'

The Flagship didn't rate as huge by *A New Life*'s standards, but she was still plenty of city to explore on foot. Naively they'd been banking on a *take me to your leader* scenario. In certain glassy-eyed moments as kilometres ticked by, they had even scripted a thankyou speech. Now you could put your tongue to the breeze and practically taste precious seconds squirting by. So far they had one awkward home invasion, and a dead clockwork man to show for it.

'As a matter of fact I do.' Smugness, your name is Lars. 'I reckon it will be just like *The Cutters*: not quite where the la-di-dah hang out, but close enough should they get any urgent haemorrhoids need looking into. As the houses get fancier we'll know we're going the right way.'

'Is that it, then? We're assuming they're all dead here, and going on our merry way? Everybody's dead?'

'He's right,' the Captain admitted reluctantly. Points to John were always difficult to concede. 'Head up that street. Random sampling, two houses each.'

One, two, skip a few. Lars wisely refused to set foot in anything that had a miniature bike or toys on the veranda. The investigation was really about letting brains confirm what sinking guts suspected. This time they kept off the lawns. What you don't know can certainly hurt you. Fortunately it was enough to open the door and shout, 'Hello?' Your voice failing and dying, along with hope. Answered only by a patient metallic ticking.

The eye refused to stop noting. Framed portraits in the halls. Those shoes lined up by the door. Terrible trespass, and they got it over with as quickly as possible. The only things that moved in the neighbourhood were bits and bobs of bafflingly pointless machinery, whittling the hours busily doing nothing. Waiting to be freed from flesh. It was an oppressive reality come home to roost. This house here contained dead people. And that one, and that one there. The same all the way and down the block, horrible, inexplicable, and so quiet. Enough to make you scream; except the Captain was no screamer and the others had to bide by her example.

A map would have been wonderfully convenient, but if wishes were horses they'd never go hungry. Instead at every third intersection they each chose a direction, advanced a block or so, then reconvened to discuss the lay of the land. Those mini-expeditions were the worst. Nobody liked splitting up, it was obviously a crap idea. John especially dragged his heels.

Any time he was on his own he seemed to catch a whiff of burning. Out of place in these wide, neat streets where not a single overhead light was cracked. Sent him scuttling back to the others every time. Nicer houses, and especially shops beckoned them onward. Money attracted commerce.

Depressingly, commerce garnered foot traffic, and so their other marker of success came to be bodies in the street with faint gold about their nostrils and lips. Pretty confident now that a fertiliser-eating trend hadn't swept the city. Nobody breathed a word of it yet, but their thoughts were beginning to flutter about the word *epidemic*. Epidemic was a bad word. Epidemic meant nobody would be going home.

Each body they came across became a delay because the Surgeons couldn't help examining them. The taboo of interference weaker for those sprawled on the pavement, as opposed to tucked away in the sanctity of one's house. These people had been shopping or promenading or whatever one did on the Flagship with leisure and credit on hand. Worrying the whole spectrum of human thought where *mine* is inevitably more critical than *yours* … Then suddenly they keeled over. Caught forever in that moment, train of thought halted.

'They weren't sick!' Lars yelled from the other side of the street.

'What?'

'They didn't feel ill, whatever it was, or they would have gone home.'

'You can't rely on folk to be sensible with their health. Remember, you came to work cranking a fever three days in a row, before I slipped you a roofie and took you home.'

'Yeah, but that was the flu. I wasn't *dying*.'

'So maybe these people didn't feel so bad, until it was too late. Or perhaps no symptoms at all, it was just really quick.'

He gently tapped the cheek of a young girl who appeared to have the lattice of a skeleton fob watch recessed into her face. The bones of her skull were holding it nice and firm, no sign of inflammation. You could pop the hood and see the void of her sinus behind gleaming, busy workings.

'How'd you avoid breaking your teeth on that? Eating very gingerly, I'd imagine.'

Each was so different with their ornate implants. Their own expression of permanence in flesh. Grotesque and dazzling. He'd only seen similar before in a museum, jewellery that had alternated exquisite beads and human teeth.

Yet they were also all wrapped in those mysterious scars, that bore no relation to the sprockets seated in muscle and bone. Something else had been done to them. Something not beautiful, that twisted and rippled their bodies.

John, the Captain and Lars peered through the display window of a top end jeweller. Here were all the nonsense widgets, inset with precious stones and laid out on velvet ready for implantation. True luxury items. The proprietor had slumped against the inside of the glass as he died, protecting his glittering stock to the end, and his eyes wept oxidised tears.

The Captain mused. 'Have you noticed their clothes, their hair? So plain. Plenty of wealthy seeming young people here and I've not seen one sporting a lick of makeup. It's like the clockwork was all that mattered.'

Lars stood back, blowing exasperated air to cover his fear. 'They can't *all* be dead, surely? It's not fair! I wanted to talk to them, ask them things …'

'I only wish to ask what happened,' she murmured. 'I'm beginning to fear we're too late.'

As it turned out the Flagship didn't have a surgery, not quite the same as *A New Life*. Blasphemy to say, but maybe they didn't even have proper Surgeons.

Instead the wanderers came upon a white marble building that looked grandiose enough to have collapsed the city's poor trembling legs all on its own. According to a large plaque set into the square outside it was rather imposingly called "The Lab." Inaugurated at the launch by a list of long-dead names. *This building stands as a monument to the endurance of the human spirit.* They were hardly likely to strike any richer. Luxury emporiums crowded on all sides.

A stinking, pinkish fluid had seeped out of the foundations of the structure as though forced from its pores by the great weight, to head downhill in long runny streaks. Staining the creamy blocks of construction. No tidemark indicated past floods, so this wasn't normal. No—along with the bodies littering the streets with their silent gold mouths, this was new.

Lars wrung his hands unhappily. It didn't take a genius to scry out their near-future. 'We're going in there, aren't we?'

John looked appalled, but the Captain merely nodded sternly. They were there for their city and no indignity, no disgust was too far. Couldn't afford squeamishness and, well sunshine, if you couldn't hack the course you shouldn't have signed on in the first place. Too late for turning up one's delicate pink nose now.

The Lab loomed, waiting patiently for them to make up their minds. Gleaming pale as chalk in the quiet. It stank, and would be like crawling into the worst part of yourself. Yet they were going in. The Captain said so.

John wanted to use the revolving door, because who wouldn't, it was just more fun. But a push found it to be mired in the congealed flood as though in honey, not worth the effort to get it turning. One more black mark against small pleasures.

Big glass entryways into the imposing lobby, which went up several stories just to make you feel small. Clear paths of exit, all up to code, but it hadn't done those inside any good. They hadn't even known that they should be fleeing. They had merely collapsed softly where they stood.

So gentle, no cranial trauma, more of a light swoon. They'd got hands out to cushion themselves, thinking muzzily "Well this is embarrassing" as the world went away. And they never woke up. No apologies and dusting yourself down as somebody brings a glass of water, and maybe someone else dials your loved ones despite your protests.

'What killed them came from outside the building, whatever it was.' Lars paced, his brow furrowed. 'Look at them, lined up at the glass. They were watching people on the street go down, wondering what was happening. And then it got to them.'

Wasted, John thought grimly, surveying the folk mired into the sticky mess on the floor. What a waste. Look at that receptionist behind his desk forever now. For all his duties he was probably considered no better than an ornament. And now all the dark and bright secrets tucked inside the lad were lost.

Their shoes went *schliik, schliik* peeling free of the tile, a noise guaranteed to drive you out of your ever loving mind. At least nobody could be sneaking up on them.

'But the pink stuff came from inside. It came through after everyone had died.'

'Now you're just making it up.'

'You know your problem, John?'

'Charm?'

'You've never had an eye for small detail. See how the wave pushed out through the lobby: it's built up on one side of the bodies. They were already lying here when it happened.'

One fellow close to John had come to rest with his face toward the incoming flood. It'd piled deeper on that side and buried his expression.

John shuddered. 'I suppose if we take a look at this one's pipes, we could confirm if he was still breathing when the stuff came through.'

'Do you really want to know that?'

'God no. I'd like to un-know it. Has anyone invented a scalpel that can slice out memories?'

'It's certainly at the top of my Christmas list right now.'

'Let's find out where the pink stuff came from, first.'

They backtracked the murky fluid's progress through The Lab, before it had spread out through the lobby. Offices, hallways and a jellified path under flickering lights. Splashes up the wall, where it had rounded corners.

Not too far in they started traipsing through actual laboratories—so it wasn't just a pretty name. Looking in every door with that uneasy paranoia that creeps up when moving through an institution you know nothing about; one with shiny sharp tools set on every bench. Nothing so sophisticated as a scalpel. These were unforgivingly solid, hack-and-slash sort of tools. Not far up from a hammer and chisel. As well batter someone to death in the hope they get better.

Until unexpectedly amid the strangeness they came upon something familiar, to the Surgeons at least. Heart animals. *Huge* versions of the heart animals, big enough to saddle up and ride. The friend would have shrieked for joy at the idea, missing the larger repercussions.

Here at The Lab they'd been growing organs on an industrial scale. Rows and rows of pens, floor after floor of them. You couldn't ask for easier subjects: uncomplaining, quiet, serious faces and big eyes taking it in as you went about your work. Kept in clean room conditions, they'd survived at least a while longer than their masters.

But the heart animals had never been intended to exist without care. Eventually in the absence of people The Lab's pens had become an abattoir. Pinkish fluid bursting from them in a great wave upon death.

'Organs.' Lars' curiosity was tempted to get into one of those stalls for a prod around, but if he did he'd never sleep again. 'The godawful scars—they were implanting organs. In *everybody*. I don't understand.'

'Then we keep going 'til we do.' Bewilderment didn't serve the Captain's purposes.

It turned out to be a case of following the bodies. Some sort of alarm had sounded, and a whole lot of people had piled down the same corridor. Attitudes of panic, grasping fistfuls of one another's apparel or hair, dragging them down as they fell.

In all the city this had been the only warning, and it hadn't been enough, for not a single soul was living. All the way to the heart of the organ farm. Most disturbingly their ticking had synchronised, every one of them. It beat loud against the ears, and nobody knew what it meant.

A final room, here, where everyone had been trying to get to. John thought of saying, *This must be where the party was*; but he'd stepped around and through a tangle of imploring limbs snatching after one more second of life. Willing to rip it from their neighbour if needs be. Levity wouldn't make him any less sad.

The room had a few lights out, a bit of damage, fittings dangling from their wires, but it was largely whole. Largely business-as-usual, even with the business all gone. It contained a massive cylinder of glossy black marble, a small room in its own right. At odds with the rest of the pale building with its efficient fussy spaces, it *looked* like it had been transplanted straight from the Captain's cold house.

You could tell the same idea occurred to her as she stared at her reflection in the polished surface. Like she'd come home.

One huge door to access the cylinder. And by the looks of it, only to be opened by a key of peculiar design.

'Mm,' Lars grunted, getting his nose practically inside the mechanism. 'Let me show you a trick.'

Putty from his belt, carefully poured into the lock. A hardening agent, and presto. He withdrew an ornate, wobbly lump.

'Amazing. Do you do children's parties?'

'Ah ha ha, you're hilarious. This is the shape of the key we need to find.'

'Hold it up, then.'

It was, they realised, a design they had already seen, all unknowing. Observed over and again in their journey through the Flagship. A shape embossed and ticking within the flesh of every good citizen.

'Oh gross. Are we going to have to violate some poor dead person to open this?'

There were plenty heaped up in the hall, but hadn't they suffered enough? John inspected Lars' face, pale and sweating like greasy tallow—Hadn't they all?

'Don't bother, hon.'

That voice. Disembodied and eerie in the gloom, and no longer even the slightest bit human.

'They were all built in imitation of a template. And you can't beat the genuine article.' From the far side of the room Mary stepped into the light. As genuine as you could get.

She was a smouldering jelly-mould of machinery and melted plastics in the vague shape of a woman. Her hair, all that exuberant gold hair burned right away. Nothing to hide her nature now. A thick toxic smoke poured off her. Somewhere inside she was still burning.

She had no face, but there were still some teeth pushed into that slurred mass and when they flashed John knew that she smiled. Instead of a loud tearing from the sticky floor, her feet made a faint *fss* each step as they caramelised it. A row of smoke detectors ripped from the ceiling in her wake. So that was how she'd been creeping around.

It was Lars she approached first. Ordinary Lars, who she'd taken a shine to because he was just a guy. He had no part in her centuries-spanning narrative. Not too close. His hair was already curling up in the heat that baked off her. To Lars she offered a loose handful of pitted marbles, like bright reflections of the sun.

Huge-jawed ants marched up and down that arm, and across her blackened scalp, biting, biting hopelessly. Hanging from their pincers with all their strength even though they must have known she could never be stopped. Their treasures were stolen.

She managed to roll the little balls of colour from her fused mitt into his cringing hand without sharing any of her passengers, and he juggled the hot glass frantically. Transferred them to his pocket before they seared through his gloves.

Then with a mad laugh she turned to the door. 'Let's see what's in here, shall we? Somebody meant for me to be able to get in.'

She plucked something free from her smouldering-coal face, a small piece of metal. With it she unlocked the door. The mechanism grumbled, stone grating on stone. The door came forward in one solid panel, then slid aside. Mary led them in.

Hard to process what the eye was seeing.

It looked like a man had exploded inside a machine. And that moment, that perfect hurricane of metal and flesh had been frozen, filling the room. It dwarfed the four intruders on their frail scale. So still you could hear a pin drop; yet the implied motion was so ferocious it almost threw them to the floor.

You would have to be a Surgeon to still see a man in all that. To trace the explosion back to its source and original form. A Surgeon, or something stranger. Mary, who saw without eyes, was incredulous.

'Son?' she whispered. As though she'd had no part in creating what spanned the room. 'How is this possible? Son, what have you done?'

Of course. It made a sick kind of sense. Who else but Son could captain the Flagship? Except it was also horrible that he'd hidden himself away in here, slowly turning into this … this thing. That made him hideously old. Almost as old as Mary herself. And despite his state, more of Son remained human.

For all his efforts he'd failed to shed as much. Mortal parts were splayed glistening before their eyes, wrapped in a sort of preservative cling film. Dissected from any coherence with the form that was meant to protect them. They hung exposed and pitiably vulnerable, looking tarry and mummified beneath their wrappings.

Mary's smoke crept among them.

'You left me. You all left me.' If grief had a voice surely this was it. Look what he'd done in the name of grief. Son could still talk, he'd made sure of that. Larynx and lungs were on opposite sides of the room, cable strung about like bunting.

He could make the case he'd been dwelling on for hundreds of years. 'I was afraid of my flesh, Mum. If I died, I didn't know where I'd go. All I wanted was to escape into the metal. But it couldn't be done anymore, no matter what

Disher said. I tried. I tried so *hard*.'

The boy raised by machines.

There had always been a quiet reverence to it, a sense of being special, but now John was getting an inkling of how things had truly been. Son had grown fitfully, stunted, and in strange directions.

And it had all led to this.

'Oh my baby, I'm so sorry.'

How do you put loving arms around an entire room? Mary ought not to be able to step forward at all. He'd ordered her away, just as he'd ordered all the machines, it was in her programming.

But little by little, as though battling her own limbs, she reached a wall. A wall that was more skin than wall, sagging in liver-spotted wrinkles. And she laid her loving cheek against it.

The sizzle filled the room, but Son cried out with as much joy as pain. With all he'd endured, what was a little more suffering?

'How? How can you now ..?'

'I'm burning up inside,' she murmured, nuzzling against him. 'It's all burning away. Oh Son, I thought you'd had a family. That you'd grown old and died. I couldn't have guessed … this.'

'Uh—excuse me?' John ventured.

The Captain put out her hand to block him. 'Don't you think they deserve the decency of some hush?' she asked hoarsely.

'We didn't come all this way to be spectators at a family reunion. We need *answers*. *A New Life* needs answers. We need to know what happened to the Flagship.'

'All my people,' Son mourned in a sing-song voice. A voice that was not entirely sane. 'They called me their saviour. Sang my praises, can you believe that? Even in schools, a chorus in praise of *me* at assembly, every morning.'

'It's tradition. We do the same in our city.'

'Well look about you, then. Look what I've done to my people. Their *saviour*. This is what I do, what I always do. No matter how I try.'

'But what *happened*?'

'I caught wind of some rumours at one of the farms. Judgment. Something I'd never heard before. Something about a celebration.'

With a wretched noise Mary buried her not-face in her burning, dripping hands.

'I grew obsessed with it. I had to know more. This Lady Joy, she was my real mother.'

'The only decent thing that bitch ever did was to give you up at the hospital! *I* stayed for you, *I* loved you!'

'But you left me. You left me, and it was like a … a sickness I couldn't let go of. The *human* part of me.'

'That woman was a sickness, but not you. Never you. Your humanity was what was *important*.'

'My sickness killed everybody. I thought I'd been so careful changing the route. If anyone could do it, should be me, right? I'd set the damn things going in the first place. But our passage cracked the ground, and poison began spewing out. Golden clouds of poison. It would have been beautiful if it weren't so terrible. And the city couldn't go any faster.

'All our plans had always been about papering over the past's poison. Whoever fixed up the landscape did such a good job of it, I'd no idea what was below until it was too late.'

John sagged. 'It was all just an accident? Our city is safe?'

We can go home?

'Eventually somebody on your city will make a mistake, just like I did. Maybe your Captain here, maybe someone else. It's so *human*.' Ants were climbing from Mary to Son. He paid them as little attention.

'Sweetheart, we didn't want you to be like us. We wanted you to be yourself. Human.' And look how he'd ended up, for their meddling. Neither one nor the other.

'Captain.' Lars was fidgeting, unhappy with the answers, unhappy with everything. 'Captain, we've stayed too long. We need to go.' Trajectories in his head, the two cities pulling apart.

'We're well past that now,' she answered serenely. She'd known it for some time, but her rage at failing had been stolen by the sight of two old bodies peacefully entwined on a bed. A fate not for her, but merely knowing it existed made the world easier to bear. 'You two go home.'

Oddly enough it was Mary who weighed in. Mary who'd no vested interest one way or the other. Mary who had never particularly liked other women.

'You can't do that, hon. Giving up when things seem hopeless is the most human mistake of all.'

'I've done enough. I've done more for that city than anyone else would have managed in three lifetimes. I've tended that cold heartless bitch, and she's never answered me. I've given her my husband and I'm *tired*.'

'You've never understood her, have you? Your city loves you, Captain. She wants you to come home. I don't think she'll be able to go on without you.'

At that the Captain, the woman of elderly steel, wept. It was a threadbare gesture. John and Lars almost broke down with her; they were so tired and emptied out themselves. Facing the prospect of trying to make their way home alone. All this grief split them wide open.

When the Captain wiped her splotched face you could already see the brief peace she'd been granted was torn up by the roots. Tossed aside. It hadn't been of use to anyone but her. 'How can I make it?'

'There is a way. It'll get you home ... But after that, I don't know how you'll live.'

'I'll live as I've always lived.' She made it sound like a curse. 'Do your worst, then.'

CHAPTER ELEVEN

ONE OF THEM

WHAT THEY did to the Captain was terrible.

The Surgeons were party to it. They stood by in that room and stopped nothing. Said nothing, even as the iodine splattered drill began to whine. Lars only stepped forward when the juddering probe took up a saw, slotting it into place with an audible *click* that promised horrific intrusions. Instead of crying out for sanity, he held up his field scalpel.

'I'll do that. She doesn't … she doesn't need your butchery.'

Candy bright blood flowed on the clean ceramic table.

Pushed aside the Captain's flesh thudded to the floor, discarded and already grey. Thrown away, become trash, just like that: part of the body that had served her faithfully, done its best. The skin that covered it, her lost husband had known it as intimately as his own, and with its sacrifice more of his memory was gone forever.

It was a rush job. She ought to have wept again, seeing it; that's what John and Lars did, violently. But she stayed grim. Lost in her own world. Perhaps it was the only place left to retreat to. This was her life's reward for devotion and struggle. The world always asked for more, and if you didn't give it would take.

Lars cut off her legs, but only to spare her what Son would have done, the Surgeon's every motion loathing. Son, he replaced them with machine legs.

A tripod of big ugly piston things that leaked and stank of oil, on a rotating base that swivelled to place each leg forward. Great swathes of tissue were cropped from her back and sides, replaced with alloy more apt to support and operate the new clanking limbs.

In place of the more normal months of intensive therapy she got drugs. Experimental chemicals. A horde of soft baggies strapped all over and piped into her withered form anywhere they could find a vein; the body that had endured so much and did not deserve this.

Son had never been blessed with the machines' talent for creating beauty. And his years of obsessive emulation had left little free time for developing his own aesthetic—otherwise, looking at himself sliced and wrapped to hell and back, he would have gone mad. He seemed quite pleased with his work. Other people's horror didn't mean much to him.

'You're going to need doctors when you reach *A New Life.*'

The Surgeons stood to either side of their Captain, loyal dogs. 'We'll take care of her.'

'There'll be no trouble with immune rejection. Once the drugs wear off, however, she's going to need to relearn … well … everything. From scratch. Do you understand me?'

'How can you be so sure about compatibility?' Lars demanded indignantly. 'You've just … mashed the bits together!' He could barely look at Son, and could not stop gazing at the Captain with great sorrowful eyes as she rattled and twitched.

Son sounded amused. 'It's quite the Flagship speciality. With such a small population we ran into gene pool issues early on, even with visits to the other cities. Kidneys especially haven't developed well in any resident for an extremely long time. Liver. Teeth. The heart. It all puts pressure on the heart.

'Our solution was to mature tissue here at The Lab and have it stitched in. Sadly, that cemented the problem. Our citizens could no longer leave to marry; not enough medical support elsewhere, not enough organs. And hardly any wished to cross over to our side once they got a whiff of the situation. They didn't want that for their children. The Flagship wouldn't exist without The Lab.'

'Wouldn't that be a crying shame.'

John saw trouble. 'Lars, let's just get the Captain out of here.'

'She's as ready as she'll ever be,' Mary confirmed, running the final checks with geisha deliberation.

The slower Mary moved, the brighter she glowed, with less smoke, but dripping trails of what looked like sizzling mercury. Smiling with those few teeth, no longer restraining the chemical inferno underway inside. Their faces and arms looked sunburnt from exposure to it.

'Get out of here, then, if we offend you. Go as fast as you can and you might make it.'

'Might?' John asked piteously. She'd tried to help him, once.

'What are you after, hon, promises? I can do that. I promise everything will be alright, and you'll all ride home on ponies made of fairy floss.'

'Oh yes, I feel scads better.'

'You lot aren't my issue anymore; I've already made it home. So now I guess it's your turn. If you can.'

'People usually get where they're headed,' Son sneered, and she turned her loving attention back to him, stroking the wall. 'Sooner or later.'

With a disgusted noise the Surgeons left Son to his mother, the door grating closed to shut out the world and keep them safe within his cylinder of black marble. To contain the heat, while it could. Son the entire room, and Mary like a radioactive coal in the palm of his hand.

As they exited through the glass lobby, the first of The Lab's fire alarms began to whoop.

John and Lars trailed a bit, unsure what to say. *Sorry* could hardly be enough. They couldn't believe they were leaving. The Captain's footsteps came in triplets now, with the heavy clank of a press stamping out numberplates. Step too close and she could catch your foot under one of those. Then you wouldn't be going anywhere.

On their way back down the silent street she ducked into one of the houses she had checked, huge clunking legs and hips barely fitting through the door. She emerged triumphant with two metal sleds on wheels, kids' toys for loading up with dolls and dragging about.

Words spilled out frenetically, the first she'd spoken. 'I saw these hanging in the hall when we came through and thought my God, the only way I'm making it home is if they pull me on one.' The shoe was on the other foot now. 'Don't look so sour. We need these. By my reckoning even the best case scenario will see the incense run out some hours before we're back.'

Lars quivered like a terrier. 'Shouldn't we be running?'

'Only if you think you can run all day and night, because that's what it would take. Let's be smart, instead of dashing about in a flap. Set a brisk pace to the end of the garbage, no stopping.'

'And then?' Because *that* wouldn't kill them.

She brandished the sleds. 'And then I take over.'

She was fishing out a poo-bar as she spoke, tearing at the wrapper ravenously. Part of the procedure had involved pumping her stomach.

'Captain, I don't think you should eat while on all those drugs …'

'Of course not!' she burst out, throwing the bar back in the bag. 'Anything *else* I shouldn't do, have or be?'

Sorry wouldn't cut it.

Back Outside the fresh rain of droppings rattled against the first layer, which had dried their clothing to a hard rigid shell. They had to take two trips down, as nobody could fit on the balcony with the Captain anymore, it had been bad enough trying to get back down the service corridor. The sound of her feet on bugs was the *crrunch* of fresh celery snapping.

John couldn't believe here he was, on the go, *again*. He thought lovingly of his apartment. Thought lovingly of just laying down in the debris right here. Draw a blanket of bugs to his chin and let it all stop.

They parted ways with the Flagship. Let her go on her journey, it was of no good to them. Let her carry her new cargo for as long as she was able. The canyon had lost enthusiasm and petered out, so at least they didn't have to climb.

John had become purely leg now, the only bit he was using, the rest was vestigial. But looking at the Captain, he knew it wasn't funny. Her movements weren't right anymore. Something to do with the nerves and the new signals they had to carry. A hack job, to get her walking out of the Lab. There'd be consequences.

To call their journey across the trash vortex "hell" would be an understatement. En route to the Flagship the Captain's pace had kept them back, made it bearable. Now she was the one flogging them along. The horror of the insects kept them on their feet for part the way. Fear was a wonderful goad, but it couldn't go on forever. Not the least because the bugs didn't go on forever, and there wasn't much terrifying about slogging your way through plain trash.

'Fifty-seven … hundred and fifty-eight … ooh, a pink one.' Lars' voice was a dull murmur to his right. He could barely crank his neck to look.

'What … What are you doing?'

'Counting toothbrushes. Pick something in the trash to count—keeps you awake.'

'God.' John rubbed his face. His legs plodded on. 'I still can't believe there wasn't … wasn't *anything* at the Flagship. No answers.'

'Maybe answers were too much to hope for.'

'WHY'D WE SODDING GO THERE, THEN!'

'Shh. It's ok, John. Just keep walking.'

'Why did we ..?' The air was rasping in his bone-dry throat, heaves. 'Why did we go there, if ..?'

'It will be ok. I promise.'

'Just walk.' The Captain cut across their chatter. It was easy for her to say. She was *built* to walk, now. 'Give me everything you have, Surgeons. We're going home.'

What she had, once they stumbled off garbage onto scabby grass, were two walking zombies. She had to tell them to stop, then physically halt them, both too far gone to understand. Operating at a level no better than trancers. No ribbon to pull them back. Her little wind up toys would have staggered on forever, trying to comply.

But now it was her turn.

Packs and all she got each Surgeon laid down in a sled. No matter if their legs dangled off the end. They went down blank-faced, then all of a sudden their clenched bodies seemed to realise it was ok to let go, and away they dropped into sleep.

The Captain set her face toward her city, and gathered up the ropes to pull.

Jolting and bumping across the ground had been soporific for a long time. This, however, was a different type of motion. Herky-jerky. Hysteric.

John opened his eyes to night, stared up at a full moon, buttery yellow as Mary's gleaming curls, and wondered where he was. His mouth had dried out. His eyes had dried out.

'John,' Lars croaked weakly.

Turning his head he found him, the two sleds side-by-side. The wheels had snapped off long ago, sliding directly on the cradle but brute force had managed where engineering let the team down. Forward motion had stopped. But they were being jerked and tilted from side to side. 'Are we there yet?'

'Shh. Oh please, just shh.'

Limbs responded on a definite delay, prying him up to spy about. They were so *close*. Bathed in moonlight *A New Life* lumbered and she was so beautiful. Two kilometres, maybe three. What did it matter among friends.

Lars urged quiet because the Blessed were out there already, pale escorts to the much larger shape. No more incense. Bowels clenching he lowered himself back down to reduce his profile. Bird shit and machine grease had to be all that was masking their scent.

'She's right there,' he moaned.

'Did I say shh? I have eyes. But we've got to find a way to get the Captain past these monsters.'

'Captain?'

Another cautious peek, scarcely daring to raise his head. The Captain twisted and jerked on the ground, entangled in the tow ropes. She trembled like someone having a small fit, although her eyes were terribly aware. All the baggies of medicine that had been tied to her were flat and drained.

'Please tell me there's some potion in your belt to fix this.'

'What? *No*, John. Bruises, a scraped knee, I'll fix them right up. But *this*.'

'I hate to ask, but what about your ..?'

'If I thought it would help I'd take this scalpel right now and slice those things off her, and you and I would carry her home. But this isn't something we can make better.'

The Captain raised her hand weakly. 'He knows we're out here,' she grated. 'Our downstairs man. He knows from the map, how close we came to making it.'

'We're not supper yet, ma'am.' Defying creeping terror. The feeling that closed down your airways, made you want to dig to the centre of the earth and never come back.

She shook her head, teeth gritted. 'I fear he's going to do something horrendous. To save us.'

The little bag of hair burst into flame against John's chest and he yelped, hurling it to the ground.

Smoke came down. It poured out of the night air itself and spread quickly, smothering the Blessed, smothering the city. The lungs wanted to hack it out; acrid and sweetish at the same time, a cooking pork sort of smell. They couldn't risk a single cough.

'Fire, again,' the Captain groaned. 'He's burning. We don't have much time.'

Lars crouch-walked to her side. 'It's not enough to get by them. Even if I can get her going these legs were made for travel, not sneaking.'

Sitting up John nodded, blew out a breath. 'Not sneaking, then.' He began stripping his pack off.

'What are you doing?'

'Well, you know how much I love running. Like, it's my *favourite* thing.'

'No, John. No. I've wiped out better plans on a bog roll.'

'You're not the boss of me. Get the Captain to the city.'

'Stupid, stupid …'

'Now's where you get to be a hero, Lars. Try not to ass it up.'

Before brains could reassert themselves John dashed into the smoke.

No visibility. No breathability. Only his heartbeat pattering away, and vague distant noises all around. You couldn't tell which direction they were coming from. One, at least, was comforting: *A New Life* was groaning somewhere out there. He'd been so close.

And soon, the following *thud thud* of cloven feet on sod. Rank breath stirring the smoke. They wanted him. Ooh, they wanted him so *badly*. Knew he was there. His taste in their mouths. But they couldn't quite locate him, not yet.

Shapes barely glimpsed—he'd lurch and backtrack, change direction frantically. His terrified, exhausted sweat falling in patters to the ground, whiskers huffing over it eagerly, they didn't need sight to follow. Pressing closer through his zigs and zags. Grunts. And excited whinny. Teeth clapped, so close!

John didn't want to die.

They were going to find him.

A flank brushed him, almost shunted him aside. The beast spun with an electrifying squeal but he'd already jumped back and let the smoke wind around. Eyes were useless, they couldn't see him.

He had to become one of them. Close enough that they couldn't tell.

Stumbling and weaving he stripped off his gloves. Hunched, shivering lightly. A hand extended, thumb jutting out in approximation of a horn. Still he sensed them feeling for him, for a mind sick with hot terror, for a screaming victim who would run, run, run.

One of them. He opened the floodgates and let all the rottenness fill him right up. The lust. The hatred, envy, the sly fear of discovery that prompted one to act normal. Grasping selfish brutality, the drive to take, to rent, to tear …

Another flank jostled him, softer this time. He ran his bare hand along it, luxuriating in rippling hide and bestial heat, muscles poised to explode in pursuit. Hot sickness flooding through his brain. The Blessed snorted, moving on, disregarding him as it would any of its ilk. All of them, crowding around. He touched them, plunged into their midst.

Charles, pissing in the street. Mary's hand shoving a girl back into her flat, for use. The rave, the rave. *Things* would be offered to him, tied to poles and he would take them, he'd *take*, screaming between his teeth he'd bite down and the veil all wet with blood, face revealed, the friend's face the Captain's face Mary's face the sister's face his face his his his.

A flare!

Lighting the way. Lars and the Captain had reached the city. They were trying to bring him home. Only, part of John *was* home amidst the rotting carnivorous breath, the impatient stamping and squeals. Bare hands, bare flesh.

That part of John wasn't *John*. It wasn't the sum of him. He wouldn't let it be.

He began shoving his way through. Raw livid hate at the top of his mind, where the Blessed's tongues flickered across it uneasily. But the man beneath, the thinking man, passionate for life, fixated on that flare and moved toward it.

A growl. A foot lashed out, not aimed but catching his thigh and numbing it, the worst Charley horse of all time. They were starting to suspect the trick. The smoke began to lift and he broke into a run, bare palms slapping the entryway and he was in, he was in. John was home. He gasped, the beginning of a sob.

A crowd awaited him. Not cheering but ugly in the way only herds of folk can achieve, passing it back and forth between them. The friend's mother stood at the fore, her hand clamped to the living sister's arm like a claw. Her eyes were two holes punched through into malice, and she jerked the sister's hand out to point at him.

'False Surgeon!' they screamed triumphantly, in unison, the sister under a new thrall.

And the crowd surged forward to take him.

CHAPTER TWELVE

GHOST

JOHN'S NEW DIGS weren't all that. He had settled on the finest moth infested rat-trap he could secure, four doors down from the sister's old flat. It was a quiet neighbourhood. The buildings between here and there stood tantalisingly vacant, but he could venture no nearer. The way some did with bee stings, by exposure he had developed a violent allergic reaction to ghosts. It was sure to be the death of him someday.

From his own window he could gaze freely at the ghost, staring back at him from her own prison. Funny how she looked so clear. Nothing else did. The heavily ridged tissue around his eyes ached, slow to heal. It had been intended that way, so he could think about what he had done.

John's eyes had been scoured with acid. Not enough to fully blind him, no, that would be *inhumane*. They had taken his ability as a Surgeon, and they had taken visual pleasure away, too. Clarity.

It was months before Lars could calm down enough to contact him. He was becoming afraid he was never going to visit at all.

'You're wearing gloves!' Was the first thing out of his mouth when John opened the door.

He was. Full of holes and tears, but gloves were expensive. He couldn't replace them on a whim.

'Yeah. I thought my skin was bad when I got to swap them out regularly.'

The Surgeon snorted softly through his nostrils, but he came inside. That had to count for something. 'Why bother?'

The question was confounding. He had to think long and hard about it. That was ok. Plenty of time these days.

'Familiarity, maybe? Nobody will touch me now. Not ever.'

'The city isn't the whole world. You could go to Judgment. Sing sad old songs with that little friend of yours.'

'When folk spit on me, I earned every bit of it for myself.'

Lars skidded to a stop in his pacing and faced him, utter agony on his face.

'How could you do it, John? She was your patient, you were supposed to care for her wellbeing!'

A creaky smile. 'Word for word what the mother said. I have to congratulate you on your memory.'

'Charles was a knob shine for ever letting that harpy into his house to speak with the girl. But it doesn't make her wrong.'

John studied his poor, ragged gloves. Flexed his fingers to hear them squeak, but got more of a tired rustling from the dried latex.

'I didn't rape that woman, Lars.'

And just when he had thought nothing else could hurt, it stung like hell to see that Lars had never doubted he'd done it, even for a second.

'But … At the trial … they said …'

'She remembered being drugged. All the rest was sheer poison the mother poured in her ear. Wanted to pin her daughter's disappearance on me, too.'

'That … *bitch*!'

'You want to hear what I did in that flat, with that poor drugged woman? I sat and I held her hands. Her warm living hands, left my gloves at the door. Quietly, for hours on end, and it was like heaven.'

'Then why didn't you say so?' He looked on the verge of crying himself. 'For crying out loud, nobody's going to believe the truth now! This can't be taken back, not ever.'

'Lars, calm down. Just sit, take a deep breath. Look, I still *drugged* her. Pure intent or no, that time I spent holding her hands I took without her consent. I took her rights as a person, a human being, away from her because it was easier to take from a *thing*.

'Truth is, I've been pretending ever since I was a boy. I was never going to be good enough, Lars. I was too weak to be a Surgeon. Too lonely. This is all for the best.'

Right off the side of the chair Lars collapsed to the floor like his spine wouldn't hold him. He buried his face in his hands, and he was crying. Sobbing the way a child would, completely wretched and without hope.

'Hey. Hey, stop that. Shall I get you a beer? They taste like lightly salted piss around here, a real delicacy.'

'I have a husband,' Lars sobbed through his hands.

Unreality shot through John and he wavered in front of the coolbox, wondering if his ears were failing to go with his damaged eyes. It felt as though the entire building had lurched meters to the left with everything in it, leaving him standing on empty air.

'What?' He asked intelligently.

'We all do. In secret, we all do. All the Surgeons. Husbands, wives, families. Everyone but you.'

'That can't be.'

'It's true.'

'But that's sick! Why wouldn't you tell me!'

'Because you were always the best! You were the purest, the most evangelical. John, you *believed*. It's still illegal. Folk die. Your own aunt was trying to prove the tradition wrong, that no patients are in danger, and they framed her for a death.

'All the others were afraid of you, of what you might do. We wanted to protect our loved ones. I was scared for my fucking husband, but John, I swear, none of us wanted any of this to happen to you!'

So. The revelation felt hollow. As did his outrage. They'd both come too late to matter. He sat on the floor opposite Lars, the squat so narrow their feet almost touched. They were quiet a while.

Then John took a deep breath.

'So. What's he like?'

'Huh?'

'Your husband?'

Lars hiccupped, then laughed. 'He's wonderful. He's kind, and funny, and patient like a stone, and so generous. It helps me look forward to every day, just to know he'll be there. He means the world to me, you know?'

Crying again. 'Oh God, I'm sorry. Of course you don't know.'

'Good. That sounds good.'

John reached across and patted Lars' shoe. Surgeon or not, he didn't pull away.

'You know, I think that's all I ever wanted.'

The world is frozen
The animals ascendant
And Jim will do anything
to keep his daughter alive

FLORA
& jim

BP GREGORY

The world is frozen. The animals ascendant. And, locked in desperate pursuit of the "other father" across a grim icy apocalypse, Jim will do anything to keep his daughter alive.

KATE KNOWS
WHAT SHE
SAW

The
T**O**WN

BP GREGORY

Kate knows what she saw: a burned out ruin. But the evidence is gone, and nobody else believes the town was ever there.

She knows the town exists. Determined to prove it at any cost, in poking around the outback Kate risks exposing herself and her friends to the slew of horrible urban legends, reticent locals, and too many people who vanished over the years with nowhere to go.

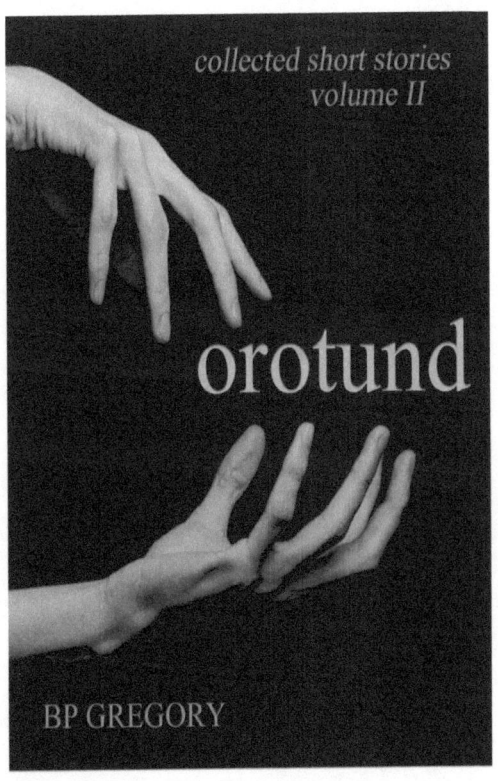

collected short stories
volume II

orotund

BP GREGORY

A paroled monster, a prostitute and a policeman all see a little girl lost, but this isn't the start of a joke. An isolated, frail old man trapped in his apartment; what possible threat could he pose to the sociopaths next door?

Take time for a stroll down humanity's eerie back alleys and enjoy BP Gregory's newest short science fiction, urban fantasy and horror stories neatly packaged together in Orotund: Collected Short Stories Volume Two.

www.bpgregory.com

Author and avid reader BP Gregory brings monsters, machines and roaming cities, insanity, betrayal and lust! With such tales you shouldn't always feel comfortable or safe.

For sneak peeks, more stories, reviews and recommendations as she ploughs through her to-read pile visit bpgregory.com.

www.ingramcontent.com/pod-product-compliance
Lightning Source LLC
Chambersburg PA
CBHW031954130726
47904CB00013B/1465